TO
ALL THE CHILDREN
IN THE WORLD

DANNY KAYE'S

AROUND
THE
WORLD
STORY
BOOK

RANDOM HOUSE, NEW YORK

ACKNOWLEDGMENTS

We owe a very special debt to Maria Cimino and Helen Masten of the New York Public Library's Central Children's Room. We have bothered them for so long that they have become our friends—in self-defense. But even when we were just beginning to haunt their domain, they were wonderfully patient and cheerful, and unfailingly knowledgeable and helpful. Without their assistance, the research work would have taken twice as long, and it wouldn't have been half as pleasant.

Margaret Bevans and Barbara Klaw

Thanks are extended to the following authors, publishers, translators, and organizations for allowing the use of their stories in this book:

THE BEDCATS is from *Ol' Paul, the Mighty Logger*, by Glen Rounds. Copyright 1936, 1949 by Holiday House, Inc. Reprinted by permission of the publisher.

THE CREATION OF MAN, copyright © 1960 by Margaret Bevans and Barbara Klaw, is an adaptation of a story from *The Folklore Record*.

THE FIRST WOMAN, copyright © 1960 by Margaret Bevans and Barbara Klaw, is an adaptation of a story by Katharine Berry Judson.

THE TALKING EGGS is from *Memoirs of the American Folklore Society*.

AMBROSE BIERCE'S FABLES are from *Fantastic Fables* by Ambrose Bierce.

THE GIRL WHO DANCED WITH THE DEVIL is adapted from "The Story of Rose Latulippe" in *Baptiste Laroque — Legends of French Canada* by Paul A. W. Wallace, published and copyrighted by the Musson Book Company, Toronto, Canada. By permission of the author and the publisher.

SENORITA CUCARACHITA is slightly adapted, with the kind permission of the author, from "La Hormiquita and Perez the Mouse" in *Picture Tales from Spain* by Ruth Sawyer. Copyright 1936 by J. B. Lippincott Company. Published by J. B. Lippincott Company.

HOW RABBIT GOT OUT OF A TIGHT PLACE is reprinted with the permission of Charles Scribner's Sons from "How Mr. Rabbit Got Out of a Tight Place" in *Indian Tales from Guatemala* by M. H. Jessup and L. Simpson, copyright 1936 by Charles Scribner's Sons.

THE VEGETABLE TREE is from *Bright Feather and Other Mayan Tales* by Dorothy Rhoads. Copyright 1932 by Dorothy Rhoads. Reprinted by permission of Doubleday and Company, Inc.

THE COYOTE AND THE DOGS is adapted from "The Coyote and the Two Dogs" in *Picture Tales from Mexico* by Dan Storm. Copyright 1941 by J. B. Lippincott Company. Published by J. B. Lippincott Company.

JUAN BOBO, from *The Rabbit and the Tiger and Other Tales* by Pura Belpré, copyright 1944, is reprinted by permission of and arrangement with Houghton Mifflin Company, the authorized publishers, and adapted by permission of the author.

ANANSI AND BABOON, copyright © 1960 by Margaret Bevans and Barbara Klaw, is an adaptation of a story by Sir George Webbe Dasent.

THE BEST MEAL AND THE WORST, copyright © 1960 by Margaret Bevans and Barbara Klaw, is translated and adapted from a story by Ramon Guirao.

BOUQUI AND THE ENORMOUS YAMS is slightly adapted from "The Yams That Were Twice as Large as Bouqui" in *Children of Yayoute* by François Marcel Turenne des Prés, published by Henri Deschamps, Haiti. Copyright 1949 by François Marcel Turenne des Prés.

THE TALE OF THE LAZY PEOPLE is based on a story of the same title in the Newbery Award book *Tales from Silver Lands* by Charles Finger, copyright 1924. By permission of Mrs. Charles J. Finger.

WHY THE URUTAU BIRD MOURNS, copyright © 1960 by Margaret Bevans and Barbara Klaw, is based on a note in a folklore dictionary.

THE TALENTED COMPANIONS is adapted from "The Boy with the Gun" in the *Pan American Union Bulletin* of February, 1937. It was translated by the Pan American Union from *Cuentos de Mi Tio Ventura* by Ernesto Montenegro. Copyright 1932. By permission of the author and the translators.

THE CAT WHO USED HIS HEAD is from "The Cat and the Tiger" in UNICEF's *Hi, Neighbor, Book 1*, as told by Miguel Solano-Lopez of the Paraguayan Mission to the United Nations, by courtesy of the U.S. Committee for UNICEF.

AYAYMAMA is adapted from *Broad and Alien Is the World* by Ciro Alegría. Copyright, 1941, by Rinehart & Company, Inc. By permission of Rinehart & Company, Inc., New York, publishers.

WHY DEER AND JAGUAR CAN'T BE FRIENDS, copyright © 1960 by Margaret Bevans and Barbara Klaw, is based on an undated, unpublished manuscript, *Brazilian Folklore*, in the New York Public Library.

THE HUNGRY OLD WITCH is based on a story of the same name in the Newbery Award book *Tales from Silver Lands*, by Charles Finger, copyright 1924. By permission of Mrs. Charles J. Finger.

THE FIVE EGGS is reprinted with the permission of Charles Scribner's Sons from *Stories from the Americas* by Frank Henius, copyright 1944 by Charles Scribner's Sons.

THE GULLIBLE MOUSE, copyright © 1960 by Margaret Bevans and Barbara Klaw, is based on a story in the *Pan American Union Bulletin* of February, 1937. By courtesy of the translators, the Pan American Union.

TWO FEASTS FOR ANANSI and WHY WISDOM IS FOUND EVERYWHERE are from *The Hat-shaking Dance* by Harold Courlander and Albert Kofi Prempeh, copyright © 1957 by Harold Courlander. Reprinted by permission of Harcourt, Brace and Company, Inc.

WAKAIMA AND THE CLAY MAN is a shortened version of a story of the same name in *Wakaima and the Clay Man* by E. Balintuma Kalibala and Mary Gould Davis, copyright 1946, by permission of Longmans, Green & Co.

THE CONCEITED SPIDER is slightly adapted from *West African Folk Tales* by W. H. Barker and C. Sinclair, reproduced by permission of George G. Harrap & Co., Ltd., London.

THE TALE OF THE NAME OF THE TREE is slightly adapted from *Bantu Tales* by Pattie Price. Copyright 1938 by E. P. Dutton & Co., Inc. Reprinted by permission of the publishers.

THE RAM AND THE LION'S SON, copyright © 1960 by Margaret Bevans and Barbara Klaw, is based on a story by Sir James E. Alexander.

THE SULTAN'S FOOL is from *The Sultan's Fool: and Other North African Tales* by Robert Gilstrap and Irene Estabrook. Copyright 1958 by Robert Gilstrap and Irene Estabrook. By permission of Henry Holt and Company, Inc.

ABU NOWAS AND HIS WIFE is reprinted from *Crimson Fairy Book* by Andrew Lang, copyright 1903, 1948, by permission of Longmans, Green & Co.

THE JUDGMENT OF KARAKOUSH is reprinted with the permission of Charles Scribner's Sons from *Arabian Romances and Folk Tales* by Habib Katibah, copyright 1929, Charles Scribner's Sons; renewal copyright © 1957, H. I. Katibah.

THE CANDLE IN THE DARKNESS is adapted from "The Candle Gives Out Heat" in *Stories from the Near East* by Leslie W. Leavitt, by permission of Longmans, Green & Co., Ltd., London.

THE FARMER OF BABBIA is from *The Fire on the Mountain and Other Ethiopian Stories* by Harold Courlander and Wolf Leslau. Copyright 1950 by Henry Holt and Company, Inc. By permission of the publishers.

RIQUET WITH THE TUFT, copyright © 1960 by Margaret Bevans and Barbara Klaw, is adapted from the story by Charles Perrault.

THE PRIEST AND THE SERVANT is from "The Padre and the Negro" in *Tales of Old Lusitania* by Francisco Coelho, 1885.

THE TAMING OF THE TERRIBLE BRIDE, copyright © 1960 by Margaret Bevans and Barbara Klaw, is based on a story by Don Juan Manuel.

BASTIANELO, copyright © 1960 by Margaret Bevans and Barbara Klaw, is adapted from a story by T. F. Crane.

PIPILO is adapted from Margaret Hasluck's *Albanian-English Reader*, Cambridge University Press, 1932. By permission of the publisher. Adaptation copyright © 1960 by Margaret Bevans and Barbara Klaw.

THE STORY OF PERSEPHONE has been retold by Anne Ross from several sources, including an ancient hymn to Demeter. © 1960 by Anne Ross.

THE FOX AND THE GRAPES is from William Caxton's *The Fables of Aesop*.

THE CROW AND THE PITCHER and THE LIONESS are from Thomas James' *Aesop*.

ASHPUTTEL is adapted from *German Popular Stories and Fairy Tales as Told by Gamer Grethel*. Adaptation copyright © 1960 by Margaret Bevans and Barbara Klaw.

TILL AND THE ASSES OF ERFURT, copyright © 1960 by Margaret Bevans and Barbara Klaw, is based on a story by Kenneth R. H. Mackenzie.

TILL'S CHANGEABLE HORSE, copyright © 1960 by Margaret Bevans and Barbara Klaw, is based on a story by Thomas Roscoe.

WILLIAM TELL, copyright © 1960 by Margaret Bevans and Barbara Klaw, is retold from various old sources.

THE KING WHO BELIEVED EVERYTHING is from *In the Land of Marvels* by Theodor Vernalaken.

TOM AND THE LEPRACAUN is adapted from "The Field of Boliauns" in *Celtic Fairy Tales* by Joseph Jacobs, by permission of G. P. Putnam's Sons.

THE BIRTH OF OISIN is adapted from *The High Deeds of Finn* by T. W. Rolleston, George G. Harrap & Company, Ltd., London, and Thomas Y. Crowell Company, New York.

KING ARTHUR AND THE STRANGE KNIGHT, copyright © 1960 by Margaret Bevans and Barbara Klaw, is adapted from a story by Sir James Knowles.

MASTER OF ALL MASTERS is from *English Fairy Tales* by Joseph Jacobs, by permission of G. P. Putnam's Sons.

THE FEARFUL BATTLE OF SONG, copyright © 1960 by Margaret Bevans and Barbara Klaw, is retold in prose from *Kalevala* by Dr. Elias Lönnrot.

THE PRINCESS ON THE PEA is by Hans Christian Andersen.

THE COLLAR, copyright © 1960 by Margaret Bevans and Barbara Klaw, is adapted from a story by Hans Christian Andersen.

THE THREE AUNTS is from a story by Sir George Webbe Dasent.

OF GRETTIR AND THE TROLL-WIFE, copyright © 1960 by Margaret Bevans and Barbara Klaw, is retold from *The Story of Grettir the Strong*, a translation from the Icelandic.

NAIL BROTH is from a story by G. Djurklo.

THE THREE LESSONS OF GOD, copyright © 1960 by Margaret Bevans and Barbara Klaw, is based on a story by A. H. Wratislaw.

THE TSAR TRAJAN'S EARS is reprinted by permission of the Oxford University Press, London, from *Yugoslav Folk Tales* by Nada Curcija-Prodanovic, 1957.

THE REAL AND THE UNREAL DEVILS is from a story by Adolf Wenig.

THE WOLF AND THE CAT is by Ivan Krylov.

THE OLD FATHER WHO WENT TO SCHOOL, copyright © 1960 by Margaret Bevans and Barbara Klaw, is adapted from a story by R. Nisbet Bain.

THE BIG OVEN is by Leo Tolstoi.

THE LAZIEST MAN IN THE WORLD, copyright © 1960 by Margaret Bevans and Barbara Klaw, is adapted from a story by Rosika Schwimmer.

WHY THE WOODPECKER HAS A LONG BEAK is slightly adapted from *Roumanian Bird and Beast Stories* by Dr. Moses Gaster, Sidgwick & Jackson, Ltd., London. By permission of the Folk-Lore Society, London.

THE LANGUAGE OF ANIMALS is reprinted from "How a Sensible Peasant Cured His Wife's Curiosity" in *The Gypsy and the Bear* by Lucia Merecka Borski and Kate B. Miller, copyright 1933, by permission of Longmans, Green & Co.

PINYA'S TRIP TO WARSAW is from *The Wise Men of Helm* by Dr. Solomon Simon, Behrman House, Inc., New York. Copyright 1945 by Solomon Simon. Reprinted by permission of the author.

DEATH AND DOCTOR is from *Lithuanian Folk Tales* by Stepas Zobarskas, published by Gerald J. Rickard, 1959. Reprinted with the permission of the author.

A GUEST FOR HALIL is reprinted from *Once the Hodja* by Alice Geer Kelsey, copyright 1943 by permission of Longmans, Green & Co.

SOHRAB AND RUSTUM is retold in prose by Anne Ross from *Poems of* Matthew Arnold. © 1960 by Anne Ross.

SINDBAD AND THE OLD MAN OF THE SEA is adapted from Richard F. Burton's *Arabian Nights*. Adaptation © 1960 by Anne Ross.

THE IMAGINARY WEDDING, copyright © 1960 by Margaret Bevans and Barbara Klaw, is based on a summary of a story by Wadia Shatara of Jordan and is printed with her permission.

THE CAMEL AND THE CAT is from *Stories from the Near East* by Leslie W. Leavitt, published by Longmans, Green & Co., Ltd., London. Reprinted by permission of the publishers.

THE HORSE WITHOUT A MASTER is from *Wonder Tales of Horses and Heroes* by Frances Carpenter. Copyright 1952 by Frances Carpenter Huntington. Reprinted by permission of Doubleday & Company, Inc.

THE PRINCESS AND RABBI JOSHUAH is by Hyman Hurwitz.

THE LION-MAKERS is reprinted from *The Panchatantra* translated by Arthur W. Ryder, by permission of the University of Chicago Press. Copyright 1925 by the University of Chicago.

THE TIGER, THE BRAHMAN, AND THE JACKAL is reprinted from *Indian Fairy Tales* by Joseph Jacobs with the permission of G. P. Putnam's Sons.

THE BRAHMAN'S DREAM is reprinted from *The Panchatantra* translated by Arthur W. Ryder by permission of the University of Chicago Press. Copyright 1925 by the University of Chicago.

THE ALLIGATOR'S COURTSHIP, copyright © 1960 by Margaret Bevans and Barbara Klaw, is adapted from a story by William Goonetilleke.

THE PRINCESS WITH THE GLITTERING EYES is based on "The Chinese Princess" in *Folk Tales of Pakistan*, compiled by Zainab Ghulam Abbas, Pakistan Publications, Karachi, with the permission of the Embassy of Pakistan. Adaptation copyright © 1960 by Margaret Bevans and Barbara Klaw.

THE MAIDEN OF THE SEA, copyright © 1960 by Margaret Bevans and Barbara Klaw, is adapted from a story by A. G. Seklemian.

THE MAN WHO WENT TO FIND HIS LUCK, copyright © 1960 by Margaret Bevans and Barbara Klaw, is based on a story by R. H. Malyon in the *Memoirs of the Royal Asiatic Society of Bengal*, by permission of the Asiatic Society, Calcutta.

THE SILLY FELLOW WHO SOLD HIS BEARD is reprinted by permission of the publishers, the Vanguard Press, from *The Gypsies' Fiddle and Other Gypsy Stories* by M. A. Jagendorf and C. H. Tillhagen. Copyright 1956 by M. A. Jagendorf and C. H. Tillhagen.

THE RABBIT'S CLEVER NOSE is from "The Rabbit Has a Cold" in *Burmese Folk Tales* by Maung Htin Aung. Copyright by Oxford University Press, Bombay, 1948.

THE MOST REMARKABLE CAT is a translation of *Le Chat si extraordinaire* by Madeleine Riffaud, published by Editions la Farandole, Paris, 1958. Translation © 1960 by Spencer Klaw.

THE PRIEST'S MANGOS, copyright © 1960 by Margaret Bevans and Barbara Klaw, is adapted from a story by K. N. Fleeson.

WHY THE MYNAH BIRD MIMICS MAN, copyright © 1960 by Margaret Bevans and Barbara Klaw, is adapted from a story by K. N. Fleeson.

THE DONKEY AND THE ROCK is by A. L. Shelton.

THE WONDERFUL PEAR TREE, copyright © 1960 by Margaret Bevans and Barbara Klaw, is adapted from a story by Herbert A. Giles.

IN THE SHADE OF A DONKEY is from *Below the Great Wall* by R. Pierce Beaver, Christian Education Press, Philadelphia, 1947. Reprinted by permission of the publisher.

THE WOODCARVER AND THE PAINTER, copyright © 1960 by Margaret Bevans and Barbara Klaw, is adapted from a story by R. H. Busk.

THE TONGUE-CUT SPARROW, copyright © 1960 by Margaret Bevans and Barbara Klaw, is adapted from *Japanese Fairy Tales, Series No. 2*.

THE BRIDEGROOM'S SHOPPING is from *The Story Bag* by Kim So-Un, 1955. By permission of Charles E. Tuttle Co., Rutland, Vermont and Tokyo, Japan.

SALAM AND THE HORNET'S NEST is adapted from a story in *Salam, The Mouse-Deer* by A. Hillman and Walter W. Skeat, by permission of Macmillan & Co., Ltd., London.

THE FIRST NOSES is from "First Noses" in *The Beginning: Creation Myths Around the World* by Maria Leach. Copyright 1956. Reprinted by permission of the publishers, Funk & Wagnalls, New York.

BRANCHES OF THE HAND is adapted from "The Cause of the Separation of the Five Fingers" in *Madagascar Before the Conquest* by James Sibree, 1896. By permission of Ernest Benn, Ltd., London. Adaptation copyright © 1960 by Margaret Bevans and Barbara Klaw.

THE PHANTOM BULLOCKY is adapted from *The Australian*, edited by Bill Wannan. It is an anonymously printed variant of "The Champion Bullock Driver" by Lance Skuthorpe in *Twenty Great Australian Stories*, edited by J. L. Waten and V. G. O'Connor, Melbourne, 1946. With the kind permission of Bill Wannan.

MA-UI AND THE LONG EEL is from "How Ma-Ui Overcame Kuna Loa the Long Eel" in *Legends of Hawaii* by Padraic Colum, Yale University Press, copyright 1937. By permission of the publisher.

THE TIGER'S TAIL and GUNO'S HUNGER are from *Kantchil's Lime Pit* by Harold Courlander, copyright 1950 by Harcourt, Brace and Company, Inc.

Photographs of Danny Kaye by permission of Black Star.

PUBLISHED IN NEW YORK BY RANDOM HOUSE, INC. AND SIMULTANEOUSLY IN TORONTO, CANADA, BY RANDOM HOUSE OF CANADA, LIMITED.

LIBRARY OF CONGRESS CATALOG CARD NUMBER: 60-15897

DESIGNED BY BEVANS, MARKS & BARROW, INC.

MANUFACTURED IN THE UNITED STATES OF AMERICA

FOREWORD

I think I can safely say that I do not know all the stories in the world and that I haven't even come close to meeting all the world's children. But I have, indeed, traveled through almost every country in the world several times and heard quite a few tales—tall, small and indigenous—and met quite a few youngsters of every size, shape and state of mind; and it was in the course of one of my far-flung junkets for UNICEF that it occurred to me how wonderful it would be if it were possible to introduce all the children in the world to all the stories ever told. It would be almost as wonderful as introducing all the children to one another.

And that's how this book came to be. It came out of a deep and growing conviction that all the world's children are very much alike—their needs, loves, fears, even their stories. And if these children—the adults of tomorrow—begin to understand this, even through the simple process of exchanging favorite stories, then perhaps tomorrow will see a world in which similarities rather than differences are emphasized.

You will see that the 104 stories in this book are both vastly different and amazingly alike—as alike as people all over the world, as different as the people in the next house. Almost all of them have been told in many lands and many tongues at varying times and by people of every color and belief.

When I was telling the story of "Cinderella" through an interpreter to a group of children in Germany, I noticed that they started to laugh and poke

PHOTOGRAPH BY VYARAWALLA

PHOTOGRAPH BY ARA GULER

PHOTOGRAPH BY GENE DANIELS

PHOTO BY E. SCOTT

PHOTO BY VYARAWALLA

each other. To my delighted amazement, I was told that I was telling them their own story of "Ashputtel." I had a similar experience in Africa when the children assured me that the name was not "B'rer Rabbit," but "Wakaima" and that it wasn't a tar baby but a clay man.

It's easy for me to tell you without immodesty about the stories in this book because I neither wrote nor originated them. Friends and strangers, United Nations delegations, foreign embassies and consulates, librarians and travelers, children and grownups, writers and readers were asked to suggest their favorite legends, fables and folk tales—and they did. Stories by the thousands were considered.

With Margaret Bevans and Barbara Klaw, to whom most editorial honors go, we read and picked and edited and asked and read and picked again. We had translations made and often went through many different versions of a story before we decided which to include.

Because there isn't room in one book or in five books to include all the stories we considered, we regret that there were many fine ones that couldn't be used and many countries that couldn't be represented separately. We do thank the army of people around the world who helped so tremendously. The stories and the pictures in the book are almost as wonderful as the children for whom they were collected, and I hope those children will laugh and cry and be pleased at reading them just as we were in making the collection for them.

DANNY KAYE

CONTENTS

PART 8   ILLUSTRATED BY Louis Glanzman

PART 9   ILLUSTRATED BY Tom O'Sullivan

PART 10   ILLUSTRATED BY Leonard Everett Fisher

PART 1 THE UNITED STATES: NORTH AMERICAN INDIAN: ESKIMO: CANADA

ILLUSTRATED BY LEONARD EVERETT FISHER

THE BEDCATS

THE UNITED STATES: Compared to most of the characters in this anthology, Paul Bunyan is a newcomer. Stories about him sprang up in Northwestern logging camps after the Civil War. The tales got taller and taller as the loggers tried to top each other's yarns. This retelling is by Glen Rounds.

OL' PAUL had quite a time with the Bedcats one winter, when he was using one of his old camps that had stood deserted for thirty years or more. It happened this way. As everyone knows, most bunkhouses have a certain number of bedbugs. These don't annoy a real lumberjack to amount to anything, although you'll hear the greenhorns holler plenty when they first come into camp. But they either make friends with the little beasts or they don't last long. The story is that the loggers all had their pet bugs that followed them around camp and out in the woods like dogs, some even being trained, it is said, to steal blankets off adjoining bunks for their masters on especially cold nights. However, that is as it may be; I never saw it.

But it is a well-known fact that the intelligent little beasts always knew when camp was to be moved, and the night before would come out of wherever they were in the habit of staying and climb into the bedding rolls so as not to be left behind. Then when the new camp was set up, there they were, jumping up and down with excitement to greet the men when they came in from their first day's work.

One time, though, they got fooled. That was the time the Indian, Squatting Calf, comes running into camp just after breakfast with the news that gold has been discovered in the Black Hills. Right away all the men tear out over the hills without even waiting to pick up their blankets. Within three minutes the camp is as empty as an old maid's letter box on Valentine's Day. That night at sundown the little bugs are all lined up at the bunkhouse door waiting for the men to come home as usual. But they don't come.

Ol' Paul's in town at the time, and when he hears the news, he knows there's no use figuring on logging till the gold fever passes, so he goes on a timber cruising trip. He locates some fine timber down Kansas way, and when he finds his men ready to work, he starts a new camp there, as he has a ready market for his lumber in the new gold towns. And, what with one thing and another, it's about thirty years before he comes back to the old camp. But when he does, he finds trouble waiting for him.

He and the men get there about noon and start cleaning out the old buildings. They're a little surprised to find the bunks filled up with the bones of rabbits and other small animals, but suppose that owls or bobcats have been living there. By night the camp is ready, and after supper the men turn in early. Ol' Paul suddenly wakes up, hearing wild yells and snarls from the bunkhouse, and comes running out of his office to see the men clawing over one another in their underwear, trying to get out in the open. They swear that their bunks are full of wildcats which have been crawling all over them. Now Paul knows wildcats, and he's never heard of one that'll come within a hundred yards of a logger if it has its 'druthers. As he can find nothing in there when he looks, he figures that being as it's the day after payday, the men have probably eaten something that disagrees with them. But they won't go back in the bunkhouse, so he lets them sleep in the stables that night.

But the next night the same thing happens, so Paul decides to get his pistol and sleep in the bunkhouse himself. When a bunch of lumberjacks are scared to sleep in a place there must be something wrong somewhere. For a time things are quiet enough to suit anybody, and Paul finally decides that the men have been reading too many old mystery magazines, and dozes off. But he wakes up mighty soon. What feels like a couple of full-grown wildcats seem to have gotten tangled up in his beard, and his blanket is heaving around like he has a runaway cat show under it. The whole bunk is full of animals of some kind, hissing and snarling like all get out. It's none too comfortable there, but Ol' Paul doesn't lose his head. He grabs out in the dark and gets a couple of the beasts and stuffs them into a sack he's got handy. Of course as soon as he starts floundering around the things clear out, like any wild animal, and by the time the men come running with lanterns the place is quiet again.

They carefully open up the sack to see what they've caught. The animals inside are not bobcats. In fact, nobody has ever seen anything like them. They are the size of bobcats, but they have several pairs of legs. They are covered with a heavy coat of reddish-brown fur, which is quite long on the back, but due to the shortness of their legs, is worn down to the length of plush on the bottom. Naturally Paul and the men are more than a little puzzled.

It is not until the Indians come into camp that they find out what it is they have caught. The Indians call them Bedcats, and from them Paul learns the story.

It seems that the little bugs, being left alone in camp, had to forage for themselves. At first many died, but the stronger ones survived and grew larger, soon attacking small mice and sparrows. As the years passed, they grew fur to keep them warm, and became more and more savage, each generation a little larger and wilder than the one before. Eventually they were bringing in gophers and small rabbits to feed their young. Later, it seems, they crossed with bobcats and the half-breeds were really fierce hunters. They took to running in packs like wolves, baying at the moon, and in a pitched fight a full-grown bobcat was no match for even an ordinary-sized Bedcat. The Indians set deadfalls for them, and made warm fur robes and mittens from the pelts. But with the return of the lumberjacks, some forgotten instinct seemed to urge them into the blankets in the bunks, which upset even the soundest sleepers.

Something had to be done. Ol' Paul buys the Indians a lot of number four wolf traps and offers a five-dollar bounty for the scalps, so they are soon trapped out. I haven't heard of any quite that big being seen since.

THE CREATION OF MAN

NORTH AMERICAN INDIAN: People everywhere have invented stories to explain what they couldn't understand about the beginnings of the world. Such stories are called "creation stories." North American Indian creation stories are mostly very serious. This one is unusual in that it is humorous.

AFTER THE COYOTE had finished the work of creating the world, he called a council of the inferior animals to decide how to create man. They sat in a circle in a forest clearing, with the lion at the head. On his right sat the grizzly bear, next the cinnamon bear, and so on around according to rank, ending with the little mouse, who sat at the lion's left.

The lion was the first to speak, and he de-

would pay particular attention to man's ears and eyes, giving him ears like a spider's web and eyes like fire.

The mountain sheep protested that great antlers branching out in every direction only got caught in thickets. Man's horns, he said, should be rolled up. They should be like stones, one on each side of his head, so he could butt powerfully.

clared he should like to see man created with a mighty voice like his own. He should also be well covered with hair and have terrible claws and fangs.

The grizzly bear said it was ridiculous to give man a lion's voice, for the lion was always roaring with it and scaring away his prey. He said man ought to be enormously strong and move about swiftly and silently, so that he could catch and grip his prey without making a noise.

To his way of thinking, the buck said, man would look very foolish unless he had a magnificent pair of antlers on his head. He also thought it was absurd to roar so loudly. And he

The grizzly bear broke in again, speaking out of turn, to object to the whole idea of horns. He had never seen any point, he said, in walking around with all that weight on the head. He would like to add, however, that man should have feet shaped like a bear's so he could stand erect. And he certainly shouldn't be burdened with a tail, which was of no use except as a home for fleas.

The beaver said he had never heard of such nonsense and twaddle in his life. No tail, indeed! He would make man with a broad, flat tail so he could haul mud and sand with it.

The owl said all the animals seemed to have

16

lost their senses. None of them had said a thing about giving man wings. For himself, he couldn't see what good any creature would be without wings.

The mole said it was perfect folly to talk of wings. With them, man would be certain to bump his head against the sky. Besides that, if he had both wings and eyes, he would get his eyes burnt by flying too close to the sun. But without eyes, he could burrow in the cool, soft earth and be happy.

The little mouse couldn't agree with that. He squeaked out that man must have eyes, of course, so he could see what he was eating. And as for burrowing in the ground, that was absurd.

took a lump of earth and started molding a man according to his own idea, exactly like himself. It was so late when they started to work that nightfall came before any of the models were finished, and the animals lay down to sleep. But the cunning coyote stayed awake.

When all the other animals were sound asleep, the coyote went around and poured water on their models and spoiled them. Then he went back to work on his own.

He gave it four feet with five fingers on each, shaped like the grizzly bear's so that man could stand upright. He gave it a powerful voice, but sense enough not to use it all the time. He left off the tail, for he knew from experience the

At last the coyote spoke. He said that all these were the stupidest ideas he had ever heard, and that he could hardly keep awake listening to such a pack of idiots and nincompoops. Every one of the animals, he said, thought his own kind was perfect and wanted to make man just like himself. They might as well take one of their own cubs and call it a man.

At this, there was such an uproar that the council broke up. The coyote flew at the beaver and nipped a piece out of his cheek. The owl jumped on top of the coyote's head and tugged at his hair. There was complete confusion.

Finally, the animals stopped fighting. Each

grizzly bear was right about tails collecting fleas. He gave it eyes and ears like the buck because he knew the buck's were better than his own. And he left it naked like a fish because hair was a burden most of the year. He made man's claws as long as the eagle's so he could hold things. And last of all, he gave man brains like his own, for surely there was no other animal as cunning and crafty as himself. He finished his model just as the sun rose and, quickly, before any of the other animals awoke, he held it up and gave it life.

And thus it happened that man was made by the coyote.

THE FIRST WOMAN

O ESKIMO: This myth, although it is very old, has only recently been written down because the Eskimos themselves have no written language.

NCE, IN THE FIRST TIMES, there were many men living in the northland, but they were lonely, for there was no woman among them. At last, when one of the young men could stand his empty igloo no longer, a traveler brought the news that far away in the southland there was one woman. So the young man went south to the home of the woman and married her.

He thought, "Now I have a wife, while the son of the headman has none." And he was very pleased.

A few days later, the son of the headman also started to travel south in search of the woman, but when he arrived the young man and the woman were already married. Nevertheless, he went to the tent where the couple were staying and waited patiently outside until all was quiet and he knew they were asleep.

Then he crept into the tent, and caught the woman by the shoulders and began to drag her away. She cried out and woke the husband. He jumped up and caught his wife by the feet.

Both men struggled and pulled with all their strength until at last they pulled the woman in two.

The husband took the lower half into the tent and immediately began to carve an upper part out of wood. He worked for hours until he had made a statue of half a woman. Then he joined it to the waist of his half-wife.

The headman's son carried the upper part of the woman back to the home of his father, and, as soon as he arrived, he took his knife and carved a wooden lower half and fastened it on at the waist. When the two men had finished each woman was complete. There were now two women.

The young man in the southland soon found that his wife could dance as lightly as a breeze and run as nimbly as a hare. But she must ask for help with fine needlework in sewing the furs, for her wooden hands were stiff and clumsy.

The headman's son in the north was proud of his wife. She was the envy of the village and her stitches of caribou-nerve thread were the finest ever seen. But her wooden feet moved with effort to the rhythm of the tambourine and she must always walk slowly and with dignity.

These two women were the first in the land, and all the women who came after them were their granddaughters. That is why all the women in the north are skillful with their hands and all the women in the south are good dancers, even to this day. Thus you may know that the tale is true.

THE TALKING EGGS

THE UNITED STATES: Stories change as they move around the world. This one came to this country from France long ago, but a Frenchman would hardly recognize this version, with all of the Southern details that have been added by Creole storytellers of Louisiana.

THERE WAS ONCE a lady who had two daughters. They were called Rose and Blanche. Rose was bad and Blanche was good. But the mother liked Rose better because she was her very picture. She would compel Blanche to do all the work, while Rose was seated in her rocking chair. One day, the mother sent Blanche to the well to get some water in a bucket.

When Blanche arrived at the well, she saw an old woman who said to her, "Pray, my little one, give me some water. I am very thirsty."

"Yes, aunt," said Blanche, "here is some water." And Blanche rinsed her bucket and gave the old woman good fresh water to drink.

"Thank you, my child. You are a good girl. God will bless you," the old woman said.

A few days after, the mother was so bad to Blanche that she ran away into the woods. She cried and knew not where to go, because she was afraid to return home. She saw the same old woman walking in front of her.

"Ah, my child, why are you crying?" the old woman said. "What hurts you?"

"Oh, aunt, mamma has beaten me, and I am afraid to return to the cabin."

"Well, my child, come with me. I will give you supper and a bed. But you must promise not to laugh at anything you see." She took Blanche's hand, and they began to walk in the woods.

As they advanced, the bushes of thorns opened before them, and closed behind their backs. A little further on, Blanche saw two axes which were fighting. She found that very strange, but said nothing. They walked further and behold! it was two arms which were fighting. A little further, two legs. At last, she saw two heads which were fighting and which said, "Blanche, good morning, my child. God will help you."

At last they arrived at the cabin of the old

woman who said to Blanche, "Make some fire, my child, to cook the supper." And she sat down near the fireplace and took off her head. She placed it on her knees and began to delouse her hair.

Blanche found that very strange, but she said nothing. The old woman put her head back in its place and gave Blanche a large bone to put on the fire for their supper. Blanche put the bone in the pot. Lo! in a moment the pot was full of good meat.

She gave Blanche a grain of rice to pound with the pestle and thereupon the mortar became full of rice. After they had taken their supper, the old woman said to Blanche, "Pray, my child, scratch my back."

Blanche scratched her back, but her hand was all cut because the old woman's back was covered with broken glass. When she saw that Blanche's hand was bleeding, she only blew on it, and the hand was cured.

When Blanche got up the next morning, the old woman said to her, "You must go home now, but as you are a good girl, I want to make you a present of the talking eggs. Go to the chicken-house. All the eggs which say 'Take me,' you must take them. All those which say 'Do not take me,' you must not take. When you will be on the road, throw the eggs behind your back to break them."

As Blanche walked, she broke the eggs. Many pretty things came out of those eggs. It was now diamonds, now gold, a beautiful carriage, beautiful dresses. When she arrived at her mother's, she had so many fine things that the house was full of them. Therefore, her mother was very glad to see her.

The next day, she said to Rose, "You must go to the woods to look for this same old woman. You must have fine dresses like Blanche."

Rose went to the woods, and she met the old

woman who told her to come to her cabin. But when she saw the axes, the arms, the legs, and the heads fighting, and saw the old woman taking off her head to delouse herself, she began to laugh and ridicule everything she saw. Therefore the old woman said, "Ah, my child, you are not a good girl. God will punish you."

The next day she said to Rose, "I don't want to send you back with nothing. Go to the chicken-house and take the eggs which say 'Take me.'"

Rose went to the chicken-house. All the eggs began to say "Take me," "Don't take me," "Take me," "Don't take me." Rose was so bad that she said, "Ah, yes, you say 'Don't take me,' but you are precisely those I want." She took all the eggs that said "Don't take me," and she went away with them.

As she walked, she broke the eggs, and there came out a quantity of snakes, toads and frogs, which began to run after her. There was even a quantity of whips, which whipped her. Rose ran and shrieked. She arrived at her mother's so tired that she was not able to speak.

When her mother saw all the beasts and the whips which were chasing her, she was so angry that she sent her away like a dog, and told her to go live in the woods.

AMBROSE BIERCE'S FABLES

A LION AND THORN

THE UNITED STATES: Ambrose Bierce, a journalist and short-story writer, made fun of practically everything, including fables—Aesop's and all others.

A LION roaming through the forest got a thorn in his foot and meeting a Shepherd asked him to remove it. The Shepherd did so and the Lion, having just surfeited himself on another Shepherd, went away without harming him. Some time afterward the Shepherd was condemned on a false accusation to be cast to the lions in the amphitheatre. When they were about to devour him one of them said:

"This is the man who removed the thorn from my foot."

Hearing this, the others honorably abstained, and the claimant ate the Shepherd all by himself.

A WOLF AND OSTRICH

A WOLF who in devouring a man had choked himself with a bunch of keys, asked the Ostrich to put her head down his throat and pull them out, which she did.

"I suppose," said the Wolf, "you expect payment for that service."

"A kind act," replied the Ostrich, "is its own reward; I have eaten the keys."

THE DISINTERESTED ARBITER

Two Dogs who had been fighting for a bone, without advantage to either, referred their dispute to a Sheep. The Sheep patiently heard their statements, then flung the bone into a pond.

"Why did you do that?" said the Dogs.

"Because," replied the Sheep, "I am a vegetarian."

AN UNSPEAKABLE IMBECILE

A JUDGE said to a Convicted Assassin:

"Prisoner at the bar, have you anything to say why the death-sentence should not be passed upon you?"

"Will what I say make any difference?" asked the Convicted Assassin.

"I do not see how it can," the Judge answered, reflectively. "No, it will not."

"Then," said the doomed one, "I should like to remark that you are the most unspeakable old imbecile in seven States and the District of Columbia."

THE GIRL WHO DANCED

ROSE LATULIPPE was one of the prettiest girls in all of French Canada. Her cheeks were round and plump, her disposition was cheerful, and when she danced her graceful feet skimmed over the floor, hardly touching the boards. Rose loved to dance. She loved it so much, in fact, that it was almost her undoing.

Now, Rose was engaged to Pierre Lebourveau, a good, handsome boy, but she was in no hurry to get married. It was too much fun dancing with all the boys who looked at her as she laughed and flirted, twirling to the music with one partner after another.

On the evening of the Mardi Gras, the day before the beginning of Lent, Pierre came in his sleigh to take Rose to a big dance. There would be lots of people and plenty of music, for the Mardi Gras dance was always the best dance of the year.

"Don't forget now," her mother warned her, as Pierre bundled the robes around her in the sleigh, "that it's Mardi Gras. You must stop dancing at midnight when Lent starts, or something bad might happen."

Rose promised, and Pierre clucked to the horse. They drove off with Rose singing like a bird in his ear. When they got to the dance, it was just as wonderful as Rose had hoped. She danced with all the boys, the music was fast and lively, and everyone said nice things to her. She had never been so happy in her life, and she forgot all about Mardi Gras until she heard the clock strike twelve. All the young people were having such a good time they couldn't bear for the dance to end, and finally some of the boys begged the fiddler to play just one more tune. And the fiddler obligingly took up his fiddle again.

At that moment, the door opened and a stranger came in. He was a tall man in black clothes, very handsome to look at. He said he had left his horse at the door, and had just come in for a moment to get warm.

"You will excuse me, won't you," said the stranger politely, "if I keep my hat and gloves on, for I have a bad cold." He looked around at all the pretty, laughing girls, and he said, "And could I, perhaps, have a dance with one of these charming young ladies?"

"Why, of course, stranger," the boys said gaily. "Come right in and welcome."

Well, the stranger looked around the room until his eyes lit on Rose, and then he didn't look any further. He went over and whispered something nice in her ear, and she blushed. Then when he asked her to dance with him, of course, she couldn't say no. So she took his hand, gloved in fine black leather, and they danced around the room.

The stranger was a dancer to match Rose.

WITH THE DEVIL

CANADA: In the small farming villages of French Canada, the conteurs—or storytellers—love to tell stories about the Devil. The stories are full of superstition and magic, and, to the delight of the audiences, the Devil usually gets the worst of it. Adapted from a story by Paul A. W. Wallace.

He skimmed and twirled just as lightly as she did, and the fiddler kept right on playing, his music getting louder and faster all the time. As they danced, the stranger whispered sweet things in Rose's ear.

Watching them whirling and whispering that way, Pierre Lebourveau got so angry he could hardly speak. He saw Rose's eyes shining up at the stranger, and her cheeks pink with blushing and laughing. Finally he went outside, slamming the door behind him and stamping his feet on the porch.

Close beside the porch, he noticed the stranger's horse, a powerful, tall, black horse, unlike any Pierre had even seen. And then Pierre noticed a funny thing. It was a very cold night, and the snow lay deep on the ground. But under the hoofs of the stranger's horse the snow was all melted away to the ground, so that the horse stood in deep holes, while all the other horses tied to the hitching rail stood on top of the packed snow.

Pierre stood for a moment, puzzled. Then a look of terror spread over his face, and he ran as fast as he could run to the priest's house. Breathlessly, he told the priest all about the stranger with the gloves on his hands and the horse with the hot hoofs. The priest didn't even stop to put on his coat. He just got some holy water, and jumped into his sleigh.

All this time at the dance, the music was going on and Rose Latulippe was still dancing with the stranger. Finally, whispering into Rose's ear, the stranger squeezed her hand. And Rose, through the fine black glove, unmistakably felt a sharp claw! With a scream, Rose fell to the floor in a faint.

Hastily the Devil—for it was he—leaned down to pick her up. But at that moment the door opened and the priest and Pierre rushed in. The priest sprinkled holy water on the girl, and held up his cross before the Devil's face. Groaning, the Devil tried to duck away, but the priest followed him, holding the cross in front of him.

Suddenly, with a howl, the Devil was gone. The room was filled with evil-smelling smoke and a tremendous hole appeared in the roof. The people ran to the door. The horse was gone, too. All they could see were the holes melted in the snow where he had stood.

Well, Rose Latulippe quickly came to her senses. She looked at the hole in the roof, and she smelled the foul smoke, and she rushed into Pierre's arms and stayed there. He drove her home to her mother's, and they were married the next month.

Rose still likes to dance, but she doesn't dance with strangers whether they are wearing gloves or not. And on Mardi Gras night, Rose and Pierre stay at home.

SENORITA CUCARACHITA

COSTA RICA, PANAMA AND EL SALVADOR: In Spain, the heroine of this story was an ant, not a cockroach. By Ruth Sawyer.

LA CUCARACHITA was a little brown cockroach — very enchanting, very agreeable, very industrious. She could not have been more charming if she had been a fairy.

One day as she was sweeping behind the door of her little house she found a *centavo*. A *centavo* is almost the smallest piece of money in the world, but it filled the little brown claw of La Cucarachita and she drew in her breath in ecstasy as she looked at it.

"What luck! What shall I do with this *centavo?* Shall I buy pine-nuts? No, for I have nothing to crack them with. Shall I buy meringues? No, for that would make me a glutton. Let me think harder."

She leaned her dainty head on her claw and thought very, very hard. *"Por dios,* now I know. I will go to the store and buy me a pot of rouge."

She washed herself all over. She combed her hair. She dressed herself in a new, red, ruffled dress and put on her high comb and black *mantilla.* On each cheek she put a touch of the rouge, and a touch of powder on her very distinguished nose. She was then content. She sat herself down in the balcony to watch all of God's world pass by.

Now, it happened that she was so exquisite, so beautiful, so wholly desirable, that all who passed fell at once in love with her.

There passed a handsome bull. "Marry me, Cucarachita?"

"And if I do, how will you make love to me?"

"Like this!" And the bull roared handsomely.

So terrible was the sound that La Cucarachita clapped her claws over her ears and said in distress: "Continue on your way, Señor Bull. I

could never live to
be loved that way."

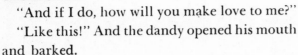

There passed a
dog who was
a dandy.

"Marry me,
Cucarachita?"

"And if I do, how will you make love to me?"

"Like this!" And the dandy opened his mouth
and barked.

"I do not like your wooing. Keep on your
way," said La Cucarachita.

There passed a mincing cat—all grace and
sleekness. "Marry me, Cucarachita?"

"And if I do, how will you woo me?"

"Like this!" And the cat caterwauled until
the little brown cockroach shook in her balcony
with fear. "Señor Cat, I beg you to stop. Go also
on your way."

There passed a pig who grunted his love.
There passed a cock who crowed his to the sky.
But none of them pleased La Cucarachita. She
turned her head sadly and rested it on her little
claw in despair. But by and by there passed a
handsome mouse, so gallant, so beseeching.

"Marry me, Cucarachita *mia.*"

"And if I do, how will you woo me?"

"Like this!" And he laid his gray paw to his
cheek as if it had been her brown one, and he
caressed it so gently. Then he looked up at her
with his soft, engaging eyes.

"I will marry you, Señor Mouse," said La
Cucarachita. "Come right in."

They lived together in the little house very,
very contented. All the things that La Cucarachita wanted to cook were the very things the
Mouse wanted to eat. The way La Cucarachita
wanted to pass the day was precisely the way
the Mouse wanted to pass it. Time went through
from their front door to their back door on soft,
slippered feet.

At last there came a day of misfortune. La
Cucarachita went alone to mass. But first she
put the *olla,* the big stew kettle, over the fire,
filled with rice and cabbage and sausage and
garlic, to make a good dinner for them. And she
said to the Mouse, "You must stir this with the

great spoon and not with the small one. Then you will be quite safe."

But the Mouse did not listen well, or at all. When the time came to stir the *olla*, he took the small spoon. He had to stand on his toes to reach the rim of the *olla*. He had to climb on the rim to reach the bottom of the *olla*. The steam and the smell made him giddy and in he fell. Alas! There was no little brown cockroach there to pull him out.

La Cucarachita returned. She called from the street, "Husband *mia*, I am here." She called from the patio, but no answer came. She went into the kitchen. She looked into the *olla*, and what did she see: What misfortune! What sorrow!

She drew a rocking chair into the patio. She sat down in it, all in the little black dress that she had worn to mass. She drew her *mantilla* over her face and she rocked and she wept for the Mouse, who had wooed her more enchantingly than had all of God's world passing by. She rocked and she wept, "Ah, alas, alas!"

A small bird came to the patio, flying.
"Dear Cucarachita, why are you crying?"
"My husband the Mouse in the *olla* lies dead.
"So I rock and I weep and I cover my head."
"I will cut my small bill, then,"
   the little bird said.

A white dove perched on the patio sill:
"Small bird, oh, small bird, why cut you your bill?"
"Her husband the Mouse in the *olla* lies dead,
"La Cucarachita has covered her head."
"I will clip my long tail," the white pigeon said.

The dove-house above gave a pitiful wail:
"White pigeon, white pigeon, why clip your long tail?"
"Her husband the Mouse in the *olla* lies dead,
"La Cucarachita has covered her head."
"I will shake myself, break myself up,"
   the house said.

The clear, happy fountain shed tears in her sorrow.
The little Infanta kept a fast till the morrow.
La Cucarachita still covers her head,
Her husband the Mouse in the *olla* lies dead.

HOW RABBIT GOT OUT OF A TIGHT PLACE

GUATEMALA AND HONDURAS: Like our Br'er Rabbit, this rabbit can outthink his enemies. By M. H. Jessup and L. Simpson.

ON THE ROAD Mr. Rabbit had to take over the mountains to get to his brother's house, there was a great stone, called by the Indians Li Nem Pec, which hung in such a way that it seemed about to fall at any moment, although, to be sure, it is hanging there to this day. The weather was so warm and the shade of the rock so inviting that Mr. Rabbit sat down under it to eat his lunch and take his siesta. He was in the middle of a sound sleep when he was rudely awakened by the growl of a jaguar close at hand. The beast was so near that Mr. Rabbit saw at once that it would be useless to try to escape. He thought fast. Putting his shoulder to the rock, he stood as if straining with all his strength, while he watched the jaguar out of the corner of his eye.

"Oh dear, oh dear!" he wailed, as the jaguar came near. "Oh dear! To think I must stand here and die to save my wife and babies! Oh, how tired I am!"

The jaguar stopped a few paces off.

"What's the matter with you?" he asked suspiciously.

But Mr. Rabbit pretended not to hear and redoubled his cries. So the jaguar drew nearer and asked again, "Say, what's the matter with you?"

"It's too terrible," gasped Mr. Rabbit. "To think that my wife and babies must die when my strength gives out, to say nothing of myself!"

The jaguar's curiosity was fully aroused, and

he insisted on knowing Mr. Rabbit's story.

"Oh, Mr. Jaguar," said Mr. Rabbit, between gasps, "unless I hold up this rock it will fall and kill me and my whole family down below! And I shall soon give out, for I am dying of thirst. It's all up with me!"

The jaguar was touched.

"I'll tell you what I'll do," he said, after thinking it over. "I'll hold up the rock for you while you go get a drink of water from the brook."

"You are very kind, dear Mr. Jaguar, indeed you are," answered Mr. Rabbit, "but I couldn't allow you to take my place, for you might let the rock fall, and if you did . . ."

At this point Mr. Rabbit's voice failed him and he began to tremble at such a rate that the jaguar expected to see him drop at any moment.

"Please, Mr. Rabbit," insisted the jaguar, "let me take your place until you get a drink of water. I promise I won't let the rock fall."

"Well," consented Mr. Rabbit, "if you really wish to save us you may come over here and put your shoulder under the rock while I slip out."

The jaguar did as he was told.

"Do be careful while I am gone," said Mr. Rabbit, as he limped painfully away. "So much depends upon your holding up the rock. Stand just as you are until I get back. I shan't be gone long."

"That's all right," answered the jaguar. "I can hold it for you."

Mr. Rabbit walked away, after thanking him, but, instead of stopping at the brook, he jumped over it and hastened to his brother's house, where he arrived after sundown.

When Mr. Rabbit did not return, the jaguar began to fear that he had fallen into the brook from weakness and drowned, but, being afraid to leave the rock for fear it would fall and kill him as well as the rabbit family, he continued faithfully at his post until he fell asleep from exhaustion. He was surprised and delighted when he awoke to find the rock still in place and himself still alive. He lay for a long time thinking it over, but finally got up and stretched.

"Well," he said to himself, "I always thought that Mr. Rabbit was a fool. If he is dead it's bad luck for him, but what a blessing for the rest of us!"

THE VEGETABLE TREE

MAYAN: The Mayans liked to tell how things began. An old story retold by Dorothy Rhoads.

I HAD THE TALE from my mother, who heard it from her mother. And she, no doubt, had heard the tale from her own mother, and so back through the centuries.

It was in the very beginning of the world. . . . There were no coconut trees and no mango trees or orange trees or bananas as there are today. And there were no bean plants or squash or chili or cassava. All the vegetables and all the fruits in the world (except corn) grew on one enormous tree which stood in the exact center of the world. And every day the animals came to the tree and ate from it. But man did not know the tree existed.

Who the first man was who found the tree, no one knows. Long ago his name was forgotten. But the man came to the tree, and he saw the vegetables and fruits that drooped heavily from the branches. And he decided to chop down the tree and plant the seed.

All day the man chopped and cut at the tree trunk with his machete. And at the end of the day he was weary, and he went to sleep. And in the morning he awoke. And there was no trace in the tree of the work he had done the day before.

All the second day the man chopped at the tree, and he cut into the trunk a few inches. And when the sun went down he was weary, and he went to sleep. And on the next day when he arose, there was no trace in the tree trunk where the man had worked the day before.

And the man brought one of his friends. And the two men cut and chopped at the base of the tree with their machetes. And they cut away several inches. And when the darkness fell they were weary, and they went to sleep. But when they awoke in the morning, there was no mark or cut in the trunk of the tree.

And the two men called other men. And they chopped and cut at the tree, and by the end of the day the men had cut halfway through the tree trunk. And they were weary, and they went to sleep. And in the morning there was no trace of their work of the day before.

And the whole village set to work to chop down the tree, and they cut and chopped all the day. And when the darkness fell, only a small piece of the tree trunk remained to be cut. And the men were weary from their work. And they lay down and went to sleep. And in the morning there was no trace of the cutting and chopping of the day before.

Then one of the men suggested wisely:

"Let us chop again at the tree. And if it happens that we do not cut through the trunk, let us remain awake and see what takes place during the night."

And all day the men cut and chopped at the tree. And when darkness fell they were weary. And they remained awake.

And in the darkness of the night the animals of the bush gathered about the tree. The jaguar was there, and the deer; and the fox and wild pig and ocelot and serpent and tepizcuintle and the armadillo. Every animal and every bird and every crawling thing of the bush gathered about the tree. And the animals began to work. They took up from around the base of the tree the chips that the men had cut out the day before, and they replaced the chips in the trunk of the tree. They worked all night, each animal and crawling thing and bird, replacing the chips. And before the light returned they had replaced all the chips, and the tree was whole.

All the next day the men worked chopping and cutting at the tree. And when the evening came there was only a small bit of the tree trunk that remained to be cut. And the men were weary, but they did not stop. They cut and chopped at the tree in the darkness, and the tree trunk was cut through. And the tree fell. And the men gathered the fruit and hurried away to plant the seed.

Today there are coconut trees and mango trees and orange trees and bananas. And there are beans and squash and chili and cassava. Each fruit and each vegetable grows on its own plant and on its own tree.

I heard the tale from my mother, who had it from her mother. And her mother had had it from her own mother back and back through the centuries.

It was in the very beginning of the world. . . .

THE COYOTE AND THE DOGS

MEXICO AND NICARAGUA: The coyote is clever, but vain, and sometimes his vanity proves his undoing. Adapted from a story by Dan Storm.

ONE DAY Señor Coyote was walking along the level valley between two mountains when two dogs sprang from behind a rock and almost caught him before he could get away.

He wanted to run to the woods, but the dogs had planned it so he would have to take to the open country. He ran around bushes and jumped over rocks and across dry arroyos, and soon he could tell that he was leaving the dogs behind. Their yelps were getting a little fainter, he thought. He gasped for breath and looked for the best direction for escape.

But while he was trying to make up his mind, two other dogs, red and white spotted and larger than the first pair, rose up in front of him out of nowhere and made up his mind for him. He was forced to turn and run back toward where he had come from. The dogs had planned to take turns racing him back and forth across the desert until he was too tired to go any farther, and the new pair was already gaining on him. Coyote knew he must act fast.

Up on the side of the mountain, he saw the dark, round entrance to a cave and he took heart. The second pair of dogs was behind him and the first pair was coming up slowly in front of him.

Coyote made a sharp turn and raced for the foot of the mountain. The dogs yelped and ran faster as he bolted up the mountainside toward the cave. They were now so close behind him that he could feel their breath upon him as each tried to be the first to get him.

A chill of fear went through Coyote when he suddenly realized that the cave entrance might be big enough to allow the dogs to get through it too. But he could not hesitate, for the dogs were now snapping hairs out of the end of his tail! With a flying dive, Coyote sailed into the mouth of the cave. Fortunately, the hole was just big enough to let him in. The dogs howled and whined and pawed around the cave while Coyote crouched as far back as he could get. After a time he heard nothing more from them.

Now that Coyote was safe, he began to be brave again. He began to think he was quite a fellow to get rid of the dogs. As his tired legs became rested, he began to feel like bragging about his success. There was no one in the cave to talk to, so he began chatting with the parts of himself which had helped him in his race with the dogs.

"Feet," he said, looking at them one at a time, "what did you do?"

"We carried you away," said the feet. "We kicked up dust to blind the dogs. We jumped the rocks and bushes, and brought you here."

"Good! Fine!" said Coyote. "You feet did very well."

Then he spoke to his ears. "Ears, what did you do?"

"We listened behind to see how close the dogs were, so that Feet would know how fast to run."

"Splendid!" said Coyote. "And Eyes, what did you do?"

"We pointed out the road and looked out for your safety. We saw this cave."

"Marvelous!" said Coyote. "What a great fel-low I am to have such fine feet and ears and eyes." And he reached over his shoulder to pat himself on the back approvingly.

Then he saw his tail. "Aha!" he said. "I had almost forgotten about you. Tell me, Tail, what did you do in this battle with the dogs?"

The tail did not answer.

"You don't know? I'll tell you," said Coyote. "You added to my load and held me back. You almost got me caught, too. You let the dogs grab the end of you. Let's hear from you! Speak up!"

The tail was angry. "You have just told me what I did. But I did even more. I motioned to the dogs to come and get you. They could follow you through the dust by my whiteness. I urged them on!"

"Silence!" shouted Coyote, stammering with anger. He reached back and slapped his tail, then he turned and bit at it. "You traitor!" he shouted. "You do not belong here with the rest of us!" He backed toward the entrance of the cave. "Out!" he said, "get outside with the dogs. You are on their side. You tried to help them. Now stay with them!"

Coyote backed his tail out the door into the open air. The dogs, who had been listening to his talk, were waiting hidden outside. When Coyote's tail appeared through the hole, the dogs grabbed it. With a mighty jerk, they pulled Coyote out of the cave by his tail.

And what the dogs did to him, you can well imagine.

JUAN BOBO

PUERTO RICO, THE DOMINICAN
REPUBLIC: This story is from
Puerto Rico, but Dominicans also
love stories about Juan Bobo. By
Pura Belpré.

THERE WAS ONCE a boy so dumb and dull-witted and so stupid that soon people called him Juan Bobo.

He lived with his mother on the hillside of a town. One day his mother sent him to the city to buy meat, molasses, and needles. Juan Bobo saddled his donkey and fixed the baskets lightly. Once in the city, he took his time seeing the sights and enjoying the shop windows. Then he bought the meat, the molasses, and the needles and brought the packages to where the donkey patiently waited. He unwrapped the meat and put it into one basket. Then he poured the molasses over it. He spread the needles into the other basket, mounted the donkey, and turned towards home.

Now the sun was shining and as he jogged home, the heat of the day began to rise. Flies, attracted by the molasses, buzzed about him and clung to the basket, which was to them like honeycomb.

Poor Juan Bobo! He spent the time wiping his forehead and fighting them. When he finally arrived home, he brought in the meat and gave it to his mother.

"Where are the molasses and the needles?" she asked.

"In the basket, Mother," he answered.

But though the mother looked and looked, she found no trace of either of them, for the molasses had melted and been eaten by the flies and the needles had slipped through the basket.

"Oh, stupid one!" she roared.

When Juan Bobo saw that his mother could not find the molasses, he remembered the flies and how he had struggled to fight them.

"Do not fret, Mother," he said. "Tomorrow I will go to the judge and denounce the thieves who attacked me on the way and stole my goods."

Next day, Juan Bobo, true to his promise, appeared before the judge and explained how he had been accosted on the road by a group of black-veiled ladies who drank up all the molasses he was taking home to his mother. He demanded their punishment and complete payment of his bill.

"Black-veiled ladies?" asked the judge. "Who are they, and where do they come from?" He began to laugh, knowing what a simpleton the boy was.

Poor Juan Bobo! He looked around the court and soon discovered two flies alighting upon the tables nearby.

"There, your Honor," he said triumphantly, "are two of them now. They must have followed me here."

The judge looked around, expecting to see two persons. Then his eyes followed Juan, who was now taunting the flies with his stick.

The judge pounded his desk with his mallet and laughed until his eyes filled with tears. "Juan Bobo," he called, amid his great laughter, "I cannot make them pay you the bill, but I give you leave to execute the law. Let the weight of your stick fall on them now and wherever you may find them hereafter."

"Yes, your Honor," said Juan Bobo.

At that very moment, he ran to the judge and, raising his stick, gave him a fierce blow on his head, for three black-veiled ladies had just settled on the judge's bald head.

ANANSI AND BABOON

THE WEST INDIES: Anansi is a West African folk hero, transplanted to the New World by slaves. He is a spider with many greedy human traits.

Anansi and Baboon were arguing one day about who was fattest. Anansi said he was sure he was fat, but Baboon insisted he was fatter. So Anansi suggested that they should prove it, and Baboon agreed.

Anansi said the way to prove it was to build a fire and hang themselves up before it and see which of them would drip the most fat. Baboon said it seemed a good idea.

Baboon hung Anansi up first, but no fat dropped.

Then Anansi hung up Baboon and very soon the fat began to drop. It smelled so good that Anansi cut a slice out of Baboon and said, "Oh, brother Baboon, you're fat for true!"

But Baboon didn't speak.

Anansi was very hungry and very greedy, so he said, "Well, speak, or I'll eat you every bit today."

But Baboon didn't speak.

So Anansi ate him. But when he had eaten up all of Baboon, the pieces joined themselves together in his stomach and began to pull him about so much that he had no rest and was obliged to go to the doctor.

The doctor told him not to eat anything for several days, then to get a ripe banana and hold it to his mouth. By this time Baboon would be hungry. He would smell the banana and would be sure to run up to eat it, and so he would run out of Anansi's mouth.

Anansi suffered and starved himself for several days. Then he got the banana and did as the doctor had told him. But when he put the banana to his mouth, he was so hungry he couldn't help eating it. So he didn't get rid of Baboon who went on pulling him about until he was obliged to go back to the doctor.

This time the doctor, knowing of Anansi's greed, held the banana himself. Very soon Baboon jumped up to catch it and ran out of Anansi's mouth. And Anansi was very glad to be rid of him.

And Baboons to this very day like bananas.

THE BEST MEAL AND THE WORST

CUBA: In folklore, hundreds of ways have been devised to test wisdom. This ancient Indian legend from Cuba tells of such a test—a highly original one.

IN THE DAYS when Obatalá ruled the universe, he had as his helper a younger god named Orula. Obatalá thought highly of his young helper. He observed him carefully and found his judgments fair and his actions praiseworthy. It was natural, therefore, that when Obatalá decided to appoint a ruler of the world, his first thought was of Orula. But Obatalá was not sure that Orula was old enough for a position of such importance, and he decided to test the young god's wisdom.

So Obatalá called Orula to him, and ordered him to prepare the finest meal that could be devised. Orula went to the nearby market, and thoughtfully looked over all the many foods for sale there. Finally he bought an ox tongue. He seasoned it with delicate herbs, and cooked it slowly in its own juices. Then he presented it to Obatalá. The supreme God thought it was delicious, and he smacked his lips with pleasure and satisfaction. When he had finished eating, he asked Orula why, in his judgment, ox tongue was the best meal that could be devised.

"Honored Obatalá," Orula answered, "what can be more important than the tongue? With it, one can teach virtue and manners. One can proclaim good works, and talk of great matters. With it, deserving men can be praised."

Obatalá was pleased at Orula's answer, but he wanted to test him still further, so in a few days he called the younger god to him again. This time, he asked him to prepare the worst meal that could be made.

Orula went back to the market, again thoughtfully considered what to buy, and finally bought another ox tongue. Again he seasoned it delicately and cooked it with care, and served it to Obatalá.

When Obatalá saw that Orula had set ox tongue before him again, he said in great surprise, "Orula! How is it possible for the best to be also the worst?"

"I have already told you how tongue could be the best, great Obatalá," Orula said. "But it can also be the worst. For with it, people can be slandered, good reputations can be destroyed, whole nations can be ruined and sold. That, Sir, is why I am serving you the same meal again."

And Obatalá marveled at Orula's wisdom and maturity, and, without further hesitation, he proclaimed him Ruler of the World.

BOUQUI AND THE ENORMOUS YAMS

HAITI: "Bouqui" means old goat, and "Malice" means malicious, which explains practically everything about these two characters. Adapted from a story by M. Turenne des Prés.

BOUQUI once owned a pig which he fed on avocado pears.

Everybody in Haiti knows that pigs fed on this fruit can get so fat that they must lie on the ground and never stand up on their feet. And also, when a finger is pressed on their backs there is a dent which stays there a long time. These are two ways to know when a pig is ready for butchering.

That was about how fat Bouqui's pig was.

For some time Malice had been scheming to eat that pig. Being Malice, it was not hard for him to think of a plan.

He went to Bouqui and said, "Uncle Bouqui, I've just returned from my godmother's house where something amazing happened."

"What happened? Tell me quick, Malice!" Bouqui said.

"For four days they have been digging one single yam in her field, and they have just finished. This fruit of the earth is twice as large as you! It is so large that it took ten men to carry it. And now my godmother has to build a special house to put it in, because the one she lives in is too small. The most interesting thing is that she felt the vines of the other yams in her field, and they all seem to have yams just as big," Malice said.

"What!" cried Bouqui, "a yam twice as large as me? My! Your godmother must have fertilized them with cow, horse, and hog manure."

"No, not cow, horse, or hog manure. She butchered her pig, cut it up, seasoned and cooked it, and buried some of it around each yam patch. That's how she fertilized her yams," Malice explained.

"Oh, what a wonderful idea!" Bouqui said. "I'd like to have my yams twice as big as me, too, Malice. I have a pig, too, you know. Maybe the fatter the pig is, the larger the yams will be. Don't you think so, Malice?"

"Yes, that's what my godmother said."

When Malice had gone, Bouqui hurried to butcher his pig. He cut the meat up, seasoned and cooked it well, and buried it around his yam patches.

But Malice had not gone far. He had been hiding and watching everything Bouqui did. When night came, he went back to Bouqui's yam field and dug up every piece of pork and every yam and took them home.

Early next morning, Bouqui ran to the field to see if the yams were bursting the ground. Even the leaves should be greener, he thought. But at the sight of his torn-up yam field, with its dying plants and gaping holes, he fainted.

When he came to, he knew that Malice had done it. He cried aloud to the sky against him. He swore to get revenge.

"Death to Malice!" he cried.

Malice, who had been hiding in the bush behind Bouqui's house, heard every cry and every curse that Bouqui used against him. He heard what Bouqui was going to do to him, and he had to find a way to save his neck. He ran to his own house and filled his mouth with a liquid mixture the local voodoo doctor had made for him. It smelled to high heaven. Then he lay down in bed and began to groan loudly.

Bouqui came, and, from outside the house, he could hear Malice groaning. He called, "Malice, you thief, you crook! I can hear you groaning, carrying my heavy yams to hide them from me! I've come to make you pay for stealing my yams," and he burst in the door.

It was hard for Malice to speak with the liquid in his mouth, but he croaked pathetically, "Ah, Bouqui, I'm dying. That yam and pig meat of yours is killing me. I'm going to get you arrested for putting poison in there to kill people."

"Hah! Law or no law, you've stolen my yams. . . . But, tell me, is it really true that my yams made you sick?"

"O-o-o-o-h, I'm dying!" Malice groaned again. And he spit out the evil smelling liquid at Bouqui's feet.

Bouqui jumped back, lifting his nose away from the smell. "Oh, Malice," he said, "did my pig—my yams—give you that awful sickness? I wonder if it is catching?"

Malice said nothing except, "Oh, my stomach! Ow, I'm dying!"

Bouqui, afraid of catching the disease, ran away as fast as he could.

"That was Papa God who is punishing Malice for stealing my yams," he said to himself as he hurried away from Malice's house. "He is good to me to let that thief try them first and keep me safe. Now I don't mind that they're gone."

As soon as Bouqui was out of sight, Malice got up and washed out his mouth. He rubbed his hands together in a pleased way, licked his lips with relish, and sat down to a heaping gourd of delicious pig and yam.

37

EL TORO

THE TALE OF THE LAZY PEOPLE

COLOMBIA: The details of this Indian story are so intriguing that they almost hide the fact that—like most Indian stories—it is an explanation of how something came to be. Based on a story by Charles Finger.

LONG AGO in Colombia there were no monkeys. At that time the trees were so full of fruits and the vines of grapes, that the people grew lazy. At last they did little but eat and sleep, being too idle even to carry away the rinds of the fruits, and much too lazy to clean their thatched houses.

It was pleasant at first, but soon winged things that bit and stung began to buzz around the fruit rinds. Flies and mosquitoes came, and worst of all, great wasps with pink heads. The people were so irritated that they moved their flimsy houses to new spots because it was less trouble than cleaning up the piles of rinds. But since they had to stay near the lake where they got their drinking water, they soon had built all around its edge and were back again at the starting place.

With so much to eat, the flies and mosquitoes soon grew lazy themselves, and the people could hardly shoo them away. Finally, it was clear that something must be done. But what that something should be, the people were too lazy to decide.

One day, late in the afternoon when the people were still resting after the noon meal, there came to the village a queer, rather faded old man. He was ragged and torn, with rough yellow hair, and a mouth that always seemed to smile. The people paid little attention to him as he walked around the lake looking at things, and did not become really curious until he made a basket and started gathering up the fruit rinds. Then the people were tempted to question him. But it was too much trouble, so everyone went back to sleep.

The old man worked very diligently all night, but the refuse was so thick that he managed to clear only a small space, after all. In the morning, Tera, the headman, was astonished at the very thought that anyone would work all night for strangers, and he questioned the old man.

"What is your name, where do you come from, and what do you want?" Tera asked him, all three questions at once to save trouble.

"I want to work," said the old man. "I want to be told what you want done and to see that it is done."

"What is your trade?"

"I have no trade," said the old man. "I just get things done."

Then, whistling gaily, the old man went to the place he had cleared. He took flat pieces of wood and began cutting out figures like little men, except that each figure had a kind of handle that looked like a long tail. When he had whittled twenty figures for each man in the village, the old man stood up and stretched. Then, ignoring the questions of the villagers, he set the figures, alike as so many pins, in a long row and stood before them like a general.

After admiring the line for a moment, the old man made a signal with his hand, spoke a magic word, and the figures all came to life. Twenty manikins gathered around each of the village men, bowing up and down so that their wooden tails waved like pump handles.

"Since you do not like to work," the old man said to the villagers, "I have made these manikins to work for you. You must give only one job to each figure, so tell me what you want done, and I will assign them their work." The villagers thought of every job they could imagine, and, in a commanding voice, the old man called out to his manikins: "Armadillo-hunters, come forth. Come forth breadmakers, cassava-gatherers, dust-collectors, goat-shearers, amusers, bakers, odd-job-doers, burden-carriers, garbage-clearers, corn-grinders, story-tellers, pot-makers, pig-tenders, cheese-makers, paraders, food-carriers, errand-runners, cow-tenders." The manikins assigned to each job scurried to group themselves together like soldiers.

So everyone was well pleased, and that day there was a great cleaning and carrying and bustling. Silently, the little figures worked, never tiring, never getting in one another's way. And all the living men had to do was rest and watch and keep their brains free for higher things.

Not two days had passed before the children came to the old man to complain that they had too much to do. What with remembering what they were told, hunting for lost objects, and a dozen other tasks, they said they had no time for play. So the old man carved many more figures—palm leaf-pickers for making fans, figures to hunt for things in the dark, private teachers who never scolded, flower-gatherers, clowns, cake-makers, game-planners, keepers of things, story-tellers and nurses to look after younger brothers and sisters, figures to make

unclean, or disorderly. Soon, however, the people wanted even more service and, as the wooden figures became more numerous and no figure could do more than one task, the old man had to make figures to serve the figures. Then, too, the figures learned to eat and drink, so there had to be more fruit-gatherers, more water-carriers, and more cooks. Before long, there were sixty or seventy figures for each person, and the old man was whittling new ones every day.

The lively manikins were everywhere, as thick as the flies had been among the fruit rinds. Many houses were quite cluttered with them, rushing about until it made the head swim to look at them. And those manikins who were resting or sleeping were lying on the floors, piled

up in corners, or hanging from rafters by their tails.

There was so much confusion that the old man had to make a thousand or more order-keepers. These were everywhere, watchful and officious, so that the real people had to step very gingerly to avoid treading on them and annoying them.

At last there came a day when the people grew tired of doing nothing. They said that a little help was a good thing, but this was too

others obey, figures to buy things, and rememberers, singers, pie-makers, servants.

Things seemed to go very well and before a month passed not one thing was out of order, soiled, bent, broken, lost, misplaced, undone, much of a good thing altogether. So there was a meeting, and the manikin message-and-gossip-carriers were very busy, rushing here and there with their little scraps of information.

"You must let us do something," Tera finally said to the old man.

"I'm afraid there is nothing you can do," he said, "because, you see, everything is done, and when everything is done, something cannot be left undone. So it is clear that there is nothing left to be done."

At this, the meeting broke up and each man went back to his hammock to think. Soon the general cry was, "We must have elbow room!"

Immediately, the old man whittled ten new figures for each man, woman and child. In voices that creaked like wooden machinery, the new figures marched about crying, "Elbow room, elbow room!" The elbow-roomers thrust and pushed the other manikins, clutching them and sometimes falling down with them. Every house became a jangling tumult of running manikins and men. Everywhere the cry was "We want elbow room!"

Soon frantic men were running out of the houses with manikins hanging on to them, beating them, pursuing them. Other manikins

began throwing food and household things out of the windows. The excited children fled, too, followed by their clowns doing tricks and their story-tellers chattering stories as they ran. And everywhere the order-keepers ran about, trip-

ping people and manikins alike in their efforts to restore order.

When that day was over, there were no people in the houses or the hammocks. All the men, women, and children, even grandmothers and grandfathers, had fled to the far side of the lake and left everything to the manikins.

The next day, the people plucked fruit for themselves, and it had never seemed sweeter. The water they carried for themselves tasted clearer and cooler than ever before. At night they were happily tired and slept well with no manikins to swing their hammocks and sing to them. In the morning, they discovered that the sunrise was wonderful to see, and they were amazed at the beautiful things they had almost forgotten—the butterflies, the shadows on the hills, the green earth and blue sky, the rippling water and bending trees. Indeed, the memory of the manikin days was like a fearful nightmare. Very lightheartedly they set to work to build new houses and make things to put in them.

In the deserted village, the elbow-roomers went on pushing the manikins who went on trying to do their jobs. Those manikins who had nothing to do became quarrelsome and mischievous. The pot-cleaners broke the pots, and the pot-makers had to make more. That meant the clay-diggers had to work harder, and they wanted more to eat. So the fruit-gatherers and cooks had to work harder. This kept the fire-makers and wood-gatherers busy, which meant more work for the food-bringers. And always the elbow-roomers rushed about in groups of ten, driving and commanding. Everywhere were the little wooden figures with their pump handle tails rushing about, busy at nothing, quarreling about nothing, fighting about nothing.

The real trouble came when the manikins started pushing and hustling the dogs and cats, the goats and hens. The animals resented it and fell upon the manikins. Seeing that, the pots and kettles joined in and ran or rolled or fell, spilling hot water over the manikins. The very embers from the fire leaped into the fray. Then the stones between which the corn had been ground began to turn by themselves, all the while growling of their hate for the corn-grinders, who had tortured them every day.

Presently an elbow-roomer who was tussling with a corn-grinder stumbled between the grinding stones and was crushed to powder. In a flash, animals and pots and pans learned the trick and, in every house, manikins were pushed between the grinding stones. Then sparks began to fly and roofs caught fire and the manikins bolted here and there, falling over one another and jamming in doorways.

Suddenly, there came a dazzling lightning flash and a great rain and the manikins fled to the forest for safety, and climbed the trees. There they have lived ever since, and as time went by, they grew hair and became monkeys.

But, to this time, they remember all that has passed and they have no love for men. For that reason, a man who goes through the forest must look well to himself, less the vengeful manikins cast nuts and branches at his head in memory of the sorry days of the lazy people.

42

T WHY THE

HERE WAS ONCE a young Indian girl named Urú who was the daughter of a Guaraní chieftain. She was a girl of rare beauty and sweetness, and she had never displeased her parents in any way until she fell in love.

For Urú did not fall in love with one of the suitable young warriors of her tribe, or of some neighboring tribe. She gave her heart to Cuimaé, an enemy warrior whom her father had taken prisoner. She could see no man but Cuimaé, nor even think about any other, and she finally asked her father's permission to marry him.

Such a marriage was unthinkable to the

URUTAU BIRD MOURNS

ARGENTINA: This sad legend is told by the Guaraní Indians.

chief, and he answered his beloved daughter almost curtly, "Urú, you know well that my daughter cannot marry our enemy. I want to hear no more of this."

The girl said no further word, but she turned and ran into the forest. The chief did not follow her. He thought she would weep out her grief and then return to her home. But when night came and then morning, and the girl had not returned, the chief grew worried. Calling his sons, he set out to search for her. They hunted all day without finding a trace of Urú.

The next day, all the men of the village joined the search. They went deeper and deeper into the woods, right to the edge of the Great Forest where Kurupira, the evil gnome of the forests, reigned. Finally, two of the searchers spied the girl. She was sitting in the crotch of a tree, staring off into the distance, quiet as a stone.

The men called to her, but Urú did not seem to hear. She just sat there without moving. But when they approached, she fled, and before they could stop her, she darted into the Great Forest and climbed up into the crotch of an ancient, spreading willow tree. Not daring to follow into Kurupira's domain, the men

43

hurried back to report to the chief at once.

The chief and his wife came immediately. They did not even pause at the edge of the Great Forest, but, heedless of their own danger, they hurried to the foot of the willow tree where their daughter sat.

"Urú," they pleaded, "come down! Come quickly from the Great Forest while there is still time!"

The girl sat like a stone, appearing not to hear them.

"We fear for you, Urú," her mother wept. "Kurupira allows no human being in the Great Forest. You know that. You must come quickly while there is still time to flee. Oh, he will come for you with his horrid gnome's body and his evil laugh and his feet turned backwards, and we will never see you again. Come home, my beloved daughter!"

But the girl did not move. And as they sadly turned away, they heard Kurupira's wicked laugh sounding far away in the Forest.

The next day, Urú's brothers and sisters came bravely to the Great Forest to plead with her.

"Sister," they called, "please listen. We miss you so. Please come home." They told her of her pet wild pig which had been snuffling about searching for her ever since she had left. They told her of the new sandals her mother was making for her.

But Urú sat motionless, not seeing or hearing them, and the horrid laugh of the gnome could again be heard.

The third day, the medicine men came. They mumbled incantations to ward off Kurupira's magic power, and they tried all the magic they knew to break the spell that seemed to hold Urú. But she just sat there, staring off into the distance. And Kurupira appeared from behind a tree, laughing at the medicine men, and hopping up and down on his backwards-turned feet.

That night Urú's mother begged the chief to let Cuimaé go to their daughter. "Only her lover's pleas will move her," she said. "Let him go, I beg you!"

"He is our enemy," the chief said. "Why should he help us?"

"Because he loves Urú," the mother said. "He is sick with grief. He has not eaten or slept since she ran away."

So the chief released Cuimaé and, without waiting for daylight, the young warrior ran off to find Urú. The Great Forest was strange to him, and the night was starless. And Kurupira heard him coming and cast a spell over him, clouding his mind so that he forgot to take care in the dark. He came to a ravine and, in his desperate, unseeing haste, he ran over the edge and was killed on the black rocks below.

The next day the medicine men found Cuimaé's body when they went again to the Great Forest. But they went on to the willow tree where Urú sat and tried again to rouse her. Again, she sat like a stone.

Finally the chief medicine man said gently, "You must go home now, Urú. It is senseless to resist any longer, for Cuimaé is dead."

Instantly, there was a piercing shriek from the girl. The whole forest trembled, and before the eyes of the terror-stricken medicine men, Urú vanished. On the branch where she had been sitting there appeared a bird, a strange weeping bird that men had never seen before. And off deep in the forest could be heard the sound of Kurupira's vengeful laughter.

In Urú's honor, the bird was named Urutaú, which means the ghost of Urú. And to this day, the urutaú perches on the branches of willow trees and mourns with anguished cries of grief.

There are dozens of South American Indian stories in which a human being is turned into a bird. There is even an entirely different legend about the urutaú bird.

THE TALENTED COMPANIONS

CHILE: Stories very much like this one are still told in Europe, and it was probably brought to Chile by early Spanish settlers. Adapted from a story by Ernesto Montenegro.

THERE WAS ONCE a blacksmith's apprentice who decided to make a gun. "A special gun," he told the blacksmith, "that will shoot three miles."

The blacksmith wanted to encourage the boy so he gave him permission to work in the smithy on Sundays. It took the boy a whole year to make the gun, but when it was finished and the boy took it out to test it, he hit a target three miles away on the first try.

The blacksmith gave the apprentice fifty pesos because he had learned his trade so well. Then he said, "The best thing for you to do is to go out and see the world. There is really nothing more that I can teach you now."

So the boy set out on his travels, with his gun over his shoulder. He had not gone far when he met a chunky fellow who was carrying two whole tree trunks, one on each shoulder. Every so often, the chunky boy would throw one of the logs in the air, twirl it on his hand when it came down and put it back on his shoulder.

"Please tell me, my friend," said the boy with the gun, "what on earth you are doing?"

"Getting a bit of exercise, that's all," the other boy replied.

"And what is your name?"

"My name is String-Strang, son of the Strong

45

Man," the husky boy answered cheerfully.

"Why not join me, then?" said the apprentice. "I am on my way to see the world."

"I would be delighted," said String-Strang.

So the two boys walked on together, and soon they saw a very thin youth stretched out on the bank of a river, with his mouth down in the water. They watched for a long time as the thin boy gulped the river dry, waited for it to refill, and then gulped it dry again. Finally the boy with the gun said, "Are you planning to drink the whole river, my friend?"

The drinker looked up then, and said, "For a start, yes. Although this little thread of water is just enough to moisten my mouth."

"And what is your name?" asked the boy with the gun.

"I am Drenk-Dronk, son of the great Drinker."

"Won't you join us?" the two companions said. "We are on our way to see the world." So the three boys walked on together.

As they were passing through a lane, they saw a boy running toward them across a wheat field. He started up some partridges as he ran and caught one in each hand as they flew away.

"How can you run so fast, friend?" they asked him.

"I'm just stretching my legs a little," said the boy, without even breathing hard.

"What is your name?"

"I am called Rin-Ren, son of the great Runner," the boy answered. So the three companions asked Rin-Ren to come with them. "Why not?" he said, as he jumped over the wall to join them.

They walked until dusk, when suddenly they almost fell over a boy lying in the road.

"What in the world are you doing," they said, "stretched out in the middle of the road that way? And what is your name?"

"Ssshhh," the boy in the road said, not even raising his head. "Ssshhh." Finally he got up. "Excuse me, friends, for shushing you. I am called Listen-Lesten, son of the Listener. I was very much interested in a conversation that was going on in the land of the Pygmies on the other side of the world. It is said there that the king will give his daughter in marriage to the one who beats her in a three-mile race."

"Let us try our luck," said the boy who had caught the partridges. So Listen-Lesten joined them and they went to the land of the Pygmies.

There they told the king they had heard his daughter would be given in marriage to the man who could outrun her.

"It is true," said the king, "but I must warn you. I will cut off the head of any man who tries and fails."

This didn't worry Rin-Ren a bit, and at the appointed hour, the companions went to the race track. The princess came out dressed in a pink gown that made her look like an angel. She and Rin-Ren stood on the mark, and the judge gave them the word to go. Rin-Ren had no more than started when he arrived at the goal, all in one jump. The princess was so slow that he became tired of waiting for her and, lying down on the ground, he went to sleep. Listen-Lesten, who was listening to the judges talking two miles away, heard them say that since the young man had gone to sleep, the race wouldn't count.

"Quickly!" he said to the boy with the gun. "Shoot a bullet past Rin-Ren's ear and wake him." So the boy with the gun whistled a bullet past Rin-Ren's ear, and the runner arose just in time to greet the princess as she finished the course.

"Well," said the king. "You won, and I must keep my word. But you boys seem a little young for marriage, so I will pay you a ransom for the princess instead."

"That was just what we were going to suggest, your Royal Majesty," said the boy with the gun.

"It would be best if you pay us in silver, Your Majesty," said the boy who lifted logs, "so we can divide the prize without quarreling. Give us what I can lift on each one of these logs."

"Agreed, my good youths," said the king, thinking to get off cheaply.

The servants placed a dozen bags of silver on each log. String-Strang hoisted up the logs, and threw them higher than the tower and then twirled them in the air as though it were child's play. The king commanded that twelve more bags of silver be placed on each log, but the same thing happened again.

"You are going to ruin me," said the king in despair. "Tell me what else I may give you besides silver."

"Let us go into your wine cellar to quench our thirst, Your Majesty," said Drenk-Dronk.

Again the king thought that this would be an easy ransom. So he gave the boys the keys to the wine cellar. Drenk-Dronk stopped in front of a hundred gallon barrel and said, "Take the spigot out of this." With one swallow he left it dry. They opened another and then another, and still Drenk-Dronk drank. The king had to beg them to leave one little ten gallon keg for his household.

Finally the companions were satisfied, and they divided the silver fairly and squarely, said goodbye to the pretty little princess, and each one went his own way to enjoy his money.

THE CAT
A WHO USED HIS HEAD

PARAGUAY: Another story of a little animal who outwits a big one—in this case, a tiger. Reprinted from *Hi, Neighbor, 1958*, a UNICEF publication.

ALONG, long time ago all the animals of the world could talk to one another. Even if they happened to be of entirely different species—like monkeys and turtles—they could understand each other. At that time, the cat and the tiger looked very much as they do today. The cat was small and the tiger was big; but both were very strong, had fine big muscles and sharp big teeth.

The cat had learned how to use his strength, his big muscles, and his sharp teeth. He had no trouble getting food. And even though he was small, he had the respect of the largest of the animals. He led a smooth and easy life. The tiger, on the other hand, was thin and hungry. He could not seem to learn how to use his muscles, or even his teeth, very well.

One day the tiger went to the cat and said, "Please, friend cat, help me. We look the same. But even though I am bigger, you are a much better hunter. Would you teach me some of your tricks?"

The cat thought a minute and then said, "Yes, friend tiger, I will teach you how to be a good hunter. You must promise to work hard and practice every day."

Of course, the tiger agreed, and day after day, with great patience, the cat showed the tiger his tricks. He first taught the tiger how to creep up behind something without making a sound. Then he taught him how to bite and claw. They climbed trees, and the cat showed the tiger how to hide on a branch without making a move and without making a sound. The cat knew the best way to sharpen his teeth and his claws, and this, too, he taught the tiger. The last lesson was jumping. Day after day they practiced jumping, first sideways, then forward; forward and then to the side. If the cat was a good teacher, the tiger was a better pupil.

Finally the day came when the cat said, "Friend tiger, you have been a good student. You have worked hard and now you know all my tricks. I can teach you no more."

The tiger was surprised. He thought quickly. All that the cat said was true. He no longer needed the cat. It would be better to eat him. Then none of the other animals would learn that he, the big tiger, had been taught everything, even how to jump, by the little cat. Fast as lightning, the tiger jumped on top of the cat. But the cat, with the same speed, jumped back. The tiger landed with an awful thud—flat on the ground!

He cried out, "You didn't teach me to jump backwards!"

"That's right," said the cat, laughing. "I didn't and I wouldn't. If I had, I would be dead right now. I know you as well as I know myself."

From that day on, these two animals have hunted for their food in the same way—but the tiger has never, never learned to jump backwards.

AYAYMAMA

PERU, BOLIVIA: This mournful tale of evil spirits is typical of the legends told by South American Indians. Adapted from a story by Ciro Alegría.

WHEN THE MOON silvers the tops of the trees and the waters of the vast rivers the *ayaymama* sings long and mournfully. It is a bird nobody has ever seen, and it is recognized only by its sad call of "Ay, ay, mama!" All this comes from an evil spell cast by Chullachaqui. This is how it happened.

Long ago there was a chief named Coranke. He had a cabin of palm tree trunks, thatched over with palm leaves. There he stayed with his wife who was called Nara, and their little daughter. He was a strong, brave man who was always in the jungle fighting or hunting. Wherever he turned his eye, there his arrow flew, and he wielded his wooden club with a strength nobody could equal. His enemies fled from him.

Nara was beautiful and industrious. Her eyes were deep, her hair was black, and her skin was as smooth as cedar wood. She could weave and plait and mold clay and cultivate the garden beside the cabin where corn, yuccas, and bananas flourished. Their little daughter had Coranke's strength and Nara's beauty, and was like a beautiful jungle flower. And the family lived in happiness until the day Chullachaqui happened to see Nara.

Chullachaqui is the evil spirit of the forest. He looks like a man except that one of his feet is the hoof of a goat or a deer. When men go into the jungle to cut mahogany or hunt or gather rubber, Chullachaqui drowns them in swamps or rivers, makes them lose their way, or attacks them in the shape of a wild animal.

Chullachaqui loved Nara the moment he saw her. To see her and fall in love with her was all one. And, as he can take any form he wants to, sometimes he changed himself into a bird, and at other times into an insect, to be near her as much as he wanted to without frightening her.

But soon he tired of this and wanted to take Nara away with him. So he changed himself back to his own shape and, not to appear before her naked, he lay in wait in the forest for a poor Indian who was hunting there. He killed him and stole his tunic, which was long and covered his goat foot. Disguised this way, he went to the river and took a canoe that had been left on the bank. He thought nothing of killing the Indian or of stealing the canoe.

He rowed along until he came to the chief's house on the riverbank. "Nara, beautiful Nara," he said as he drew in, "I am a hungry traveler. Give me food. . . ."

Beautiful Nara filled half a gourd shell with yuccas and sweet corn and bananas. Sitting at the door of the cabin, Chullachaqui ate slowly, looking at Nara, and then said, "Beautiful Nara, I am not really a hungry traveler. I am only here because of you. I adore your beauty and I cannot live without it. Come with me!"

Nara answered, "I cannot leave Chief Coranke."

Then Chullachaqui began to weep and plead with Nara to go away with him.

"I will not leave Chief Coranke," said Nara.

Chullachaqui went sadly to the canoe and rowed down the river.

Nara noticed the footprints the visitor had left in the sand on the riverbank, and when she saw that one was the print of a hoof she exclaimed, "That was Chullachaqui." But she did not say anything to Chief Coranke when he came back so as not to expose him to the wrath of the evil one.

Six months went by and late one afternoon, a mighty chief stopped his great canoe in front of the cabin. He wore a rich tunic and his head was adorned with beautiful plumes, and his neck with heavy necklaces.

"Nara, beautiful Nara," he said, "you can see that I am powerful. The jungle is my domain. Come with me and it will be yours."

He had brought a thousand gifts—the most

beautiful flowers and the sweetest fruits of the forest and the most beautiful blankets, dishes, and tunics that the jungle tribes make. On one of his hands sat a white parrot and on the other a wild turkey, black as night.

"I see and know you are powerful," answered Nara, glancing at the hoofprint in the sand, "but for nothing in the world will I leave Chief Coranke."

Then Chullachaqui called out and the anaconda came out of the river, and he gave another cry and the jaguar came out of the forest. And on his one hand the anaconda rolled up its huge flexible body, and the jaguar arched its back on the other.

"You see now," said Chullachaqui, "I am also the master of the animals in the jungle. I will

50

kill you if you do not come away with me."

"I don't care," answered Nara.

"I will kill Chief Coranke," said Chullachaqui.

"He would prefer to die," said Nara.

Then the evil one pondered a moment and said, "I could take you by force, but if you were sad with me, it would be unpleasant. I will return in six months and, if you refuse to come with me, I will give you a terrible punishment." Carrying away his gifts, very sad, he disappeared down the river.

When Coranke returned from his hunting Nara told him everything, for she had to, and the chief decided to stay home to protect Nara and their daughter when the time came for Chullachaqui to return.

When the six months were nearly gone, Coranke put a new cord on his bow, sharpened his arrows and stayed around the cabin.

Then one day, when Nara was in the cornfield, Chullachaqui suddenly appeared before her. "Come with me," he said. "It is the last time I am going to ask you. If you don't come, I will turn your daughter into a bird who will mourn forever in the forest and will be so shy that nobody can ever see her; for the day she is seen the spell will be broken, and she will resume her human shape. Come, come with me. If not. . . ."

But Nara, mastering her fright, began to cry out, "Coranke! Coranke!"

The chief came quickly with drawn bow and swift arrow, ready to pierce Chullachaqui's heart, but the evil one had already fled into the jungle.

The parents ran to the spot where their little daughter lay sleeping, but the hammock was empty. And out of the rustling depths of the jungle they heard, for the first time, that mournful cry, "Ay, ay, mama," which gives its name to the enchanted bird.

The *ayaymama* still sings, especially on moonlit nights, and the men of the jungle always peer into the thick foliage in the hope of freeing the unfortunate child. It is very sad that nobody has yet been able to see it.

WHY DEER AND JAGUAR CAN'T BE FRIENDS

BRAZIL: In old stories, animals that are natural enemies often live together in harmony. This explains how one such friendship broke up.

ONE DAY many years ago the deer decided to build a house. "I am tired of living in the woods," he said, "with the rain pelting down on me and the wind chilling my bones. It is a very trying way to live. I shall find a place to build myself a snug house." He searched through the jungle and finally came to a sunny clearing on the river bank. "This is a fine place," he thought. "I shall build my house here."

On the same day a jaguar was wandering along the same river bank, and he paused to enjoy the sun in the little clearing. "What a splendid spot this is," thought the jaguar. "I would like to stay here always. I think I will build a house here and settle down."

So on the following day the deer came, ready for work, and he cleared the ground with his strong horns, and pawed the dirt smooth in the clearing. When the jaguar appeared to start work on the following day, he was surprised to find the ground all prepared. "The God Tupan is helping me!" he thought gratefully, and he set to work and laid out the floor of the house.

The next day the deer came again and said, "Look, the floor is laid! Obviously it is right for me to build this house, for Tupan must be helping me." And he put up the walls of the house, making two fine rooms, one for himself and one for Tupan.

On the day after that the jaguar came again and, thanking Tupan for his assistance, he finished the house, putting on the roof and the doors. It was evening when he finished his work, so he went into one of the rooms of the new house and fell asleep. Presently the deer arrived, admired the finished building, and settled down to sleep in the other room.

At dawn the two animals woke up and were amazed to see each other. "Was it you who was helping me with this house?" asked the jaguar.

The deer answered, "It was I. And all the time I thought Tupan was helping me."

The jaguar admitted he had had the same thought. "Anyway, we have a fine house," said the jaguar. "We must live together." The deer agreed, and they settled down to live amiably

51

in their comfortable house on the river bank.

One day the jaguar said, "I am going hunting for our dinner. Get the pots ready and get in the water and wood, for when I return, I shall be very hungry." And the jaguar went into the jungle, killed a large deer and dragged it home to his companion.

The deer was afraid when he saw what the jaguar had brought home. He prepared the meal and watched sadly as the jaguar ate, but he wouldn't touch the deer meat himself. That night he could not sleep for fear the jaguar would creep into his room and kill him as he slept.

The next day it was the deer's turn to hunt, so he went off into the jungle where he saw a great jaguar. The deer called to his friend the anteater, a powerful animal with great claws, and said to him, "Do you see that jaguar over there? Well, he has been speaking evil of you."

The anteater was furious, and he crept up behind the jaguar and seized him and killed him.

When the anteater had gone, the deer picked up the dead jaguar and carried it to the house. "Light the fire and get everything ready," he said to his companion. "I have brought home a fine dinner for us."

The jaguar was frightened when he saw the deer come in carrying a dead jaguar on his back, but he silently prepared the meal and watched, without eating any jaguar meat, as the deer enjoyed his dinner.

That night neither of the companions could sleep. They lay fearfully, each in his own room, listening. In straining to catch the slightest sound from the jaguar's room, the deer accidentally struck his antlers against the wall, making a clattering noise. When the jaguar heard this, he was sure the deer was coming to kill him, and he let out a shriek. The shriek, in turn, terrified the deer, and both animals ran for their lives out of the house and disappeared into the jungle in opposite directions.

And so it is that since that time, the deer and the jaguar have never lived together or trusted each other again.

THE HUNGRY OLD WITCH

URUGUAY: This tale of magic is based on a story by Charles Finger.

SHE WAS A WITCH, very old, always hungry, and she lived in the days when mighty beasts moved in the marshes and great worms bored through mountains and rocks. Her strength was such that she once caught one of the giant worms and killed it to get the green stone in its head, for he who has such a stone may fly through the air between sunrise and sunset, though never in the night. She had, too, a secret powder made of dried tree frogs mixed with goats' milk. With it she could turn plants to animals, vines to serpents, and grass into ants.

The old witch had lived for hundreds of years, devouring cattle and pigs and goats, sometimes carrying off in one night all the animals of a village. In time, it came about that men would put outside the village, in a corral, half of what they raised, hoping she would take it and leave them in peace.

At last there grew up a lad who refused to take animals to the corral for the old witch to eat. "It is not right," he said, "that we should give up that which we have tended and learned to love. Nor is it right that we should feed and fatten the thing that destroys us."

So the wise men called him Stout Heart, and he took his lance and went alone into the forest to put an end to the witch's evil work. After three days, he came to a lake. As he was tired, he climbed into a tree, which overhung it, to sleep.

While he slept the old witch came to fish, and she sang a charmed, unpleasant song which lured the fish into her basket-net. Soon the croaking song woke Stout Heart and he looked down and saw the wrinkled crone and the great pile of fish on the bank, and his heart was grieved at the waste of good life.

Stout Heart was weak and hungry from his long walk, and he had left his spear hidden nearby in the grass, so he sat very still in the tree hoping the old witch would not see him until he was better prepared. But she saw his shadow on the water and looked up at him. Since she did not have her magic stone with her and could not climb trees, she tried to coax the lad down with fruits and honey and with wheedling pleas of loneliness. But, although Stout Heart's hunger increased, he only laughed and said, "Have you any other trap to set for me?"

The witch fell into a black rage, gnashing her teeth and hooking her nails at him like a cat. Then suddenly she went on her hands and knees and fell to gathering up blades of grass into a little heap. When she had enough, she sprinkled a powder over the heap, mumbling, "Creep and crawl, creep and crawl! Over leaf and over twig. Seek and find the living thing. Pinch him, bite him, torture him! Make him drop like rotting fruit!"

Presently the grass blades moved, became smaller, rounded themselves, and turned brown. Fine hairs shot out and became legs, and each blade turned into a stinging ant. Up the trunk they swarmed, over every leaf and twig, and louder and louder the old witch screamed, "Up the tree trunk, on the branch! Creep and crawl, creep and crawl." The nearer to Stout Heart they came, the louder she shrieked, "Seek and find the living thing!" Stout Heart avoided them for a time, going higher and higher, crawling along a branch that hung over the lake, but as the ants came nearer, the witch bade them, "Pinch him, bite him, torture him!" And at last, when the ants were swarming over his hands, there was nothing to do but loose his hold on the branch.

He dropped into the cool green-blue lake with a splash and tried to swim under water for a way, but he seemed to be caught in some-

thing. With a sudden leaping of the heart, he knew he was in the old witch's basket-net. He was drawn ashore, all mixed up with fish and scum, with water beetles and sticky weed, and presently he was toppled head first into the witch's basket. He was dazed and weak and he fell into a trance, or slept. When he came to himself, he was in an evil smelling stone house. Through a small hole in the wall, he could see only bare earth and great rocks and he sank down in grief and despair.

But then a door opened and a lovely maiden appeared. She took his hand and led him out

53

of the dark into a great hall with a vast fireplace. Having heard his story, she showed him a little room where he might hide.

"When I came to this place long ago," she said, "the old witch killed the one who was her slave before me. But before that girl died, she told me of the witch's green stone and her magic powders. Since then, I have been the witch's slave. But now she will kill me and you will take my place until she catches another. For many, many years, each one who has died has revealed the power of the green stone to the other, though none has dared to use it."

Stout Heart argued with the maiden, telling her that he would not let her die, that they must escape together. Suddenly, they heard the voice of the witch, and the maiden said, "Hide quickly. I will steal the green stone so we may fly. With you I dare to try it."

She thrust him into the little room and closed the door, and he could hear the witch enter and throw a pile of wood on the hearth.

"I have a new prize," the hungry witch said to the maiden. "You have fattened long enough and must now be my meal. Go, then, fetch red pepper and black, and salt. And hurry, for I am hungry and cannot wait."

The girl went into another room, but soon returned running lightly. As she passed the old witch, she cast some of the magic powder on her. The witch thought she had spilled the salt and pepper and angrily took her by the hair and cast her into the room where Stout Heart was, screaming, "Stay there until I am ready to roast you!"

By means of the green stone, Stout Heart and the maiden at once flew through the window and up into the sky. The powder did its work on the witch and she began to swell so that she could not pass through any of the doors. But the boy and girl looked down from the sky and saw her burst through the roof. Then they flew

swift and high. But the witch was also swift, and she ran under them, gleefully aware in her wicked heart that the power of the green stone would soon disappear with the setting of the sun. No deer, no huanaco, could have bounded lighter over the ground than she did, and no ostrich could have moved more swiftly.

The boy and girl flew lower and lower as the sun dropped toward the horizon. Finally, the maiden thought of a plan. She scattered some of the magic powder on the earth. They rejoiced to see the leaves on which it fell turn to rabbits. The witch could not resist stopping to catch and swallow some of them and the fliers won a little time. But the witch was soon under them again, running as fast as ever. The maiden scattered more powder, and this time some thorn bushes turned into foxes. Again the hungry witch stopped to eat, but the sun was lower and the boy and girl were dropping ever nearer to the earth, now barely higher than the trees. Ahead of them was the lake where Stout Heart had been caught. The old witch was so near by they could hear her horrible breathing.

They cast the last handful of powder on the lake shore. The grass turned to ants and the stones to great turtles as the lad and maiden passed over the water, now just skimming the surface. The old witch stopped to swallow the turtles, shells and heads, and the girl and boy just reached the far shore before the power of the stone gave out. Weeping, the maiden clung to Stout Heart as they watched the old witch plunge into the lake.

She cut through the water so swiftly that a great wave leaped up on either side of her. But when she was in the middle of the lake, the turtles, like great stones inside of her, began to weigh her down. She made such an uproar of lashing hands and feet that the water became hot and steam rose up. But then her force was spent. She sank beneath the water, and was seen no more.

Great was the joy of the villagers when Stout Heart brought the maiden home. She became his wife and was loved by all there as the fairest woman among them.

THE FIVE EGGS

ECUADOR: There must be a lot of stubborn women; at any rate, they appear in folk tales all over the world. In this story a stubborn wife gives up but she doesn't give in. By Frank Henius.

IN THE FIELDS near the city there lived two poor peasants, named Juan and Juanica. They loved each other devotedly, but since they were very poor they would sometimes go two or even three days without eating.

Once after they had had nothing to eat for three days, Juanica asked her husband: "How are we going to keep on living if we don't eat?"

"Don't worry," said he, "I will go this very day to town to see if I can manage to find money to buy five eggs for us to boil and eat."

boil the eggs at once, for he was so hungry he could eat a burro. When the eggs were all boiled, his wife said to him, "Juan, come eat your two eggs; I shall eat three because I cooked them."

But he immediately said no, that he was the one who was to have three eggs, and she should have only two. And he kept on insisting, saying: "Three for me and two for you." But his wife was stubborn, maintaining that she was to have three and he two. And that went on and on.

Immediately he set out for town. On arrival, he stood on a corner to wait for a passer-by from whom he could ask alms. When he saw a man coming, he said to him: "Listen, my friend! Would you be good enough to give me four cents to buy an egg?" And the man, who was very charitable, gave him the four cents. That happened five times, and the peasant was fortunate enough not to have one of the five refuse him. When he had enough to buy the five eggs he went on and bought them. And when he had bought them he returned home to tell his wife the good news.

When he reached home he told his wife to

After they had wasted a good deal of time talking, Juanica decided to tell Juan that if he did not give her the three eggs to eat she would die. But he said to her, very indifferently: "All right, that makes no difference to me. Go ahead and die!"

So she fell to the ground as if dead. Then he began to weep: "Oh, my poor wife, I loved her so. Oh, my poor wife!" And after he had wept until he was tired, he whispered in her ear: "Juanica, don't be so silly. I'll eat three and you two." But she answered: "No, I am going to eat three and you two, or else you can bury me." But he kept on weeping.

After he saw that his wife refused to come to life again, he decided to go and look for his best friend. But he had five friends, and when he reached their homes he told them that he had come to ask them please to bury his wife, who had just died, and that he was counting on them, for he did not have a single cent to buy the casket. But his friends said not to worry, that they would see to that.

On his return home, he found her still playing dead. Then Juan burst into tears again: "Oh, Juanica, do not leave me alone, please!" And so that no one would see him, he slipped near where she lay to whisper in her ear: "I am going to eat three and you two." But she said no, that she was to eat the three and he the two. Then he said to her: "Take care, for we are going to bury you." And she replied: "That's nothing; bury me whenever you like."

After waiting a good while, they put her in the casket to carry her to the cemetery. And on the way Juan kept on crying: "Oh, my poor wife, don't leave me!" And he made them stop the funeral procession, supposedly so that he could kiss her, but really to tell her that he was going to eat three and she two. But her reply was always the same. When they reached the cemetery they bore her to the edge of the grave they had dug to receive her. Then he went up to her and whispered in her ear: "Look, you are on the edge of the grave, and we are about to put you in it." Then, when she realized that he was telling the truth, she sat up in the casket and said, "All right, then; you can eat all five of them."

So she got up out of the casket and they both went home. But once arrived there, Juanica set the five eggs on the table—and ate *three!*

THE

VENEZUELA: In this story, unlike many folk tales about animals, the smaller animal does *not* outsmart his larger opponent.

T HERE WAS ONCE a fine cat, a clever and aristocratic cat, who spent his idle hours in a well-stocked pantry. The pantry was full of sausages, hams, preserves, cheese, oysters, corned beef, and a thousand other delicacies, but everything was hung from the rafters, well above the reach of even the most aristocratic cat. The cat came to the pantry, therefore, not so much in the hope of stealing food, but simply because the odors of the place were so delicious to his nostrils.

One moonlit night, as the cat rested in his accustomed place, sniffing and sighing, he spied a fat, self-satisfied mouse who was perched on top of a cheese up near the ceiling. The cat knew it was useless to try to jump that high, so he decided to resort to flattery.

"Dear sir," the cat called in his most pleasing tones. "Your distinguished appearance and your high position in life attract me enormously. I would like to offer, in all sincerity, my affection and friendship."

From his safe perch on top of the cheese, the mouse answered suspiciously. "I can see your claws too well to have much faith in your friendship, Cat. And I know for a fact that you breakfasted on my uncle last week."

"It is true," said the cat repentently, "that I have eaten a mouse or two in the past, but all that is behind me. I have reformed, dear friend!

GULLIBLE MOUSE

The divine light of religion has come to me. I am now a more humane and sensitive cat. Look down from your great eminence and see how I have changed." The cat moved into a ray of moonlight where the mouse could see him clearly, and he stood looking humble, with his tail drooping and his eyes pleading. "Can you see me, dear Mouse?" the cat asked. "Can't you see how I long for your friendship? Ah, if only I could be always at your side, to learn from you, and to admire your rare perfection."

The mouse looked down at the cat, preened himself, and answered in a friendlier way. "You do, indeed, look different, my poor friend with the claws. And although it's not for me to say, you are right in recognizing me as a superior specimen of my race. My gleaming fur and the length of my whiskers are much admired all over the city, not to mention my quick wit. But tell me, what do you think of my tail?"

"It is a tail to put all other tails to shame," the cat said. "Surely, your tail must have been a direct gift from heaven, presented to you as a mark of your superior Mousehood. I have always thought," the cat went on conversationally, "that man lacked a certain grace by not having a tail, don't you agree? How I would like to discuss these serious matters with you, dear Mouse, but I must say this calling from floor to ceiling destroys the privacy of our conversa-tion. And, although I don't like to mention it, my neck is getting awfully tired looking up so far. Come down, good Mouse, so I can delight in your presence while we talk."

"I would like to, my friend, I really would," said the Mouse. "I am enjoying our talk enor-mously, but I can't forget what happened to my uncle."

At this, the cat beat his breast and wailed: "Oh heavens, poor miserable creature that I am, I deserve this! I deserve to be reviled and mis-trusted!" And tears came to the cat's eyes. "I am unworthy of your trust. I can never live down my past sins. I can never aspire to the friendship of a blameless hero like yourself."

"Ah now, my friend—" the mouse began.

"No, no, don't try to comfort me merely out of kindness," the cat cried. "If my deep respect and affection can't persuade you to trust me, if you feel it would lower you to come down and talk to a sinner like myself, then I accept your verdict! I shall retire to a black hole and live far from the world until death at last puts an end to my miserable fate." And the cat sobbed piti-fully.

The mouse was greatly moved. "No, no, dear Cat," he said. "I believe you. Truly I do. I can see now that you are goodness itself. And you shall have the pleasure of my company."

With that the mouse strutted down from his perch on top of the cheese, like a king deigning to mingle with his subjects. But hardly had he touched the floor when the cat sprang, caught the mouse and promptly ate him. Proving that mice are, after all, mice, and that cats are for-ever cats, no matter how foolish the one, or how convincing the other.

PART 5 GHANA: TOGOLAND REPUBLIC: REPUBLIC OF GUINEA: CAMEROONS: LIBERIA: BRITISH EAST AFRICA: NIGERIA: BANTU: UNION OF SOUTH AFRICA ILLUSTRATED BY PAUL BAC

TWO FEASTS FOR ANANSI

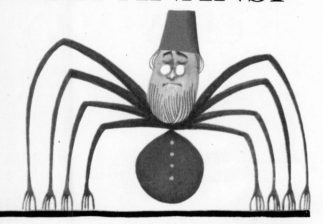

LIBERIA: The greedy and clever Anansi is West Africa's animal hero. This story and the one that follows are from *The Hat-Shaking Dance* by Harold Courlander and A. K. Prempeh.

KWAKU ANANSI'S thin belly came from greed. It is said that one year there was a wedding feast in the town of Kibbes, and another wedding feast in the town of Diabee, and they were both on the same day. Anansi asked himself, "Which feast will I go to?" He thought, and then he said, "I am very hungry, I will go to both. I will eat first at the place where the food is served first, and afterwards I will go to the other place and eat again."

But Anansi couldn't find out which of the feasts would come first. He went to Diabee and asked: "When will the food be served?" But they couldn't tell him. So he went down to the town of Kibbes and asked: "What time will the food be given out?" But they didn't know. He went back and forth between the two towns, first one and then the other, until he was weary. But still he knew nothing about where the food would be given out first.

So Kwaku Anansi bought two long ropes, and he sent for his sons Intikuma and Kweku Tsin. He tied both ropes around his middle. He gave the end of one rope to Intikuma, saying: "Take this end of the rope with you and go to Diabee. When they start giving out the food, pull hard on the rope and I will come." He gave the end of the other rope to Kweku Tsin, saying: "Take this with you to Kibbes. When the feast begins, pull hard and I will come. This way I will know where the food is given out first."

So Intikuma went to Diabee, taking the end of one rope with him, and Kweku Tsin went to Kibbes, taking the end of the other rope with him. Each of them stood in the town and waited to give the signal.

But when the feasts began in Diabee and Kibbes, they began at the very same moment. Intikuma pulled and Kweku Tsin pulled. As they both pulled very hard, Anansi couldn't go one way or another. He was halfway between and he couldn't move. His sons pulled harder and harder, and they didn't stop until the feast was over and the food was gone. Then they went to see what had detained their father.

They found him where they had left him, but he didn't look the same. Where the ropes had squeezed him around the middle he had become very small. And this way he has always remained. The spider carries with him forever the mark of his greed.

WHY WISDOM IS FOUND EVERYWHERE

GHANA, TOGOLAND REPUBLIC, REPUBLIC OF GUINEA, CAMEROONS.

KWAKU ANANSI regarded himself as the wisest of all creatures. He knew how to build bridges, to make dams and roads, to weave, and to hunt. But he didn't wish to share this wisdom with other creatures. He decided one day that he would gather together all the wisdom of the world and keep it for himself. So he went around collecting wisdom, and each

bit he found he put
in a large earthen pot.

When the pot was full, Anansi prepared to carry it into a high treetop where no one else could find it. He held the pot in front of him and began to climb.

Anansi's son Intikuma was curious about what his father was doing, and he watched from behind some bushes. He saw Anansi holding the pot in front of him against his stomach. He saw that this made it hard for Anansi to grasp the tree he was climbing. At last he couldn't keep quiet any longer and he said: "Father, may I make a suggestion?"

Anansi was startled and angry, and he shouted: "Why are you spying on me?"

Intikuma said to him: "It's only that I see you are having difficulty. When you climb a tree, it is very hard to hold a pot in front. If you put the pot on your back, you can climb easily."

Anansi tried it. He took the pot from in front and put it on his back. He climbed swiftly. But then he stopped. He looked at Intikuma and was embarrassed, for although he carried so much wisdom in the pot, he had not known how to climb with it.

In anger, Kwaku Anansi took the pot and threw it from the treetop. It fell on the earth and shattered into many pieces. The wisdom that was in it scattered in all directions. When people heard what had happened, they came and took some of the wisdom Anansi had thrown away. And so today, wisdom is not all in one place. It is everywhere. Should you find a foolish man, he is one who didn't come when the others did to take a share of the wisdom.

WAKAIMA AND THE CLAY MAN

BRITISH EAST AFRICA: In the United States, the elephant has become Br'er Fox, Wakaima is called Br'er Rabbit, and the clay man is a tar baby, but the story has hardly changed at all. By E. B. Kalibala and Mary Gould Davis.

LONG AGO in Africa there was a very lazy rabbit called Wakaima. He lived with his greatest friend, a hard-working elephant called Wanjovu. They had a farm.

Now Wanjovu grew tired of doing all the work for his lazy friend, so one day he said, "Let us each have his own farm and share what we grow."

Wakaima agreed.

They each selected a plot of ground, prepared the soil and planted the seed. Wanjovu worked hard on his farm, but Wakaima spent his days in the jungle eating wild fruit and sleeping. When evening came, he would rub dirt on himself and come in, rubbing his back and groaning about how tired he was.

Wanjovu cultivated his corn and potatoes and peas. He was really tired in the evening, but he said nothing. He prepared supper for both of them while Wakaima lay before the fire.

This went on for weeks. Finally the crops were ready. The time had come to gather in the harvest.

One evening Wanjovu came in with a large basket filled with beautiful corn and fine white potatoes. He cooked them very carefully and he and Wakaima ate every one.

"How good the corn is, how sweet!" said Wakaima. "And I have never eaten finer potatoes."

The next evening Wakaima came in with a basket full of corn and potatoes. "These are probably not as good as yours," he said. "But we will try them."

Wanjovu looked them over. They looked very

much like those from his own garden. But he said nothing. He cooked them, and they ate them for supper.

The next morning, when Wanjovu went to his farm, he saw that someone had been there in the night and stolen some of his corn and potatoes. That evening he told Wakaima about it.

Wakaima pretended to be very much excited. "Some thief got into my farm, too," he said. "What are we going to do about it?"

"We must do something to keep the thief away," Wanjovu said. "I will think it over and work out a plan."

The next day Wanjovu went to the river and got a large quantity of clay. With it he made a clay man with arms outstretched. Carefully he carried the clay man to his farm and set it up between the corn and the potatoes. When he had finished it was quite dark. Wanjovu went home, cooked supper and he and Wakaima went to bed.

Later, when the moon had risen, the thief stole into Wanjovu's potato patch. It was Wakaima. He saw the clay man looming up in the moonlight and he was frightened. Could it be Wanjovu waiting to punish him for stealing his vegetables? He dared not move. The clay man did not move, either.

Finally Wakaima gathered courage to speak. "Hullo, Wanjovu," he called, "what are you doing here at this time of night?"

The clay man did not answer.

Wakaima grew angry. "You are not Wanjovu!" he shouted. "You are a thief who has come to steal his corn. Tell me what you are doing, or I will go at once and tell Wanjovu."

The clay man did not answer.

Wakaima drew nearer to him. He was puzzled. "Who are you?" he said. "Why do you not answer?"

The clay man did not answer.

Wakaima walked cautiously all around him. The clay man looked very large in the moonlight.

"If you do not answer me, I will hit you!" shouted Wakaima.

The clay man did not answer.

Wakaima went up to him and struck him as hard as he could with his paw. And his paw stuck to the soft clay.

"Let me go!" he screamed. "Let me go, or I will hit you with my other paw!"

But the clay man did not let him go.

Wakaima lifted his other paw and punched the clay man in the stomach as hard as he could. And his other paw stuck in the soft clay. He was getting more angry every minute.

"Let me go, I tell you!" he shouted. "If you do not let me go, I will kick you with my foot."

But the clay man did not let him go.

Wakaima raised his foot and kicked the clay man. And his foot stuck in the soft clay. He tried his best to pull his foot away.

But the clay man would not let it go.

Wakaima was now very angry and very tired. He lifted his other foot and kicked the clay man with all his strength. And the other foot stuck in the soft clay.

"I will bite you with my teeth!" screamed Wakaima. "I will bite you in the stomach with my long, sharp teeth unless you let me go."

But the clay man did not let him go.

Wakaima butted his head against the clay man and set his long, sharp teeth into the clay. And the clay held him fast. He could not draw his teeth away. He could not draw his head away. His feet and his paws were held fast. He could not move or call for help. He was held as if in a trap.

The moon sank low in the sky. Darkness came. There was Wakaima, held by the clay man.

When the sun rose and the birds began to sing their morning songs, Wanjovu got up and went to his farm. And there he found Wakaima, held by the clay man.

"You wicked fellow!" he thundered. "So you are the thief who has stolen my food. It was easier to steal my corn and potatoes than to work on your own farm. What a lazy, good-for-nothing you are! Now I shall punish you."

He pulled at Wakaima until he had freed him from the clay man.

"What are you going to do with me?" sobbed the wretched Wakaima.

Wanjovu thought for a while. Finally he said, "I really ought to eat you. You have lied to me and eaten my crops, so I should eat you."

"But you cannot eat me alive," protested Wakaima. "I will have to be dead before you eat me."

"Well, what do you want me to do?" asked Wanjovu uneasily. He was not very happy about eating his friend.

"Throw me over there among the trees," said Wakaima. "Throw me very high among the branches. By the time I hit the ground, I will be dead. Then you can eat me."

Wanjovu lifted Wakaima. He threw him high among the branches of the trees. But when Wakaima struck the ground, he was not dead. He was not even hurt. He landed lightly on his feet and scampered away into the jungle. Wanjovu knew that he could not catch him. He went back to his farm.

Since that time, Wanjovu and Wakaima have not spoken to one another.

THE CONCEITED SPIDER

NIGERIA: It is no accident that so many stories are told about Anansi. By W. H. Barker and C. Sinclair.

I N THE OLDEN DAYS, all the stories men told were stories of Nyankupon, the chief of the Gods. Anansi the Spider, who was very conceited, wanted all the stories to be told about

him. So one day he went to Nyankupon and asked that, in the future, all tales told by men might be Anansi stories instead of Nyankupon stories.

Nyankupon agreed, on one condition. He told Anansi the Spider that he must bring him three things: the first was a jar full of live bees, the second was a boa-constrictor, and the third was a tiger. Anansi gave his promise.

He took an earthen jar and set out for a place where he knew there were numbers of bees. When he came in sight of the bees, he began saying to himself, "They will not be able to fill this jar." "Yes, they will be able." "No, they will not be able."

Finally the bees came up to him and said, "What are you talking about, Mr. Anansi?"

He then explained to them that Nyankupon and he had had a great dispute. Nyankupon had said the bees could not fly into the jar. Anansi had said they could. The bees immediately declared that, of course, they could fly into the jar. And they did. As soon as they were safely inside, Anansi sealed up the jar and sent it to Nyankupon.

Next day, he took a long stick and set out in search of a boa-constrictor. When he arrived at the place where one lived, he began speaking to himself again. "He will be just as long as this stick." "No, he will not be as long as this." "Yes, he will be as long as this."

He repeated these words several times, until the boa-constrictor came out and asked him what was the matter.

"Oh, we have been having a dispute in Nyankupon's town about you," said Anansi. "Nyankupon's people say you are not as long as this stick. I say you are. Would you please let me measure you by it?"

The boa innocently laid himself out straight, and Spider lost no time in tying him on to the stick from end to end. Then, when the boa was helpless, he sent him to Nyankupon.

The third day, he took some gum and glued his eye shut. He then set out for a den where

he knew a tiger lived. As he approached the place, he began to shout and sing so loudly that the tiger came out to see what was the matter.

"Can you not see?" said Anansi. "My eyelids are glued together and now I can see such wonderful things that I must sing about them."

"Glue my eyelids," said the tiger, "so that I, too, may see these amazing sights."

Anansi immediately did so, and having made the tiger helpless, he led him straight to Nyankupon's house. Nyankupon was astonished at Anansi's cleverness in accomplishing the three tasks.

"From now on," Nyankupon said, "you have my permission to call all the old tales Anansi tales."

And that is why, in Nyankupon's country, all the stories are Anansi's.

THE TALE OF THE NAME OF THE TREE

BANTU: As in most primitive stories, men and animals are mixed together rather indiscriminately in this one. By Pattie Price.

THERE WAS at this time, my friend, a great famine in the land. Now, in the land there grew a great tree with fine fruit, but it was known that this fruit would only drop when someone spoke the name of the tree. So as the famine grew worse and worse, the people all came and lived near the tree, waiting for the fruit to ripen. When the fruit was almost ripe, it was found with dismay that no one knew the name of the tree!

So they said, "Let us send the Hare to the Chief over the Mountains in order that he might tell us the name."

The Hare accordingly set forth and soon reached the kraal of the Chief over the Mountains. When he asked the Chief for the name of the tree, the Chief replied, "That tree is called U-wun-ge-lay-ma. When you get back, stand beneath it and say 'U-wun-gay-lay-ma' and the fruit will fall."

So the Hare hurried on his way back to his people. But he had not gone far on the path when he tripped over a root and rolled down the hill. And before he reached the bottom, the name of the tree had gone out of his head!

He tried all the names he knew and many others as he went along. He said, "Is it U-wun-tu-le-gay-le, or U-wayn-gay-le-tu-la, or what?' All the way, he tried to remember, but when he arrived at the tree, although he tried many words, not a piece of fruit fell!

Now the people said they would send the Springbok, for he was so swift he would return before he had forgotten the word. So the Spring-bok set out and arrived there in no time. Then the Chief told him, "That tree is called U-wun-ge-lay-ma."

And he started back as fast as he could to return to his people. But in his haste he tripped over an ant hill and before he could pick himself up, the name was gone! He tried all the names he knew on the way, but in vain. When he got back, all he could say was, "U-wun-ge-lay-tum-ba," and *that* was no use!

So the people said they would send the Kudu, for he was stronger and would not fall on the way. So the Kudu set out and soon arrived at the Chief's kraal. The Chief over the Mountains told him, "The name of that tree is U-wun-ge-lay-ma," and the Kudu thanked him and started back.

But on his way, he caught his horns in the branches of a tree. While he was freeing himself, he forgot to say the word and it went out of his head! When he had freed himself, it was gone. And when he returned to his people, he had to admit that he had forgotten it.

The people now said they would send the Lion, for he was both swift and strong, and he had no horns to catch in trees. The Lion got the word from the Chief over the Mountains and started home, repeating the word to himself. But the sun was hot and he was tired. He lay down to rest in the shade of a bush. And he slept. But when he woke, the name was gone out of his head!

Now the Lion was too proud to admit he had forgotten the word, so he made up a word and said it many times to the tree. But no fruit fell. Then the people said, "Nonsense! There is no such word! You are no better than the others, for you have forgotten also." And they were very sad, for their hunger was growing and the fruit was ripening.

At last the Elephant said, "Let us send the Tortoise." All the animals laughed for they were sure no one so slow could remember.

But the Lion said, "Let him go. Since we have all failed, it is best that he should fail also."

But before the Tortoise left, he went to his mother and asked her, "How does one remember a very hard word?"

His mother said, "If you wish to remember it, do not stop saying it for any reason."

After a long time, the Tortoise reached the kraal of the Chief over the Mountains and the Chief told him, "That tree is called U-wun-ge-lay-ma." The Tortoise asked him again and the Chief told him yet again. The Tortoise asked him a third time and the Chief said the word yet again.

So then he set out, saying the name to himself. When he came to the ant hill, he said "U-wun-ge-lay-ma," as he went around it. When he came to the tree, he just went on saying it. And again when he came to the bush, although he was very tired and it was very hot, he only said "U-wun-ge-lay-ma," and kept on.

At last he reached his home and his wife said, "You are very tired. Will you not rest?"

But the Tortoise said, "U-wun-ge-lay-ma," and went on.

When he reached his friends underneath the tree, they all said, "What is the name? Tell us the name of the tree!"

And he said, "U-wun-ge-lay-ma."

And the fruit immediately began to fall. And the people ate and were hungry no longer, and they said, "We will make the Tortoise Chief over all the people for he has brought us the name of the tree!"

And now, my friend, can *you* remember what was the name of that tree?

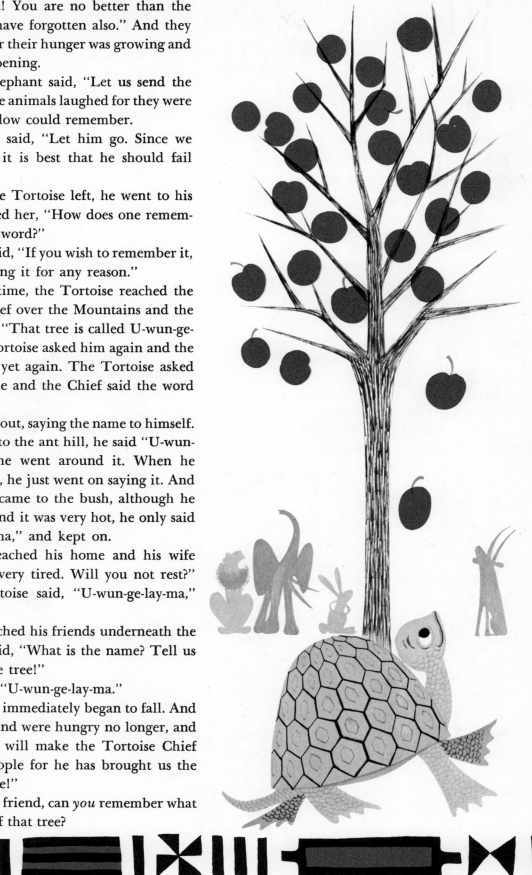

THE RAM AND THE LION'S SON

UNION OF SOUTH AFRICA: The Bushmen of South Africa tell this particular story, but animal stories much like it turn up in other countries, too.

THE LION'S son had become old enough to hunt for himself and not to wait upon the pleasure of his father and mother. One day, when he was returning home from hunting by himself, he came upon the home of a Ram. Now this young Lion had never before seen a Ram and, therefore, approached him timidly.

"Good day, friend," he said. "And what may your name be?"

The Ram was terrified, for the Lion's son, though young, was large and strong, with mighty claws and teeth, and his muscles rippled slickly under his yellow hide. But the Ram was too clever to let the young Lion know of his feelings, so he struck his chest with his forefoot and said in his gruffest, most menacing voice, "I am a Ram. Who are you?"

66

"A Lion," the young one whispered, frightened out of his wits by the Ram's voice and actions. "Good-bye friend!" And he ran home as fast as he could.

When the young Lion was almost home, he met his friend, the Jackal. "Slow down, friend," the Jackal said soothingly, standing squarely in his path. "From what do you flee in such a panic?"

"Oh, friend Jackal," the Lion's son gasped, panting and puffing, "I am half dead with fright, for I have just seen the most dreadful creature, the like of which I've never seen before. He looked as though he would attack me with his huge, thick head and, when I asked his name, he thumped his chest and growled, 'I am a Ram!' "

"A Ram!" cried the Jackal. "Do you mean to say you went off and left a delicious meal like that just standing there? For goodness' sake, where are your brains? Come, we will go back together and eat it."

"Oh, no, friend Jackal, I couldn't," moaned the Lion's son. "From the looks of this fierce beast, I think we may be the ones who will be eaten."

"Nonsense!" said the Jackal. "Come, we will tie ourselves together with this leather thong.

Then you will know I will always stay with you."

"Well, if you really think it's all right," said the Lion's son. "But I am no less frightened to know he will eat us both instead of only myself."

They started off for the home of the Ram, and the Ram, who was out looking for the tenderest greens for supper, saw them coming over the crest of the hill. He whirled and ran to his wife, calling, "Wife! Wife! I fear this is the last day of our lives, for the Lion is coming back, and this time he has brought a Jackal with him! What shall we do?"

"Don't be afraid," said his wife. "Take the child in your arms and, when you see them coming near, pinch it to make it cry as if it were hungry. I'll do the rest."

The Ram did as his wife said, and went out with the child in his arms toward the approaching companions. When the Lion's son saw the Ram, his legs began to go weak and he shivered all over with fright. He tried to turn back, but the leather thong held him fast to the Jackal, who continued to walk toward the Ram saying, "Come on, friend, there's nothing to fear!"

When the Lion's son and the Jackal were near, the Ram pinched his child and the child bellowed in anger and pain. The wife came running out, saw the approaching companions and called above the uproar, "You have done well, friend Jackal, to have brought us such a fine supper as Lion meat. And just in time, too. Hear how the child cries for food!"

On hearing these dreadful words, the Lion's son turned tail and set off the way he had come, dragging the Jackal after him. There was no time in his terrified flight to stop and let the Jackal loose, even though he begged and pleaded. He dragged the howling Jackal over hill and valley, through bushes and over rocks. And he never stopped to look behind him until he and the half-dead Jackal came to the home of his father.

But the Ram and his wife comforted their offended child, and they all spent the rest of the day eating the most delicious greens for supper.

THE SULTAN'S FOOL

LIBYA, TUNISIA: Folklore is full of stories about weird characters that various kings and sultans kept around their courts. By Robert Gilstrap and Irene Estabrook.

Long ago in the Kingdom of Algeria, there lived a mighty sultan. He was not only wise and good, but he was also very wealthy. He lived in a palace of gold that was surrounded by picturesque gardens. There, multicolored birds sang and raised their young, and tropical flowers bloomed perpetually. His life was surrounded by unparalleled beauty.

Because of his fame as a wise and good sultan, scholars, poets, scientists, and writers from the surrounding countries came to his palace where they could learn from him and from each other. His palace became the mecca of learning in North Africa.

Among the people who gathered in the Sultan's court, there was one whom the Sultan liked better than the others. This was a man who could say things to make the royal ruler laugh. He did funny tricks, sang silly songs, and did daffy dances. He could make his fat, little body shake like gelatin and the serious Sultan would laugh with delight. The funny one's name was Mahboul, but he was known to all as "the Sultan's fool."

Mahboul had one trait, however, that bothered the Sultan. And that was his ravenous appetite. He ate from the time he got up in the morning until he went to bed at night. At regular meals he ate three times as much as anyone else in the court, and between meals he ate what one man would normally eat in a day.

Thus the Sultan was forced to spend quantities of gold paying for his clown's food. Being a wealthy man he did not mind the money that was spent, but he feared that one day the little fat man would explode.

One day the Sultan decided to break Mahboul's eating habits once and for all. He called together the wise men and poets, the scientists and all his court servants and said, "I have an order for you! For one whole day you are to see that Mahboul has no food to eat. Do not set a place at the table for him. Do not bring wine for him, nor baskets of grapes nor pomegranates. Do not give him even a bite of bread. He must learn that he cannot eat from dawn to dusk. So see that my order is obeyed."

"Yes, your majesty," all the courtiers said as they bowed before the throne. "He is fat like a goat, anyway."

So it was that the servants and the courtiers began to carry out the Sultan's order. At the dinner table no place was set for Mahboul. Finding no place at the table, he stood against the wall. For he was certain the servants had merely forgotten his place but surely would serve him food and drink.

But time after time the servants passed by with delicious food loaded on their trays. Not once did they stop.

Each time a servant passed, Mahboul's eyes begged for food, but he dared not speak. He feared the Sultan's anger. And if anyone made the Sultan angry he could lose his head. Mahboul grew worried and very, very hungry.

The meal continued for hours and Mahboul's legs grew weak. He was not used to going without food. He watched the servants closely, and as one passed by him a piece of bread happened to fall to the floor. Mahboul reached down quickly, picked it up, and slipped it into the pocket of his coat.

"At last a bite of food," Mahboul said to himself, as he clutched the piece of bread. "But I must wait until later to eat it, for the others have stopped eating. It is now time for the entertainment."

But as the guests moved back from the tables and the dancing girls began to perform their exotic dances, Mahboul's stomach began to pain with hunger. He could think of nothing but the piece of bread and the fragrant aroma which came from his pocket.

"Maybe while the Sultan is busy watching the dancing girls I will be able to take just one small bite of bread," Mahboul thought to himself.

So when Mahboul thought no one was looking he took out the piece of bread and put it to his lips. Just as he was about to bite into it, the Sultan who had been watching Mahboul out of the corner of his eye, signaled that the music stop. He called to the clown, saying, "Tell me, Mahboul. I hear you have bought a fine donkey. Where did you get it?"

Mahboul jumped with surprise, but quickly put the bread back in his pocket, and answered the Sultan's question.

"I bought it in Tripoli," he answered.

"Oh, I see," the Sultan said with a smile. "Come. On with the entertainment."

Thus the entertainment continued, and Mahboul breathed a sigh of relief. Again when the music became loud and the dancing girls moved faster and faster, Mahboul reached into his pocket and pulled out the piece of bread which by now had become quite ragged.

Just as he started to bite, the music stopped, and the Sultan said, "I forgot to ask you something, Mahboul. How much did you pay for this donkey you bought in Tripoli?"

Mahboul nearly choked on his tongue when the Sultan called out his name, and hastily he placed the bread back in his pocket and replied, "Fifteen dinars, sire. A good price."

The Sultan nodded his head, winked at his courtiers, and commanded the entertainment to proceed. But Mahboul had only time to catch his breath and try again for the long-awaited bite when the Sultan asked him another question. And so it went throughout the afternoon. The Sultan continued to question the clown each time he saw him getting ready to take a bite and Mahboul's hunger continued to grow.

As evening approached, Mahboul was so hungry and so weary that he found it difficult to stand erect at his post near the wall. His tongue swelled. His feet ached. His stomach pained. But still he could not ask for food or seem displeased by the Sultan's actions.

Finally the Sultan decided to retire. *At last I can get some food*, Mahboul thought. But the hour was so late that the kitchen was locked, and Mahboul had only his small piece of bread.

He went to his room and tried to sleep, but he could not. He was too hungry, and his hunger had turned him into a desperate man willing to do anything for food.

Suddenly an idea came to him that offered a way to relieve his torture. Jumping out of bed, he ran through the palace corridors and up the steps that led to the Sultan's sitting room. He knew that the Sultan often invited several friends to his sitting room to discuss the activities of the day. And he knew, too, that the Sultan disliked very much being disturbed.

So, as loudly as he could, Mahboul knocked on the huge golden door that led into the Sultan's chambers. The Sultan was much surprised when he heard the sound, for he had given orders not to be disturbed.

"Oh, sire, pardon me for disturbing you," Mahboul said, bowing low. "But I have just remembered that I gave you incorrect information this afternoon. I did not buy my donkey in Tripoli. I bought it in Benghazi."

The Sultan was not amused, but since it was his favorite courtier speaking, he thanked him for making the correction and returned to his friends.

After Mahboul had given the Sultan time to again become involved in conversation with his friends, he went back to the golden door and knocked vigorously.

"Pardon me for interrupting you a second time," murmured Mahboul. "I would not disturb you but you seemed so anxious to know all about my donkey today. I just remembered that something else I told you was untrue. I did not pay fifteen dinars for the donkey as I told you. I paid twenty dinars."

The Sultan frowned and shut the door angrily. Mahboul stood outside for several more minutes, and then knocked again. The Sultan rushed to the door, threw it open, and grabbed

Mahboul by his robe. As he did this, Mahboul kneeled and mumbled another correction in the story of his donkey.

"You swine," screamed the Sultan, as he jerked Mahboul to his feet. "Not once, not twice, but three times you have disturbed me with some wild tale about this donkey you have bought. I'm going to have your head cut off at once so I can finish my conversation. Then you shall be thrown to the jackals. And then to the birds who will pick your bones."

Mahboul listened patiently to the Sultan's shouting, and never said a word nor stopped smiling. Finally, the Sultan stopped and as he was catching his breath, Mahboul spoke softly, " 'Tis true. I have sorely tried your majesty, and if you think I should be killed, so shall it be. But I beseech your majesty, the condemned man's last wish is always granted. Grant me this, I pray you. Before I die I should like just one good meal."

As Mahboul spoke the Sultan realized what he had forced his clown to do. "You are a true clown," he shouted. "What a magnificent fool! Anyone who would pull a trick like this because he so loved to eat should have all the food he wants."

The Sultan called his servants to fix a sumptuous meal, and he and Mahboul, his favorite courtier, sat in the middle of his ornate chambers. There they remained, eating and laughing, until the sun came up over the Mediterranean.

And Mahboul never again was without food. Nor did he ever explode.

ABU NOWAS AND HIS WIFE

ALGERIA, MOROCCO: Abu Nowas, the court jester, is a favorite Arab character. Many stories are told about him, and in most of them, he gets away with some outrageous scheme. By Andrew Lang.

ONCE UPON A TIME there lived a man whose name was Abu Nowas, and he was a great favorite with the Sultan of the country, who had a palace in the same town where Abu Nowas dwelt.

One day Abu Nowas came weeping into the hall of the palace where the Sultan was sitting, and said to him: "Oh, mighty Sultan, my wife is dead."

"That is bad news," replied the Sultan. "I must get you another wife." And he bade his Grand Vizier send for the Sultana.

"This poor Abu Nowas has lost his wife," said he, when she entered the hall.

"Oh, then we must get him another," answered the Sultana. "I have a girl that will suit him exactly," and clapped her hands loudly. At this signal, a maiden appeared and stood before her.

"I have got a husband for you," said the Sultana.

"Who is he?" asked the girl.

"Abu Nowas, the jester," replied the Sultana.

"I will take him," answered the maiden; and as Abu Nowas made no objection, it was all arranged. The Sultana had the most beautiful clothes made for the bride, and the Sultan gave the bridegroom his wedding suit, and a thousand gold pieces into the bargain, and soft carpets for the house.

So Abu Nowas took his wife home, and for some time they were very happy, and spent the money freely which the Sultan had given them, never thinking what they should do for more when that was gone. But come to an end it did, and they had to sell their fine things one by one, till at length nothing was left but a cloak apiece, and one blanket to cover them. "We have run through our fortune," said Abu Nowas. "What are we to do now? I am afraid to go back to the Sultan, for he will command his servants to turn me from the door. But you shall return to your mistress, and throw yourself at her feet and weep, and perhaps she will help us."

"Oh, you had much better go," said the wife. "I shall not know what to say."

"Well, then, stay at home, if you like," answered Abu Nowas, "and I will ask to be admitted to the Sultan's presence, and will tell him, with sobs, that my wife is dead, and that I have no money for her burial. When he hears that perhaps he will give us something."

"Yes, that is a good plan," said the wife; and Abu Nowas set out.

The Sultan was sitting in the hall of justice when Abu Nowas entered, his eyes streaming with tears, for he had rubbed some pepper into them. They smarted dreadfully, and he could hardly see to walk straight, and everyone wondered what was the matter with him.

"Abu Nowas! What has happened?" cried the Sultan.

"Oh, noble Sultan, my wife is dead," wept he.

"We must all die," answered the Sultan; but this was not the reply for which Abu Nowas had hoped.

"True, O Sultan, but I have neither shroud to wrap her in, nor money to bury her with," went on Abu Nowas, in no wise abashed by the way the Sultan had received his news.

"Well, give him a hundred pieces of gold," said the Sultan, turning to the Grand Vizier. And when the money was counted out Abu Nowas bowed low, and left the hall, his tears still flowing, but with joy in his heart.

"Have you got anything?" cried his wife, who was waiting for him anxiously.

"Yes, a hundred gold pieces," said he, throwing down the bag, "but that will not last us any time. Now you must go to the Sultana, clothed in sackcloth and robes of mourning, and tell her

72

that your husband, Abu Nowas, is dead, and you have no money for his burial. When she hears that, she will be sure to ask you what has become of the money and the fine clothes she gave us on our marriage, and you will answer, 'before he died he sold everything.' "

The wife did as she was told, and wrapping herself in sackcloth went up to the Sultana's own palace, and as she was known to have been one of the Sultana's favorite attendants, she was taken without difficulty into the private apartments.

"What is the matter?" inquired the Sultana, at the sight of the dismal figure.

"My husband lies dead at home, and he has spent all our money, and sold everything, and I have nothing left to bury him with," sobbed the wife.

Then the Sultana took up a purse containing two hundred gold pieces, and said: "Your husband served us long and faithfully. You must see that he has a fine funeral."

The wife took the money, and, kissing the feet of the Sultana, she joyfully hastened home. They spent some happy hours planning how they should spend it, and thinking how clever they had been. "When the Sultan goes this evening to the Sultana's palace," said Abu Nowas, "she will be sure to tell him that Abu Nowas is dead. 'Not Abu Nowas, it is his wife,'

he will reply, and they will quarrel over it, and all the time we shall be sitting here enjoying ourselves. Oh, if they only knew, how angry they would be!"

As Abu Nowas had foreseen, the Sultan went, in the evening after his business was over, to pay his usual visit to the Sultana.

"Poor Abu Nowas is dead!" said the Sultana when he entered the room.

"It is not Abu Nowas, but his wife who is dead," answered the Sultan.

"No; really you are quite wrong. She came to tell me herself only a couple of hours ago," replied the Sultana, "and as he had spent all their money, I gave her something to bury him with."

"You must be dreaming," exclaimed the Sultan. "Soon after midday Abu Nowas came into the hall, his eyes streaming with tears, and when I asked him the reason he answered that his wife was dead, and they had sold everything they had, and he had nothing left, not so much as would buy her a shroud, far less for her burial."

For a long time they talked, and neither would listen to the other, till the Sultan sent for the door-keeper and bade him go instantly to the house of Abu Nowas and see if it was the man or his wife who was dead. But Abu Nowas happened to be sitting with his wife behind the latticed window, which looked on the street, and he saw the man coming, and sprang up at once. "There is the Sultan's door-keeper! They have sent him here to find out the truth. Quick! throw yourself on the bed and pretend that you are dead." And in a moment the wife was stretched out stiffly, with a linen sheet spread across her, like a corpse.

She was just in time, for the sheet was hardly drawn across her when the door opened and the porter came in. "Has anything happened?" asked he.

"My poor wife is dead," replied Abu Nowas. "Look! she is laid out here." And the porter approached the bed, which was in a corner of the room, and saw the stiff form lying underneath.

"We must all die," said he, and went back to the Sultan.

"Well, have you found out which of them is dead?" asked the Sultan.

"Yes, noble Sultan; it is the wife," replied the porter.

"He only says that to please you," cried the Sultana in a rage; and calling to her chamberlain, she ordered him to go at once to the dwelling of Abu Nowas and see which of the two was dead. "And be sure you tell the truth about it," added she, "or it will be the worse for you."

As her chamberlain drew near the house, Abu Nowas caught sight of him. "There is the Sultana's chamberlain," he exclaimed in a fright. "Now it is my turn to die. Be quick and spread the sheet over me." And he laid himself on the bed, and held his breath when the chamberlain came in. "What are you weeping for?" asked the man, finding the wife in tears.

"My husband is dead," answered she, pointing to the bed; and the chamberlain drew back the sheet and beheld Abu Nowas lying stiff and motionless. Then he gently replaced the sheet and returned to the palace.

"Well, have you found out this time?" asked the Sultan.

"My lord, it is the husband who is dead."

"But I tell you he was with me only a few hours ago," cried the Sultan angrily. "I must

get to the bottom of this before I sleep! Let my golden coach be brought round at once."

The coach was before the door in another five minutes, and the Sultan and Sultana both got in. Abu Nowas had ceased being a dead man, and was looking into the street when he saw the coach coming. "Quick! quick!" he called to his wife. "The Sultan will be here directly, and we must both be dead to receive him." So they laid themselves down, and spread the sheet over them, and held their breath. At that instant the Sultan entered, followed by the Sultana and the chamberlain, and he went up to the bed and found the corpses stiff and motionless. "I would give a thousand gold pieces to anyone who would tell me the truth about this," cried he, and at the words Abu Nowas sat up. "Give them to me, then," said he, holding out his hand. "You cannot give them to anyone who needs them more."

"Oh, Abu Nowas, you impudent dog!" exclaimed the Sultan, bursting into a laugh, in which the Sultana joined. "I might have known it was one of your tricks!" But he sent Abu Nowas the gold he had promised, and let us hope that it did not fly so fast as the last had done.

THE JUDGMENT OF KARAKOUSH

EGYPT: This highly satirical story is typical of North African folk tales. By Habib Katibah.

A MAN OF THE EAST who says, "Like the Judgment of Karakoush," is speaking of something so unreasonable and unjust that it may be ridiculous. Karakoush was, long ago, the governor of Cairo in Egypt, and there is a story which shows why his judgments became a symbol of injustice.

It is said that a thief in Cairo broke into a house to steal. He climbed a wall and tried to pry open a window. But the window frame, being weak, suddenly gave way and the thief fell into the house and broke his leg.

On the next day the thief, wobbling on his sound leg, appeared before Karakoush and, showing his broken leg to the governor, said, "Your Excellency, I am a thief by profession. Yesterday I entered a house. As I was prying the window open, it caved in and I fell and broke my leg."

Karakoush shouted to the guards to bring the owner of the house to him. Presently the owner, trembling with fear, not knowing what he was accused of, was dragged before the governor. Karakoush repeated the charge of the thief, adding, "Why did you make your window so loose that it caved in and caused this thief to break his leg?"

What answer could the owner make? And since when had thieves the right to accuse their victims? But the owner knew better than to argue with Karakoush. He thought for a moment and then said, "Your Excellency, it was no fault of mine that the window of my house was put loosely in place. I swear that I paid the carpenter sufficiently to make me a window strong enough to prevent such an accident."

"Bring the carpenter, then," thundered Karakoush.

And when the carpenter appeared, the governor sternly addressed him, saying, "This houseowner claims that he paid you enough to construct him a strong window. Why did you then make so weak a one that this poor thief broke his leg when he tried to pry it open?"

The carpenter's face turned pale at this unexpected accusation. But he, too, knew how useless it was to argue with Karakoush, so, after a little hesitation, he said, "Your Excellency, it was not my fault that the window frame was not fastened properly. I was driving a nail when a beautiful young lady with a red dress passed under the window, and the nail went crookedly into the frame."

Karakoush found out the name of the young

lady with the red dress and sent for her.

When the young lady appeared, the governor repeated the charge of the carpenter, saying that if it weren't for her beauty and her red dress, the carpenter would not have been distracted, the window would not have been loosely made, and the poor thief would not have broken his leg.

To this the young lady answered with a smile, "My beauty is from Allah, but my red dress is from the dyer. It was he who dyed it red and made me distract the carpenter."

"Then bring the dyer," Karakoush ordered.

A few minutes later the dyer stood trembling before the awful Karakoush.

"Oh, villainous dabbler in dyes," cried the governor. "Why did you dye this young lady's dress red so that she attracted the attention of the carpenter, so that he drove the nail crookedly and caused a weakness in the window frame, so that this thief broke his leg when he tried to pry it open?"

The poor dyer stood speechless and stunned with bewilderment. He stammered one excuse after another, but none appealed to the relentless governor, who finally shouted out, "Take this fellow and hang him at the door of the prison!"

Now, the dyer happened to be an extraordinarily tall fellow, and when the soldiers took him to hang him at the door of the prison, they found that the doorway was too low, allowing no space for the rope. So they hurried back to the governor and told him that they could not hang the dyer because he was too tall for the prison doorway.

But Karakoush, not to be daunted so easily, bellowed at the terrified soldiers, "Go out and look for a short dyer and hang him in place of this one!"

The soldiers went out and found a short dyer. Without listening to his wild protests and pleadings, they dragged him to the prison and hanged him on the door.

Thus it is that the name of an ancient governor of Cairo is spoken, even today, to describe capriciousness and lack of reason.

THE CANDLE IN THE DARKNESS

ETHIOPIA, SUDAN, SOMALIA: This gentle, pleasant joke is a favorite in North Africa. Adapted from a story by Leslie W. Leavitt.

O<small>N A COLD EVENING</small>, Yasu and several of his friends were gathered about the fire in Yasu's house, toasting themselves and telling stories. The wind whistled around the corner of the house and spatters of snow could be heard against the windows. But inside the men were comfortable and warm.

Soon each man's story telling turned upon himself, and the friends were vying with one another with tales to prove their bravery and strength. As they went on, they became boastful, not about what they had done, but about what they could do if the occasion arose. Finally, Yasu, having listened to the boasts of the others politely, said, "I, too, am exceedingly strong. And I have great courage and fortitude."

His friend, Mikael, scoffed, for Yasu was not a powerful or outstandingly bold man. "What can you do," he said, "that would show you are particularly fearless?"

"Well, let me see," said Yasu. "Can any of you think of a deed I could perform now?"

None of his friends could.

"Nevertheless," said Yasu, "since Mikael seems to doubt my courage, I must prove it. Will this convince you, Mikael? I will stay out all night in the snow with no fire to give me heat."

"Yes, my friend," said Mikael, "it would convince me. But I have no desire to see you freeze to death to prove your point."

Ali joined Mikael in protesting, "Don't do it, Yasu. The night is becoming colder every minute and the snow falls more thickly. You will freeze with no fire."

"Not I," said Yasu. "I am very strong. I know I can do it, and I intend to prove it to all of you this very night."

"Please, Yasu," said Mikael, "I do not want to be responsible for the death of my friend."

"You will not be, Mikael. I will stand out in the cold all night. I will have no fire for warmth, and I will come in when the sun rises, as healthy as I ever was. If I do not succeed—and I have no doubt that I will—I shall . . . shall give you all a big dinner here at my house."

"All right, then," said Yasu's friends, "since you insist on being stubborn, we will admit that you have great strength and great courage if you can stay all night in the cold. But remember, you cannot have any kind of fire to warm you, and you cannot go indoors, or we will demand the dinner in payment."

Yasu's friends left then, to go to their own houses and their warm beds. Yasu went out into the snow. At first, the air felt like ice and he shivered. After a few minutes, he became more accustomed to the cold and did not mind it as much. Then he settled down to wait out the night. He walked slowly up and down watching the lights in the houses go out. Soon there was no light to be seen, only darkness and the cold wet snow falling about him and melting on his shoulders and back. The town was silent. A great loneliness came over him, and he wished he could see the stars, but snow clouds covered the sky.

He realized his fingers were icy. He thrust them into his sleeves for warmth and walked more briskly to warm his legs and feet. Back and forth, back and forth, across the open square he paced. The hours must be passing, he thought, but how slowly they went! There was no sign of light in the eastern sky—only cold, gray darkness. Yasu's hands and feet grew numb. The snow had become too deep to walk through easily, so he stood in one place, stamping off the minutes. He removed his hands from his sleeves and rubbed his legs until they tingled, then covered his hands again.

How unfriendly the night was, and how dreadfully dark! A strong urge came over him

to lie down where he was and sleep, but he knew he must keep moving or he would surely freeze to death. The thought frightened him and he started walking again, kicking his way through the snow, stumbling and slipping. Then he stopped. Far off, in a window of one of the village houses, a candle had been lighted. He could barely see its tiny glow through the falling snow. But it burned steadfastly—warm and somehow friendly. The person who had lit the candle hadn't even known he was there, but the little flame was like a magic sign that he was not all alone in the dark. There were other people near him and awake.

Now he was no longer afraid. He watched the candle every minute, and its light helped him to fight off sleep. Its friendliness told him that he could last out the night. Four o'clock . . . five o'clock . . . a glimmer of light showed in the eastern sky. The light grew brighter and the candle went out, but by now it was almost time for sunrise. With a surge of triumph, Yasu knew he had succeeded!

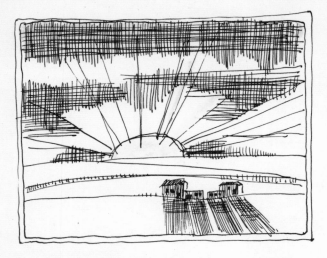

With the first blaze of the sun over the horizon, Yasu turned and plodded back to his house on feet that felt nothing. It seemed he would never be warm again, but when he reached his comfortable house and stirred up the embers of his fire, a glow came over him. It was partly the warmth of his hearth, but it was also the knowledge that he had proved his courage and strength to his doubting friends.

At about ten o'clock, there was a knock on Yasu's door and his companions of the night before came in. "Did you manage to stay out all night, Yasu?" Mikael said.

"Yes, I stayed out until the sun rose," said Yasu.

"And you had no fire to keep you warm?"

"No, not the smallest fire."

"How did you ever do it?" asked Ali wonderingly. "Wasn't it terribly hard?"

"It certainly was," said Yasu. "I am very strong and I am very brave, but I confess there was a time when I thought I might have to give up. But then someone lit a candle in a window far across the village. It was amazing what encouragement the sight of that little flame gave me. . . ."

"Did you say a candle, Yasu?" Mikael broke in.

"Yes, a candle."

"Ah, but a candle gives out heat. And you said you would stay out all night with no heat of any kind. You did not do what you said you would do."

Yasu snorted. "How can a candle all the way over on the other side of the village warm someone who is standing in the square?"

"You can argue if you like, Yasu. But a candle gives out heat. You may have felt very little, but you did get some heat from it. You must give us that dinner as you promised."

Yasu turned to the others for support, but they laughed and said, "He's right. You had the heat of the candle. We want the dinner you owe us. We want it tonight."

Yasu argued and protested, but none of his friends would listen. Finally he said sadly, "All right. Come for dinner when the sun goes down."

When the door had closed behind his friends, Yasu sat down to think. He thought and thought. . . .

Just as the sun was going down, all the men

arrived at Yasu's house laughing and talking. "Here we are, Yasu," they shouted to him as they took seats around the room. "Is the dinner ready?"

"No," Yasu called from the next room, "not yet. But please sit down."

They sat back comfortably, chatting with one another, and waited. From time to time they could hear Yasu moving about in the next room, but, curiously, there was no smell of cooking food.

They waited and waited. They began to be restless, and they were very hungry. Every man there had eaten lightly during the day so that he would be able to do justice to the big dinner at Yasu's house. After a long time they called to Yasu, "Can we help you get it ready?"

"No thank you," Yasu called back.

Later they called again, "Yasu, could we perhaps have part of the dinner now and the rest when it is ready? We are terribly hungry."

"I'm sorry, but all the dinner is in one pot."

At last, when Yasu's friends could wait no more, they got up and went to the next room. They crowded into the doorway and then stood speechless. Finally they looked at one another and laughed until tears flowed from their eyes at the sight they saw. Hanging from the ceiling, higher than their heads, was a big pot. Under the pot, on the floor at their feet, was one very small lighted candle. Yasu was standing on a stool, craning his neck to see into the pot. He turned to them and said innocently, "I'm sorry, my friends, that the food is cooking so slowly. But wait a little more, please. I know a candle gives out heat. You told me so."

THE FARMER OF BABBIA

ETHIOPIA, SUDAN, SOMALIA: This is an Ethiopian version of a story that is popular in many parts of the Arab world. From *The Fire on The Mountain* by Harold Courlander and Wolf Leslau.

ONCE IN THE TOWN of Babbia there was a farmer named Tesfa. He was known as an enthusiastic but silly man.

One day Tesfa's wife told him they would soon have a baby. Tesfa was highly elated. Nothing like that had ever happened to him. But very shortly he began to worry about what kind of child they would have, and so he questioned his wife:

"What kind of child will it be?"

But his wife couldn't give him any kind of a satisfactory answer.

"Stupid woman!" he said. "We are having a baby and you don't know what kind! Well, I will have to go to the wise monk in the mountains. He will know."

So he took one of the young bulls from his herd and drove him to the cave in the mountains where the monk lived. The monk looked at Tesfa inquiringly.

"I come to you for information," Tesfa said. "My wife tells me we are going to have a baby, but the stupid woman doesn't know what kind of baby it will be. Please let me know the answer. I have brought you a bull for payment."

The monk took out his divining board, and threw seeds upon it. This was the way he foretold the future. As the seeds fell upon the divining board, the monk shook his head. Tesfa shook his head, too. The monk clucked his tongue, and Tesfa clucked his tongue also.

The monk took up the seeds and threw them again.

"Aha!" he said.

"Aha!" Tesfa echoed.

Once more the monk threw the seeds on the divining board.

"Ho!" he said.

"Ho!" Tesfa replied expectantly.

At last the monk looked up at Tesfa. He was very serious.

"The child your wife will bear will be either a boy or a girl," he said.

Tesfa clapped his hands.

"A boy or a girl! How fortunate I am!" he said happily. He gave the monk the bull and ran home breathlessly to tell his wife the good news.

And true to the monk's words, in the course of time a child was born, and it was a boy.

"What a brilliant man the monk is!" Tesfa said over and over. "How truly he spoke!"

Soon the time came when they had to christen

the child, but they couldn't think of a suitable name for him. When Tesfa proposed a name his wife didn't like it, and when his wife suggested a name Tesfa didn't like it. They couldn't agree at all, and finally Tesfa said:

"I'll ask the monk. He is so wise. The monk shall be godfather."

So he took another young bull from his herd and went again to the cave of the monk.

"You have been so helpful in the past, help me again," he said. "Please tell us our boy's name."

The monk brought out his divining board and threw seeds on it.

"Aha!" he said.

"Aha!" Tesfa echoed.

"Ho!" the monk said.

"Ho!" Tesfa replied.

The monk looked at Tesfa wisely.

"Well, what is his name?" Tesfa asked.

"Come close," the monk said.

Tesfa came close.

"I have the name," the monk said. "I will put it in your hands so that you won't lose it."

Tesfa cupped his hands and held them out. The monk leaned forward and whispered into them.

"Close your hands quickly, so that you don't lose it now," the monk said aloud.

"Yes, yes, I am always losing things!" Tesfa said enthusiastically. "Thank you, we are deeply indebted! May you have many children and cattle!" And holding his hands together, he turned and ran homeward.

When he came to a place near the village where the farmers were threshing their grain, he raced toward them shouting:

"I have it! I have it! How lucky I am! I have my son's name!"

But as he ran through the straw and chaff he slipped and fell, and as he did so his hands came apart.

"Now I've lost it," he shouted at the farmers. "See what you made me do!"

He picked up a threshing fork and began to sift through the straw and chaff.

Some of the farmers came to help him.

"What does it look like?" they asked Tesfa.

"How do I know? I hadn't even opened it," Tesfa said with irritation.

As they sifted through the straw, a woman of the village came by. She asked what they were doing.

Tesfa explained everything. The woman shook her head.

"It's simply ridiculous," she said, and went on her way.

"Is it really?" Tesfa said with amazement. "Oh, thank you!"

And he dropped his fork and went home. His wife was waiting for him.

"Well," his wife asked, what is it?"

"I got it from the monk, but I dropped it in the straw," Tesfa said. "While I was looking for it our neighbor came by and told me it was Ridiculous. So I didn't have to look any more. How do you suppose she knew?"

PART **7** FRANCE: LUXEMBOURG: MONACO
PORTUGAL: SPAIN: ANDORRA: ITALY:
SAN MARINO: ALBANIA: GREECE: CYPRUS
ILLUSTRATED BY ANTHONY D'ADAMO

RIQUET WITH THE TUFT

FRANCE, LUXEMBOURG, MONACO: Charles Perrault, a 17th century French lawyer, is one of the world's best-known story-tellers, though he wrote only nine stories. He made up his fairy tales as bedtime stories for his son. Americans all know his Cinderella. This one, however, is a favorite among French children.

THERE WAS, once upon a time, a queen who had a son so hideously ugly that it was long disputed whether he was human. A fairy who attended his birth assured the queen that he would be very charming for all that, since he would be endowed with an abundance of wit. In addition, the fairy told the queen, he would be empowered to bestow on the person he most loved as much wit as he pleased. All this somewhat comforted the poor queen, who was grief-stricken at having brought into the world such a deformed dwarf.

As the fairy had predicted, no sooner did the child begin to prattle, than he said a thousand pretty things of such wittiness that he charmed everybody. (I forgot to tell you that he came into the world with a little tuft of hair upon his head, which made people call him Riquet with the Tuft, for Riquet was the family name.)

Seven or eight years after this, the queen of a neighboring kingdom was delivered of a daughter. The infant was more beautiful than the day. When the queen saw her baby, she was so very glad that it seemed her excess of joy might injure her health. At her bedside was the same fairy who had assisted at the birth of little Riquet with the Tuft, and this fairy, to moderate the queen's gladness, declared that the new princess should have no wit at all, but be as stupid as she was pretty. This distressed the queen extremely and she begged the fairy to grant her baby some portion of sense.

"I can do nothing for her, madam, as to wit," answered the fairy, "but everything as to beauty. Furthermore, to comfort you, I hereby grant her the power to make handsome the person who shall best please her."

As the princess grew up, her perfection grew with her. All the public talk was of her beauty. It is true also that her faults increased considerably with her age and she became every day more stupid. She either made no answer at all to what was asked her, or said something very silly. She also was so unhandy that she could not place four pieces of china upon the mantlepiece without breaking one of them, nor drink a glass of water without spilling half of it on her clothes.

But although she was unaccountably dull, she realized her defects and would have given all her beauty to have half the wit of an ordinary person. Kindly as the queen was, she could not help reproaching the little princess several times, and the poor child wanted to die for shame.

One day, as the princess wandered in the woods, grieving over her misfortune, she saw a little man coming toward her. His figure was very disagreeable, but he was most magnificently dressed. This was the young prince, Riquet with the Tuft, who had seen a picture of the lovely princess, fallen promptly in love with her beauty, and left his father's kingdom to find her. Overjoyed to discover her thus all alone, he addressed her with all imaginable politeness and respect. He soon noticed, however, that in spite of his graceful compliments she remained silent and melancholy.

"I cannot understand, madam," he said, "how a person so beautiful as you are can be so sorrowful as you seem to be; for though I have seen great numbers of exquisitely charming ladies, I

have never beheld one whose beauty approaches yours."

"You can say that if you wish," answered the princess sullenly, and here she stopped.

"Beauty is such a great advantage," said Riquet with the Tuft, "that it takes the place of all things. And since you possess this treasure, what could grieve you?"

"I had far rather," cried the princess, "be as ugly as you are and have wit, than have beauty and be as stupid as I am."

"There is nothing, madam," replied Riquet with the Tuft, "which proves more surely that we have intelligence than to believe we have none."

"I do not know that," said the princess bitterly, "but I know very well that I am senseless and miserable because of it."

"If that is all that troubles you, madam," Riquet with the Tuft said, "I can easily put an end to your sorrow."

"And how will you do that?" asked the princess.

"At birth I was granted the power to give to that person I love best as much wit as can be had," he said. "And it shall be yours if you will marry me."

The princess was dumbfounded at this offer, and she could not answer a word.

"I see," said Riquet with the Tuft, "that this proposal makes you very uneasy, and I do not wonder at it. I will give you a whole year to consider it."

But the princess had so great a longing to become intelligent that she agreed to marry Riquet with the Tuft on that same day twelve months later.

No sooner had she spoken the words than she found herself transformed. She could say whatever she pleased—politely, easily, naturally. She began at that moment a courtly conversation with Riquet with the Tuft in which she spoke with such grace that Riquet wondered if he had given her more wit than he had reserved for himself.

When she returned to the palace, the whole court was astounded at the extraordinary change in the young princess. She spoke now as many sensible words and as many witty turns of phrase as she had spoken stupid and silly impertinences before. Her parents and the members of the court were overjoyed beyond imagination. The king looked on his daughter with new eyes, took to asking her advice in affairs of state, and sometimes even held council in her apartment. In the satisfactions of her new life, the princess quickly forgot the promise she had made to Riquet with the Tuft. In fact, the ugly little dwarf who had transformed her faded almost entirely from her memory.

Word of the change in the princess quickly spread throughout the land, and all the young princes of neighboring kingdoms strove to gain her favor. They begged for her hand in marriage, but although she gave each a courteous hearing, none seemed intelligent enough to her and she refused them all.

Finally, however, there came a prince so rich, powerful, witty, and handsome that she could not help being attracted to him. Her father noticed it and told her that she was free to choose her own husband and that she should declare her choice when she was ready. She thanked her father and asked for time to consider.

One day while she was trying to make up her mind, she happened to go walking through the same wood where she had met Riquet with the Tuft. Deep in meditation, she was startled to hear a noise under her feet. It sounded as though great numbers of people were busily running backwards and forwards. Thoroughly alarmed, she stood absolutely still, listening.

"Bring me that pot," she heard a voice say. "Give me that kettle!" "Put some wood on the fire!" other voices shouted. At that moment, the ground under her feet seemed to open, and she saw a great kitchen full of cooks and scullions making preparations for a magnificent banquet. There came out of the hole a company of meat-cooks, with their larding pins in their hands.

They set to work to prepare great sides of meat for roasting.

The princess, astonished at this sight, asked them whom they worked for.

"For Riquet with the Tuft," said the chief cook, "who is to be married tomorrow."

At the sound of that name, the princess remembered her promise. Realizing that it was now exactly twelve months from the day she had promised to marry Riquet with the Tuft, she would have liked to sink into the ground with shame.

In a daze, she walked on, but she had not taken thirty steps before Riquet with the Tuft appeared before her, bravely and most magnificently dressed as befits a prince who is about to be married.

"You see, madam," said he, "I am very exact in keeping my word. And I see that you have come hither to keep yours and, by giving me your hand, to make me the happiest of men."

"I have to admit," answered the princess, "that I cannot make up my mind to marry you."

"You astonish me, madam!" said Riquet with the Tuft.

"I believe it," said the princess, "and I know that if I were speaking to a dullard, I would be unable to explain myself. 'A princess always keeps her word,' he would say to me, 'and you must marry me since you promised to do so.'

But as you are a man with the greatest sense and judgment, I believe you will hear my reasons. You know, when I was but a fool, I could hardly make up my mind to marry you. Now that I have the good judgment you have given me (which makes me a much more difficult person than when I was stupid), it is even harder for me to give my consent. If you sincerely wanted me for your wife, you should have left me witless."

"If a dullard could hold you to your promise, madam," said Riquet with the Tuft in an anguished voice, "why cannot I have this privilege? All the happiness of my life is at stake. Do you mean to say that a dullard is better off than a person of wit? Can you pretend this? Let us be honest, if you please. Is it only my ugliness and deformity which displeases you, or are you dissatisfied with my birth, my wit, my humor or manners?"

"I love and respect you in all those last qualities," said the princess.

"If that be so, I am happy," said Riquet with the Tuft, breathing a great sigh of relief, "for it is in your power to make me the most handsome of men."

"How can that be?" asked the princess, unable to hide her surprise.

"All you need to do is wish it so," said Riquet with the Tuft. "Did you not know, madam, that we have gifts from the same fairy? The fairy who gave me the power to make witty and wise the person I most love, gave you the power to make the man you love extremely handsome."

"In that case," said the delighted princess, "I bestow my gift on you, sir. I wish with all my heart that you may be the handsomest prince in the world."

The princess had no sooner said these words than Riquet with the Tuft appeared to her the finest prince on earth, the handsomest and most charming man she had ever seen. Some people say that this transformation was not due entirely to the gift of the fairy, but also to the eyes of love with which she now saw him. They say that the princess, impressed by her lover's perseverance, his tact, and all the good qualities of his mind, his wit and his judgment, no longer saw the deformity of his body or the ugliness of his face. These doubters feel that his hump suddenly seemed to her no more than the grand air of one who has a broad back; that his limp suddenly appeared as nothing more than a charming sidling gait. They say further that his squinty, crossed eyes appeared to her most bright and sparkling, irregularly focused only because they expressed such a wealth of love. And finally, they say that his great red nose suddenly struck her as heroic.

Howsoever that may be, the princess immediately promised to marry him on condition he get her father's consent. The king received him for his son-in-law with pleasure. And the next morning their wedding was celebrated, as Riquet with the Tuft had foreseen, and according to the orders he had given a long time before.

THE PRIEST AND THE SERVANT

PORTUGAL: Everyone always enjoys the underdog outsmarting the top dog, or as in the case of this old Portuguese folk story, the servant outsmarting the master. By Francisco Adolpho Coelho.

Once upon a time, a certain Priest had a servant who thought himself very sly and clever. One morning the Priest told the servant to cook a chicken for his dinner. The servant did so, but when he dished it, the savory smell from the roast chicken so whetted his appetite that he cut off a leg and ate it, and then arranged it on the dish so that his master should not detect what was wanting.

The Priest, however, soon discovered that there was a leg wanting to the bird, and, turning to his servant, he asked him, "Did you cut a leg off the chicken and eat it?"

"No, sir, I did no such thing; the chicken had only one leg when it was alive."

"Do you think I am such a fool as to believe that?"

"Oh, dear Father, there's a number of other hens in the poultry yard strutting about with only one leg, and the next time I notice one, I will call you out to see it."

"Very well, do so."

When the servant by chance saw a hen standing with one of its legs drawn up under it, he called out to his master, "Oh, dear master, come out and see a hen with only one leg!"

The Priest ran out and cried out to the bird, "Cho', cho', chuckie!" and the hen instantly putting its leg down, the Priest said to the servant, "You rascal! do you think I am a donkey?"

"No, indeed, Father, by no means! But when the chicken was on your table, you did not say 'Cho', cho', chuckie!' so it did not find its other leg!"

THE TAMING OF THE TERRIBLE BRIDE

SPAIN, ANDORRA: Written by Don Juan Manual, a 14th century ruler of Spain, this violent story probably gave Shakespeare the idea for his "Taming of the Shrew."

THERE ONCE LIVED, in Spain, a Moor of very modest means. He had a son—a most promising youth—and the father was sad that he was not rich enough to procure for the young man an honorable position in life. In the same city, there lived another Moor, a man of greater wealth than the first, and the two had been neighbors and trusted friends for many years. The second Moor would have been a happy man but for his daughter, a shrewish, disobedient young woman. She was beautiful to look at, but was so violent and ill-tempered that no man would consider marrying her.

One day, the son of the first Moor confided to his father that he would like to marry a woman richer than himself so that he could

afford to live quietly and well. The father approved the plan (which was thought to be a reasonable way of improving oneself in those days) and the son said, "Then with your consent, Father, I would like to marry the daughter of our neighbor."

The father was astonished. "How can you think of such a union?, You know very well that no man can be induced to marry her."

But the son insisted, and finally the father gave his consent. "Thank you, Father," the son said. "And now I want to tell you my scheme, for I will need your help. . . ."

After hearing his son's plan, the father went to ask his neighbor about the marriage.

"By heaven, my friend!" the neighbor said. "Were I to consent to such a marriage, I would prove myself a false friend indeed. I know for certain that any man who tried to live with my daughter would soon sicken and die. Or death, at least, would be preferable to life. Don't think, good friend, that I say this because I object to such a marriage. I should be only too grateful to any man who would take her out of my house."

So the marriage was arranged.

After the wedding, the bride was taken to the house of her husband. Friends and relatives returned to their own homes and waited anxiously for the following day when they feared they would find the bridegroom either dead or injured.

When they were left alone, the young couple sat down to supper. No sooner were they seated than the bridegroom, looking behind him, saw his mastiff and said to him, "Bring me a basin of water to wash my hands." The dog naturally took no notice of this command, and the man repeated the order sternly. When the dog still sat unheeding, the young man rose in a rage, drew his sword, and, grabbing the dog by the collar, dragged him out of the house. Soon he returned, wiping the blood from his sword, and sat down again with his astonished wife.

Looking around, he next saw a cat. "Bring me a basin of water for my hands," he commanded sharply. The animal, needless to say, paid not the slightest attention. "You fool!" the bridegroom said angrily. "Did you not see that the mastiff died for disobeying me?" The cat still did not move, and the man snatched up the animal and stamped out of the door, drawing

his sword. He soon returned, and his wife, sup-
posing he had lost his senses, dared not say
a word.

Next he saw his horse and called fiercely to it
to bring a basin of water. When the animal did
not obey, the man cried out in a rage, "How is
this? Do you think that you, too, can disobey
my orders?" Raging, he drove his horse from the
room, and returned a few minutes later with
his sword dripping blood. When the wife saw
this, she became dreadfully alarmed.

Again he sat down at the table, and as there
was no other living creature in the room, he
next ordered his bride to bring him water to
wash his hands. The wife, trembling and speechless, immediately brought him the water.

"Thank God you have obeyed me," he said.
"I was so irritated by these senseless brutes that
I might have treated you in the same way." He
then commanded her to serve his meat, and she
hastily arose to wait on him.

Thus passed the night, she not daring to
speak, but hurrying to obey his orders. After
letting her sleep for a short time, he said to her,
"Get up. I have been so annoyed that I cannot
sleep. Take care that nothing disturbs me, and
in the meanwhile prepare me a good breakfast."

Early in the morning, the bride's relatives
same stealthily to the door of the young couple's
house, fearing for the bridegroom's safety. When
the bride came to the door alone, they were at
first alarmed. But she came cautiously and
tremblingly toward them and said, "What are
you doing here? Speak not a word or all of us,
you as well as I, will die!" Then, in a frightened
whisper, she told them what had happened the
night before.

They withdrew, astonished at the change that
had come over the girl, and full of respect for
the young man who had started his married life
so well. For from that day on, the wife was
obedient and pleasant, and the couple led a
long and happy life.

And no one—not the bride's relatives, nor her
friends, and certainly not the bride herself —
ever learned the truth about that violent wedding night. For the mastiff, the cat and the horse

had not really been killed at all, but had merely
been led away by the groom's father who had
been hiding outside the house. As for the bloody
sword that had so terrified the bride, it had
simply been dipped in chicken blood to make
the lesson more convincing. For such was the
scheme that the clever young man had devised
to tame his terrible bride.

BASTIANELO

ITALY, SAN MARINO: This story, by T. F. Crane, is an Italian favorite, but it is told in many other countries, too.

ONCE UPON A TIME there was a husband and wife who had a son. This son grew up and said to his mother one day, "Do you know, Mother, I would like to marry!"

"Very well, marry. Whom do you want to take?"

"I want the gardener's daughter," he answered.

"She's a good girl," the mother said. "Take her. I am willing."

So the son went and asked for the girl, and her parents gave her to him. They were married, and when they were in the midst of the wedding dinner, the wine gave out.

Anxious to show what a good housekeeper she was, the bride hopped up and said, "I will go and get some more wine." She took the bottles and went to the cellar. As she was turning the cock of the wine cask, she began to think,

"Suppose I should have a son, and we should call him Bastianelo, and he should die. Oh, how grieved I should be! Oh, how grieved I should be!" And thereupon she began to weep and weep, and meanwhile the wine was running all over the cellar.

When the others saw the bride did not return with the wine, the mother said, "I will go and see what the matter is." So she went into the cellar and saw the bride with a bottle in her hand, weeping, while the wine was running all over the cellar.

"What is the matter with you that you weep so?" asked the mother.

"Ah, my mother, I was thinking that if I had a son and should name him Bastianelo and he should die, oh, how I should grieve! Oh, how I should grieve!"

The mother, too, began to weep and weep,

90

and meanwhile the wine was running all over the cellar.

When the people at the table saw that no one brought the wine, the bride's father said, "I will go and see what is the matter. Certainly something has happened to the bride." He went and saw the whole cellar full of wine, and the mother and bride weeping. "What is the matter?" he said. "Has anything happened to you?"

that no one returns." He went down the steps and saw the wine running all over the cellar. He hastened to shut off the cock and then asked, "What is the matter that you are all weeping and have let the wine run all over the cellar?"

Then the bride said, "I was thinking that if I had a son and called him Bastianelo and he should die, oh, how I should grieve! Oh, how I should grieve!"

"No," said the bride, "but I was thinking that if I had a son and should call him Bastianelo and he should die, oh, how I should grieve! Oh, how I should grieve!" Then the father, too, began to weep and all three wept, and meanwhile the wine was running all over the cellar.

When the groom saw that neither the bride nor the mother nor the father came back, he said, "Now I will go and see what the matter is,

"You stupid fools!" the groom said, "are you weeping at this, and letting the wine run into the cellar? Have you nothing else to think of? It shall never be said that I remained here with you! I will roam about the world and, until I find three fools greater than you, I will not return home."

He had a bread-cake made, took a bottle of wine, a sausage, and some linen, and made a bundle, which he put on a stick and carried over his shoulder. He journeyed and journeyed, and began to despair of finding a fool greater than his wife. He thought of turning back, but at that moment, he saw a man in his shirt sleeves at a well, all wet with perspiration and water.

"What are you doing, sir, that you are so covered with water and in such a sweat?"

"Oh, let me alone," the man answered. "For I have been here a long time drawing water to fill this pail and I cannot fill it."

"What are you drawing the water in?" the groom asked.

"In a sieve," the man said.

"What are you thinking about, drawing water in a sieve? Just wait." The groom went to a house nearby and borrowed a bucket with which he promptly filled the pail.

"Thank you, good sir," said the man. "Heaven knows how long I should have had to remain here!"

"Here is one who is a greater fool than my wife," thought the groom.

He continued his journey and after a time he saw a man in his shirt who was jumping down from a tree. As he drew near, he saw a woman under the tree holding a pair of breeches. He asked them what they were doing, and they said they had been there a long time and that the man wanted to try on those breeches, but did not know how to get into them.

"I have jumped and jumped until I am tired out," said the man. "And I cannot imagine how to get into these breeches."

"No wonder," said the groom. "You will never get into them that way. Come down and lean against the tree." Then he picked up the man's legs and put them one by one into the breeches. After he had pulled the breeches up, he said, "Is that right?"

"Very good, bless you, for if it had not been for you, heaven knows how long I should have had to jump."

The groom said to himself, "Now I have seen two greater fools than my wife." Then he went on his way, shaking his head in astonishment.

As he approached a city, he heard a great noise. When he drew near, he asked what it was and was told that it was a marriage and that it was the custom in that city for brides to enter the city gate on horseback. On this occasion, there was a great discussion between the husband and the owner of the horse, for the bride was tall and the horse high and they could not get through the gate. They argued that they must either cut off the bride's head or the horse's legs. The husband did not wish his bride's head cut off, and the owner did not wish his horse's legs cut off — hence the disturbance.

Then the groom said, "Just wait." He went up to the bride and gave her a slap that made her lower her head, and then he gave the horse a kick and so they passed through the gate and entered the city.

The husband and the owner of the horse asked the groom how they could reward him, for he had saved the husband his bride and the owner his horse. He answered that he did not wish anything and said to himself, "Two and one make three! That is enough. Now I shall go home."

He hurried home and said to his wife, "Here I am, my wife. I have seen three greater fools than you. Now let us remain in peace and think about nothing else." They renewed the wedding and always remained in peace. After a time, the wife had a son whom they named Bastianelo, and Bastianelo did not die, but still lives with his father and mother.

In other versions, the stupidities are different, but the husband always finds that the world is full of silly people and decides that he might as well return to his silly wife.

PIPILO

ALBANIA: This story comes from an Albanian-English reader. It was written by an Albanian boy who had heard it from his grandparents.

ONCE UPON A TIME in a small village in Albania, there lived three brothers. The youngest and tallest of the three was named Pipilo. Although they were hard-working young men, they were often hungry, for an Ogress who lived in their quarter of the village, stole everything she could lay her hands on. The villagers were afraid to oppose her, because if she could not find chickens or sheep to steal, she would snatch a child for her dinner. The villagers got so they quivered at the sound of her voice, and mothers made children hide under the beds when the Ogress walked abroad.

Pipilo, who was as brave as he was tall, decided to get revenge on the Ogress. Working at night while she slept, he dug a tunnel. It started at his house and came out inside the Ogress' walled courtyard, where he carefully covered the opening with branches and leaves.

The first night he stole into the courtyard, he saw her shepherd and said to him, "Come with me, shepherd. I will free you from the power of the Ogress."

The shepherd did not heed his words, but at once called out, "Pipilo is trying to carry me off!" Pipilo quickly dived back into the mouth of the tunnel and, when the Ogress stormed out of her house, he was safely hidden.

"Where are you hiding Pipilo, fellow?" the Ogress demanded of the shepherd. When he could not tell her, she beat him unmercifully.

The second night, Pipilo returned and repeated the same words to the shepherd. This time, the shepherd, remembering the beating of the night before, gladly came with Pipilo, herding the sheep before him down the tunnel. When the Ogress woke the next morning, she saw her sheep and shepherd were missing.

"Oh, Pipilo! Oh, Pipilo!" she screamed.

"Sheep and shepherd and all you've taken from me."

After two or three nights, Pipilo went again to the Ogress' house and called to her doves, throwing down grain for them. The doves, however, did not heed the grain, but trembled with

fear and cried out, "Pipilo is trying to carry us off!"

Pipilo again hid in the tunnel, and when the Ogress appeared, she was unable to find him.

"Where is Pipilo hiding?" she demanded of the doves angrily, and when they could not tell her, she hit them with a stick.

The next night, Pipilo returned and threw more grain for the doves. This time they followed him into the tunnel.

After keeping quiet for some nights, Pipilo went through the tunnel again to lure away the Ogress' horse. He threw raisins and chickpeas to it to persuade it. The horse, however, neighed loudly and said, "Pipilo is trying to carry me off!"

When the Ogress appeared this time, she said, "Yes, yes! Pipilo has got into the habit of carrying off my livestock." Then she beat the horse saying, "What do I want with you when my sheep and doves are gone? You go, too, with Pipilo."

So the next night, Pipilo came and led the horse through the tunnel.

After two or three months, Pipilo dressed himself like a carpenter and went to the Ogress' forest to saw some planks. As soon as the Ogress saw him, she said, "Hi! you there, what do you want in my forest?"

"I've come to saw some planks," said Pipilo in a disguised voice. "An evil man named Pipilo has just died and I need planks for his coffin."

The Ogress was delighted. "Oh, take all the planks you want," she said. "Here, let me help. We'll make the coffin together. Pipilo was indeed an evil man. He stole my sheep and shepherd from me. He took my doves from me. And he even led my horse away."

After they had made the coffin, Pipilo said to the Ogress, "Hop in a moment to see if the coffin is long enough. Pipilo's very tall, you know, just about your size."

"Yes, yes," said the Ogress. "He is very tall," and she hopped into the coffin.

Quickly Pipilo nailed down the lid and carried the coffin to his own house where his brothers had built a great fire. They threw the coffin, Ogress and all, into the blaze and burned her up.

And ever since then, Pipilo and his brothers and the rest of the village have been happy and prosperous.

94

THE STORY

ON THE ISLAND of Sicily, high in the mountains, lay the Valley of Enna. It was so high that no mortal climbed to it, only goats and sheep and swine. No wind except the gentle Zephyrus visited it and its grass was forever green, its flowers forever in bloom.

The Valley of Enna was the home of Demeter, the Earth Mother, who was the goddess of all things that grew — the wheat, the fruits, the flowers, and the lambs. She lived there with her beautiful daughter Persephone whom she treasured above everything else.

One day, Persephone and her young companions, the daughters of the river nymphs, were playing in the Valley of Enna, gathering flowers for their delight. They roamed across the valley, picking the hyacinths, lilies and purple irises for their baskets and skirts and twining sprays of wild roses in their hair. Persephone, wandering off a little from her companions, saw one particularly magnificent flower, a kind of narcissus, purple and white, with a hundred blossoms branching from one stem. Its sweet odor was more heavenly than anything she had ever experienced.

With joy, she started to pick the flower for her basket and, as she tugged at it, she heard a rumbling underground. Then the earth suddenly opened and from beneath it sprang a golden chariot, drawn by black horses. It was driven by a dark stern-faced man with a crown on his head. He was Hades, king of the underworld and of the dead. When he saw Persephone, he loved her instantly and determined that she should be his bride. He grasped her around her slender waist and drew her up beside him in his chariot to re-enter the dark passages beneath the earth with her. As he departed, the earth closed behind him and none of Persephone's companions could tell where she had gone.

OF PERSEPHONE

GREECE, CYPRUS: This myth is an early Greek explanation of why winter is barren and summer is fertile. There are many different versions of Persephone's story, but they are all based on an ancient hymn to Demeter, her mother, which celebrates the gathering of the harvest.

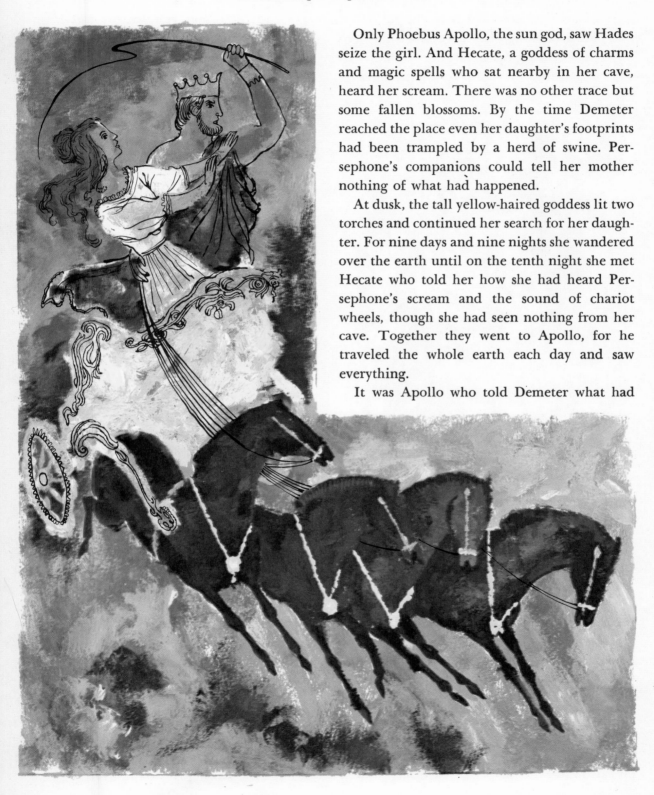

Only Phoebus Apollo, the sun god, saw Hades seize the girl. And Hecate, a goddess of charms and magic spells who sat nearby in her cave, heard her scream. There was no other trace but some fallen blossoms. By the time Demeter reached the place even her daughter's footprints had been trampled by a herd of swine. Persephone's companions could tell her mother nothing of what had happened.

At dusk, the tall yellow-haired goddess lit two torches and continued her search for her daughter. For nine days and nine nights she wandered over the earth until on the tenth night she met Hecate who told her how she had heard Persephone's scream and the sound of chariot wheels, though she had seen nothing from her cave. Together they went to Apollo, for he traveled the whole earth each day and saw everything.

It was Apollo who told Demeter what had

happened to her missing daughter: that Hades had carried her down to his underworld kingdom. When Demeter heard this, she lamented deeply, for she knew her daughter was indeed lost to her.

For her mourning, she wrapped herself in dark blue draperies so that all her bright beauty was hidden, and she went down into a dark cave where she would speak to no one, neither laughing nor smiling, but completely numb. And the

earth, now neglected, suffered from her grief. The cattle died, the ploughs of men broke in their furrows, there was too much sun or too much rain, or it was cold and dark. The birds stole the seeds of the crops and only brambles and thistles grew.

From Mount Olympus, Zeus, the father of the gods, saw that without Demeter everything on earth must die. So he sent Iris, the rainbow goddess, down to Demeter to persuade her to go back to the fields. Iris' brilliance lighted up the cave, but Demeter would not smile or speak to her. One after another, Zeus sent the gods down to comfort the sorrowing mother, but nothing could penetrate the depths of her mourning.

Finally Zeus sent Hermes, the messenger of the gods, down to the underworld to ask Hades for Persephone's return. Hades agreed to restore the girl to her mother, but he cunningly gave her a pomegranate to eat before she left, knowing that whatever she ate in the underworld would enforce her return to him. Persephone innocently sucked the sweet pulp from six of the seeds before she left. Then Hermes, driving Hades' chariot with its black horses, took the girl up beside him and returned her to earth and her goddess mother.

When Demeter saw her daughter, she ran out of the cave where she had been mourning and the world lighted up with her joy. She embraced the girl fervently, stroking the yellow hair that was like her own, while Persephone told how Hades had carried her away to the underworld.

Then Demeter asked her anxiously whether she had eaten anything during her stay and Persephone confessed that she had eaten the six pomegranate seeds just before she left.

At this, Demeter despaired, fearing that she would again lose her daughter, this time forever. She went to Zeus to appeal to him for help. When he heard her story, he told her that Persephone must indeed return to Hades, but only for six months of the year—one for each seed she had eaten. For the other six months she might remain with her mother in the beautiful Valley of Enna.

In her happiness at hearing this, Demeter smiled upon the earth again and the trees bore fruit once more, and the flowers blossomed, and the wheat tasseled in the fields as yellow as the goddess's hair.

Ever after that, the earth has come to life again in the spring when Persephone returns to her mother, and in the winter months when she returns to Hades, the earth lies dark and cold and fallow, waiting for the following spring.

AESOP'S FABLES

GREECE: In the fifth century B.C., the Greek slave Aesop wrote his famous fables. They have provided writers with plots ever since.

THE FOX AND THE GRAPES

A HUNGRY FOX stole one day into a vineyard where many bunches of grapes hung ripe and ready for eating. But as luck would have it, they were fastened upon a tall trellis, just too high for Reynard to reach.

He jumped, and paused, and jumped again, in the attempt to get at them. But it was all in vain. At last he was fairly tired out, and thereupon 'Take them who will,' he cried, 'THE GRAPES ARE SOUR!'

THE CROW AND THE PITCHER

A CROW, ready to die with thirst, flew with joy to a Pitcher, which he saw at a distance. But when he came up to it, he found the water so low that with all his stooping and straining he was unable to reach it. Thereupon he tried to break the Pitcher; then to overturn it; but his strength was not sufficient to do either. At last, seeing some small pebbles at hand, he dropped a great many of them, one by one, into the Pitcher, and so raised the water to the brim, and quenched his thirst.

Skill and Patience will succeed where Force fails. Necessity is the Mother of Invention.

THE LIONESS

T HERE was a great stir made among all the Beasts, which could boast of the largest family. So they came to the Lioness. 'And how many,' said they, 'do you have at birth?' 'One,' said she, grimly; 'but that one is a Lion.'

Quality comes before quantity.

PART **8** GERMANY: LIECHTENSTEIN: THE NETHERLANDS:
BELGIUM: SWITZERLAND: AUSTRIA
ILLUSTRATED BY LOUIS GLANZMAN

ASHPUTTEL

GERMANY, LIECHTENSTEIN: There are over 300 known versions of the Cinderella story. It is told by Turks, Canadian Indians and Koreans, to mention only a few. No one knows where or when the story originated. It was centuries old when Jakob and Wilhelm Grimm wrote this version in about 1815.

THE WIFE of a rich man fell sick and, when she felt her end was near, she called her only daughter to her bedside and said, "Always be a good girl, and I will watch over you from heaven." Soon afterwards she died and was buried in the garden. The little girl went every day to the grave and wept. And she was always good and kind to everyone.

Winter came, and then spring, and by the time the sun had melted the snow on the grave, the little girl's father had married another wife. This new wife had two daughters of her own who were fair in face but cruel in heart, and now began a sorry time for the little girl.

"What does this good-for-nothing want in the parlor?" her new sisters said. "They who would eat bread should first earn it. Away with this kitchen maid!" They took away her fine clothes and gave her an old gray dress to wear. Then they laughed at her and pushed her into the kitchen.

There she was forced to rise before daylight, to bring the water, to make the fire, to cook and wash. And the sisters annoyed her in many ways and laughed at her. In the evening, she had no bed to lie on, but was made to lie by the hearth among the ashes. This made her always dusty and dirty and they called her "Ashputtel."

It happened once that the father was going to the fair and he asked all his daughters what he should bring them. One of his wife's daughters said, "Fine clothes," and the other said, "Pearls and diamonds." But Ashputtel said, "Bring me the first twig, dear father, that brushes against your hat when you turn homewards."

He bought the fine clothes and the pearls and diamonds at the fair. On the way home, as he went through a green wood, a hazel twig brushed against him and almost pushed off his hat. So he broke it off and took it home to his daughter. Ashputtel planted it on her mother's grave and cried so much that it was watered with her tears and became a fine tree.

Soon a little dove built its nest in the tree and talked with Ashputtel and watched over her and brought her whatever she wished for.

It happened that the king of that land held a feast which was to last for three days, and of the girls who came, the king's son was to choose a bride for himself. When Ashputtel's sisters

were asked to come, they called her from the kitchen and commanded, "Comb our hair, brush our shoes, and tie our sashes, for we are going to dance at the king's feast."

She did as she was told, and when all the work was done, she begged the mother to let her go too.

"You, Ashputtel!" said the mother. "You have nothing at all to wear and you cannot dance. Why should you want to go?"

But finally, to stop Ashputtel's begging, she said, "I will throw this dishful of dried peas into the ash heap, and if you have picked them all out in two hours, you may go to the feast." And she threw the peas among the ashes.

The little maiden ran out of the back door into the garden and called to her dove for help. Immediately came two white doves, flying in at the kitchen window, then came two turtle doves, and after them came all the little birds under heaven, chirping and fluttering. They flew into the ashes and set to work. Among them all, they soon picked out all the peas and put them in a dish. Long before even one hour was done, the work was finished and they flew out of the window.

Then, happily, Ashputtel took the dish of peas to the mother. But the mother said, "No, no! You have no clothes, you are dirty, you cannot dance. You shall not go."

But when Ashputtel begged very hard, she finally said, to get rid of her, "If you can pick two of those dishes of dried peas out of the ashes in one hour, you shall go."

The little maiden went out into the garden and called to the bird as before. Again, all the little birds under heaven came and set to work in the ashes. The work was done before half an hour was gone, and the birds flew out of the window.

When Ashputtel joyfully showed the mother the dishes of peas, the mother said angrily, "It is useless to beg. You cannot go, for you would

only put us to shame." Then off she went with her two daughters to the feast.

When everyone was gone, Ashputtel went sorrowfully to her hazel tree and cried out again for help. Then her friend the dove brought a gold and silver dress and slippers of spangled silk. Ashputtel put them on and followed her sisters to the feast, but they did not know her. They thought she must be some strange princess in her beautiful clothes.

The king's son soon saw her. He came and took her by the hand and danced with her, never leaving her. And when anyone else asked her to dance, he said, "This lady is dancing with me."

When it was time to go home, the king's son said, "I shall take you to your home," for he wanted to see where the beautiful maiden lived. But she slipped away from him and when she reached home she heard the prince following her, so she jumped up into the pigeon house and bolted the door.

The prince waited until her father came home and told him that an unknown maiden

who had been at the feast was hiding in his pigeon house. Together they broke open the door, but no one was inside. Ashputtel had run through the pigeon house into the garden. There she had put her beautiful clothes under the hazel tree for the dove to carry away, and she was now lying in her dirty gray dress sleeping, as she always did, among the ashes.

On the second day of the feast, when her father, mother and sisters were gone, Ashputtel again cried out to the dove for help. This time the dove brought a still finer dress and more beautiful slippers. The king's son was waiting for her when she got to the feast and again he danced with no one else. When anyone asked

her to dance, he said, as before, "This lady is dancing with *me!*"

When the feast was over, Ashputtel again slipped away from the prince. She ran into the garden and, knowing the prince was following her, she sprang into a large pear tree full of ripe fruit. The king's son lost sight of her, so he waited until her father came home and said, "I think the unknown lady is now hiding in your pear tree."

The father thought to himself, "Can it be Ashputtel?" He had an ax brought and he cut down the tree, but they found no one in it, for Ashputtel had slipped down the other side, put her fine clothes back under the hazel tree for the bird, and was now asleep among the ashes in her gray dress.

On the third day, waiting until everyone was gone, she called to her kind friend, the dove. He brought her an even finer dress than the last one, and slippers of pure gold. When she got to the feast, everyone was speechless with wonder at her beauty. And when anyone else asked her to dance, the king's son said, "This lady is *my* partner, sir."

This time the prince was determined not to lose her, so she was obliged to hurry. In her haste she dropped the golden slipper from her left foot upon the stairs. The next day, the prince picked up the shoe and said to his father the king, "I will take for my wife the lady this golden slipper fits."

The news of his decision soon spread and the sisters were overjoyed to hear it, for they were both sure they could wear the golden slipper.

The king's son took the slipper to their house and placed it in a room. The eldest sister went first to try it on, while her mother stood by. But try as she might, she could not fit her big toe into it, for the slipper was much too small.

But her mother gave her a knife, saying, "Never mind, cut it off. When you are queen, you will not care about toes, for you will have no need to walk."

The stupid girl cut off her big toe and thus was able to squeeze into the slipper. Then the king's son set her beside him on his horse and rode away with her homewards. But on their way they passed the hazel tree Ashputtel had

planted. On a branch sat the little white dove singing:

"Prince, prince, see the foot of your bride,
For she's not the true one that sits by your side!"

The prince stopped his horse and looked at the eldest sister's foot. When he saw the blood on it, he realized what a trick she had played on him and he took her back home.

"This is not the right bride," he said to her mother. "Let the other sister try on the slipper."

The younger sister went to the room with the shoe and pushed and pushed. But she could not get her heel into it. So her mother squeezed until the blood came and finally forced the heel in. Then she took her daughter to the king's son. He set her on his horse and rode away with her.

But when they came to the hazel tree, the dove was still there and it sang:

"Prince, prince, see the foot of your bride,

For she's not the true one that sits by your side!"

The prince looked down and saw the bloody heel. Again he turned his horse back. "This is not the true bride," he said to the father. "Have you no other daughters?"

"Only the child of my first wife, dirty little Ashputtel," said the father. "I am sure she cannot be the bride."

"Nevertheless, send her to me," said the prince.

"No, no!" cried the mother. "She is much too dirty to show herself." But the prince insisted and Ashputtel was summoned.

She first washed her face and hands, then went in and curtsied to the king's son, and he handed her the golden slipper. She took the clumsy shoe off her left foot and put on the shoe the prince had given her. It fitted as if it had been made for her.

Seeing this, the prince drew near to her and gazed into her face. Then he knew her and said, "Now, at last, this is the right bride."

The mother and sisters were pale with anger as the prince took Ashputtel on his horse and rode away with her. This time, when they came to the hazel tree, the white dove sang:

"Prince, prince, take home your bride,

For she is the true one that sits by your side!"

And with that, the dove came flying down and perched on Ashputtel's right shoulder, and so went to the home of the prince with her.

TILL AND

IN THE COURSE of his travels, Till Eulenspiegel came one time to Erfurt where there was a great university full of learned professors. Till, who liked nothing better than a little sport with those who considered themselves extraordinarily wise, let it be known that he was quite a scholar himself. In fact, he had a marvelously decorated sign made up to advertise his abilities and hung it on the church door.

When they saw his sign the professors, who

had heard something of Eulenspiegel's tricks before, realized that Till was trying to make fools of them. So they set themselves to figure out a problem that he would never solve, thereby making him look foolish instead.

After thinking and weighing and conferring, they finally hit upon a plan that pleased them. They bought an ass, and dragged the unwilling creature to the inn where Till was staying.

"We see by your advertisement," the Rector of the university said to Till, "that you have extraordinary powers as a scholar. We have therefore brought you this pupil. We will pay you handsomely if you will receive him, and, by your great learning, teach him to read."

Till looked into the beast's drowsy eyes thoughtfully, as though studying the ass's intellect. "Yes," he said finally. "I will teach him,

THE ASSES OF ERFURT

THE NETHERLANDS, BELGIUM: The favorite folk hero of Flemish children is Till Eulenspiegel, a peasant trickster who delights in making fools of city people.

but as an ass is not known for its eagerness to learn, it might take some time."

"How long?" asked the Rector. "Would twenty years be sufficient, Herr Professor?"

"Yes, I should think so, yes indeed," said Till solemnly. To himself he thought, "Twenty years is a long time. By then the Rector may well be dead, which would settle the matter. Or I might be dead, or most likely the ass will be dead, which would be the best solution."

So they agreed on the terms, the professors gave Till a goodly sum of money on account, everyone bowed respectfully to everyone else, and Till led his new charge off to the stable.

The next day, Till bought an enormous old book, and placed it in the ass's manger. Between the pages Till sprinkled oats. The ass was quick to smell the food, and, with his tongue, he started turning the pages to lick up the grain. When the creature could find no more, he let out a great disappointed bray — "Eee-aaa, eee-aaa!" Till was delighted, and he made the ass practice with the book and the oats every day for a week.

Then he went to see the Rector. "Herr Rector," he said, most respectfully. "Won't you drop by and observe my pupil's progress?"

"Indeed I will," said the Rector. "And I will bring my colleagues, if I may. Do you find your scholar a good pupil, Herr Professor?"

"He is not exactly an eager student," said Till, "but he already knows a few of his letters, and that is fine progress for an ass in a week's time."

The Rector and the other professors came to see Till the very next day, and Eulenspiegel led them straight to the stable. He had not fed the ass that day, and when the beast saw Till set down the great book in his manger, he hungrily turned through the pages with his tongue. But this time Till had not put any oats between the pages, so the ass started braying, "Eee-aaa, eee-aaa, eee-aaa, eee-aaa," in his loudest tones.

Thereupon, Till patted him and removed the book.

"His 'E' and 'A' are still a little broad, as you see, most learned doctors," Till said modestly, "but I hope to improve his pronunciation as he masters the other vowels."

At this, the visitors went away furious. The Rector, soon afterwards, had a stroke and died, and on hearing the news, Till packed up his belongings, including the money the Rector had given him, and let the ass out of his stall.

"Go away, my good scholar," he said, slapping him affectionately on the rump. "Go and join the other asses of Erfurt." And with that, Till hastily left town.

TILL'S CHANGEABLE HORSE

THE NETHERLANDS, BELGIUM: Till Eulenspiegel again, with another trick

SOME TIME LATER, Till turned up in the city of Halberstadt where he took a room at one of the city's best inns. He lived grandly for a while, ordering his favorite dishes and drinking wine, whenever he was thirsty. But after eight days his money was gone.

Till had been such a good customer that the innkeeper continued to serve him, however, and soon Till had run up a large bill, not only for himself but also for the keep of his horse.

Finally the innkeeper began to be suspicious, and one day he refused to give Till any more wine until the bill was paid.

"I happen to be a little short of money at the moment," said Till. "But I assure you, you will be paid if you are patient."

"Patient?" the innkeeper shouted angrily, waving the bill in Till's face. "I have been patient."

"Well, be patient a little while longer," Till said. "I have a scheme."

Eulenspiegel then arranged with the town crier to proclaim throughout the city the arrival of a stranger who had brought with him a marvelously curious animal — an animal closely resembling a horse but with its head placed where its tail should be. While the town crier was announcing this message in every street and square, Till went to the stable, turned his horse around in its stall, and tied its tail to the manger. Then he closed the stable door and occupied himself with writing out intriguing handbills about his new exhibition.

The townspeople came running from all sides, expecting to see a monster, or at least a rare freak. Till passed out his handbills and collected a penny a head, with no reduction for children. Then leaving a friend to guard the stable door and collect the pennies, Till conducted the assembled customers into the stable to see his horse with its tail where its head should have been.

After their first shock, the townspeople couldn't help laughing at the hoax, and Till laughed the loudest of everyone.

"And now, good people," he said to the group in the stable, "you wouldn't want those waiting outside to miss this marvelous show, would you? You wouldn't want them to learn the secret without paying their penny as you have paid yours? And certainly, good citizens, I know you wouldn't want to ruin my business."

Still laughing and feeling a little sheepish to have been fooled so easily, the people agreed not to tell a soul about Till's hoax. Till led them out the back door of the stable, and they all hurried away, telling everyone they met not to miss the unique exhibition.

In this way, Eulenspiegel raised a good round sum of money, paid his bill at the inn, and rode merrily out of town on his changeable horse, whose head was now once more in front where it ought to be.

WILLIAM TELL

SWITZERLAND: William Tell was a 14th century Swiss mountaineer, who fought for Swiss independence. His legend is known throughout the world.

CENTURIES AGO, in the beautiful mountainous region of Uri in Switzerland, there was terror and despair among the people. It was not sickness or famine that frightened the goatherders, the chamois hunters, or the villagers of the region. It was the Austrian governor, Gessler, who had been sent with his soldiers to subdue the citizens and make them bow to the Austrian crown.

Gessler was a cruel man. He bound men in chains and threw them in jail to starve when they couldn't pay their taxes; he permitted his soldiers to steal and loot at will; and he tortured or murdered all who spoke out against his tyranny.

Not satisfied with the misery he had spread throughout the district, Gessler finally devised a scheme to humiliate the proud Swiss. He had his soldiers erect in the village square in Altdorf, where all the citizens came to draw their water at the public fountain, a tall pole with a golden, feathered hat set on top of it. To this symbol of Austrian rule each villager must kneel as to a king every time he passed by. He set two soldiers on guard by the pole to see that his order was obeyed.

At this time, in the mountains near Altdorf, there lived a chamois hunter named William Tell. Tell was a large man, tall and broad, and a marksman so expert that he could bring down a running chamois with one arrow. He was also a gentle and proud man who loved his family and prized his freedom. He hated Gessler's cruel governorship, but he knew that one man alone could do little, and that until the freemen of the region banded together there was no hope of throwing out the tyrant. In the meantime, Tell and his family stayed away from Altdorf where the governor and his soldiers made their headquarters.

One day, however, William Tell had to go to the blacksmith's in the village to get steel tips for his arrows. He took with him his eldest son, Walter, and he cautioned the boy to stay quietly by his side.

Not knowing about Gessler's newest scheme, Tell and his son were astonished to find the village square deserted but for two bored soldiers sitting on the edge of the fountain near a pole topped by a golden hat. No children played in the water, no dogs shuffled about in the dust, no women gossiped as they filled their buckets.

As Tell stopped to wonder at this unusual stillness, he and Walter saw an old woman walk quickly and timidly into the square and hurry toward the fountain, carrying her water bucket. She stopped, dropped to one knee and bowed her head in front of the pole, and then quickly got to her feet and started to fill her pail.

"Hey, you there, woman," one of the soldiers bawled. "Down on both knees! Show proper respect for the ducal hat!" At the same time, he

shoved her with his staff till she fell in the dust before the pole. The soldiers laughed as the old woman got to her feet, still bowing her head nervously as she hurried away.

Tell, watching all this from the shadow of a house on the edge of the square, grew stiff with anger. Suddenly he gripped Walter's hand and strode out into the square. Without paying any attention to the pole, the hat or the soldiers, he marched straight across in the direction of the blacksmith shop.

"Stop, knave!" the soldiers yelled. "Stop and salute the hat." They ran toward him with their spears poised. "Bow down, goatherder, you and your sniveling brat. Down on your knees and show respect!"

"Respect for what?" Tell said quietly. "Respect for a hat wiggling at the top of a pole? I get down on my knees before God, not before a hat." And he started to walk on, pulling his frightened son along by his side.

The soldiers tried to bar his way with their staffs, but Tell, towering above them, pushed them aside as though they didn't exist. They cursed Tell and shouted again for him to stop. Heads appeared at windows, and people started to gather on the edges of the square. Hearing the shouts, more soldiers came running. Finally, when he was surrounded, Tell stopped, laying one arm protectively over Walter's shoulders.

The soldiers took away his crossbow and his quiver and led him before the governor, followed by a crowd of nervously muttering villagers. When the guards had described Tell's defiance, Gessler rose from his brocaded chair, and stared angrily at the powerful prisoner.

"What is this disrespect?" Gessler demanded. "Are you too noble to bow down before the sacred badge of your sovereign?"

Tell glared back at Gessler and said nothing.

"You are a fool, goatherder," Gessler said furiously. "A fool and a traitor. If you have nothing to say for yourself, then you shall die silent." With a wave of his hand, Gessler said to the captain of the soldiers. "Let the people see that I will tolerate no disobedience of my orders. Run him through!"

The captain raised his spear and advanced toward Tell. The big man, gently pushing his son aside, stood without flinching, contemptuous of the advancing soldier.

"Stop," Gessler commanded, watching Tell in surprise. The soldier lowered his spear and stood at attention. "Obviously, this man doesn't fear death. We will have to think of some more subtle punishment." And he regarded Tell thoughtfully.

Walter crept back to Tell's side, and slipped his hand into his father's. Tell squeezed the small trembling hand reassuringly.

"What is your name, goatherder?" Gessler snarled at the prisoner, "and who is this brat by your side?"

"William Tell, sir," Tell answered calmly. "And my eldest son, Walter."

"So you're William Tell, are you?" the governor said. "I have heard of you. I have heard it boasted that you are a great bowman, a cleverer shot than my soldiers, perhaps. Is that true?"

"I know not how your soldiers shoot, sir,"

Tell said. "I shoot chamois to make my living. That is all."

"He's the best of us all," a villager yelled.

"Ah, so, your friends have confidence in you," Gessler said. "Well, we will give them a little show. While seeing justice done, the people of Altdorf shall also admire your skill." And the governor smiled cruelly. "This is how we will do it. Your son shall be placed one hundred yards away from you. We will put an apple on his head—a fine, big red apple—and you will shoot it off with one arrow. If you miss or harm your son, we will kill you for a braggart or for the murder of an innocent child. If you refuse the test, you shall see your son slain before your eyes. But if, by good fortune, you should shoot off the apple cleanly, I will pardon you both and set you free."

A gasp of horror went through the crowd, and William Tell turned pale.

"Your honor," he pleaded, "you can not ask this of me. Kill me, if you will. But let my boy go home. He has done nothing."

"Your honor, is it now?" Gessler sneered. "Already he is finding respect for his betters. No, I like this punishment. What do you say, Tell?"

"Father," Walter said urgently tugging at his father's hand. "I am not afraid. You can do it. You always bring down a chamois that is running with one shot, and I will stand perfectly still."

Miserably, his eyes on Walter, Tell nodded his head. As though in a daze, Tell let himself be led to the public square. A soldier seized Walter and tied him to a stake in front of a linden tree, while another paced off a hundred yards, and a third returned Tell's crossbow and gave him one arrow.

The villagers pressed close, murmuring and shocked, until the soldiers forced them back with spears. A man cursed, and a woman sobbed.

"Quiet!" Gessler shouted angrily. "Stand quiet and see justice done."

A soldier placed an apple on Walter's head, and the boy stood as still as the tree behind him, looking directly at his father and smiling. The villagers grew quiet.

William Tell shook his head as though confused, and rubbed one hand over his eyes. He looked at the arrow in his hand as if it were something strange that he had never seen before.

"It's all right, Father," Walter shouted. "You will not miss."

Tell looked at Walter, then at Gessler. He shuddered and straightened his shoulders. He tested the point of the arrow, and it broke under the pressure of his powerful thumb.

"Bring me my quiver," he said. "Let me choose my own arrow."

A soldier brought the quiver and emptied it on the ground before him. Tell knelt to examine the arrows, and, taking a long time to select one, he quickly slipped a second into his girdle. He strung his bow, while the soldier cleared away the other arrows. He raised the heavy crossbow to his shoulder, and sighted on the apple set on his son's head. The silence in the square was profound, no foot moved, no one seemed to breathe.

Tell stood for a moment as though without strength. Then suddenly he drew the bow and shot. The arrow sped through the air, pierced the apple through the core, and stuck into the linden tree behind Walter, with the apple still trembling on its shaft.

A shout of triumph and relief arose from the crowd, and Tell dropped to one knee as though about to faint. A guard untied Walter, and the boy plucked the apple off the shaft and carried it joyfully to his father.

"See, Father, right through the core," he said excitedly, jumping up and down in front of him. "You didn't even break it."

Tell climbed wearily to his feet and kissed his son. He didn't notice that the second arrow fell from his girdle to the ground as he rose. But Gessler, who had walked over to stand before him, saw it instantly.

"Well, Tell, you are indeed a bowman," the governor said, reluctantly. "But tell me, what of that second arrow, there, on the ground, the one you hid in your girdle?"

Tell, shaken and still pale, looked at Gessler.

"That is just the custom of the bowmen of Uri, sir," he said hesitantly.

"Come, Tell. You are a poor liar. I want the truth," Gessler said. "You have my word that your life will be spared, but tell me why you hid a second arrow."

Tell stared at the governor, and the color came back into his face.

"The second shaft, Governor," he said slowly, "was to pierce your heart, if I had harmed my son. And I would not, sir, have missed twice."

The legend goes on to describe how Gessler, in fury, arrests Tell in spite of his promise, and how Tell escapes, kills him, and leads a rebellion.

108

THE KING

Once there was a king who believed everything he was told. But he hated believing everything, and finally he promised the hand of his daughter and his throne to the man who could tell him something he would not believe.

Then there came men from all quarters of the world. They told him fabulous stories of extraordinary places and people and happenings. He believed them all. So he proclaimed that any man who tried and did not succeed should die. But his daughter was so beautiful and his kingdom so rich that many men were willing to take the risk of dying to gain them.

Many heads were lost in the trying until one day a workman called Hans heard of the king and his promise. He was a stranger to that land and was pleased with its prosperity and richness. He went to the gates of the king's palace and saw the princess ride out. He was dazzled by her beauty and modest manner.

He thought, "To gain such a wife and such a kingdom is well worth the chance of losing my head. I will try my luck." So he went before the king and said, "O, king, I will tell you something you will not believe."

"Good," said the king. "But you know, do you not, that if I believe all you say, you will lose your head?"

"I know," said Hans, and began his story. "Once I went out into the field and sowed hemp. Lo, before I had finished the far end of the field, the first seed had sprouted and shot up as high as a church tower!"

"Yes, I believe you," said the king.

"Then I tried to climb up the hemp," Hans went on. "I managed very well, for the hemp was so thick and strong, and grew straight as a pine up toward heaven. When I had got to the top, I looked over towns and villages, meadows and forests, mountains and valleys, brooks and rivers. Then, having filled my eyes,

AUSTRIA: Even today contests are held by "liar's clubs" to see who can tell the most unbelievable story. This is a very early example.

I wanted to slide down to earth again. But, mercy on me! I slipped, let go the hemp and fell so hard that I sank twenty feet into the earth. I was very frightened to be in such a deep hole, so I ran as quickly as I could to my house, fetched a spade, and dug myself out of the ground. Then I went home, quite tired."

"I believe that, too," said the king.

Hans continued: "When I went to the field the next day, I noticed to my great surprise that the hemp had grown so tall overnight that the top of it disappeared into the clouds. I had long ago made up my mind that some day I would visit heaven, and it occurred to me that this might be the best way. But the hemp did not seem to me to be quite high enough, so I waited a few days. Then I went to the field again, sure that the hemp had by now reached heaven, and I started climbing. The journey took me a year."

"I believe you," said the king, solemnly.

"In heaven," Hans said, "everything was so beautiful and splendid that I could not stop wondering and admiring. Angels flew about in the air singing and playing lovely music. Then I saw many old friends, all in the finest clothes, riding in silver coaches. And what joy! I saw my beloved parents sitting in a golden chariot, taking a drive.

"Then I went on further and saw your father and your mother, O king—covered with rags, caring for a herd of swine."

"That's false!" cried the king in anger. "You did not see it!"

"O, yes, I actually saw it," replied Hans, laughing. "But now do not forget your promise. Give me your daughter and your throne."

And the king had to do so, because he would not believe what Hans had said.

TOM AND THE LEPRACAUN

IRELAND: Celtic tales often deal with Fairy Folk. This one is adapted from a story by Joseph Jacobs.

ONE FINE DAY in harvest—it was indeed Lady-day in harvest, which everybody knows to be one of the greatest holidays in the year—Tom Fitzpatrick was taking a ramble through the ground, and went along the sunny side of a hedge; when all of a sudden he heard a clacking sort of noise a little before him. Tom stole on, going on the tops of his toes to try, if he could, to get a sight of what was making the noise. The noise stopped; but as Tom looked sharply through the bushes, what should he see in a nook of the hedge but a little wee teeny tiny bit of an old man, with a little *motty* of a cocked hat stuck upon the top of his head, and a deeshy daushy leather apron hanging before him, who was working at putting a heel-piece on a bit of a brogue just fit for himself.

"Well, by the powers," said Tom to himself, "I often heard tell of the Lepracauns, and, to tell God's truth, I never rightly believed in them —but here's one of them in real earnest. If I go knowingly to work, I'm a made man. They say a body must never take his eyes off them, or they'll escape."

Tom now stole on a little further, with his eye fixed on the little man just as a cat does with a mouse. So when he got up quite close to him, "God bless your work, neighbor," said Tom.

The little man raised up his head, and "Thank you kindly," said he.

"I wonder you'd be working on the holiday!" said Tom.

"That's my own business, not yours," was the reply. "And as for you, young man, it would be fitter for you to be looking after your father's property than to be bothering decent quiet people with your foolish remarks. While you're idling away your time here, the cows have broke into the oats, and are knocking the corn all about."

Tom was taken so by surprise with this that he was just on the very point of turning round when he recollected himself; so, afraid that the like might happen again, he made a grab at the Lepracaun, and caught him up in his hand. He then swore that he would kill the tiny man if he did not show him where his money was. Tom looked so wicked and so bloody-minded that the Lepracaun was quite frightened; so, says he, "Come along with me a couple of fields off, and I will show you a crock of gold."

So they went, and Tom held the Lepracaun fast in his hand, and never took his eyes from off him, though they had to cross hedges and ditches, and a crooked bit of bog, till at last they came to a great field all full of boliauns, and the Lepracaun pointed to a big boliaun, and says

he, "Dig under that boliaun, and you'll get the great crock all full of guineas."

Tom in his hurry had never thought of bringing a spade with him, so he made up his mind to run home and fetch one; and that he might know the place again he took off one of his red garters, and tied it round the boliaun.

Then he said to the Lepracaun, "Swear ye'll not take that garter away from that boliaun." And the Lepracaun swore not to touch it.

"I suppose," said the Lepracaun, very civilly, "you have no further occasion for me?"

"No," says Tom, "you may go away now, if you please, and God speed you, and may good luck attend you wherever you go."

"Well, good-bye to you, Tom Fitzpatrick," said the Lepracaun, "and much good may the money do you when you get it."

Not sure what a Lepracaun's word was worth, Tom ran for dear life till he came home and got a spade, and then away with him, as hard as he could go, back to the field of boliauns. When he got there, he stopped and stared. To be sure, the Lepracaun had kept his word; he had not untied Tom's garter. But lo and behold, the whole field was now blooming with red garters. There was not a boliaun in the whole vast meadow but had a red garter, the very model of Tom's own, tied round it.

So Tom came home again with his spade on his shoulder, a little cooler than he went, and many's the hearty curse he gave the Lepracaun every time he thought of the neat turn the tiny man had served him.

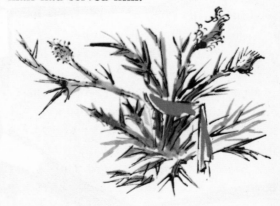

THE BIRTH OF OISIN

IRELAND (CELTIC): The deeds of Finn and his followers, the Fianna, make up one of Ireland's great and ancient sagas. The sagas are romantic and sad and filled with magic. Adapted from a story by T. W. Rolleston.

ONE DAY as Finn, his companions and their dogs were returning from the chase to their Dún—or castle—on the Hill of Allen, a beautiful fawn started up on their path. Excitedly the hunters and dogs took up the chase, with the fawn leading them straight toward their home. So swiftly did she run that soon all the pursuers

were left far behind save only Finn himself and his two hounds Bran and Sceolaun.

Now these hounds were of a strange breed. For Tyren, aunt to Finn, had herself been changed into a hound by the enchantment of the Fairy Folk, and Bran and Sceolaun were her children. Of all the hounds in Ireland they were the best, and Finn loved them dearly.

With Bran and Sceolaun in pursuit, Finn watched the fawn race down the side of a valley,

and then suddenly stop and lie down. And the two hounds, when they came upon her, began to play around her and to lick her face and limbs. Finn gave them command that none should hurt her, and the fawn followed them to the Dún of Allen, playing with the hounds as she went.

The same night Finn awoke and saw standing by his bed the fairest woman his eyes had ever beheld.

"I am Saba, O Finn," she said, "and I was the fawn you chased today. Because I would not give my love to the Dark Druid of the Fairy Folk, he put a deer's shape upon me by his sorceries, and I have borne it for three years. But a slave of his took pity on me. He revealed to me that if I could win my way into your great Dún of Allen, O Finn, I should be safe from all enchantments and my natural shape would come to me again. But I feared being torn to pieces by your dogs or wounded by your hunters. So I kept away until I could let myself be overtaken by you alone and by Bran and Sceolaun, who have the souls of men and would do me no harm."

"Be afraid no longer, maiden," said Finn. "No one shall harm or frighten you here."

Thenceforth Saba dwelt with Finn, and he made her his wife. So deep was his love for her that neither the battle nor the chase had any delight for him, and for months he never left her side. She loved him deeply in return, and their joy was like that of the Immortals in the Land of Youth.

But at last word came to Finn that the warships of the Northmen were in the bay of Dublin, and he summoned the Fianna to the fight. For, he explained to Saba, the Fianna had pledged themselves to defend Erin from the foreigner. And bidding Saba stay inside the Dún, Finn took his leave of her.

Seven days was Finn absent, and he drove the Northmen from the shores of Erin. Joyfully he rode home on the eighth day, expecting to see his bride watching for him from the rampart. But he could see no sign of her, and when he entered the Dún, there was a troubled sadness in the eyes of his men and their womenfolk. He bade them tell him where his wife was.

"While you were far off fighting the foreigner, my lord," one of the men said, "Saba stood ever on the ramparts looking down the pass for your return. One day we saw a man of your exact likeness approaching, with two hounds, the images of Bran and Sceolaun, at his heels. And we seemed also to hear the notes of the Fian hunting call blown on the wind. Then Saba hastened to the great gate, and we could not stay her, so eager was she to rush to the phantom. But when she came near, she halted and gave a loud and bitter cry, and the phantom, in your likeness, smote her with a hazel wand. And lo, there was no woman there any more, but a doe. Then the hounds chased the doe, and though she tried repeatedly to reach the gate of the Dún, they drove her away. We seized what arms we could lay hands on and ran out to drive away the enchanter. But when we reached the place there was nothing to be seen. In the distance we could hear the rush of flying feet and the baying of dogs, and at last, as we pursued, the sounds died away and all was still. What we could do, O Finn, we did. But Saba is gone."

Finn then struck his hand on his breast. He spoke no word, but went to his own chamber. No man saw him for the rest of that day, nor for the day after. Then he came forth, and led the Fianna as of old. But for seven years thereafter he went searching for Saba through every remote glen and dark forest and cavern of Ireland, and he would take no hounds with him except Bran and Sceolaun.

When the seven sad years of searching were ended, he renounced all hope of finding her again, and once more he went hunting, as of old. One day as he was following the chase on

the Ben Gulban of Sligo, he heard the musical bay of the dogs change suddenly to a fierce growling and yelping as though they were in combat with some beast. Running up hastily, he and his men saw a naked boy with long hair standing under a great tree. The hounds were struggling to seize him, while Bran and Sceolaun fought to keep him safe from the jaws of the other dogs. The lad was tall and shapely, and as the hunters gathered round, he gazed undauntedly at them, ignoring the mob of snarling hounds at his feet.

The Fians beat off the dogs and brought the lad home with them. Finn was very silent and continually searched the lad's countenance with his eyes. In time, the boy learned to speak, and he told them his story.

He had known no father, and his mother was a gentle doe with whom he lived in a green and pleasant valley shut in on every side by towering cliffs. In the summer he lived on fruits and nuts, and in the winter food was brought to him in a cave. There came to them sometimes a tall dark-visaged man, who spoke to his mother, now tenderly, and now in loud menace, but she always shrank away in fear, and the man always departed in anger.

At last there came a day when the Dark Druid spoke at great length with his mother, first pleading, then tenderly, and then in rage. But she still kept aloof and gave no sign except of fear and loathing. Finally the Dark Druid drew near and struck her with a hazel wand. With that he turned and went away. This time she followed him, repeatedly looking back at her

son and sighing piteously. The boy tried to follow her, but he found himself unable to move a limb. Crying out with rage and despair, he fell to the ground unconscious.

When he came to his senses, he found himself on the mountain side, on Ben Gulban. For days he searched in vain for the green and hidden valley where he lived with his mother. Then the dogs came upon him. But of the doe, his mother, and of the Dark Druid, there is no man knows the end.

Finn knew then that this was his son, and he named him Oisin. Oisin grew to become a warrior of fame, but more famous yet was he for the songs and tales that he devised. And to this day, when men speak of the Fianna of Erin, they always end their tales, "So sang the bard, Oisin, son of Finn."

KING ARTHUR

EARLY IN THE REIGN of King Arthur, the youthful king was enraged by the exploits of a strange knight. The king did not know who this stranger was. He knew only that the knight had built a pavilion by a fountain near the royal court at Camelot, and that the stranger waited there, challenging all passing knights to battle. When one of the knights of the Round Table was killed, and a second, the youngest of King Arthur's knights, was grievously wounded, the king swore personal vengeance on the intruder. He vowed to himself that he would not allow any more of his knights to risk their skins in combat with this stranger, but would punish the impudent one himself.

So as not to inform his followers—not even the great wizard Merlin who guided and protected him—that he planned to fight the strange knight, King Arthur secretly ordered his chamberlain to take his horse and armor outside the city walls before sunrise one morning. The King even left behind Excalibur, his sword of magic power, so as not to arouse suspicion that he was going forth to do battle.

Rising before the sun appeared, the King mounted his waiting horse, took his shield and spear and ordered his chamberlain to wait until he returned. He then rode off at a soft pace through the dawn.

A short way from the palace, he suddenly came upon three villains who were chasing Merlin as if to attack and slay him. Clapping spurs to his horse, the king rushed toward them and cried out in a terrible voice, "Flee, churls

AND THE STRANGE KNIGHT

ENGLAND, WALES: King Arthur—with his knights, his Round Table, his wizard Merlin and his magic sword—is almost as well known in America as in England. Whether such a man ever actually lived is uncertain, but tales of his adventures have been told for more than 700 years.

or you will die." And the three villains fled away with the haste of hares.

"O Merlin," cried the King, "had I not happened to pass, you would have been slain, despite your wizard powers."

"Not so," said Merlin calmly. "For when I would, I could have saved myself. But you are nearer death than I, for without special help from heaven, you are now riding toward your grave."

And as they were thus conversing, they came to the fountain with the rich pavilion pitched beside it. A great horse stood nearby, well saddled and bridled, and on a tree close to the pavilion hung a shield of many colors and a long lance. On a chair in the opening of the tent sat the strange knight, completely armed.

"Sir knight," said King Arthur, "why do you sit there thus? To challenge every knight that passes by? If so, I warn you to quit that custom."

"That custom," said the knight coldly, "have I followed and will follow. Let whoever objects try to prevent me, if he should be so bold."

"I will prevent you," said King Arthur.

"Try if you will," answered the strange knight, not knowing who his challenger was.

When the knight of the pavilion had mounted his horse and made himself ready, the two knights charged at each other and came together with such force that both of their lances splintered into pieces. King Arthur drew his sword, but the knight cried out, "Not so. Let us run another tilt together with sharp spears."

"I would gladly," said King Arthur, "but I have no other spear."

"I have spears," replied the knight, and called a squire, who brought two good new lances.

Spurring their horses, the two knights rushed together again with all their might, and once more both spears broke off short. Again the king put his hand to his sword, and again the strange knight protested. "Nay, abide a while," he cried out. "You are the best jouster I have ever met.

115

For the love of knighthood, let us joust yet once more."

So once again they tilted with the fullest force, and once again King Arthur's spear was shivered. But this time the other knight's lance held whole, driving so furiously against the king that both his horse and he were hurled to the ground.

At that, King Arthur was enraged. He drew his sword and said, "I will attack you now on foot, Sir knight, for on horseback I have lost the honor."

When the strange knight saw King Arthur advance on foot, he dismounted, thinking it unfair to have so great an advantage, and drew his sword in turn. They began a strong battle, with many great strokes and grievous blows, and so hewed with their swords that the fragments of their armor flew about the fields, and both bled so that all the ground around was like a marsh of blood. Thus they fought long and mightily, and, after a brief rest, fell to again. Finally they hurtled together like two wild boars and both rolled to the ground. Their swords clashed furiously until, at last, the knight's sword shivered the king's in two.

Then the knight said, "Now you are in my power to save or to slay. Yield therefore as a coward, or you shall surely die."

"As for death," replied King Arthur, "welcome be it when it comes. But as for yielding as a coward because of this poor accident to my sword, I had far rather die than be so shamed."

So saying, the king sprang on the knight, and took him by the middle and threw him down, tearing off his helmet. But the knight, being a huge man, wrestled and struggled in a frenzy with the king until he downed him, and tore off his helmet in turn, and made ready to smite off his head.

Then Merlin spoke up and said, "Knight, hold thy hand. For if you slay this knight, you put all the realm to greater loss and damage than ever realm was in. For he is a man more greatly worshiped than you dream of."

"Who then is he?" cried the knight.

"Arthur Pendragon!" answered Merlin. "The King!"

The strange knight was frightened and would have slain King Arthur for fear of his royal wrath, but Merlin cast a spell upon him, so that he fell suddenly to earth in a deep sleep. Then, pulling the King to his feet, Merlin led him away.

"Alas," said King Arthur, "what have you done, Merlin? Have you slain this good knight by your magic? There never lived a better knight. I had rather lose my kingdom for a year than have him dead."

"Do not be afraid," said Merlin. "He is more whole and sound than you are. He is only asleep, and he will awake in three hours' time. I told you how near you were to death. For there lives not a better knight than he in all the world. His name is Pellinore, and hereafter he shall do you good service with no equal in prowess."

So they rode on to Camelot, and all the knights grieved greatly when they heard that the king had endangered himself thus alone. Yet they could not hide their joy at serving under such a noble chief, who would risk his own life as readily as that of the poorest knight among them.

MASTER OF ALL MASTERS

SCOTLAND, ENGLAND: This story, which makes fun of people who are never satisfied to say something simply, is an old one, found in many languages. By Joseph Jacobs.

A GIRL ONCE went to the fair to hire herself for servant. At last a funny-looking old gentleman engaged her, and took her home to his house. When she got there, he told her that he had something to teach her, for that in his his house he had his own names for things.

He said to her: "What will you call me?"

"Master or mister, or whatever you please sir," says she.

He said: "You must call me 'master of all masters.' And what would you call this?" pointing to his bed.

"Bed or couch, or whatever you please, sir."

"No, that's my 'barnacle.' And what do you call these?" said he pointing to his pantaloons.

"Breeches or trousers, or whatever you please, sir."

"You must call them 'squibs and crackers.' And what would you call her?" pointing to the cat.

"Cat or kit, or whatever you please, sir."

"You must call her 'white-faced simminy.' And this now," showing the fire, "what would you call this?"

"Fire or flame, or whatever you please, sir."

"You must call it 'hot cockalorum,' and what this?" he went on, pointing to the water.

"Water or wet, or whatever you please, sir."

"No, 'pondalorum' is its name. And what do you call all this?" asked he as he pointed to the house.

"House or cottage, or whatever you please, sir."

"You must call it 'high topper mountain.'"

That very night the servant woke her master up in a fright and said: "Master of all masters, get out of your barnacle and put on your squibs and crackers. For white-faced simminy has got a spark of hot cockalorum on its tail, and unless you get some pondalorum high topper mountain will be all on hot cockalorum!"

. . . That's all.

PART 10   FINLAND: ESTONIA: DENMARK: NORWAY: ICELAND: SWEDEN

ILLUSTRATED BY LEONARD EVERETT FISHER

THE FEARFUL BATTLE OF SONG

FINLAND, ESTONIA: This is an incident, written in prose, from the *Kalevala*, an epic poem based on old Finnish chants and ballads. Americans are more familiar with this poem than they realize; in writing *Hiawatha*, Longfellow not only used the meter of the *Kalevala* but many of its characters and incidents.

LONG AGO in the dismal cold of Lapland, where minstrels were wizards and worked magic by their singing, there lived a young and reckless minstrel named Youkahainen. He prided himself on his sweet voice, on his knowledge, on his strength in battle and, most of all, he prided himself on the magic power of his songs. He boasted that there was no minstrel to equal him in all of Lapland.

One day, when he was feasting in the village, he heard his friends talking of another minstrel, Wainamoinen, who lived in Kalevala, the Land of Heroes.

"He sings more sweetly than you, Youkahainen," the young girls teased him.

"He is better skilled in chanting legends," the old men said. "He has all the wisdom of the world. For Wainamoinen is the oldest magician, the son of the Mother of Waters."

The young minstrel grew envious and angry at these words, and he hurried home to tell his parents he was journeying southward to Kalevala to meet the famed Wainamoinen in a minstrel's battle of song.

"I will prove who is the wiser and braver," he said. "I will prove who sings more sweetly. I will show who is more skilled in chanting legends."

"Do not go to Kalevala, my son," said his anxious father.

"Do not go," his fearful mother begged. "You do not know the power of Wainamoinen. He will bewitch you with his singing. He will sink you in a snowdrift, and turn your feet and fingers to ice. He will send you home dishonored. Do not go, my son."

"I must do as I think best," Youkahainen insisted. "Do not fear for me. I will challenge old Wainamoinen to sing in contest, and I will best

him. I will sing until his feet and hands have turned to flint, and his breeches to oak."

Then the young wizard brought from the stable his magic stallion, with fire streaming from its nostrils. He hitched it to his golden sleigh and, touching the horse with his jeweled whip, he sped away upon his journey. For three days the stallion galloped, until at twilight of the third day, they reached the plains of Kalevala.

As it happened, Wainamoinen was driving slowly across the plains that evening, enjoying the beauty of the peaceful meadows. Youkahainen saw the other sleigh approaching on the road, but he would not turn his frothing, racing stallion aside, and the two horses met in head-on collision. The shafts and collars wedged together, the reins tangled, and the horses stood locked together, steaming with sweat.

"Who are you and where do you come from, with your stupid, careless driving?" said Wainamoinen. "Look what you have done. My harness is ruined and my golden sleigh is broken."

"I am Youkahainen," said the young minstrel. "And who are you? From what low tribe do you come?"

"If you are Youkahainen," said the old man more gently, "you should move aside, for my name is Wainamoinen and I am many years older than you."

"Young or old, it doesn't matter," the young man said. "Let the wiser man and the sweeter singer keep the road and the other take the ditch. If you truly are Wainamoinen, let us sing so that one may judge the other in a war of wizard songs."

"What I know is very little," said Wainamoinen modestly, "and hardly worth the sing-

ing. I live quietly in my cottage and only know the cuckoo's songs. But since you demand a contest, I accept your boastful challenge. What is this wisdom of yours, young man? Tell me what you know."

"I know many things," Youkahainen said. "I know that every roof must have a chimney and every fireplace a hearth. I know that walruses lead merry lives feeding on careless salmon and perch. Whitings live in quiet shallows, pike spawn in icy water, and perch drop their eggs in the summer. I know that the Northmen plow with reindeer, mares pull the plows in the Southland, and the Laplanders use oxen."

"That is the knowledge of women and children," said Wainamoinen. "Give me wisdom suited for bearded heroes. Tell me the story of the world's beginning."

"I know that the titmouse is a bird and the viper a snake," Youkahainen went on. "Iron rusts and the rusting weakens it. Boiling water scalds and fire burns. I know that water was the first medicine. Copper comes from the rocks, the oldest land is marshland, and the willow was our first tree."

"I am waiting for some wisdom," said Wainamoinen. "Or is this nonsense all you know?"

"Oh, I can still tell you some small things," the young man answered. "Shall I tell you I created the lakes and heaped the mountains round them? Do you want to know how I dug the salmon grottoes and hollowed out the deepest caverns? I was there when the heavens were formed and the Moon was placed in orbit. I saw the Sun put in the sky, and the stars sprinkled through the heavens."

"You are a liar, young man," the old wizard said. "You were not present when the world was created. You were not born. Not even imagined. Stop your child's chatter!"

120

At this Youkahainen grew angry, and he drew his sword. "Then sir," he said, "since you scorn my wisdom, let us allow our blades to decide between us."

"Put down your sword," Wainamoinen said. "I respect it no more than I respect your knowledge. I will not fight a youthful braggart."

Youkahainen sneered and answered, "A man who fears to fight is a coward. By my singing I hurl such swine into the mud, into the dung where they belong."

At last Wainamoinen could stand no more. His face grew fierce with anger and before Youkahainen had sung a single note, the old wizard began his wondrous singing. Grandly he sang of bearded heroes until the mountains trembled and the ocean heaved and roared. Then he sang of Youkahainen, and he sang his golden sleigh into the water so that it floated like brushwood on the waves. He sang Youkahainen's reins into willow twigs, and his jeweled whip into a reed. He sang his horse into a statue with seaweed for a collar.

And still he sang. Youkahainen's sword he sang into lightning and hung it in the sky above him. He sang his crossbow into a rainbow spanning the ocean, and his arrows into hawks and screaming eagles. One more song he sang and Youkahainen found himself sinking into quicksand, deeper and deeper until the mud and water reached his belt. In panic, the young minstrel tried to lift his feet, but found they were shod in stone.

And at last the young man knew that he was beaten, that he could never equal Wainamoinen's song. Frightened and humbled, Youkahainen began to beg for his life.

"You are the greatest minstrel, Wainamoinen, the first and only true magician. I know it now. I pray you turn back your magic and free me from this killing torment. I will pay a golden ransom for my life."

"What ransom could you give me?" Wainamoinen asked.

"I have at home two magic crossbows," Youkahainen said. "One is so light a child can bend it, and the other needs a great man's strength.

They are yours in ransom, mighty magician."

"I don't want your crossbows," Wainamoinen said. "I have bows on every nail and rafter in my cottage. I have bows that go out hunting by themselves." And he sang Youkahainen deeper into the quicksand.

"Stop, Wainamoinen!" the young man cried. "I will give you my two magic stallions. One is a racer, fleet as lightning, and the other can pull unheard-of burdens."

"I don't need your stallions," the old man said. "In every manger of my stable magic stallions eat." And he sang again, until quicksand crept up to the young man's chin.

"I pray you, turn away your magic. Take me from this pit of horror," Youkahainen pleaded. "My corn fields you can have. All my golden corn."

"I have enough corn," the old man said. "In every field my corn grows rich and sweet." And he sang again until Youkahainen's beard sank in the quicksand, grass tangled in his teeth, and mud seeped into his mouth.

In despair, the young man wept and cried out, "Oh, Wainamoinen, turn away your magic. Free me! Save me! I will give you my lovely sister Aino for your wife. She will sweep your cottage and bake your bread, and weave the finest linens for your bed."

And at last Wainamoinen was pleased. He wanted a young and beautiful maiden to comfort his old age, to care for him and keep his cottage. And happily he started to sing a new song. He sang and paused and sang again to break the spell of enchantment.

And soon the defeated and saddened Youkahainen emerged from the quicksand. His feet dragged and his beard dripped mud and slime. Wainamoinen sang to bring to life the young man's horse, and to restore his crossbow, whip and arrows. While Wainamoinen sat on a rock and sang his song of triumph, Youkahainen in silent shame mounted his sleigh and started home. His boasting was ended forever. He was dishonored. And his heart was heavy with the knowledge that to save his life, he had sold his sister Aino like a slave.

THE PRINCESS

THERE WAS ONCE a Prince who wanted to marry a Princess; but she was to be a *real* princess. So he travelled about, all through the world, to find a real one, but everywhere there was something in the way. There were princesses enough, but whether they were *real* princesses he could not quite make out: there was always something that did not seem quite right. So he came home again, and was quite sad: for he wished so much to have a real princess.

One evening a terrible storm came on. It lightened and. thundered, the rain streamed down; it was quite fearful! Then there was a knocking at the town gate, and the old King went out to open it.

It was a Princess who stood outside the gate. But, mercy! how she looked, from the rain and the rough weather! The water ran down from her hair and her clothes; it ran in at the points of her shoes, and out at the heels; and yet she declared that she was a real princess.

"Yes, we will soon find that out," thought the

N THE PEA

DENMARK: Stories by the great Hans Christian Andersen have been printed in many different forms. This one is an exact translation of Andersen's own version.

old Queen. But she said nothing, only went into the bedchamber, took all the bedding off, and put a pea on the flooring of the bedstead; then she took twenty mattresses and laid them upon the pea, and then twenty eider-down beds upon the mattresses. On this the Princess had to lie all night. In the morning she was asked how she had slept.

"O, miserably!" said the Princess. "I scarcely closed my eyes all night long. Goodness knows what was in my bed. I lay upon something hard, so that I am black and blue all over. It is quite dreadful!"

Now they saw that she was a real princess, for through the twenty mattresses and twenty eider-down beds she had felt the pea. No one but a real princess could be so delicate.

So the Prince took her for his wife, for now he knew that he had a true princess; and the pea was put in the museum, and it is there now, unless somebody has carried it off.

Look you, this is a true story.

THE COLLAR

DENMARK: Hans Christian Andersen wrote two different kinds of stories—those based on old folk tales, such as *The Princess on the Pea*, and those he made up himself. This is one of the stories he made up.

THERE WAS ONCE a fine gentleman who owned practically nothing except a bootjack and a haircomb. But he also had a collar—the detachable kind that gentlemen wore then—and it was one of the most remarkable collars in the world. I'll tell you a story about it.

When the Collar got rather old and threadbare, it began to think of marriage. And it happened that it was thrown into the laundry one day with a lady's garter.

"Ah!" said the Collar, "I have never seen anything so slender and so fine, so soft and neat as you. May I ask your name?"

"No, you may not," said the Garter. "I won't tell you."

"Perhaps you would tell me where you live?" asked the Collar.

But the Garter was too bashful and modest to answer such an embarrassing question.

"You must be a girdle," said the Collar. "That is to say, an inside girdle. And I'm sure you're as useful as you are beautiful, my dear young lady."

"I will thank you not to speak to me," said the Garter. "I'm sure I've given you no excuse for such forwardness."

"Your loveliness is excuse enough," said the Collar.

"Don't come near me, I beg of you," said the Garter. "You look so terribly masculine."

"Oh, I'm a fine gentleman, I assure you," said the Collar. "I even have a bootjack and a comb." This was not exactly true, for it was his master who had them. But the Collar was a boastful fellow.

"Don't come so close," said the Garter. "I'm not used to masculine things."

"Prude!" exclaimed the Collar as he was lifted from the washtub. He was starched, hung over the back of a chair in the sunshine, and was then laid on the ironing board. He saw the Iron approaching.

"Dear lady!" said the Collar. "Dear widow lady! I am warmed to the heart at your approach. I'm a changed Collar since I've met you. I feel all smoothed out. I am burning for you. Oh dearest, won't you marry me?"

"Rag!" said the Iron as she steamed over him, leaving him stiff and flat, "rag!" she said scornfully.

The collar was a little frayed, so out came the long scissors to trim off the jagged edge.

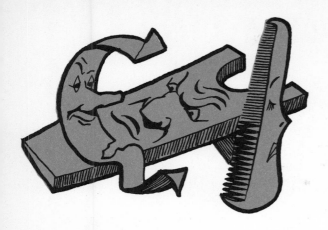

"I'll never forget my first love — she was a Girdle — so fine, so soft, so charming. She threw herself into a tub of water for my sake. There was also a widow. She glowed with love for me, but she didn't interest me, and I left her to cool off. Then there was a ballet dancer — ferocious with love! Look, you can see the scar she left on me. Even my own comb was in love with me. She lost all her teeth from despair. Yes, I have left much grief behind me. But the lady I feel worst about is the Garter — I mean the Girdle — who drowned herself in the washtub. I have much on my conscience in this life. I want to repent my sins by becoming white paper."

"Oh," said the Collar, "you must be a ballet dancer. How well you can stretch your legs! It is the most graceful performance I have ever seen. No one can equal you."

"I know it," said the Scissors.

"You deserve to be a princess," said the Collar. "All that I can offer is my fine gentleman, my bootjack and my comb. If only I were a prince!"

"Are you, by any chance, asking me to marry you?" asked the Scissors angrily. And without more ado, she cut a large gash in him so that he was useless.

"I shall now have to ask the Comb," said the Collar calmly. "It is surprising how well you've preserved your teeth, my dear," he said to the Comb. "Have you ever thought of becoming engaged?"

"Why certainly," said the Comb. "I am engaged — to the Bootjack."

"Engaged!" exclaimed the Collar. Now that there was no one else to woo, he decided that he loathed the whole idea of marriage.

A long time went by and finally the Collar turned up in the rag bin at the paper mill. There was a large company of rags, the fine ones in one bin and the coarser ones in another, just as it always is. They all had much to say, but the Collar talked most, for he was the greatest boaster.

"I have had hundreds of sweethearts," said the Collar. "The ladies couldn't leave me alone. To be sure, I was a finely starched gentleman, with a bootjack and comb which I never bothered to use. Oh, you should have seen me then!

And that is just what happened. All the rags were turned into white paper. And the Collar came to be this very same piece of paper on which this story is printed, condemned to tell its whole life history, to expose its own outrageous lies, for the rest of time.

THE THREE AUNTS

NORWAY: This story is particularly popular in Norway, but it is told in other countries, too. It is an amusing variation of those many folk tales in which hard work is shown to be a great virtue.

ONCE UPON A TIME there was a poor man who lived in a hut in the wood and got his living by shooting. He had an only daughter who was very pretty. She had lost her mother when she was a child and was now half grown up, so she said she would go out into the world and earn her bread.

"Well, lassie!" said the father, "true enough you have learned nothing here but how to pluck birds and roast them, but you may as well try to earn your bread."

So the girl went off to look for work and, when she had gone a little while, she came to a palace. There she was given work, and the queen liked her so well that all the other maids were envious of her.

So they decided to tell the queen that the lassie said she was able to spin a pound of flax in four-and-twenty hours. You must know the queen was a great housewife and thought much of good work.

"Have you said this? Then you shall do it," said the queen. "But you may have a little longer time if you choose."

Now, the poor lassie dared not say she had never spun in all her life, so she only begged for a room to herself. That she got, and the wheel and the flax were brought up to her. Then she sat sad and weeping and knew not how to help herself. She pulled the wheel this way and that, and twisted and turned it about, but she made a poor hand of it, for she had never seen a spinning wheel in her life.

But all at once, as she sat there, in came an old woman to her. "What ails you, child?" she said.

"Ah," said the lassie, with a deep sigh, "it's no good to tell you, for you'll never be able to help me."

"Who knows?" said the old wife. "Maybe I know how to help you after all."

Well, thought the lassie to herself, I may as well tell her. So she told her how her fellow servants had given out that she was able to spin a pound of flax in four-and-twenty hours.

"And here am I, wretch that I am, shut up to spin all that heap in a day and a night, when I have never even seen a spinning wheel in all my born days."

"Well, never mind, child," said the old woman. "If you'll call me Aunt on the happiest day of your life, I'll spin this flax for you. So

you may just go away and lie down to sleep."

Yes, the lassie was willing enough, and off she went and lay down to sleep.

Next morning when she awoke, there lay all the flax spun on the table. It was so clean and fine, no one had ever seen such even and pretty yarn. The queen was very glad to get such nice yarn and she set greater store by the lassie than ever. But the rest of the maids were even more envious and agreed to tell the queen that the

126

lassie had said she was able to weave the yarn that she had spun in four-and-twenty hours also.

So the queen again said that since she had said it, she must do it. But if she couldn't quite finish it in four-and-twenty hours, she wouldn't be too hard on her. She might have a little more time. This time, too, the lassie dared not say no, but begged for a room to herself and then she would try. There she sat again, sobbing and crying, and not knowing which way to turn, when another old woman came in and asked, "What ails you, child?"

At first the lassie wouldn't say, but at last she told the whole story of her grief.

"Well, well!" said the old wife. "Never mind. If you'll call me Aunt on the happiest day of

your life, I'll weave this yarn for you. So you may just be off, child, and lie down to sleep."

Yes, the lassie was willing enough, so she went away and lay down to sleep. When she awoke, there lay the piece of linen on the table, woven so neat and close no woof would be better. So the lassie took the piece and ran down to the queen. She was very glad to get such beautiful linen and set greater store than ever by the lassie.

But as for the other maids, they grew even more bitter against her and thought of nothing but how to find out something to tell about her. At last they told the queen the lassie had said she was able to make up the piece of linen into shirts in four-and-twenty hours.

Well, it all happened as before. The lassie dared not say she couldn't sew, so she was shut up again in a room by herself, and there she sat in tears and grief. But then another old wife came and said she would sew the shirts if the lassie would call her Aunt on the happiest day of her life. The lassie was only too glad to do this. Then she did as the old wife told her and went and lay down to sleep.

Next morning when she woke, she found the piece of linen made up into shirts which lay on the table — and such beautiful work as no one had ever laid eyes on. More than that, the shirts were all marked and ready for wear. So, when the queen saw the work, she was so glad at the way it was sewn that she clapped her hands and said, "Such sewing I never had, nor even saw, in all my born days." And after that she was as fond of the lassie as of her own children.

She said to her, "Now if you'd like to have the Prince for your husband, you shall have him. For you will never need to hire work-women. You can sew, spin and weave all yourself."

So, as the lassie was pretty and the Prince was glad to have her, the wedding soon came on. But just as the Prince was going to sit down with the bride to the bridal feast, in came an ugly old hag with a long nose — I'm sure it was three ells long.

So up got the bride and made a curtsey and said, "Good day, Auntie."

"*That* Auntie to my bride?" said the Prince. Yes, she was!

"Well, then she'd better sit down with us to the feast," said the Prince. But to tell you the truth, both he and the rest thought she was a loathsome woman to have next to them.

Just then in came another ugly old hag. She had a back so humped and broad, she had hard work to get through the door.

Up jumped the bride in a trice and greeted her with "Good day, Auntie!"

And the Prince asked again if that were his bride's aunt.

They both said yes, so the Prince said if that were so, she had better sit down with them to the feast.

But they had scarce taken their seats before another ugly old hag came in. She had eyes as large as saucers and so red and bleared it was gruesome to look at her. But up jumped the bride again with her "Good day, Auntie!" and her, too, the Prince asked to sit down.

But I can't say he was very glad, for he thought to himself, "Heaven shield me from such Aunties as my bride has!" So when he had sat awhile, he could not keep his thoughts to himself any longer.

He asked, "But how in all the world can my bride, who is such a lovely lassie, have such loathsome, misshapen Aunts?"

"I'll soon tell you how it is," said the first. "I was just as good-looking when I was her age. But the reason why I've got this long nose is because I was always kept sitting and poking and nodding over my spinning. So my nose got stretched and stretched, until it got as long as you now see it."

"And I," said the second, "ever since I was young, I have sat and scuttled backwards and forwards over my loom. That's how my back got so broad and humped as you now see it."

"And I," said the third, "ever since I was little, I have sat and stared and sewn, and sewn and stared, night and day. That's why my eyes have got so ugly and red, and now there's no help for them."

"So, so!" said the Prince. "It was lucky I came to know this, for if folk can get so ugly and loathsome by all this spinning and weaving and sewing, then my bride shall neither spin nor weave nor sew all her life long."

OF GRETTIR AND THE TROLL-WIFE

ICELAND: The thousand-year-old Gretta Saga tells of the deeds of Iceland's most famous outlaw, Grettir. Here, Grettir is hiding out in the mountains.

THERE WAS a widow called Steinvor who dwelt at Sand-heaps, south of Isledale-river. She had young children. Alone she managed the household of her place, for there was no master. It happened thus.

Two winters before, Steinvor, who was then young and merry-hearted, had gone at Yuletide to Isledale-river to church. But the master had remained at home with the housefolk. They lay down to sleep in the evening, but in the night, the housefolk had heard a huge crashing about the master's bed. None had dared to rise and find the cause of the noise, for they were few and the sounds were the sounds of many. In the morning, when the mistress had come home, the master was gone, and none knew what had become of him.

The next winter at Yuletide, the mistress again wished to go to worship at Isledale-river and bade her houseservant stay behind. He was loath to do so, but this he could not say, for he was but a bondman and she the mistress. So all had gone the same way. There was a crashing in the night, and the houseservant had vanished.

People thought it amazing and believed an evil witch had taken them both. The strange happenings were told through the countryside and Grettir the Strong heard of them. Grettir had come into the north country some weeks before and, when he heard of the happenings at Sand-heaps, he took his way there to find out for himself the truth of it.

He arrived on Yule eve and asked to be allowed to stay. He said his name was Guest. The housefolk were much afraid of him because of the time of his coming. They had no heart for strangers at Yuletide. But the mistress saw he was marvelous of growth and was not afraid, only glad of the presence of so strong a man.

She said there was meat for him to eat. "But," she said, "as to your safety, see to that yourself."

"That I will do," said Guest. "I will stay here, but you go to worship if you wish."

"You are a brave man," Steinvor said, "if you dare to stay to guard this place tonight. I, myself, have no desire to stay, but I cannot cross the river."

"I will go with you to the crossing," said Guest.

Then Steinvor made herself ready for worship and made her little daughter ready also, and with Guest they set out toward the river. It had thawed fast that winter and the river was in flood. The swift water carried great drifts of ice.

Steinvor said, when she saw the river, "There is no way to cross this, either for man or horse."

"There will be fords here," said Guest. "Do not be afraid."

"Carry over the little maiden first," said Steinvor. "She is lightest."

"I am loath to make two journeys of it," Guest said. "I will bear you in my arms."

She crossed herself fearfully. "That will never work," she said. "For if you bear me in your arms, what will you do with the child?"

"I see a way for that," said he. He took them both up and laid the little girl in her mother's lap. He set them both on his left arm, leaving his right arm free. Then he took the ford.

They were afraid as the river rose up to his chest, but they dared not cry out. A great ice floe drove against him, but he put forth his free hand and thrust it from him. Then the stream grew deeper and broke over his shoulder, but

129

he waded through it stoutly till he came to the farther shore. There, he set them on land and turned back. It was twilight by the time he got home to Sand-heaps and called for his meat.

When his hunger was satisfied, he bade all the housefolk go into the great hall. None dared to speak against him or utter the least sound, remembering the witch of other Yuletides. For who could know what form a witch might take? The shape of this giant man might well be false. They gathered together, silent, at one end of the

end of the hall and the housefolk trembled at the other end far on in the night.

When it drew towards midnight, Guest heard a great din outside. Into the hall came a huge

hall and watched Guest with fearful eyes.

Guest took boards and loose timber and dragged them across the room. And he built them higher and higher until he had made a wall between himself and the housefolk. For they seemed like ordinary folk, but who knew what form a witch might take on Yule eve? And if the witch approached from outside, Guest wished to face it alone.

The entrance to the hall was near the end of the side wall. There Guest lay down, but he did not take off his clothes and he left a light burning near the door. Thus Guest lay at one

troll-wife with a trough in one hand and a great chopper in the other. She peered about and saw where Guest lay and she ran at him. He sprang up to meet her and they began to wrestle dreadfully. She was the stronger, but he was the more clever, and they struggled long around the hall. Everything in their path was broken as they fell and rose and fell again. Even the wall of timbers splintered under their weight.

The troll-wife dragged Guest to the door of the hall and then to the outer door. As she strove to force him from the house, he struggled harder against her. He seized the massive frame of the outer door and braced his body in the opening. But the troll-wife made a mighty effort and the door frame split off from the house as they carried it away on their shoulders. Then she labored to drag him toward the river, and right down near the deep gulfs.

Guest was very weary, but he knew he must either gather his strength or be thrown into the river. So he found new power and fought more fiercely. Each time he felt himself grow weary, he thought of the bottomless gulfs with their sucking whirlpools and he grew stronger once more. Thus they fought all night on the river bank. Never before had Guest met with such strength. The troll-wife held him so hard in her crushing grip that he could not use his arms except to hold fast to her.

But then, toward morning, at the very brink of the water, Guest felt himself failing and a sudden huge power came to him. He gave a mighty swing of his body and, as the hag stumbled, he got his right hand free. He swiftly seized the short sword at his thigh and smote her on the shoulder and struck off her arm. Then he was free, and she fell backward into the gulf and was swallowed by the torrent.

When Steinvor came from church, she thought her house had been somewhat roughly handled, so she went to Guest. He was lying in bed. Stiff and weary, and all swollen and bruised he was. Steinvor asked what had happened that all was broken and downtrodden and he told her of the troll-wife. Then Steinvor knew Guest was no ordinary man and asked him what man he truly was. He told her he was Grettir the Strong, and she cared for him the many days he lay abed, rejoicing that no longer would men vanish from Sand-heaps at Yuletide.

NAIL BROTH

SWEDEN: Sometimes the broth is made with a stone instead of a nail. Sometimes it is not broth, but stew. One way or another, this story is told in many countries.

ONCE A TRAMP, who had plodded all day through the forest with little hope of finding shelter, saw a cottage through the trees. There was a fire on the hearth, and he thought wearily how nice it would be to roast himself before the fire and get a bite to eat. Just as he was dragging himself toward the cottage, he met an old woman coming toward him.

"Good evening, and well met!" said the tramp.

"Good evening," said the woman. "Where do you come from?"

"South of the sun and east of the moon," said the tramp. "I have been all over the world except for this parish."

"You must be a great traveler, then," said the woman. "And what may be your business here?"

"Oh, I would like a shelter for the night," he said.

"I thought as much," said the woman. "But you may as well get away from here at once. My man is not at home and my place is not an inn."

"You must not be so hard-hearted," said the tramp. "We are both human beings and we should help one another."

"Help? Who'll help me? I haven't a morsel of food in the house, even for myself. No, you'll have to find shelter elsewhere."

But the tramp was persistent, and although the old woman grumbled and complained, she at last gave in to his begging and said she would allow him to lie on the floor for the night.

When the tramp went into the house, he could see that the woman was not as poor as she had pretended to be. She was only stingy and greedy. In his most agreeable manner, he asked her for something to eat.

"Where am I to get it from?" said the woman. "I haven't tasted a morsel myself the whole day."

But the tramp was a clever fellow. "Poor old

granny," he said. "You must be starving. Well, I suppose I must ask you to have something with me, then."

"With you! What have you got to offer, I'd like to know?"

"He who far and wide does roam, sees many things not known at home," said the tramp. "Lend me a pot, granny."

The old woman was very curious so she handed him a pot. He filled it with water and put it on the fire. Then he took a four inch nail from his pocket, turned it three times in his hand, and put it in the pot.

The woman stared. "What's this going to be?" she asked.

"Nail broth," said the tramp and began to stir the water with the porridge stick.

The old woman had never heard the like of that before. "That's something for poor people to know," she said. "I should like to learn how to make it."

"You have only to watch me," said the tramp, and went on stirring.

The old woman squatted on the hearth, her eyes following every movement of his hand.

"This kind of nail generally makes good broth," said the tramp, "but tonight it is likely to be rather thin. I have been making broth for

a whole week with this same nail. If I only had a handful of sifted oatmeal to put into it, that would make it all right. But since there's none, there's no use wishing for it." And he went on stirring.

"Well, I may have a scrap of oatmeal somewhere," said the old woman. When she fetched it, it was both good and fine.

The tramp put in some of the oatmeal and went on stirring, while the woman still stared. "This broth would be good enough for company," said the tramp, adding more oatmeal, "if only I had a bit of salted beef and some potatoes. Oh well, it's no use thinking about that."

But the old woman suddenly remembered some potatoes she had put away, and perhaps a bit of beef, as well. She gave them to the tramp, who kept on stirring. She sat and stared as hard as ever.

"This will be grand enough for the best in the land," he said.

"Well, I never!" said the old woman. "And just fancy—all with a nail!"

"If only I had a little barley and a drop of milk, we could ask the king himself to have some of it," the tramp said. "This is what he has every blessed evening, I know. For I have served under the king's cook."

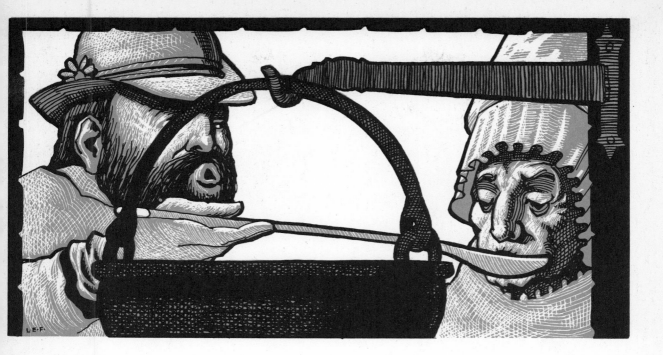

"Dear me! The king! Well, I never!" she exclaimed, slapping her knee. She was quite awestruck by the tramp's fine connections.

"But there's no use thinking about what we can't have," said the tramp.

Then the old woman happened to remember that she had a *little* barley, and that she wasn't *quite* out of milk. So she went to fetch the one and the other. The tramp went on stirring, and the woman squatted down again and went on staring.

Then, all at once, the tramp took out the nail. "Now it's ready," he said, "and we'll have a real feast. Of course, the king and queen always had a bit of brandy and a sandwich with this kind of soup. And they always used a cloth on the table when they ate. But there's no use thinking of that."

But by this time, the old woman was feeling quite grand and fine, and she thought it would be nice to have it just as the king and queen did, for once. She went straight to the cupboard and brought down the brandy bottle and glasses. She brought butter and cheese, smoked beef and veal. When she had set them out on her best cloth, and table looked as if it were decked out for company.

Never in her life had the old woman had such a grand feast! Never had she tasted such broth. And, just fancy, it was made with only a nail!

She was in such a good humor at learning how to make delicious broth so cheaply that she could´ not make enough of the tramp who had taught her such a useful thing. They ate and drank and drank and ate until they both became tired and sleepy. The tramp started to lie down on the floor, but now that would never do! Such a grand person must have a bed to lie in.

The tramp did not need much urging. "It's just like sweet Christmas time," he said, "and I never came across a nicer woman." He lay down on the bed and went to sleep.

When he awoke the next morning, coffee and a glass of brandy were waiting for him. And when he was going, the old woman gave him a bright coin.

"And thanks, many thanks, for what you have taught me," she said. "I shall live in comfort now that I've learned to make broth with a nail."

"Well, it isn't very difficult, if you only have something good to flavor it with," said the tramp, as he started on his way.

The old woman stood in the doorway, staring after him admiringly. "Such people surely don't grow on every bush!" she said.

THE THREE LESSONS OF GOD

BULGARIA: Few Bulgarian stories have been translated into English, and most of those that have are stories of God and how things began, such as this one.

AFTER the Lord had formed the world and made man, he left people to fend for themselves for a time to find their own ways of living. But, when a certain time had passed, the Lord wished to see how his newly created people fared. He came down from Heaven, first on the Balkan mountains, in the form of an old man with a long white beard. With a staff in his hand, he traveled over the Bulgarian land, first through the desolate mountains, then down to the valleys.

In the second valley, he came upon a partly plowed field and he paused to watch the plowman at his work. As with all men of that time, this plowman had no beast to draw his plow, but used a hand plow. When he had cut a furrow from one end of the field to the other, he lifted his plow onto his shoulder, trudged back to the end at which he had started and thence began to plow the next furrow.

The Lord, in the form of an old man, approached the plowman as he was about to lift his plow to his shoulder for the second time, and he said, "Not thus, my son, but when you make a furrow, turn your plow around at the same place to which you have cut, and plow back to the end at which you began."

And thus the plowman learned to plow aright, as people plow to this day.

Thence the Lord went away, still in the form of an old man, and he saw a house. When he came up to it he looked in the window and there saw a woman weaving at a loom. Each thread she bit off to the width of the cloth and put it through from her right hand to her left. Then she bit off another piece and started again at the same side.

The Lord knocked on the door and, when the woman had opened it, he said, "Let me help you, daughter, with your weaving." He picked up a smooth stick from the hearth and wound the thread over and over it from end to end. "Now," he said, "let this shuttle lead the thread. When you have reached the other side, take the shuttle in your other hand and weave the same thread back without biting it off." And the woman learned to weave as people weave to this day.

Then the Lord passed on his way, and he saw a man cutting logs of wood. Those he cut he piled in a heap, then tapped them with a stick and told them to go to the kitchen. And, because logs were things over which man had command in that day, they rose and went of themselves where they were told to go.

The Lord was pleased to see that man was willing to learn and to make good use of the gifts he had received from Heaven, so he blessed the earth and went on his way.

Some days later, thinking to see how well man had learned his teaching, the Lord disguised himself as a different old man and went again to the earth. He first came to the man chopping wood, and he watched him for a time. But now the man had grown lazy. When he had piled the logs in a heap, he no longer wanted to walk beside them to the kitchen. Instead he mounted upon the pile and tapped the logs, commanding them to carry him. But the logs resisted, so he struck them harder, but they didn't move. Then he beat them on one side and the other in a rage, but the logs were still.

Finally, the Lord came up to him and said, "I will show you how you must get the logs to the kitchen." And he removed the man's belt and tied the logs to his back. "The logs will no longer do your bidding, for you are wicked and lazy. Instead of your riding on them, they will ride on you from this day onward."

The Lord was saddened, for he had believed

no longer be trusted to fend for themselves until they know me and believe as I do. From this day, I must make laws for them to follow or they will destroy themselves and others with cruelty and deceit and selfishness."

As the Lord wandered, thinking thus, he came to the field where he had met the plowman. He noticed that the man was plowing in the way he had been shown, turning the plow and making his furrow back to the place where he had started. When the plowman came up to him, the Lord said, "Who taught you, my son, to plow thus?"

there was no wickedness on earth. But he went farther, to the house where he had taught the woman to weave. When he looked in at the window, she sat industriously at her loom, weaving in the way he had taught her. He was pleased, and he knocked again at the door. When the woman opened it, she did not know him as her visitor of the other time, for he had changed his appearance.

The Lord said, "I saw you weaving through the window. Who taught you to weave thus?"

And with no hesitation, she lied, "Myself, my very own self, and quickly, quite quickly."

Then the Lord was angry and said to her, "You are wicked, for you lie. Therefore, from this day on, it will take you a year to weave a piece of cloth you can carry under your arm!"

"Men have learned wicked ways," the Lord thought sadly, as he turned away. "They may

Not knowing this was the same old man who had taught him, the plowman said, "I was taught by the Lord God. He came to me in the form of an old man, but his disguise did not conceal his goodness."

Then the Lord knew that not all men were wicked. And he knew that some men recognized that good things came to them from Heaven and he rejoiced. So he blessed the plowman, and he said, "The land you plow in a day shall grow food enough to feed you for a year."

And, with the awe-stricken plowman gazing after him, he walked back into the desolate mountains and thence into Heaven.

THE TSAR TRAJAN'S EARS

YUGOSLAVIA: In ancient times, rulers had absolute power, but they still couldn't stop their subjects from secretly making fun of them, as in this story about the Tsar with goat's ears. By Nada Curcija-Prodanovic.

A LONG time ago there was a Tsar named Trajan. He had a vast empire and riches of all sorts, he commanded a big and brave army, and he lived in a magnificent palace. But in spite of all this he was unhappy. The cause of his unhappiness was his ears, which were not ordinary, human ears, but were shaped like those of a goat. Tsar Trajan managed to hide them under an elaborate headdress and nobody had ever seen them except his barbers, for the Tsar had to be shaved, and there was no way of hiding his misfortune from them. Whenever a new barber came to his palace—and every time it had to be a new one—Tsar Trajan would ask him, after shaving: "What have you seen, barber?" The barber, who could not help noticing the Tsar's strange ears, would answer: "I saw that you had goat's ears, Tsar Trajan." The Tsar would order him to be beheaded instantly, fearing that the truth about his ears would spread throughout his country and that he, the mighty Emperor, would be made a laughing-stock for all his subjects. So no barber who went to the Court was ever seen again.

For a long time people envied the missing men, believing them to be living in luxury as the Tsar's own barbers, but later they began to wonder. So many had gone to the palace and none of them had returned—why, surely the Tsar was not recruiting a barbers' army? Slowly it began to dawn on them that these unfortunate men must have met their death in the palace. As the rumor went from mouth to mouth, terror seized all the barbers in the empire. They lost their appetites, they were unable to sleep, and they cut such pitiful figures in every way that, when somebody came across a pale and sad man in the street, he guessed that he must be a barber. The merry songs with which they used to amuse their customers and which, indeed, they sang beautifully, for barbers have a good ear for music, were heard no more, and a gloomy shadow of death fell on the once cheerful and lively streets. However, any barber who received the Tsar's summons had to obey, although he knew that he was doomed.

One day the lot fell upon one of that brotherhood who could not bring himself to accept his death in cold blood, and he pretended he was ill—which, after all, was not far from the truth, for he lay in his bed shaking from head to foot at the idea of shaving Tsar Trajan. He had a country lad as an apprentice in his shop and, although he was sorry that the good, honest youth should die, still, preferring his own life, the barber sent him to the palace. The youth was also aware of the sad fate that was in store for him and, going to the Tsar, he decided to try every means to save his life.

As he came into the Tsar's presence, Tsar Trajan looked at him and frowned.

"Are you the barber I summoned today? You look too young," he said.

"I am his apprentice, my gracious Tsar. My master lies in his bed, sick with some dreadful ague," answered the youth, taking the razors and scissors out of his satchel.

The Tsar sat down on his chair and gave a sign to the boy to start shaving him. The boy was very skilful and, as he had delicate fingers, Tsar Trajan soon began to doze. The youth went on carefully with his operation and noticed, of course, what strange ears his imperial customer had. He finished shaving him and started packing his things in his satchel, when the Tsar asked in a stern voice:

"What did you see while shaving me, boy?"

"Nothing, mighty Tsar, except that you have regular features," answered the boy.

The Tsar was very pleased with his answer; he gave him a dozen golden ducats and told him that he was to shave him henceforward.

The lad's master was greatly astonished at seeing him again. He got up from his bed and asked his apprentice: "Well, how was it at the Tsar's?"

"Very well indeed," answered the youth.

"Did you shave him? What happened afterwards?"

"I shaved the Tsar as you had taught me, master. He seemed to have been pleased, for he gave me twelve golden ducats and ordered me to come to him again."

The barber was very inquisitive, as barbers often are, and wanted to know all about the palace, the Tsar, his dress, and many other things. The youth answered all his questions truthfully, keeping only one piece of information for himself: he never mentioned that the Tsar had goat's ears.

From that day on he went often to shave Tsar Trajan, and every time he received a dozen golden ducats as a reward. The Tsar liked him, and all would have been well had not the boy's secret begun to prey on his mind. He never confided in anybody, but somehow he could not get rid of the thought of Tsar Trajan's goat's ears. Indeed, he was unable to think about anything else, and as the other barbers recovered from their fear and became robust and cheerful again, the poor lad pined away. He was unable to eat or to sleep, and soon looked a miserable sight.

His master noticed the change in him and asked him what it was that was ailing him.

"Nothing, my master; I'm perfectly healthy," answered the boy sadly.

But the barber went on with his questions till, at long last, his apprentice said:

"The truth is, master, I have a secret preying on my mind heavily, but I dare not confide in any living soul, for if I did, it would be the death of me. Oh, but if I could, I know I should feel relieved and would go on living happily as of old," he ended, sighing and looking wistfully at the good-natured barber.

His master thought for a while, then spoke again: "Can't you confide in me? I promise I'd carry your secret to my own grave."

The boy only shook his head sadly.

"Well then, go to the priest and confess your troubles to him."

The boy shook his head again, tears brimming his eyes.

"Your secret must be of a peculiar sort if you can't do that either. Still, you can unburden yourself of it without telling it to any living soul. Go out of the town, my son; when you reach a large field go to its far end and dig a hole in the ground. When it is deep enough, put your head down and tell the earth your secret three times. Cover the hole with the clay you've dug out, level it, and come back. You will have told your secret at last, and the earth is sure not to betray you."

The boy thought about his master's advice and decided to try it. He went to the large field, dug a hole in the ground, and said three times, "Tsar Trajan has goat's ears!" There was nobody there except the sky, the field, and himself with his secret. When he had parted with it in that way, he levelled the ground and returned home, relieved.

After a few weeks an elder tree grew up in the place where the youth had dug the hole to hide his secret. Three tall stalks, straight as wax candles, shot up from the earth. The little shepherds who used to roam over the field following their flocks noticed the elder tree and cut off one stalk to make pipes out of it. It was an easy thing to do, but as the first child put one of the new pipes to his mouth and blew in it, they heard a voice coming out and saying quite clearly: "Tsar Trajan has goat's ears!"

The other children were amazed. Then they thought that the boy who held the pipe had been playing tricks on them; they snatched the instrument from him and every one of them tried to play on it. The same voice went on repeating the same words—"Tsar Trajan has goat's ears!"

When they returned to the town in the evening, the streets through which they walked resounded with the strange song of their pipe. Before the night set in, the whole town knew about the ears of Tsar Trajan. Within a day or two the whole country learnt his secret.

Before long the Tsar heard what his people knew and, seething with rage, summoned the young barber to come to him at once. As soon as the boy appeared, the Tsar shouted at him: "What did you say to my people about myself, you ungrateful devil?"

"Nothing, my gracious lord," said the boy.

"How dare you tell lies to your Tsar! You told my secret to somebody, for it's on everybody's lips." The idea of his subjects laughing at him made the Tsar still more furious, and he drew his sabre out of its scabbard angrily.

The boy went down on his knees and said:

"Forgive me, mighty Tsar! I told your secret to no human being, but to the earth—to a deep hole I dug in the ground. The secret was preying on my mind too heavily, and I'd have gone mad had I not confided it to the dumb earth."

The Tsar listened to him with interest, for the boy's voice rang true. Tsar Trajan then heard about the speaking pipes, made of elder stalks that had grown on the spot where his secret had been buried. The Tsar took the boy and drove in a chariot to that place.

As they came near, they saw that there was only one elder stalk left—the other two had been turned into many pipes by that time. The Tsar ordered one of his servants to cut the remaining stalk and to make a pipe on the spot. As soon as it was finished, the Tsar ordered the servant to play on it. He heard a clear young voice say: "Tsar Trajan has goat's ears!"

The Tsar snatched the pipe from the servant's hand and brought it to his own lips. As he blew in it the same words were repeated.

Tsar Trajan dropped the pipe and turned to the young barber. "You have been telling the truth to me, my boy, and to the earth, for that matter. Nothing can be kept secret in this world, as I see now for myself. You shall live; and," he spoke to the people who had gathered around their Tsar, having seen him in the field, "from today on no barber will perish by my hand. They can come to shave me without fear, for my secret is no secret any more."

That day was the happiest for all the barbers of his empire.

THERE was once a poor man who had a wife and five children, and they had nothing to eat. His godfather in the village was a rich landowner, but he was so miserly that he would not give the family even a piece of bread. So these people rose hungry in the morning and went to bed hungry at night.

One day, as the wife was walking along a path by a stream a great piece of earth gave way under her and she barely saved herself from falling in the water. And then she saw where the earth had fallen away there was a huge pot full of golden ducats which had rolled out of its hiding place in the bank of the stream. The woman was overjoyed. She quickly gathered the coins into her apron and ran home.

Now their misery was ended. They hid the money in a chest in the garret. Then, taking a ducat, the woman went to the godfather and asked for a loaf of bread.

The godfather began to scold, saying that he had no bread for beggars. But when the woman showed him the ducat, he brought the loaf at once. His eyes gleamed as he asked her where she got the money. The woman innocently told him how she had found the gold.

The greedy godfather begrudged them their riches, and one day he said to his wife, "I must have that money. But how am I to get it?"

She at once thought of a way. "I'll tell you," she said. "Tonight, after dark, we will kill our black cow. Then you must wrap yourself in the hide with the horns upon your head. At midnight go to your godson's house, knock on the door and tell them you are the devil and have come for the money."

The godfather waited until dark, killed and skinned the cow and, just before midnight, set out for his godson's hut. At midnight, he was pounding on the door and rattling an iron chain. Presently, the poor man put his head out of the window.

"Who is there?" he called. "And what do you want at this hour?"

"I am the devil," thundered the godfather. "I have come for my money!"

The poor man saw the black horned head and trembled with fear. "Do you hear?" he said to his wife. "The devil has come for the money. You give it to him. I want nothing to do with it."

But the wife was braver. "I will not," she said. "Who knows what all this might mean?"

So the godfather stalked about the hut, but nothing happened, and, soon after midnight, he went away. "If I come every night," he thought, as he walked home, "I will frighten them into giving me the money."

The next night, he again pounded on the door and loudly demanded the money. And again he got nothing.

But he succeeded in frightening his godson, for the next morning the poor man said, "Wife, if the devil comes again tonight, I will give him the money myself. Indeed, who knows what kind of gold it might be?"

That day the godfather came to visit them, and the poor man told him what had happened and what he intended to do that night.

"I have won," thought the godfather. "Tonight, surely, I shall get the money."

That evening, the poor man was sitting in front of his hut resting after his day's work, when a strange man in hunter's dress came up the road. He was dusty and tired and he asked the poor man to give him lodging for the night.

"If you are brave enough to stay," said the poor man, "I shall be glad to have you. Terrible things have been happening here." Then he explained about the money and the nightly visits of the devil.

The hunter seemed not at all afraid. He was eager to see this devil. So the poor man led him into the hut, glad they would not be alone.

THE UNREAL DEVILS

As it neared twelve o'clock, the loud noise and rattling of chain was heard. The poor man picked up the money and was prepared to give it up when the hunter said, "No, don't give it up! Open the door. Let him in!"

The wife objected. "Let us pay no attention," she said. "Perhaps he will go away again."

But the hunter jumped up and opened the door and the horned monster stormed into the room.

The man and his wife cowered in the corner, but the hunter stood his ground. "Who are you?" he asked. "What have you come for?"

"I am the devil, and I have come for my money," shouted the godfather.

"You are a devil?" said the hunter. "How strange that we should meet here! I am a devil, too. Well then, since we have met, let us travel together to where we both belong."

There was a sudden puff of smoke and a smell of brimstone. The hunter picked up the horned monster, rose from the floor, and flew out of the window. All that remained was the smoke, the smell, and the shutters swinging in the night wind.

THE WOLF AND THE CAT

RUSSIA: Ivan Krylov is Russia's most famous fabulist. Here is his rather gay version of an old Biblical proverb.

A WOLF ran out of the forest into a village—not for a visit, but to save its life; for it trembled for its skin. The huntsmen and a pack of hounds were after it. It would fain have rushed in through the first gateway; but there was this unfortunate circumstance in its way, that all the gateways were closed. Our Wolf sees a Cat on a partition fence, and says, pleadingly,

"Vaska, my friend, tell me quickly which of the moujiks here is the kindest, so that I may hide myself from my evil foes? Listen to the cry of the dogs and the terrible sound of the horns! All that noise is actually made in chase of me!"

"Go quickly, and ask Stefan," says Vaska the Cat; "he is a very kind moujik."

"Quite true; only I have torn the skin off one of his sheep."

"Well, then, you can try Demian."

"I'm afraid he's angry with me, too. I carried off one of his kids."

"Run over there, then. Trofim lives there."

"Trofim! I should be afraid of even meeting him. Ever since the spring, he has been threatening me about a lamb."

"Dear me, that's bad! But perhaps Klim will protect you."

"Oh, Vaska, I have killed one of his calves."

"What do I hear, gossip? You've quarrelled with all the village," said Vaska to the Wolf. "What sort of protection can you hope for here? No; our moujiks are not so destitute of sense as to be willing to save you to their own hurt. And, really, you have only yourself to blame. What you have sown, that you must now reap."

THE OLD FATHER WHO WENT TO SCHOOL

THE UKRAINE: The "school" that the old man is sent to in this story is obviously a local poor house where orphans and old people are boarded.

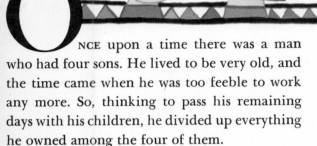

ONCE upon a time there was a man who had four sons. He lived to be very old, and the time came when he was too feeble to work any more. So, thinking to pass his remaining days with his children, he divided up everything he owned among the four of them.

First, the old man went to live with his eldest son, and the son treated him with respect and affection. "It is proper that we should feed and clothe our father," he said. "And we shall see that he has clean, new shirts on festival days." So the eldest son and his wife set a place for the old man at their table and welcomed him warmly.

But after a few months, the eldest son began to regret his hospitality and became rough with his father, sometimes even shouting at the old man. The father's place was no longer set at the table, and no one would cut up his food for him. As the days went on, the eldest son came to grudge every morsel of bread that the old man ate. The old man had no choice but to move to his second son's house.

At the second son's house, however, the old man soon discovered that he had only changed wheat for straw. Whenever he began to eat, his second son and his daughter-in-law looked sour and murmured something disagreeable between their teeth. "We can hardly make ends meet," they complained. "And now we have old men to keep into the bargain."

The old man soon had enough of it there also, and he went on to his next son's house.

And so it went. One after another, the sons grudgingly took their father to live with them, and he was glad to leave each house. All four made him feel unwelcome and burdensome. Each had some reason not to keep him. This one had too many little children. That one had a scold for a wife. This house was too small, and that house was too poor.

Finally, the old man wept and did not know where to turn. He could argue with his sons no more, but let them do with him as they wanted. So the four sons met and agreed to send their father away to school. When they told the old man about their decision, however, he wept again and begged them not to send him.

"Now that I am so old I can hardly see the white world," he said, "how can I see a little black book? All my life, I have never learned my letters. How can I begin now?"

But his sons would not listen, and he was too feeble to argue very long. He was packed off down the road to walk to the school in the next village. The road ran through a forest and, as the old man trudged sadly along, he heard a carriage coming behind him. He respectfully stepped aside to let it pass. The carriage drew up and a nobleman got out.

"Where are you going, old man?" the nobleman asked. "And why do you look so sad?"

At the sound of a kind voice, the old man broke down and poured out all his misery. "I don't understand it, kind sir," the old man said, with tears running down his cheeks. "If the Lord had left me without children, I should not complain. But I have four grown sons, thank God, and all four have houses of their own, and yet they send their poor old father away to school. How can it be?"

When the nobleman had heard the whole story, he looked thoughtful for a moment. Then he said, "Well, old man, it is silly for you to go to school, that's plain. Don't be troubled. I have a plan."

The nobleman then took out his purse—a real nobleman's purse of fine soft leather. And, turning his back so the old man could not see what he was doing, he filled it full of something. Then he gave it to the old man.

"Take this and go home to your village," he said. "Call all your sons together and say to them . . ." and the nobleman spoke long and earnestly to the old man. "Remember," he finished, "as long as you live, never let this purse out of your sight."

The old man listened carefully. Then he thanked the nobleman several times, tucked the beautiful leather purse under his arm, went back to his village, and called all his sons together.

"My dear children," he began, when they all gathered around him and stood eyeing the purse. "Years ago, when I was much younger,

I made a little money. I decided to save it for my old age, so I went to the forest and hid it in a hole in an oak tree. I didn't think about it for years because I had such good children. But when you sent me away to school, I happened to pass by this same oak, and I said to myself, 'I wonder if those few silver pieces have been waiting for their master all these years? Let me look and see.' And there they were.

"I have brought them home to you, my children. I shall keep them until I die, but after my death, whichever one of you has cherished me most, has taken care of me and not grudged me a clean shirt now and then, he shall have the greater part of my money. So now, my children, receive me back again. It is not right that I should seek a home among strangers. Which one of you will be kind to your old father—for money?"

From then on, the four brothers could not take good enough care of the old man, and he was happy. But he remembered the nobleman's advice and never let the purse out of his sight.

After a few years, the old man died peacefully. His children bought him a fine casket and took his body to the church for a proper burial. They held a splendid funeral, and paid the priest to say forty days of prayer for their father's soul. Then, when the old man was buried, they hurried home to open the purse, followed by the curious villagers.

They picked up the purse, stroked its fine leather, and they shook it to hear the promising rattle inside. Finally, all standing around a table, they opened it and poured out the contents . . . it was full of nothing but bits of glass!

They couldn't believe their eyes. They rummaged through the glass, looking for coins. When they finally realized that the treasure was worthless, they got so angry that they would have come to blows but for the crowds of people standing around them, watching. And then the villagers started to laugh.

"That was a good school you sent your father to," the villagers said mockingly. "Yes, indeed. He didn't start learning until he was old, but when he learned, he really learned!"

THE BIG OVEN

RUSSIA: Leo Tolstoi, whose novels are among the greatest books in the world, also wrote stories and fables for children. Here is one of his fables.

ONCE upon a time a man had a big house, and in the house there was a big oven; but this man's family was small—only himself and his wife.

When winter came, the man tried to keep his oven going; and in one month he burnt up all his firewood. He had nothing to feed the fire, and it was cold.

Then the man began to break up his fences, and use the boards for fuel. When he had burnt up all of his fences, the house, now without any protection against the wind, was colder than ever, and still they had no firewood.

Then the man began to tear down the ceiling of his house, and burn that in the oven.

A neighbor noticed that he was tearing down his ceiling, and said to him:

"Why, neighbor, have you lost your mind?— pulling down your ceiling in winter. You and your wife will freeze to death!"

But the man said:—"No, brother; you see I am pulling down my ceiling so as to have some-thing to heat my oven with. We have such a curious one; the more I heat it up, the colder we are!"

The neighbor laughed, and said: "Well, then, after you have burnt up your ceiling, then you will be tearing down your house. You won't have anywhere to live; only the oven will be left, and even that will be cold!"

"Well, that is my misfortune," said the man. "All my neighbors have firewood enough for all winter; but I have already burnt up my fences and the ceiling of my house, and have nothing left."

The neighbor replied: "All you need is to have your oven rebuilt."

But the man said: "I know well that you are jealous of my house and my large oven, and so you advise me to rebuild it."

And he turned a deaf ear to his neighbor's advice, and burnt up his ceiling, and burnt up his whole house, and in the end he had to go and live with strangers.

THE LAZIEST MAN IN THE WORLD

HUNGARY: Laziness, along with gluttony, stubbornness and greed, have obviously concerned people everywhere, because there are so many stories about them. In this story, the cure for laziness is very strenuous.

KING Mathias had a peculiar hobby. He collected people as other rich men might collect beautiful paintings or precious jewels. Not only did he collect wise men at his court—scientists, poets, and musicians—but he also collected freaks. And his favorite freak was The Laziest Man In The World.

This champion of laziness was so languid that he wouldn't even chew his food. He had to be fed gruel, like a toothless baby. He was too lazy to slap at mosquitoes which bit him. He was so lazy that one night when his house caught fire, he would have burned to a cinder rather than move except that a faithful servant carried him out of the flaming building.

One day, however, the King commanded the Laziest Man, along with the rest of his collection of people, to come to a state banquet. And the Laziest Man was ordered to sit up and keep himself awake. It was a gorgeous banquet, with the richest and most tempting foods, the choicest wines, and as guests, all the fairest men and women in Hungary. The orchestra played lovely music, soft melodies and lively dances that set every foot to tapping. Every foot, that is, except the Laziest Man's. He had trouble enough keeping his eyes open.

During the soup course, his spoon slid twice from his hand and splashed into his soup because he was too lazy to hold it firmly. And between the soup and fish course, he fell asleep just as the young lady on his right started to converse politely with him.

Instead of being offended, the young lady was amused at her sluggish dinner partner, and she started to laugh. Somehow this silvery peal of laughter penetrated the hearing of the Laziest Man. He made an effort to open his eyes and talk with the girl, but the conversation was jerky because the Laziest Man could not speak two sentences without falling asleep in between.

After the feast the Laziest Man fell into his bed like a log. But a strange thing happened to him. Though his eyes closed, he did not really sleep. In his mind, he kept hearing silvery peals of laughter. Limply—for he never moved fast—he pulled the blanket over his head, but the laughter continued in his brain.

And, for the first time in his lazy life, he became awake. As the hours passed he became more and more awake. In fact, he did not sleep a wink all night.

In the morning he shambled in to see the King.

"Well, friend, what's the matter?" King Mathias asked with a broad smile. He could

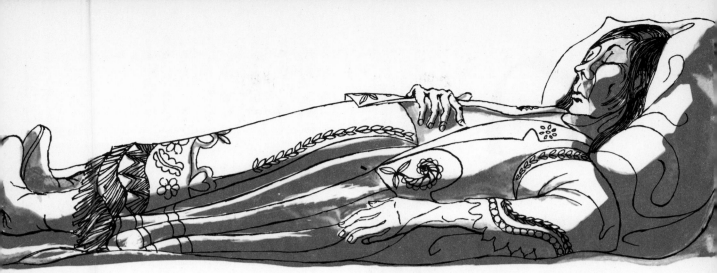

never look at the Laziest Man without amusement.

"Your Majesty," said the Laziest Man in his lazy, drawling speech, "I don't know what the matter is, but I couldn't sleep a wink last night."

"Good Heavens," said the King. "This is serious. You better see the court physician. Are there any other symptoms?"

"Well, yes, Your Majesty," said the Laziest Man. "I kept hearing laughter, like the laughter of the girl who sat next to me last night. It . . . makes . . . me . . . very . . . tired," the Laziest Man concluded, starting to fall asleep.

The King roared with mirth. "You, my friend," he finally said, "are in love! That's what it is! Nothing else is the matter with you." And the King, convulsed by the idea of his Laziest Man being in love, almost fell off his throne.

But it was not funny at all to the Laziest Man himself. In his vague mind he had a vague notion that being in love was not restful. He morosely withdrew and went straight to bed.

But, as soon as he lay down, he began to hear that laugh again, and it came between him and sleep. He tossed sluggishly, but he couldn't shake off that lovely silvery sound. As the days passed, he could hardly sleep at all.

One day he went before the King again.

"How are you, my friend?" asked the King.

"I am worse, Your Majesty, much worse," the Laziest Man said, miserably. "I am afraid you were right when you said I was in love. How can I be cured of this illness?"

"There is only one cure, my friend," the King said. "Go and ask the girl to marry you."

The Laziest Man groaned. What an idea! What energy it would take to ask the girl! What energy it would take to be married! The thought made him want to lie right down.

"There's no help for it," the King said. "I know of no other cure for you."

So the Laziest Man shuffled to the girl and asked her to marry him. The girl broke out in laughter—that same laughter that had become so painfully familiar to the Laziest Man during his sleepless nights.

"I am sorry," the girl said. "I am sorry indeed, but I can't marry you."

"Why not?" he asked, drowsily.

"Because," the girl said gently, trying not to hurt his feelings, "I can't marry the Laziest Man in the World."

Dully, the Laziest Man felt relieved and he went home and went right to bed. Now perhaps he could sleep, he thought. But the silvery laugh, now fresher than ever in his mind, echoed in his ears and sleep would not come.

Two days later he went before the King again.

"Well, my friend," said the King jovially, "are you happily betrothed and sleeping well again?"

"No, Your Majesty," the Laziest Man said. "She refused me and I am now more sleepless than ever. She said she couldn't marry the Laziest Man in the World. What am I to do now?" The Laziest Man spoke with unusual feeling, and the King stared at him in surprise.

Then the King said thoughtfuly, "I know how you can win the girl. You must catch a hare alive, with your own hands, and take it to her.

If you do that, I, the King, guarantee that the girl will marry you."

"Oooooohhhhhh," the Laziest Man groaned, and he went home exhausted and went straight to bed. Still he could not sleep. Now as well as hearing the silvery laughter, he kept seeing in his mind hundreds of scampering hares.

After a few days he knew there was no escape. The Laziest Man shambled out to a meadow and puffed his way through a wood until finally he caught sight of a hare. He shuffled toward it, but before he could decide which hand to catch it with, the nimble animal was out of sight. And so with the next hare and the next.

To his surprise, that night when the Laziest Man came home from his fruitless hunt, he was able to sleep for several hours. The next day after more rabbit chasing, he slept all night. The third day the man found himself walking faster, the next day he trotted a bit, and in a week he had learned to run.

It was exactly a year from the time the Laziest Man started pursuing hares that he finally caught one. He raced to the girl's house, put the hare into her hands, and once again asked her to marry him.

The girl couldn't believe her eyes. The Laziest Man had grown slim and muscular; his wide open eyes sparkled and shone, and his cheeks were ruddy and golden from the sun and air. The astonished girl found this handsome suitor irresistible, and she gladly consented to marry him.

The Laziest Man in the World, of course, lost his title. However, as he was now the fastest runner in the kingdom, the King appointed him to the honored position of King's Personal Courier, and his bride was made lady-in-waiting to the queen. As for the hare that had brought them together, it was lovingly cared for by the happy couple, and it lived to become the pet of their many children.

WHY THE WOODPECKER HAS A LONG BEAK

ROMANIA: "Why" stories—that is, stories about how things came to be—are told literally everywhere. This Romanian one is by Moses Gaster.

Know that the woodpecker was originally not a bird but an old woman with a very long nose. She sniffed around into everybody's pots and pans, eavesdropping, inquisitive and curious about everything whether it belonged to her or not. Constantly, her talebearing made mischief among her neighbors. When God saw her doings, he took a huge sack and filled it with midges, beetles, ants, and all kind of insects, and, tying it tightly, gave it to the old woman, and said to her: "Now take this sack and carry it home, but beware of opening it, for if your curiosity makes you put your nose into it you will find more than you care for, and you will have trouble without end."

"Heaven forbid," replied the old hag, "that I should do such a thing; I am not going against the will of God. I shall be careful."

So she took the sack on her back and started trotting home, but whilst she was carrying it, her fingers were already twitching, and she could scarcely restrain herself, so no sooner did she find herself a short distance away than she sat down in a meadow and opened the sack. That was just what the insects wanted, for no sooner did she open it than they started scrambling out and scampered about the field, each one running its own way as fast as its little legs would carry it. Some hid themselves in the earth, others scrambled under the grass, others, again, went up the trees, and all ran away as fast as they could.

When the old woman saw what had happened, she got mightily frightened and tried to gather the insects to pack them up again, and put them back into the sack. But the insects did not wait for her. They knew what to do, and a good number escaped into the field. Some she was able to catch, and these she packed into the sack, and tied it up. Then came the Voice of God, who asked her what she had done, and if that was the way she kept her promise.

"Where are the insects, beetles, and midges, which I gave you to carry? From this moment you shall change into a bird and go about picking up all these insects until you get my sack full again, and only then can you become a human being again."

And so she changed into a woodpecker; the long beak is the long nose of the old woman, and she goes about hunting for these midges, beetles, and ants, in the hope of filling up the sack, when she would again resume her human shape. But to this very day she has not completed her task and has remained a woodpecker.

THE LANGUAGE OF ANIMALS

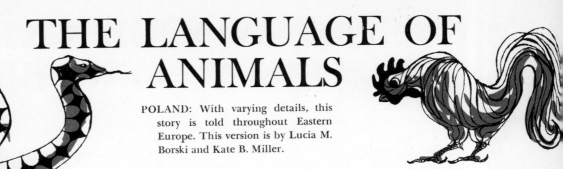

POLAND: With varying details, this story is told throughout Eastern Europe. This version is by Lucia M. Borski and Kate B. Miller.

THERE was once a sensible, well-to-do husbandman who, well along in years, took unto himself a young and handsome wife. She made a good enough wife, but she was so eaten up by curiosity that many a time she made her husband's life miserable. Often he wished to cure her of her fault, but did not know how to go about it.

One day at harvest time the husbandman watched his hired men mow his field and heard them shout: "Kill it, kill it," and saw them chase something across the field. He approached them and saw a snake with her young ones in the grass. Feeling sorry for the dumb creature, he advised the mowers to leave the snake alone, and this the men did.

At noontime, when the peasant went home for his dinner, the snake lay across his path, as if waiting for him, and spoke to him thus:

"I wish to reward you for saving me and my children from death. Tell me, which would you rather have: a long life or a load of money?"

The peasant reflected for a moment and answered:

"I have enough money to last me until my death, and I do not wish to live too long, because old age is a misery."

"Would you, perhaps, like to know the animals' language?" questioned the snake.

"That I should, and gladly."

"So shall it be, but you must not tell about it to any woman. If you do, you shall die," said the snake and disappeared in a crevice in the ground.

The peasant continued on his way home. As he came to his cherry orchard, he heard the sparrows twitter: "Twit, twit, good husbandman, nice husbandman, let us leave his cherry trees untouched, let us fly to his neighbors' instead." And the birds flew off with a loud chirping.

The peasant felt happy that the sparrows knew him and that he understood their twittering. On entering his court smiling broadly, his dog came out to greet him, barking and wagging his tail.

"Bow, wow, my beloved master! Bow, wow, how much I do like you, how glad I am that you have returned."

The peasant felt happier yet to be so much liked by his dog and to be able to understand his talk, and he played with him, laughing, for a while.

His wife saw it all from the window and wondered what had made her husband so happy that he should laugh to himself. She was so overcome by her curiosity that she dropped the things she held in her hands and followed him around the house and farm to find out the cause of his merriment.

When the plowmen returned with the oxen to be fed, the husbandman watched them and heard one of the oxen complain:

"Booh, booh, I worked so hard that all my bones ache, booh!"

In the shed with the oxen there was a buck who had been doing nothing but feeding all morning long, and he, shaking his beard, advised the ox:

"Be-eh, be-eh, you are foolish. If it were I, I should pretend to be sick and should lie on my side all day instead of working."

The husbandman listened and, chuckling, said to himself: "Wait, in the afternoon you shall plow." The wife watched him and could not make out why he laughed.

In the afternoon, after dinner, one of the plowmen came to the peasant, saying that the ox must have been taken ill, because he moaned and would not get up.

"Yes, I know, take the buck instead," ordered the master.

The buck jumped and kicked, complaining of the trick he had unwittingly played upon himself, but the plowman beat him with the whip and made off with him to plow the field. When they returned in the evening, the buck could hardly drag his feet, suffering from the beating he had received and the afternoon's hard work, though all he had done was to plow one furrow. As soon as his harness was taken off, he went to the ox, begging:

"Be-eh, be-eh, please, get up and do your work, because I'll die of it."

"So, you did not like plowing, did you?"

"Be-eh, be-eh, plowing is my death."

The husbandman laughed long and heartily, listening to their conversation, while his wife almost burned up with curiosity. She decided to find out the cause of his merriment, and so she prepared for his supper a big dish of scrambled eggs with sausage, and gave him a glass of sweet whisky, treating him to the best she had, and spoke to him tenderly, reproaching him for not loving her.

"How do you make out that I do not love you?" asked the peasant.

"Because you do not tell me what you are laughing at," she said.

She begged and prayed him so long to tell her that at last the peasant admitted that he would die if he confided his secret to her.

"Well, then, die, but tell me your secret," begged the wife, unable to restrain her curiosity.

"All right," agreed the husbandman. "If you must know, you must, but bring me a sheaf of straw, because it is easier to die on straw than on a feather bed."

The wife rushed out to get a sheaf of straw; and the dog, sitting under the table, began to howl:

"Bow, wow, such a good master, and he is going to die, bow, wow!"

"*Kuku-ryku, kuku-ryku!*" laughed the cock, clinking his spurs, as he walked across the room.

"Bow, wow, how dare you laugh at our master's death!"

"*Kuku-ryku*, because he is foolish. He has only one wife and cannot manage her, while I have four-and-twenty, and they all obey me," the cock crowed loudly.

The peasant listened to them and thought:

"True, why should I die just to satisfy her curiosity? The cock is right."

Just then the wife came in with the sheaf of straw, spread it on the floor and said:

"Well, now you can tell me."

"Wait a moment, I also need a rope well soaked in water," said the husbandman.

The wife ran out for the rope and was back with it in a moment.

"Tell me now," she called.

The husbandman took the rope, caught his wife, and beat her properly, saying:

"Such a wife as you are! Wishing for my death, do you? Take this and this and this!"

"*Kuku-ryku*, now you have what is coming to you," shouted the cock.

After that, the peasant woman lost all her curiosity and became the most loving and diligent wife, and they lived together peacefully for many years.

Iᴛ was well known to the people of the town of Helm that Pinya was a profound thinker. "Now that's a brain for you!" they said. "A veritable philosopher!" And that is why, when the Helmites were seeking a wise man to send to Warsaw to find out how fires were put out in that great city, they chose Pinya the Philosopher.

At the break of day Pinya awoke, recited his prayers, breakfasted, packed some food for the journey and set out for Warsaw.

Pinya walked. The road was dusty, the day was hot, and Pinya thought: A drink of cold water would surely be refreshing. But the road was long and dusty and there was no water.

So Pinya walked farther. Soon he came to a hill. Pinya groaned and went on. Going uphill was hard. He climbed slowly, puffing and panting all the way to the top. On the hilltop it was cooler and nearby there was a little grove. In the grove, close to the road, stood a large shade tree. Underneath the tree was a big rock and from beneath the rock gushed a spring of clear cold water.

Pinya stopped, cast off his coat, wiped the sweat from his brow and sat down. Then he took a long drink from the icy spring, washed and ate. Growing sleepy, he took another drink from the spring, yawned slowly and murmured:

"To lie down in the shade of this tree would be pleasant. It is cool and comfortable here."

Making a pillow of his coat, he was soon ready for sleep. But Pinya was not called the Philosopher for nothing, and soon his shrewd brain posed a question:

"A fine thing! Here I am going to sleep, but when I awake, how will I know which way is Warsaw?"

Then Pinya had an idea: He took off his shoes and placed them out on the road with the toes pointing towards Warsaw. Now he could go safely to sleep and when he awoke, his shoes would tell him just which way to go. And without further ado, Pinya lay down and was soon fast asleep.

Not long afterwards, a stranger happened to pass, saw Pinya sleeping under the tree and noticed the shoes out in the middle of the road. They looked so funny standing there that, for no reason at all, the stranger just had to turn them around. Then he went on his way, whistling a merry tune.

Pinya the Philosopher slept long and soundly. When he awoke, he yawned contentedly and said to himself:

"God is good to me. I have eaten well, I have slept soundly and there are my shoes pointing the way to Warsaw. God is truly good to me."

He put on his shoes and continued on his way.

WARSAW

YIDDISH: This story, by Solomon Simon, is one of a whole series of gently satirical Yiddish stories about the Jews of Helm. Helm is a town in Poland, and Yiddish is the language spoken by Eastern European Jews.

One hour passed, then two, and suddenly he glimpsed a town in the distance. The first thing he saw was the cemetery and then there appeared the roofs of the houses. Pinya clucked his tongue and marvelled—from the distance Warsaw looked exactly like Helm. But Pinya was a Philosopher, and he reasoned:

"To be sure, isn't it written in the Great Books that the world is the same everywhere? Naturally, *that* is why Warsaw looks like Helm."

The nearer he approached the place, the more he marvelled. The streets looked exactly like the streets of Helm. Even the Town Baths looked the same. And an identical Town Hall. Why, there was a post for the watchman's horse, just like the post near the Town Hall in Helm. And imagine, there in the middle of the marketplace stood a pear tree, just like in Helm. Pinya couldn't get over it. "True," he said to himself, "it is written that the world is the same everywhere, but I never expected it to be *so much* the same. That just goes to show you. When the Great Books say something, they know what they're talking about."

Pinya walked on. He gasped as he rounded the next corner. "Well, well, just such a street in Warsaw as my street in Helm." He continued walking. "Look, there is a house exactly the same as mine and standing just where mine does in Helm."

Pinya stood and stared and wondered. He stroked his curly little black beard and murmured: "Lo and behold, the whole world is like Helm."

And as he stood there, he heard a woman inside the house, shouting, "Moishe, stop that noise. Your father leaves and I think I'll get a little peace, so now *you* begin. Go bring in the goat. And don't say 'Later' or I'll—"

By this time Pinya was really impressed. Will God's wonders never cease? A scolding wife just like mine, nagging a disobedient son named Moishe, just like mine, in a house on a street just like mine. And imagine, as if all this weren't wonder enough, this Moishe says "Later" when told to do something—just like mine.

Standing with mouth agape, he scrutinized the house, the porch, the gate, when suddenly out came his wife Zlota. When she saw Pinya, she clasped her hands in amazement and shrieked:

"Pinya, back so soon from Warsaw?"

Pinya nearly dropped from shock. How does this strange woman know that I am called Pinya and what does she mean when she says, "Back so soon from Warsaw?" After all I *am* in Warsaw.

When Zlota saw her Philosopher standing there with his mouth open wide enough for a cat to walk in, she began to scold:

"Why are you standing there like a dummy, staring at me with two glass eyes? Fool! Go to the Synagogue or you'll be late for evening prayers."

All his life Pinya had obeyed his wife Zlota. So now, without another thought, he obeyed this strange woman who was so much like his Zlota and went off to the Synagogue.

There, the Helmites greeted him with surprise and joy. After the services, they crowded around him, exclaiming:

"Back so soon? Now there's a messenger for you! Goes to Warsaw in the morning and is back in Helm by evening!"

Pinya became very angry, but not being a Philosopher for nothing, he controlled himself and said calmly:

"I know that the Jews of Warsaw are clever but surely that doesn't give you the right to laugh at a stranger."

"Look here, Pinya," replied the Rabbi. "You may be a great Philosopher, but that's no reason for you to talk in riddles. Please tell us how they put out fires in Warsaw."

Spluttered Pinya:

"What are you talking about? I *am* in Warsaw!"

The Helmites became indignant. "Why are you making fun of us?" they cried. "You know you're back in Helm."

Still calm, Pinya answered.

"Jews of Warsaw, I am not called Pinya the Philosopher for nothing. I am in Warsaw and I have proof of it."

Whereupon Pinya told them how before he had gone to sleep, he had carefully placed his shoes on the road with the toes pointing towards Warsaw.

When the Helmites heard *this*, a hue and cry arose: if that's the case, then Pinya must be right and they are in Warsaw! A pretty kettle of fish! The women and children in Helm and they, the men-folk, in Warsaw, all of a sudden! Something had to be done!

Timid Berel the Beadle spoke up in a piping voice, "I think I know how we can tell where we are. Remember how I painted *This Synagogue Belongs to Helm* on the outside wall of the Synagogue. Let's go out and see if it's there. If it is, we're in Helm. If not, we're in Warsaw."

Being Berel's idea, it was naturally ridiculed, but the Helmites went out anyway. Happily, it was a bright, moonlit night, and sure enough there was the inscription on the Synagogue, clear and plain for everyone to see. It was as if a stone had been lifted from their hearts.

DEATH AND DOCTOR

LITHUANIA, LATVIA: The tales of these two countries are similar. A Lithuanian story by Stepas Zobarskas.

MANY years ago there lived a very poor man who seldom had enough bread to eat. What's more, he had a whole flock of children—every year a son was born to him. When his last son arrived the poor old man could not get a god-father to carry his child to the baptismal font. He asked one neighbor, then another, then a third—but no one would agree to be his child's god-father.

"If I only could meet someone who would be my son's god-father," thought the poor man as he returned home one day, sad and dejected.

No sooner had he said that, than Death appeared before him.

"Would you become my son's god-father?" asked the poor man.

"I wouldn't mind becoming your son's god-father," said Death. "But I'm as poor as you and I have no present to offer your son."

"I need no present," said the poor man. "Just a god-father."

"All right," said Death. "When your son grows up he'll become a doctor. And he will be able to see me. Whenever he sees me behind a patient's head he'd better give up healing him—the sick person will die anyway. But when I stand at the patient's feet—the sick person will recover. This shall be my present to your son."

The poor man returned home with Death, and the next day the child was baptised. The poor man thanked Death for his help and so they parted.

When the son grew up he became a doctor, just as Death had said. And he was considered a miracle worker, for every time he said a sick person would die, Death would come to him, and when he said a sick person would live, he would get well again.

One day the daughter of a wealthy man got sick. All the doctors in the country could not heal her because they could not diagnose her sickness and therefore did not know how to treat her. Then the people told the wealthy man about the doctor who worked miracles. The wealthy man sent his fine carriage and his servant and begged the doctor to do everything he could to cure his daughter. If he could heal her, the rich man promised him all his wealth and even his daughter's hand in marriage.

It was late in the evening when the doctor arrived at the wealthy man's palace. When he entered the sick girl's room he saw Death, his god-father, standing behind her head.

"I can't heal her," said the doctor.

The wealthy man began to kiss his hands and implored him to do everything he could to save his daughter's life, for she was his only child.

The doctor took pity on the wealthy man, and he especially felt sorry for the young daughter who was as beautiful as an angel. So he decided to cheat his god-father, Death. He told the wealthy man's servants to make a revolving one-legged bed. When the bed was made the doctor put the sick girl into it, and the moment Death approached her head, the doctor turned the bed around. Death found himself standing behind the girl's feet. As Death rushed behind the girl's head again, the doctor turned the bed, and again his god-father found himself standing behind the girl's feet. Finally Death became tired of running around and angrily left the room, never to return.

The wealthy man's daughter felt better, and soon she was as healthy as before. Her father kept his promise: he gave the young doctor all his wealth and also gave him his daughter in marriage. And from that time Death never again appeared to the doctor.

A GUEST FOR HALIL

"**H**URRY! You will be late for the banquet at Halil's house!" One person after another called this advice to Nasr-ed-Din Hodja as he jogged home from a day's work in his vineyard.

TURKEY: The "hodja," which means wise man, teacher or judge, is a popular hero of Middle Eastern stories, and dozens of tales are told about his ingenuity and wit. This one is by Alice Geer Kelsey.

"They are right," the Hodja finally admitted. The sun was almost touching the horizon. "I will be late for the dinner, unless I go now—just as I am."

He turned his reluctant donkey's head about and was soon at Halil's house. He tied his donkey in Halil's courtyard and walked confidently into the house, where the feast was soon to begin. Always sure of a welcome, he spread his smiles and his jokes to right and to left. He was so happy talking that he did not notice for some time a very strange thing. He was talking to backs instead of to faces. Not a single man was listening to him! Soon an even stranger thing happened. When the soup was brought in, Halil ushered other men to seats at the low table, but he had no word for Nasr-ed-Din Hodja.

The Hodja cleared his throat noisily. Halil did not notice. He coughed loudly. Halil paid no attention.

"Oh, Halil Effendi!" called Nasr-ed-Din Hodja cheerily. "I noticed a fine crop of fruit in your vineyard today."

Halil, busy with his well-dressed guests, did not hear.

"Oh, Halil Effendi!" The Hodja's voice was even louder this time. "Your smallest grapes are twice as big as the best in my vineyard."

Still Halil seemed unable to hear or to see the one guest who stood alone in his shabby, dirty working clothes.

The Hodja looked thoughtfully at the other guests. Each man was scrubbed till he glistened. Each man was wearing his best clothes. Then the Hodja looked at his own brown hands, caked with the honest dirt of the vineyards. He looked at his own clothes with their patches upon patches, and with the day's new holes which the patient Fatima would mend that night.

Very quietly, Nasr-ed-Din Hodja slipped out of the door, untied his willing donkey and jogged home.

"Hot water, Fatima!" he ordered. "Soap, Fatima! My new shoes! My best turban! My new coat!"

Fatima bustled and fluttered about. Soon Nasr-ed-Din Hodja looked like a new man. He preened himself before the admiring Fatima, who had not seen her husband so completely well dressed in years. He strutted out of the house. Little boys spoke to him respectfully as he swaggered back along the street to Halil's house. Women peered from behind their veils at the grand gentleman who walked with such an air.

A bowing servant ushered him into the banquet room at Halil's house. A beaming Halil hurried to meet him and escort him to the best seat in the room. Men smiled and nodded. Halil heaped his plate with goodies. Questions and stories were directed toward Nasr-ed-Din Hodja.

When he felt that all eyes were upon him, the Hodja picked up the choicest piece of meat on his plate. He did not raise it to his lips. Instead, he opened his coat and placed it in a pocket which was hidden inside.

"Eat, coat, eat!" said the Hodja.

A handful of pilaf, a square of cheese, a pickle, and a fig followed the meat into the coat.

"Eat, coat, eat!" said the Hodja as he put in each tidbit. The guests stopped eating to watch the Hodja feed his coat.

Finally, Halil could hold in no longer. "Tell me, Hodja Effendi, what you mean by telling your coat to eat."

"Why, surely, you wish the coat to eat." The Hodja raised innocent eyes to Halil. "When I came in my old clothes, there was no place at the table for me. When I come in my new clothes, nothing is too good for me. That shows it was the coat, not me, that you invited to your banquet."

SOHRAB AND RUSTUM

IRAN: This tragic story is based on one part of a sixty thousand verse poem, the *Shah Nameh*, which was written in the 10th century and tells the whole history of Persia.

On one of Rustum's missions for his king, Shah Kai Khosroo, he fell in love with the daughter of the king of Aderbaijan. He married her, but before she gave birth to their first-born child, the mighty warrior grew restless and desired to set forth on new adventures. He gave his wife a seal of onyx, bearing his own family crest, a griffin.

"If the child be a girl," he told her, "bind the seal in her hair. If it be a boy, let him wear it strapped to his arm beneath his armor so that I may know him."

After he left, the princess gave birth to a son and she called him Sohrab, which means "smiling one." But she sent word to Rustum that their child was a daughter because she was afraid he would take a son away from her.

Sohrab grew up in his grandfather's palace to be strong and skilled in the manly sports. At first his mother feared his great prowess, for she felt that like his father he would some day ride away and leave her. But gradually she knew that she could not change his nature, and he hunted and fought until he was one of the finest warriors in the land.

When he had come to manhood, his mother told him the secret of his father, and Sohrab was proud. He had heard of the mighty deeds of Rustum. He determined to attack Shah Kai Khosroo so that he could seat Rustum on the throne of Persia.

He raised an army of Tartars and went to King Afrasiab, who was at war with the Persians, to offer him aid. Now Afrasiab was a wily king. He knew that Sohrab was Rustum's son, and he hoped these two great champions would meet in battle. If Sohrab killed Rustum, it would lighten the task of Afrasiab's armies. If Rustum killed his own son, the old warrior's heart would be broken and he might well die, too. So Afrasiab welcomed Sohrab's army and they set forth together in the field.

At the banks of the river Oxus, the Tartar armies encamped, awaiting the battle. Across the plain lay the glittering forces of the Persians.

and begged him to meet Sohrab, the Tartar champion. This unknown young fighter, they said, was like Rustum himself, with the wild stag's foot and the lion's heart. Nobody else in the Persian forces could vanquish him. Only the great Rustum himself could hold his own in battle against young Sohrab.

But Rustum protested. He bore the boy no grudge. He would have liked to have a son like Sohrab, rather than a slight, helpless

This was Sohrab's first encounter with the Persian army, and he went to his general's tent. There he pleaded with him to declare a truce for the day so that he, Sohrab, might meet the Persian champions in single battle, and perhaps in this way finally make himself known to Rustum, his father.

On the Persian side, the mighty Rustum had pitched his tent apart from the main forces and sat sulkily there, his falcon on his wrist. He was aging now and he felt that Kai Khosroo preferred the services of younger men. He smiled grimly when the Persians came to him

daughter. Then he could retire to his castle and hang up his armor and rest in his old age while he listened from afar to the exploits of his son.

But the Persian warriors entreated him, saying that if he refused to take up the challenge, it would be said that Rustum was afraid to risk his reputation against a younger man.

So finally Rustum agreed to be their champion and meet Sohrab before the two armies, in hand to hand combat. Only one thing he stipulated, and that was that his name must not be known. And he dressed himself in armor of plain steel with no device upon it, and only

erful arm. But Sohrab saw it coming and leapt aside quickly and the spear buried itself in the sand. Then Sohrab in his turn struck Rustum's shield full force with his spear but the iron plates turned it aside. And Rustum seized his club, which was the trunk of a tree only he could wield, and struck forth at Sohrab. Again Sohrab leaped aside and this time Rustum fell to his knees with the force of his own blow.

Now Sohrab could have drawn his sword and killed Rustum, but he smiled and stood back courteously.

"Even though you be not Rustum," he said to the older man, "you have touched my heart strangely and, young that I am, I have fought many warriors and felt no pang. Let us strike our spears in the sand and call a truce, sit down together like old friends over a cup of wine, and you can talk to me of Rustum's deeds."

But Rustum arose, trembling with rage, and picked up his spear again. He roared at Sohrab to cease this talk of truce and fight it out hand to hand, man to man, with an end to his nimble dancer's tricks. And Sohrab, angered now in his turn, drew his sword, and they rushed together with such a hail of blows that the sand around them was caught up as if by a whirlwind, and the watching hosts could no longer see them.

Then a blow from Sohrab's sword struck the scarlet plume from Rustum's helm which had never been defiled before. And Rustum's horse, Ruksh, raised his head and uttered a great cry, so that the watching armies which heard it quaked for fear. But Sohrab paid no heed and rushed on to strike again and this time the blade of his sword shivered to pieces on Rustum's helm.

Now Rustum raised his spear, his eyes glaring with rage, and shouted "Rustum!"—his battle cry.

Sohrab, startled, stepped back, dropping his shield, and Rustum's spear pierced his side, and he fell. And then the sands died down and the watching forces could see again, Sohrab lying wounded on the bloody sand and the towering figure of Rustum standing above him.

his helm inlaid in gold, supporting a scarlet horsehair plume. So he went forth to the battle with his horse, Ruksh, following at his heels like a faithful hound.

And from the Tartar side, Sohrab came forth in armor and the two forces parted like the sea to let the champions meet upon the sands.

When Rustum saw Sohrab so slender and gently reared coming towards him, he was swept by a great wave of pity and he called out to him not to risk his life against a tried warrior like himself. "Quit the Tartar host," he cried out; "and come back to fight under our banner as my son. There are no youths in Persia as brave as you."

And when Sohrab heard Rustum's voice and saw his mighty figure planted like a tower in the sands, and saw the gray streak in his hair, he ran forward to him crying that he must indeed be the great Rustum. And he knelt at his father's feet.

But Rustum feared a trick and he turned his face away from the youth denying that he was Rustum and telling him to rise and meet his challenge like a man.

So Sohrab drew himself up again and faced the Persian warrior, and Rustum hurled his great spear at him with all the force of his pow-

And Rustum said to him bitterly, "Sohrab, you thought to challenge Rustum today so that you could boast about it among the Tartar host. But an unknown warrior has proved to be your match, and you shall die alone here by the river Oxus."

And Sohrab answered him, "You are wrong, for it was Rustum's name which you called out that defeated me and caused me to drop my shield. If it had not been for that, you would have been lying here and I would have been standing over you. But lest you boast of conquering me, you must know that the mighty Rustum is my father and that when he learns of this, he will avenge himself on you for my death."

And Rustum, standing over him, said coldly, "What talk is this of fathers and revenge? The mighty Rustum never had a son."

And Sohrab said to him faintly, "Ah yes, he had, and that son is I."

And Rustum, looking down at him now, stirred by old memories, said gently, "Oh, Sohrab, you are indeed such a son as Rustum might have had, but you must know that Rustum's child was a girl. She is with her mother now and does not dream of wounds or war."

Then Sohrab feebly untied his belt and loosened his armor so that Rustum, kneeling, could see the onyx seal emblazoned with his own crest, which the boy wore strapped against his arm. And when Rustum saw it he knew that Sohrab was indeed his son. He gave a mighty cry and called out, "Oh boy, I am your father!" and then he fainted in the sands.

But Sohrab dragged himself across the sand to his fallen father and took his head in his arms and stroked his cheeks until Rustum opened his eyes again. And when he saw the boy and realized what he had done, he was overcome with horror and seized handfuls of dust to rub it into his hair and beard and wept bitterly. Seeing his sword lying close, he grasped it and tried to drive it into his breast. But Sohrab held his hands.

"Do not do it, Father," he begged. "For what

has happened today is our Fate. When I first saw you, my heart cried out to you, as yours did to me. But Fate engaged us in battle, and it was written that this should be."

Rustum cried out, shaken by his great grief, that he would gladly die himself. But Sohrab said to him, "No, Father, for you must live to do the deeds I cannot do myself, for you were born to do great deeds and I was born to die."

Then he asked Rustum if he would let the Tartar armies pass peacefully back over the Oxus, and Rustum said that he would, and that he would burn his own tents and carry Sohrab's body back with him to his mountain home, where he would build him a mighty monument for all to see.

And Sohrab reached up and pulled the spear from his side, and as he did so, the blood gushed out and he lay back on the sands and died. Rustum covered him with his coarse horseman's cloak and sat beside him. And as it grew night, the two armies lit their campfires, preparing to move away and the plain between them darkened. Only the tiny flickering of their lights showed them, now and again, the shadowy figure of Rustum where he sat alone, his head bent in grief over the muffled body of his valiant son.

SINDBAD AND THE OLD MAN OF THE SEA

IRAQ: Sindbad is a merchant whose seven voyages are described in the *Arabian Nights*. In this story, he tells a friend of one of his adventures.

THE GIANT BIRD Ruhk had crushed our ship with the huge boulder she let fall, and we were all cast into the sea. But Allah sent me one of the planks as I struggled for life and I clung to it, paddling with my feet. The wind and waves bore me to an island and cast me up on the shore where I lay half dead with hunger and thirst.

When I revived and walked about, I found the island was a paradise. Its trees were laden with ripe fruit, its streams ran clear and bright, there were flowers to delight the eye and birds to enchant the ear. So I ate my fill of the fruits and drank from the streams and gave thanks to Allah for my deliverance. And, at nightfall, I lay down and slept as one exhausted.

In the morning, I rose and walked about until I came to a well fed by a running stream.

Crouched beside the well was an old man dressed in a waistcloth of palm frond fiber. I thought he must be one of those who were wrecked on the ship and I drew near him and greeted him courteously, but the old man did not answer except by gestures.

I said to him, "Oh, Uncle, what causeth thee to sit there?"

The old man moaned and signaled to me as if to say, "Take me up on thy shoulders and carry me across the stream."

Thinking he might be ill or crippled, I bent down and took him up on my back and carried him across the stream. Here I leaned over and told him to dismount at his leisure. But he would not get off and instead wound his legs around my neck. They were like a buffalo's hide for roughness and blackness and, fright-

ened, I tried to throw him off. But the old man gripped my neck with his legs until I was nearly choked and the world grew dark to my sight and I fell senseless to the ground. But the old man, still keeping his seat, raised his legs and drummed with his heels on my back and shoulders until I was forced to rise for the pain.

Then he signaled to me with his hand to carry him hither and thither among the trees so that he might pick the best fruits. If I refused or if I went too slowly, he beat me with his feet more grievously than if I had been beaten with whips. So I carried him about the island as if I were a captive slave and he dismounted neither night nor day. When he wished to sleep, he wound his legs about my neck and leaned back and slept awhile, then awoke and beat me so that I sprang up in haste to follow his commands.

As I continued my miserable, weary way, I reproached myself for having felt sorry for him. "I did him a favor and he repays me with ill. By Allah, never more will I do any man a service as long as I live!" I thought. And again and again I wished I might die.

One day I came with him to a place where there were many gourds and some of them were dry. I took a great dry gourd and, cutting open the head, scooped out the inside and cleaned it. Then I gathered grapes from a nearby vine and squeezed them into the gourd until it was full of juice. Then I stopped up the mouth and set it in the sun where I left it for several days until the juice became strong wine. Every day I used to drink of it, and it comforted me and seemed to make my troubles lighter.

One day he saw me drinking and signaled to me as if to ask, "What is that?"

Said I, "It is an excellent cordial which cheers the heart and revives the spirits." Then I began to caper about among the trees, clapping my hands and singing and making merry, and I pretended to stagger under him.

He signaled to me to give him the gourd that he might drink and I gave it to him. So he drained it to the dregs and cast it to the ground. Then he grew merry and began to clap his hands

and jig on my shoulders until finally the fumes of the wine overcame him and his leg muscles relaxed and he swayed to and fro on my back.

When I saw that he had lost his senses for drunkenness, I put my hand to his legs and, loosening them from my neck, I threw the devil to the ground where he lay senseless.

After that, I returned to the place where I had landed on the shore and waited, keeping a lookout for passing ships, until one day, behold!, a ship was making for the island through the dashing sea and clashing waves. When the sailors landed, I hailed them and they gathered around me, asking me how I came there.

They marveled as they heard my story and said, "He who rode on thy shoulders is called "Shayk al-Bahr" or "Old Man of the Sea," and no man who has felt those legs on his neck has ever lived until now."

So I gave thanks to Allah, for I knew my escape had been a miracle.

THE IMAGINARY WEDDING

JORDAN, SAUDI ARABIA: Stories about Juha—a man who is often tripped up by his own cunning—are so popular in Arab countries that most Arab children know dozens of them. Based on a story told by Wadia Shatara.

WHEN JUHA finished his shopping at the town market, he was tired and hot. He decided to rest for a while under a large tree before starting home. The tree cast a welcome shade, and he soon began to nod and drowse comfortably.

Soon, however, a group of boys discovered him napping there, and began to tease him.

"Hey, Juha," one small boy shouted, dancing merrily in front of him. "Hey, hey, hey," shouted another, startling Juha by poking his head suddenly around the trunk of the tree behind him.

"Go away, boys," Juha said crossly. "Can't you see I'm sleeping?" This sent the children into peals of laughter, and they danced and teased all the more. Juha decided that if he was to have his nap, he'd have to think of some clever way to get rid of them.

"Why are you wasting your time around here, children?" he said, after thinking for a moment. "Don't you know about the wedding? Don't you want any candy?"

"Candy?" the children said. "What candy? What wedding?"

"Why, everybody knows about it," Juha said. "The whole town's invited, and they are giving free candy to everyone who comes. Surely you must have heard the news. It's at the big house, down at the other end of the village."

"Do you mean it, Juha?" the boys said eagerly. "Are you sure?"

"Why, of course I'm sure," said Juha. He felt well pleased with his cleverness as he watched the boys run off in the direction of the big house—where, in fact, as Juha perfectly well knew, no wedding was even thought of, much less taking place.

Juha had just begun to nod again when he was waked by another group of boys running by, calling to all the children in the market as they passed. "Candy!" they called. "Come on, run, candy for everyone at the wedding!" He smiled to himself and closed his eyes again.

In a moment there were more running feet passing him, more children and adults, too. Juha watched them in surprise. "Juha," one of the men called to him. "Get up and come to the wedding, lazy one. Don't you know there is a wedding in the big house at the end of the village, and they have fine refreshments for everyone?"

"How do you know?" asked Juha, sitting up.

"Why, everybody says so," the man said. "The whole town is talking about it."

Juha rubbed his eyes and got up. He stood for a moment, puzzled. Then, thinking that he had better get to the wedding before all the refreshments were eaten up, he began to run after the others.

THE CAMEL AND THE CAT

SYRIA, LEBANON: The hero of this typically Arab story would never break a vow, even a meaningless one he has made only to himself. But he has no scruples about using his wits to make the vow less painful to keep. By Leslie W. Leavitt.

ALI WAS A POOR MAN who owned nothing at all but one camel and a small cat. He had owned the camel for many years and they had become good friends. He often said, "I cannot live without my camel." But one morning when he went out to give some food to his camel, it was not there. He looked everywhere for it; he asked everyone he saw. The camel could not be found.

The next day Ali walked sadly down the road, looking on every side. He had lost his camel and his friend. He said to himself, "My camel may now have an owner who is not kind to it. Or it may be lost out in the fields with no food or water. Or it may be dying. Or it may be dead." He began to cry.

Would he ever see his old friend again? "Ah," he said, "I must see my camel once more. I would not want to keep it. I would sell it for one pound. Yes, I will sell it for one pound if it will come back and I can see it once again."

Just as Ali said this he saw something coming along the road far away. It came nearer and nearer. It was a camel . . . it was a camel and a man . . . an old man leading a camel. Could it be? Yes, it was . . . it was his own camel, his old friend. Oh, how happy he was! "Where did you find this camel?" he asked the old man.

"I found it near my house last night," was the answer, "and I am looking for its owner."

"It is mine; it is my camel," said Ali. "Oh, I am so happy! How can I thank you enough!"

Ali took the camel back to his own house. He was very happy for some days, and then he remembered what he had said when he was looking for his camel. He had said that he would sell it for one pound if only he could see it again. He knew he must do what he had said. But it was very hard. Was there nothing to be done? He thought and thought for a long time.

The next morning he got up very early and went into the town to the place where animals are bought and sold. "I want to sell my camel,

THE HORSE

ONE DAY the Bedouin boy, Tamad, and his father, the Sheik, were taking a rest in their goat-hair tent. Its black roof kept off the worst heat of the noonday sun. The two were stretched out at ease on rugs spread on the sandy floor of the Arabian Desert.

Suddenly there was a noise at the open front of the tent. Sa'da, the boy's horse, thrust his golden-brown head in under its cloth roof. Little by little, the clever horse edged his way inside the tent, out of the burning sun.

Tamad and his father laughed. This often happened. They seldom drove their favorite horses out of their tent.

a very good camel," he said to the many men who were there.

"How much do you want for the camel?" they asked.

"One pound," was the answer.

"One pound!" they cried. "One pound for a camel!" People came running. "Is it strong and well? Or is it old and ill? That is very little money for a camel. Where is it?"

"I also want to sell my cat," said Ali, "a very nice cat, for one hundred pounds. And," he added, "I will not sell the camel without the cat. Who will give one hundred and one pounds for the two animals?"

The people who had come running to buy the camel now became angry. "One hundred pounds for a cat!" they said. "We will buy the camel but not the cat. Who ever heard of giving one hundred pounds for a cat!"

"No cat, no camel," said Ali, and waited for someone to buy his two animals for one hundred and one pounds. After some time he said, "Well, I have tried to do what I said I would do . . . to sell my camel for one pound. If no one wants to buy it, can I help it?" And he went back to his house and his camel and his cat, very, very happy.

WITHOUT A MASTER

YEMEN: This story, by Frances Carpenter, is an old one, and as in many of the very old tales, animals and men talk together freely.

"Sa'da knows he is well off wherever his master is," the Sheik said to the boy. The man reached out to pat the soft nose of the gentle horse.

"It was not always so," the Sheik added. "I know a tale about a horse that once thought he would be far better off without any master at all."

"What happened to that horse, my father?" Tamad asked.

"Praise Allah who made all things!" the Sheik began. "It took place in the days when horses could talk. Now this horse was not happy and gentle like Sa'da. His spirit was wild. He wanted above all things to be free. He complained to the other horses. He complained to the camels. But the only reply he got from the animals was, 'You are a fool, O Horse. You do not know when you are well off.'

"Then the Horse complained to his master, saying, 'What is the reason that I should have to carry you here and carry you there? Am I not bigger? Am I not stronger than you? A man like you is a poor, weak creature compared to a horse like me. Why should I do your bidding?'

" 'I am indeed smaller, O Horse,' his rider replied. 'I am not nearly so strong as you. That is easy to see. But yet you cannot do without me. I give you your food. I find you green grass. I bring you barley and warm camel's milk. I even share my tent with you. I hunt water holes for you that you may not be thirsty. In return for my care, is it not just that you should carry me on my journeys?'

" 'It is true that you care for me, Man, but also you make me your slave,' the Horse said, still complaining. 'I never can go and come as I like. You put a hard bit in my mouth. You tie on my saddle with tight ropes that bite into my belly. You make me gallop and gallop until my legs crumple with weariness. You even ride me into battle so that sometimes I am wounded. Who gave you the right thus to take my freedom away?'

" 'Allah, the Lord of Heaven and Earth, made me your master, O Horse,' the man replied. 'But I will not hold you if, indeed, you wish to be free.'

"So the man took off the Horse's bridle. He took off his saddle. And he took away the camel-hair rope that hobbled the animal's legs.

"With a whinny of joy, the Horse bounded away. His master was camped in a grassy part of the desert. It was then early spring. There were green bushes about. So the Horse had little trouble in getting enough food to keep him alive. There was a stream of clear water in the river bed nearby. He could drink when he liked. Oh, it was fine to be free.

"But in time, summer came. Under the heat of the desert sun, the green grass turned brown. The stream in the river bed became a thin trickle. At last, the grass was burned up. All the water was gone. Gone, too, was the camp of that horse's master. The other horses and the camels had long since been led away to better pastures and watering places.

"The Horse grew hungry and thirsty. He went this way and that way. But no water nor green grass could he find.

"The wild beasts that roamed over that part of the desert were hungry too. Foxes, hyenas, and lean, hungry wolves prowled in search of something to eat and to drink.

"One night, in the moonlight, the Horse saw five dark shapes creeping toward him. With a whinny of fear, he quickly galloped away. His keen smell had told him the five dark shapes were five starving wolves looking for meat.

"Now hungry wolves, too, can run very fast. The wolves came even more swiftly than the Horse's weak legs would take him. They caught up with that horse and they leaped on his back. Their gnawing teeth bit and bit into his flesh.

"The Horse reared and kicked. He rolled in the sand. Somehow, he managed to shake the wolves off his back. His thrashing hoofs found their heads. At last, he was safe. But he knew he would not be safe very long. Some other wild, hungry beast would surely attack him.

" 'Alas! Alas!' the bleeding Horse cried to himself. 'No bridle bit, no saddle rope, none of my master's battles ever gave me such wounds as the fangs of these hungry wolves. If only I were safe now in my kind master's camp! How happy I was there! Seldom was I hungry. Not long was I thirsty. No journey of my master's made my legs so weak as now they are. I shall go seek my master.' "

"Did the Horse find his master, O my father?" Tamad asked. He did not like to think of any horse in such terrible trouble.

"I was not there, my son. So how can I say?" The Sheik smiled at the boy's question. "But since we do not know surely, let us hope that the Horse soon found the trail of his master. Let us hope, too, that his master forgave him and took him back into his camp."

THE PRINCESS AND RABBI JOSHUAH

ISRAEL: The heroes in Jewish stories are usually wise and holy men, or clever rascals, rather than heroic warriors who do noble deeds. This story is originally from the Talmud.

RABBI JOSHUAH, the son of Cha-nan-yah, was one of those men whose minds are far more beautiful than their bodies. He was so dark that people often took him for a black-smith, and so plain, as almost to frighten children. Yet his great learning, wit, and wisdom had procured him not only the love and respect of the people, but even the favor of the Emperor Trajan. Being often at court, one of the Prin-cesses rallied him on his want of beauty.

"How comes it," said she, "that such glorious wisdom is inclosed in so mean a vessel?"

The Rabbi, no ways dismayed, requested her to tell him in what sort of vessels her father kept his wine.

"Why, in earthen vessels, to be sure," replied the Princess.

"O!" exclaimed the witty rabbi, "this is the way that ordinary people do: an Emperor's wine ought to be kept in more precious vessels."

The Princess, thinking him in earnest, ordered a quantity of wine to be emptied out of the earthen jars into gold and silver vessels; but, to her great surprise, found it in a very short time sour, and unfit to drink.

"Very fine advice, indeed, Joshuah, hast thou given me!" said the Princess the next time she saw him: "Do you know the wine is sour and spoiled?"

"Thou art then convinced," said the Rabbi, "that wine keeps best in plain and mean ves-sels. It is even so with wisdom."

"But," continued the Princess, "I know many persons who are both wise and handsome."

"True," replied the Sage, "but they would, most probably, be still wiser, were they less handsome."

169

THE LION-MAKERS

INDIA, BHUTAN, NEPAL: Most students of folklore believe that all funny European folk tales—and probably many serious ones too—came originally from India. This tale is from the *Panchatantra,* a collection of stories written in Sanskrit about 200 B.C. and intended to teach young Indian princes to be wise and good.

I
>   Scholarship is less than sense;
>   Therefore seek intelligence:
>   Senseless scholars in their pride
>   Made a lion; then they died.

N a certain town were four Brahmans who lived in friendship. Three of them had reached the far shore of all scholarship, but lacked sense. The other found scholarship distasteful; he had nothing but sense.

One day they met for consultation. "What is the use of attainments," said they, "if one does not travel, win the favor of kings, and acquire money? Whatever we do, let us all travel."

But when they had gone a little way, the eldest of them said: "One of us, the fourth, is a dullard, having nothing but sense. Now nobody gains the favorable attention of kings by simple sense without scholarship. Therefore we will not share our earnings with him. Let him turn back and go home."

Then the second said: "My intelligent friend, you lack scholarship. Please go home." But the third said: "No, no. This is no way to behave. For we have played together since we were little boys. Come along, my noble friend. You shall have a share of the money we earn."

With this agreement they continued their journey, and in a forest they found the bones of a dead lion. Thereupon one of them said: "A good opportunity to test the ripeness of our scholarship. Here lies some kind of creature, dead. Let us bring it to life by means of the scholarship we have honestly won."

Then the first said: "I know how to assemble the skeleton." The second said: "I can supply skin, flesh, and blood." The third said: "I can give it life."

So the first assembled the skeleton, the second provided skin, flesh and blood. But while the third was intent on giving the breath of life, the man of sense advised against it, remarking: "This is a lion. If you bring him to life, he will kill every one of us."

"You simpleton!" said the other, "it is not I who will reduce scholarship to a nullity."

"In that case," came the reply, "wait a moment, while I climb this convenient tree."

When this had been done, the lion was brought to life, rose up and killed all three. But the man of sense, after the lion had gone elsewhere, climbed down and went home.

171

THE TIGER, THE BRAHMAN, AND THE JACKAL

O
INDIA, BHUTAN, NEPAL: In this version of a very old story the cunning hero is a jackal. By Joseph Jacobs.

NCE UPON A TIME, a tiger was caught in a trap. He tried in vain to get out through the bars, and rolled and bit with rage and grief when he failed.

By chance a poor Brahman came by.

"Let me out of this cage, oh, pious one!" cried the tiger.

"Nay, my friend," replied the Brahman mildly, "you would probably eat me if I did."

"Not at all!" swore the tiger with many oaths; "on the contrary, I should be forever grateful, and serve you as a slave!"

Now when the tiger sobbed and sighed and wept and swore, the pious Brahman's heart softened, and at last he consented to open the door of the cage. Out popped the tiger, and, seizing the poor man, cried, "What a fool you are! What is to prevent my eating you now, for after being cooped up so long I am just terribly hungry!"

In vain the Brahman pleaded for his life; the most he could gain was a promise to abide by the decision of the first three things he chose to question as to the justice of the tiger's action.

So the Brahman first asked a pipal tree what it thought of the matter, but the pipal tree replied coldly: "What have you to complain about? Don't I give shade and shelter to every one who passes by, and don't they in return tear down my branches to feed their cattle? Don't whimper—be a man!"

Then the Brahman, sad at heart, went farther afield till he saw a buffalo turning a well-wheel;

but he fared no better from it, for it answered; "You are a fool to expect gratitude! Look at me! Whilst I gave milk they fed me on cotton-seed and oil-cake, but now I am dry they yoke me here, and give me refuse as fodder!"

The Brahman, still more sad, asked the road to give him its opinion.

"My dear sir," said the road, "how foolish you are to expect anything else! Here am I, useful to everybody, yet all, rich and poor, great and small, trample on me as they go past, giving me nothing but the ashes of their pipes and the husks of their grain!"

On this the Brahman turned back sorrowfully, and on the way he met a jackal, who called out: "Why, what's the matter, Mr. Brahman? You look as miserable as a fish out of water!"

The Brahman told him all that had occurred. "How very confusing!" said the jackal, when the recital was ended; "would you mind telling me over again, for everything has got so mixed up?"

The Brahman told it all over again, but the jackal shook his head in a distracted sort of way, and still could not understand.

"It's very odd," said he, sadly, "but it all seems to go in at one ear and out at the other! I will go to the place where it all happened, and then perhaps I shall be able to give a judgment."

So they returned to the cage, by which the tiger was waiting for the Brahman, and sharpening his teeth and claws.

"You've been away a long time!" growled the savage beast, "but now let us begin our dinner."

"*Our* dinner!" thought the wretched Brahman, as his knees knocked together with fright; "what a remarkably delicate way of putting it!"

"Give me five minutes, my lord!" he pleaded, "in order that I may explain matters to the jackal here, who is somewhat slow in his wits."

The tiger consented, and the Brahman began the whole story over again, not missing a single detail, and spinning as long a yarn as possible.

"Oh, my poor brain! oh, my poor brain!" cried the jackal, wringing his paws. "Let me see! how did it all begin? You were in the cage, and the tiger came walking by—"

"Pooh," interrupted the tiger, "what a fool you are! *I* was in the cage."

"Of course!" cried the jackal, pretending to tremble with fright; "yes! I was in the cage—no I wasn't—dear! dear! where are my wits? Let me see—the tiger was in the Brahman, and the cage came walking by—no, that's not it, either! Well, don't mind me, but begin your dinner, for I shall never understand!"

"Yes, you shall!" returned the tiger, in a rage at the jackal's stupidity; "I'll *make* you understand! Look here—I am the tiger—"

"Yes, my lord!"

"And that is the Brahman—"

"Yes, my lord!"

"And that is the cage—"

"Yes, my lord!"

"And I was in the cage—do you understand?"

"Yes—no—Please, my lord—"

"Well?" cried the tiger impatiently.

"Please, my lord!—how did you get in?"

"How!—why in the usual way, of course!"

"Oh, dear me!—my head is beginning to whirl again. Please don't be angry, my lord, but what is the usual way?"

At this the tiger lost patience, and, jumping into the cage, cried: "This way! Now do you understand how it was?"

"Perfectly!" grinned the jackal, as he dexterously shut the door, "and if you will permit me to say so, I think matters will remain as they were!"

THE BRAHMAN'S DREAM

INDIA, BHUTAN, NEPAL: Variations of this story from the *Panchatantra*, a two-thousand-year-old Indian classic, are told in dozens of languages.

IN A CERTAIN TOWN lived a Brahman named Seedy, who got some barley-meal by begging, ate a portion, and filled a jar with the remainder. This jar he hung on a peg one night, placed his cot beneath it, and fixing his gaze on the jar, fell into a hypnotic reverie.

"Well, here is a jar full of barley-meal," he thought. "Now, if famine comes, a hundred rupees will come out of it. With that sum I will get two she-goats. Every six months they will bear two more she-goats. After goats, cows. When the cows calve, I will sell the calves. After cows, buffaloes; after buffaloes, mares. From the mares I shall get plenty of horses. The sale of these will mean plenty of gold. The gold will buy a great house with an inner court. Then someone will come to my house and offer his lovely daughter with a dowry. She will bear a son whom I shall name Moon-Lord. When he is old enough to ride on my knee, I will take a book, sit on the stable roof, and think. Just then Moon-Lord will see me, will jump from his mother's lap in his eagerness to ride on my knee, and will go too near the horses. Then I shall get angry and tell my wife to take the boy. But she will be busy with her chores and will not pay attention to what I say. Then I will get up and kick her."

In his daydream he let fly such a kick that he smashed the jar. And the barley-meal which it contained turned him white all over.

THE ALLIGATOR'S COURTSHIP

CEYLON: Mouse-deer, spider, or (in this case) jackal—almost every country has its Br'er Rabbit.

WHILE HUNTING on the bank of a river one morning, a jackal overheard the water birds spreading the news that an elephant had just died on the opposite side of the river.

"What a feast!" the hungry jackal thought. "What days and days of feasting!" And he set himself to figure some way to get across the river.

Just then he spied an alligator, dozing in the sun. The jackal sat contemplating the alligator's horny skin, his vicious teeth and his evil little eyes for a moment, and then an idea came to him. From a safe distance, he called to the alligator.

"What a handsome fellow you are!" he said in awed tones. "What strength! What vigor! You deserve a beautiful wife to match your handsome figure." The alligator raised his head and looked pleased. "In fact, I know just the bride for you," the jackal went on, creeping closer. "Yonder, where you see the coconut trees across the river, is a village, and in it lives the loveliest girl you ever saw. Why not have her for your bride, you who are so beautiful, and so worthy of her hand?"

The alligator liked the idea immensely. "Yes, yes, a beautiful young bride would be pleasant," he said, preening himself. "But tell me, friend jackal, how could it be arranged?"

"Leave that to me," said the jackal. "All you have to do is carry me across the river on your back." The alligator agreed readily, and he swam with great care so as not to splash his passenger. "Now, be sure to be here at dusk to carry me home again," said the jackal, as he jumped off the alligator's back onto the other bank, "and I will bring you news of your wedding arrangements." With that, the jackal ran off, found the elephant carcass, and stuffed himself with as

much food as his stomach could possibly hold.

Long before dusk the alligator was at the appointed place, and when the jackal appeared, the alligator asked him whether the match was all arranged.

"Oh, friend," said the jackal, "there will, I fear, be some small delay. The girl and her mother were willing, but the father was absent, and without his consent nothing could be settled. I promised to return tomorrow to speak to him."

So on the following day, the alligator again ferried the jackal across the river. And at dusk, when the jackal, stuffed with elephant meat, returned to the river bank, the alligator was there waiting for news.

"Did you see the father?" the alligator asked eagerly. "What did he say?"

"Well, the father does present some difficulties, I must admit," said the jackal solemnly. "At first he said no, but I persuaded him to think it over and said I would return for his answer tomorrow. As for the girl, however, I can tell you there's no problem there, friend alligator. Why, she is head over heels in love with you from merely hearing me describe your beauty."

So day after day, inventing one delay after another, the jackal tricked the alligator into ferrying him back and forth across the river. Finally the day came when the jackal ate the last of the elephant carcass. That evening he rode home as usual, flattering the alligator with tales of the girl's burning love and complimenting him on his strength and beauty. But when he got to shore, he jumped a safe distance up the bank, and burst into laughter.

"Really, friend alligator, you are a vain fellow! Who ever heard of a girl marrying an alligator, a slimy, horny, ugly water creature? Haven't you ever seen your own reflection in the water, you great hideous brute?" And the jackal exploded once more with laughter. "Anyway, you may not be much to look at, but you make a fine raft!" And with that, the jackal ran off into the woods.

The alligator was so angry he was speechless. From that time on he thought of nothing else

but how to get revenge on the jackal, and at length he hit upon a plan.

Close to the river there was a mangrove tree. In the heat of the day, the jackal often lay in its shade and napped. So early one morning, the alligator dragged himself to the tree, and stretched out full length underneath it, lying stiff and motionless as though he were dead.

At midday, the jackal approached his accustomed resting place and saw the alligator. He stopped for a moment to consider, and then advanced slowly, talking out loud to himself.

"Well," he said. "This is strange! There seems to be a dead alligator under my mangrove tree. Strange . . . very strange. . . . Is he dead or isn't he? He looks dead, but I don't believe he could be, because dead alligators always move their tails."

The alligator, hearing this, slowly moved his tail from side to side. And once again the jackal scampered away laughing.

"My poor friend," he called from a distance. "I already knew you were impossibly vain, but I confess, I didn't realize how stupid you were!"

And the jackal disappeared into the woods, still laughing.

THE PRINCESS WITH THE GLITTERING EYES

PAKISTAN: Many Pakistan folk tales are sad stories of ill-fated young lovers. This story is about magic rather than young love, but it is characteristically somber. Adapted from a story by Zainab Ghulam Abbas.

ONE DAY, while out hunting, Ali Mardan Khan, the Governor of the Valley of Kashmir, heard the sound of a woman weeping. The crying seemed to come from a deep thicket, and he made toward it, pushing aside the bushes. There he found seated under a tree a maiden of unearthly beauty, richly dressed and regally jeweled.

Ali Mardan was dazzled by her loveliness. He dismounted and asked her who she was and why she wept.

"Oh, sir," she said. "I am the daughter of a Chinese king. My father fell in battle, our cities have been sacked, and most of our noblemen taken prisoner. Somehow I managed to escape, and since then I have been wandering like a beggar."

"Princess," Ali Mardan said. "Now you need wander no more. I am the ruler of this country, and I welcome you to the Valley of Kashmir. Please dry your tears."

But the Chinese princess still wept. "Oh, my lord," she said. "I cannot stop weeping. What will become of me, friendless and homeless? How can I live?"

"Come and stay in my palace," the Governor said. "There you will be safe and comfortable."

"That gladly will I do," said the girl, drying her tears. She gave him a strange, piercing look, but her voice was sweet and meek as she spoke. "And if you should want me for your wife, I should not be able to refuse you."

When he heard these words, and looked into the princess' glittering eyes, Ali Mardan felt as though he were in the grip of an enchantment. He took the girl's hand, and spoke in a voice he hardly recognized as his own. "Come, my be-loved. I will make you my wife." And he took her to the palace where they were married the next day.

One morning a few weeks after the wedding, Ali Mardan woke up feeling unwell.

"I have a pain in my stomach," he told his wife. The royal physician promptly examined him and gave him some medicine, but still the pain continued. Ali Mardan felt sicker on the next day, and still worse on the third. Finally, except for short walks in his gardens, he was confined to his bed, and the Chinese princess constantly attended him, hovering over him, never leaving his side.

Now it happened that a Guru, a wise and holy man, was passing by the palace one day. He wandered into the lovely gardens to admire the flowers. As the day was hot, he sat down under a tree to rest. So much at peace did he feel among the flower beds, and so sweetly did the birds sing around him that soon he was lulled to sleep.

There Ali Mardan, as he was out taking the air, happened to see him. Ali Mardan was a man of humble heart, who held holy men in great respect, and he smiled when he saw the sleeping Guru, and gave orders that he shouldn't be disturbed.

"But go and bring the best bed you can find," he said to his courtiers, "and lay this holy man gently upon it, so that he shall rest more comfortably."

When the Guru awoke, he was surprised to find himself lying in a silken bed. An attendant hurried to his side. "You are the guest of Ali Mardan, the Governor of Kashmir," the attendant said, bowing low. "And the Governor would

177

like to speak with you." He then took the Guru to the Governor's bedside.

"I am much honored by your presence, O Guru, and I hope you have rested well," Ali Mardan said with reverence.

"Indeed I have," answered the Guru, "and I have been refreshed in your lovely gardens. I thank you for your kindness, but now I must hurry on my way."

Just as the Guru was turning to leave, Ali Mardan was seized by a spasm of pain, and the Guru stopped to inquire about his illness.

"I wish I knew the nature of my sickness," the Governor said. "My doctors are mystified. They have tried one treatment after another, and I do not improve. But holy one, if you can cure me of this disease, I shall be grateful to you all my life."

The holy man then ordered everyone from the room, and told the Governor to take off his clothes. He examined the Governor's wasted body, and then asked, "Have you recently married?"

"Yes," answered Ali Mardan, and he told the Guru the exact circumstances of his marriage.

"And is your wife inhumanly beautiful?" asked the Guru.

"She is indeed beautiful," said the Governor.

"And does she hover always at your side?" the Guru asked.

"Yes, she is always near me," said the Governor.

"O Governor," said the Guru gravely. "It will not be easy. But if you will do just as I say, I can cure you. This evening," the Guru ordered, "you must have two kind of *kitcheri* prepared for your dinner, one sweet and the other salty. They must be put on one plate, so that the salty food is nearest to your wife, and the sweet food is nearest to you. Then all drinking water must be removed from your bedroom, and the doors must be locked from the outside. When all this is done, you must pretend to sleep as usual, but actually you must watch everything your wife does."

The Governor did as he was told, and that evening the dish of *kitcheri* was laid before the couple. The Chinese wife found her portion

salty, but seeing that her husband was eating from the same plate without complaint, she made no remark and ate in silence.

As was expected, the Chinese princess woke up in the middle of the night very thirsty, and finding no water, and no way to get out, she began to move around the room in a strange, sinuous manner. She looked at her husband to assure herself that he was asleep. Her eyes glittered, and suddenly, to Ali Mardan's horror, she turned into a venomous snake. She slipped through the window and slithered down to the lake to drink. In a few minutes, she returned, resumed her human form and lay down beside her husband again.

Ali Mardan was appalled at what he had seen, and early the next morning he sought the holy man and told him everything.

"Governor," said the Guru, "as you have seen, your wife is not a woman but a Lamia—a snake woman. If for one hundred years the glance of no human being falls on a snake," the Guru explained, "a crest forms on its head, and it becomes king of the snakes. If for another hundred years it does not come within sight of man, it changes into a dragon. And if for a third hundred years it has not been seen by human eyes, then it becomes a Lamia. A Lamia possesses enormous evil powers and can change its appearance at will. It is particularly fond of taking a woman's form. Such is your wife, O Governor, and her purpose is to kill you. She lingers about you always to poison you. In a few more weeks, be assured, you will be dead, and she will find another victim."

"What shall I do?" asked the terrified Governor. "Is there no way to escape from this fiend?"

"Yes, but only one," said the holy man. "A Lamia cannot stand the heat of a fire. But we must act cautiously so as not to arouse her suspicions. For if she suspects that her secret is known, she will destroy not only you but your whole country." And they laid their plans.

A house of lac—or resin—was built at some distance from the palace. A big oven was built into the kitchen. Then, on the Guru's orders, the royal physician advised Ali Mardan to confine himself in this house for forty days, and asked the Chinese princess to attend him. The snake woman was, of course, delighted to have Ali Mardan delivered into her exclusive care.

So Ali Mardan and the Lamia moved into the little house of lac. A few days later, Ali Mardan called his wife to him and said, "The physician has prescribed a special kind of bread for me. Will you make a loaf, please."

"I dislike ovens," she said, suspiciously. But since she could think of no good excuse, she went into the kitchen and mixed the loaf.

Soon it was ready, and she went to set it in the oven, holding it at arm's length in front of her. But when she opened the oven door, Ali Mardan, who had crept up behind her, seized her and held her in the wave of heat from the oven. She struggled to escape, but Ali Mardan summoned his last ounce of strength and held her fast. A minute passed, and suddenly he found himself holding a venomous snake. In another minute that, too, had disappeared, as the Guru had predicted, leaving only air between his hands. Then he hurried outdoors, and, as directed by the holy man, set fire to the house of lac, which flared up instantly.

"You have done well," said the Guru who was waiting at a distance. "You have saved not only yourself, but all those others who would have been her victims. Now go to your palace and rest there for two days, and on the third day I will come to you."

So the Governor rested for two days, and on the third the Guru came to him. "Get up now from your bed, O Governor," the Guru said.

And to the amazement and delight of the royal physician and of all his courtiers, Ali Mardan threw back the covers and jumped from his bed—once more a vigorous and well man.

THE MAIDEN OF THE SEA

ARMENIAN: This is a typical Armenian story, and it ends with the verse that traditionally closes all Armenian folk tales.

THERE WAS ONCE a poor lad who lived by himself on the seacoast. There was little comfort in his lonely cottage, nor was there ever much to eat. But in spite of his poverty, the lad never failed to throw a loaf of bread into the sea every day, as his mother had bade him just before she died.

One evening when he came home from his work, he was surprised to see that his cottage had been swept and cleaned, his bed newly aired, and his table top bleached and scrubbed. The next day he shot a rabbit and put it in the cupboard, and in the evening when he returned to his cottage, not only was the room spotless, but the meat was cooked and the table set for his supper.

For several days, this mysterious blessing continued, until finally, unable to restrain his curiosity, the lad did not go to work, but hid himself under the stairs to see who his thoughtful helper could be. Soon he heard a great splash on the shore outside, and lo, a big fish cast itself onto his threshold. At once the skin of the fish peeled off, and out of it came a maiden as beautiful as the shining moon. She swept the house clean, and washed the dishes, and prepared a tempting meal. Then, setting the table with care, she started to leave. At this, the lad jumped from his hiding place, and seized her.

"Mama, Mama, help me!" the maiden called out.

Immediately a voice came from the sea: "Be not afraid, daughter, for that lad is to be your husband."

The lovely maiden and the lad were delighted, and with the permission of the mother, they at once called the priest. The marriage ceremony was performed, and for seven days, they celebrated the wedding festival. The lad adored his lovely bride, and they lived in harmony and joy.

One day, as the bride was sitting by the window sewing, the Prince who ruled that land happened to pass by the cottage. He saw her through the window and was enchanted by her beauty. Determined to have her for himself, the

Prince laid plans to get rid of her husband.

He called the lad to the palace, and said, "I want you to make me a tent so large that it will shelter my whole army, and still be only half full. I will give you three days time to make it, and if you fail, your head shall be cut off."

Knowing that the task was impossible, the lad went home sadly to spend his last three days.

But his bride noticed his distress at once. "What is the matter, dear husband?" she asked. "Why are you so sad?" The lad could only sigh. "Pray tell me," she begged him.

So the lad told her what the Prince had ordered him to do.

"Never mind, husband, don't worry yourself," she said, and putting her head out the window toward the sea, she cried, "Mama, Mama, send us up the small tent, please. We want to go a-camping."

The small tent was thrown up from the sea onto their doorsill. The lad took it straight to the Prince. When the royal servants unfolded it, it proved to be so huge that it took them seven days to pitch it. Not only the Prince's army, but all his people could fit inside it, and it was still half empty.

"This is right well," said the Prince. "But you see there is nothing in this tent to make my army comfortable. I want you to bring me a rug that will fit the tent exactly. If you fail, you shall lose your head."

Again the lad told his wife, and again she appealed to her mother under the sea. "Send me up the small rug, Mama," she called, "so the ground won't chill us when we go a-camping." And out of the sea the rug was tossed up and landed on their doorsill. The lad took it to the Prince, and when it was unrolled, it exactly fitted the tent.

The next day the Prince summoned the lad again, and demanded food for his army to eat in the tent. "I want you to bring me a cluster of grapes so large that every man may eat his fill and there will still be grapes left on the stem."

Once more the maiden of the sea called out to her mother. "Mama," she called. "Send me a cluster of grapes off the small grape vine that

we may have food for our camping trip." At once a cluster of grapes emerged from the sea and fell so gently to the ground that not a grape was shaken loose from its stem. And when the soldiers had eaten their fill, there were still grapes enough for another army.

By now, the Prince was enraged at the failure of his schemes, and he longed more than ever to possess the beautiful maiden of the sea. So he set himself to think of a task that the lad could not possibly perform.

"I want you now," he told the lad, "to bring me a three-day-old baby who can walk and talk like a grown man. And if you fail, or if the baby be four days old or two days old, you shall lose your head."

At this, the lad was truly dismayed, and his distress was great when he told his wife the Prince's newest command.

"Why, that is not difficult, husband," the wife said. And she called out toward the sea, "Mama, send me up my three-day-old brother. We are anxious to see him."

A baby was given up from the sea, and the lad took him to the Prince, still doubting whether this sleeping bundle in his arms could do what the Prince required. But when he reached the palace and was shown into the Prince's presence, the baby suddenly awoke, threw off the blanket which was wrapped around him, walked over to the Prince and climbed up into his lap.

"Are you not ashamed, Prince," the infant said, "to make so much trouble for my brother-in-law? I know your scheme. You want to kill him and marry my sister, don't you? For shame, Prince, for shame!" And the baby raised his tiny fist and started boxing the Prince's ear.

Thereupon the Prince was suddenly filled with shame. He gave up his evil plan and begged the lad's forgiveness. So the lad and his bride were left unmolested and they are still living happily on the border of the sea.

Three apples came down from God:
   One to the one who told it
   One to the one who asked it
   And one to the one who gave ear to it.

THE MAN WHO WENT TO FIND HIS LUCK

AFGHANISTAN: The notion that every man is entitled to some luck in his lifetime is an old one, and in many folk tales, as in this one, "luck" often appears as a character with a shape and a voice. Based on a story by R. H. Malyon.

THERE ARE TWO THINGS in this world that every man needs to get along. First, there is luck. This is when a man is given an opportunity. Second, there is intelligence. This enables the man to make good use of his opportunity.

Now, there were two brothers. One of them was always lucky. As for the other, he had neither luck nor intelligence.

So he went to his brother's luck and asked, "Since my brother has luck, there must also be a luck for me. Where, then, can I find mine?"

And his brother's luck answered, "There is indeed a luck for you. It is asleep in that wood to the north." So the man turned north and set off toward the wood to find his luck.

On the way, he met a lion, stretched out in the middle of the road. It was thin and ill-looking, and it raised its head only a little to question the man, saying, "Where are you going?"

"I am going to find my luck," said the man. "It lies asleep in that wood to the north."

"If you find it," begged the lion in a weak voice, "please ask your luck for me why I am so ill and why nothing seems to make me feel better."

"Very well, I will ask," said the man.

When he had gone a little farther, he met a horse standing head down and weary by the side of the road. "Where are you going?" asked the horse, opening one eye.

"I am going north, to that wood, to find my luck," answered the man.

"Then ask your luck for me," said the horse, "why I am so weak and tired."

"I will ask it for you," said the man.

Some distance down the road, the man met a dying tree which spoke sadly to him, saying, "O, man, pray tell me where you are going." When the man had told him of his sleeping luck in the wood, the tree said, "I will be grateful if you would ask your luck for me why I am so dry and leafless."

The man agreed to ask.

Now, when he had reached the wood and walked for a time, he came upon his luck. It was sleeping comfortably curled up at the roots

of a large tree with its head pillowed on a soft hummock of moss. The man was outraged by its laziness and he seized it angrily, shouting, "Here am I, pursued by ill fortune and almost dying of hunger! And you sleep in the wood, caring nothing!"

His luck replied, "It would be useless to awake for you, for you are not clever enough to make use of the good fortune I could bring you if I did interrupt my nap for your sake."

"Nonsense!" said the man. "I never had any good fortune, so I have had no chance to use it cleverly. Awake and give me the luck which is rightfully mine!"

"Very well," said his luck, stretching and sitting up. And the man, satisfied, turned toward home. But when he had gone a few steps, he remembered his promises to the tree, the horse and the lion and he went back to his luck.

"Why is the tree leafless, the horse weak, and the lion ill?" he asked. "I told them I would ask your advice about a cure."

"Tell the tree that under its roots lies the treasure of seven kings," said his luck. "If this treasure is taken out of the ground, then the tree will flourish. Tell the horse he should take a master to ride him. Then he will grow strong. And tell the lion that he will recover when he devours a fool."

Next he came to the horse which asked, "What advice have you brought me?"

"That you should take a master to ride you. Then you will grow strong again."

"Then you take me!" said the horse. "You can be my master."

"Find another master," said the man. "My luck is now awake and it will bring me many horses." And he continued on foot, leaving the horse drooping by the side of the road.

The lion, which still lay listlessly in the road, saw the man coming and raised its head weakly to question him. "Did you find your luck?" it asked. "What did your luck say?"

The man told the lion of the advice he had received for the tree and the horse, but explained that he had no need for the treasure under the tree or for a horse to ride because all these things would come to him now that his luck was awake.

The man set out homeward and soon came to the tree. He told it what his luck had advised and the tree said, "If you will take the treasure from under my roots, your kindness will be great, and you will be as rich as seven kings."

But the man replied, "What do I want with your riches? My luck has awakened, and it will work for me." And he went on, leaving the treasure under the leafless tree.

"And what was the answer to my question?" asked the lion.

"That you will recover when you devour a fool," answered the man.

"In that case," said the lion, "you have truly brought me my cure. When I hear of what you have done with your luck, I can think of no greater fool than you!" And rising up, he devoured the man where he stood.

THE SILLY FELLOW WHO SOLD HIS BEARD

GYPSY: Gypsies, who speak a language called Romany, are thought to have come originally from India. They now live in many countries. This story is told by Swedish gypsies, and it starts with the standard phrase that gypsy storytellers use to signal the beginning of a story. By M. A. Jagendorf and C. H. Tillhagen.

IF IT HADN'T HAPPENED, it wouldn't be told.

Once there were two merchants who were good friends. One was smart and one was silly; the smart one was clean-shaven, like a young boy, and the other had a long, thick beard. Take my word for it, it was a very handsome beard.

One day they were sitting together talking of this and that. Said the one who had no beard:

"Little brother, would you like to sell me your beard?"

The one with the beard answered: "Why not, if you'll pay me a good price?"

"I'll give you whatever you ask for that fine beard of yours."

"I'll let you name the price, good friend. I know you'll be fair," said the one with the beard.

"Fine. I'll give you a good sum, but on one condition. I want the beard to keep on growing on *your* face, but *I* will take care of it—how it is to grow, how it is to be combed, what perfume is to be put on it, and how it should be cut. Everything will have to be done as I like it. You won't have the right to say anything about it. That beard will be all mine. If anyone says to you, 'What a beautiful beard!' you'll have to answer quickly, 'Sorry, my good man, it's not my beard, it belongs to so-and-so.' That's what you'll have to say."

The man with the beard had no objection to that.

"Sure, friend," he said. "You can keep looking after my beard—I mean your beard. It will be cheaper for me!"

So they wrote out a contract, and the merchant who was clean-shaven paid a good sum to the other.

Mischtó! Fine and dandy. From that day on the clean-shaven man was very particular about taking care of the beard he had bought on his friend's face and he stopped at nothing to show it. Whenever he felt like it or thought of it, which was many a time during a day, he came to tend to the beard his merchant friend had on his chin. It made no difference to him whether his friend had company or whether he was asleep. And sometimes he wasn't too gentle about the beard, either. He'd pull it and tug it. Sometimes he'd cut it to a point, sometimes in

squares or zigzag. One day he'd smear sweet-scented oil over it, and the next, he'd pour on it heaven knows what.

If the poor sufferer complained, it was like talking to the wind. His crying and wailing just struck a stone wall.

"Listen, friend; listen, you there! Are you out of your mind? You're acting like a crazy man. Leave my beard in peace."

"Well, here is something," the one who had bought the beard cried. "Grumbling and kicking! Maybe you'd like to break your contract! You'll get into trouble if you do. The law is on my side. Just keep calm. That beard belongs to me, and I have the right to do with it as I wish."

And then he went at that beard hammer and nails. He tugged it and pulled it until the poor merchant screamed to heaven.

So time went by while the one who bought the beard kept tearing and teasing the beard of the one who had it on his chin. In the end the poor sufferer couldn't stand it any longer.

"Little brother, good friend, I want to buy back my beard. For the love of our good God, let me have my beard again. You are making my life worse than if I lived with the Devil."

"Don't talk foolishly. I am very happy with my beard on your face. It's a nice beard; it's thick and glossy. Look how strong the roots of the hair are," he said as he began to pull it. "I want to keep it. Maybe later on we'll see what can be done."

And so he kept on taking care of the beard in his own way and as he felt like it. In the end it was too much for the bearded merchant.

"I want to buy my beard back," he cried. "Little brother, I want my beard, you are driving me crazy. Give it back to me and I'll pay you any price."

"How much do you offer?"

"I'll give you twice as much as you paid me."

"Twice as much for this fine, thick, glossy beard! Just feel it," and he got hold of it. "You'll have to go higher, brother."

"Ow! Let go! Name any price. I'll give you whatever you ask."

"That's talking! Give me four times as much as I gave you, and you'll pay just right for your beard—and your foolishness!"

So the bearded merchant paid the other. And then he quickly went to the barber and had his beard shaved off.

PART 14 BURMA: VIETNAM: LAOS: CAMBODIA: THAILAND: TIBET

ILLUSTRATED BY JEANYEE WONG

THE RABBIT'S CLEVER NOSE

BURMA: This version of an old tale is by Maung Htin Aung.

KING LION appointed the Bear, the Monkey, and the Rabbit to be his ministers of state, and together they roamed the forest. But one day the Lion became tired of their company, and wanted to kill and eat them. However, as he himself had chosen them to be his ministers, he had to think of an excuse which would give a semblance of legality to his unjust act.

So King Lion called his three ministers of state, and said to them, "My lords, you have been my ministers for some time, and I must now find out whether high office has spoilt you." The Lion opened his mouth wide, and asked the Bear to state what sort of smell ensued from the royal mouth. As the Lion was a great meat-eater, naturally a foul smell came out from his mouth.

The Bear, ever truthful, said, "Your Majesty, it is a foul smell."

"Rank treason," roared the Lion in anger. "You insult the king to his face. The punishment for treason is death." So saying, he pounced upon the Bear and killed him.

The Lion now asked the Monkey to say what sort of smell ensued from the royal mouth. The Monkey, after witnessing the fate of the Bear, thought that the only way to escape with his life was to resort to flattery, and said, "Your Majesty, it is a delicious smell, as sweet as the choicest perfume."

"You are a liar and a flatterer," roared the Lion in anger. "Everyone knows that only a foul smell can come out of my mouth as I am a great meat-eater. Untruthful and flattering counselors to the king are a danger to the state." So saying, he pounced upon the Monkey and killed him.

The Lion now said to the Rabbit, "Wise Rabbit, what sort of smell ensues from my mouth?"

"I am sorry, Your Majesty," replied the Rabbit, "I have a cold and my nose is blocked. May I go home and rest until my cold is cured? For only then shall I be able to use my nose and say what sort of smell ensues from the royal mouth." The Lion had no choice but to let the Rabbit go home and, needless to say, the Rabbit never went near him again.

And to this day in Burma, when a person is being cagey and won't express an opinion, it is said that "he has a cold!"

THE MOST REMARKABLE CAT

VIETNAM, LAOS, CAMBODIA: Tales like this, which end exactly where they begin, are called "circle" stories. There are lots of children's stories told in this form, particularly in the East. This one is by Madeleine Riffaud.

Once upon a time there was a mandarin who had a cat which he loved very much. He was so proud of the cat, and he considered it such a remarkable creature, that he decided to name it *Sky*.

One day a friend said to him, "Permit me to point out to you that there is something stronger than the sky—I mean the clouds, for they hide the sky."

"You are right," replied the mandarin. "And from now on I am going to give my most remarkable cat the name *Cloud*."

Some time later, another mandarin was drinking tea at his house. "Why is it," he asked, "that you call this most remarkable creature *Cloud*? For there is something much stronger than the clouds—I mean the wind that scatters the clouds before it."

So from then on his master called the cat of which he was so proud by the name of *Wind*.

But a week had not passed when the mayor of the town, whom the mandarin had invited to his house, noticed the most remarkable cat.

"*Wind*," he said, "seems to me a name that is most unworthy of the merits of this extraordinary creature. The wind meets its master every day—I mean the wall that it cannot blow through."

"Just so," said the owner of the cat. "Henceforth my most beloved pet will be called *Wall*."

A little later, a scholar who was pursuing his studies at the mandarin's house, respectfully remarked to the mandarin that there is something that can conquer even a wall—the mouse that nibbles a hole through it.

"That is true," said the mandarin. "I will name my most remarkable cat *Mouse*."

Just then the gardener's little son happened by.

"*Mouse*!" he exclaimed, laughing as hard as he could. "I know something much stronger than a mouse—I mean the cat who catches the mouse and eats him up!"

At this, the mandarin realized his folly. And from then on, he called the animal of which he was so proud by the most beautiful name that anyone had been able to bestow on it—the name of *Cat*.

THE PRIEST'S MANGOS

VIETNAM, LAOS, CAMBODIA: In folklore there are many stories—not all of them favorable—about priests and holy men. The priest in this story from Laos is undoubtedly a Buddhist.

IN THE COURTYARD of a temple there was a large mango tree, a vigorous spreading tree, whose fruit was of a juiciness and sweetness unequaled anywhere in the countryside. Everyone who passed longed to sample the ripe mangos, but the priest would allow no one to eat so much as a single one because he was greedy and selfish and wanted them all for himself.

One day two men who were passing determined to taste some of those mangos, and they devised a plan to get some without either stealing or paying for them.

The first man came to the priest, admired the lush fruit hanging from the branches, and asked if he might have some.

"Certainly not," said the priest gruffly. "I need them for my own use."

"I'm sorry to hear that," said the man. "Because I have made a splendid venison curry, and I need some mangos to eat with it. I was hoping that you would come and share it with me this evening."

The priest was immediately interested. "Ah well, friend," he said hospitably, "take all you want." The man filled his scarf with the coveted fruit and left, saying to the priest, "I will call for you then as the eye of day closes."

Shortly after, the second man came and begged the priest to give him some mangos. Again the priest refused gruffly, until the man mentioned that he wanted to eat the fruit with a rich pork curry he had at home. "It is a big curry," the man said, "and I was hoping you would do me the honor of eating it with me tonight."

At this the priest brightened and said agreeably, "Do help yourself. Take all you want." And the man filled a large basket with the choicest mangos.

As the eye of day closed, the two men came

to call for the priest. They walked on either side of him until they reached a fork in the road. Then one laid hold of the priest's right arm, and said, "Come with me first. My house is down this way."

"Oh no," said the second man, tugging at the priest's left arm. "My curry is all ready. My family will already be eating. Come this way."

"But I invited the priest first," said the first man, pulling harder on the priest's arm.

Thus they argued, pulling and tugging at the greedy old priest. They dragged him through brambles, bumped him against trees, and jerked him off his feet.

Finally the priest, bruised, tired, and scratched, cried wearily, "Stop, stop! This is enough! I will not eat either the venison or the pork."

And the men let him go, and went home laughing, for they had no curries at all, neither of venison nor of pork.

WHY THE

Long ago people caught and trained the parakeet and kept it for a pet because it could be taught the language of man. It had but to hear a word and it could easily repeat it. It could even use man's words to express its own thoughts.

Once a man who owned a parakeet stole a buffalo from his neighbor and killed it. The man cooked and ate part of the buffalo, and the rest he divided into two parts. He hid one part in the rice bin and the other over the rice house.

The neighbor came the next day seeking his buffalo, and he asked the man whether he had seen it.

"No," said the man, "I have not."

But the parakeet cried out, "He killed it. He hid part in the rice bin and part over the rice house."

The neighbor searched in these places and found the buffalo meat hidden just as the parakeet had said.

"I did not steal the buffalo," the man insisted.

But the parakeet repeated over and over again, "He killed it and put part into the rice bin and part over the rice house." So the neigh-

MYNAH BIRD MIMICS MAN

THAILAND: This story is told in many versions. Sometimes, for instance, the mimic is a parrot instead of a mynah bird. But the point is always the same: a bird who has learned that man is not necessarily honest warns another bird to keep his thoughts to himself.

bor, unable to tell the truth of the matter, went to court. The court decided that the man must be brought to trial.

The night before the trial, the man took the parakeet and put it in a pot. Then he covered the pot with a cloth so that the bird was in darkness. The man then set to beating on the pot to make a low rumbling noise like thunder. And at the same time he dropped water on the cloth to make a dripping sound like rain. All that night he continued to make the sounds of rain and thunder although the sky was clear and the moon shone brightly outside.

When the morning came the man took the parakeet out of the pot, put it in its cage, and took it to court as a witness.

When the parakeet was called on to testify, it said as before, "He killed it, and put part in the rice bin and part over the rice house."

All the people in the court believed the bird. But the man cried, "Would you condemn me on the word of a bird? Surely a man's word is worth more. Ask the parakeet some other question. Ask him what manner of night it was last night."

The question was put to the bird. And the bird, remembering the noise of the night, said, "There was a great storm. All night the sky rumbled and the rain fell."

Then the people cried, "Truly, the bird cannot be believed! A great storm in the midst of the dry season—and the moon as bright as day! It has through falsehood endangered the life of an innocent man. From this time forward, men must no longer cherish the parakeet!"

The thieving man was set free because there was only the word of the bird to name him the guilty one. The parakeet was set loose in the forest to fend for itself, no longer to be cared for by man.

When a year of living as a wild bird had gone by, the parakeet saw the black and gold feathers of a mynah bird and asked the owl and the crow what manner of bird it was. The owl and the crow said it was a bird of beautiful plumage from a strange land, and that it could speak the words of man.

"Then we must warn it," said the parakeet, and they went to meet the beautiful stranger. When they had come together the parakeet

cried out, "We come to greet you and to give you of our wisdom since you are a stranger in our land. It is said that you speak the words of man. Even so do I. I was once cherished and cared for by man because I spoke his words. But I also spoke my own thoughts, and this made man angry. So I was cruelly punished and driven from the houses of men. Therefore, I come this day to warn you that when man hears of your speaking his words, he will capture you and keep you in his home. Yet if you should speak any word but those he teaches you—if you should utter your own thoughts in his words— he will drive you, also, from his home. For man cares not for the truth or wisdom of other creatures. He loves only to hear his own thoughts repeated."

Men soon heard of the speaking tongue of the mynah bird, and they captured it and cherished it in their homes. But the mynah bird, remembering the warning of the parakeet, has never uttered his own thoughts, but only echoed the words of man.

THE

A VERY LONG TIME AGO, somewhere in that far away land of Tibet, away up so high that it seems a little nearer to the sky than any other land, in one corner was a country governed by a very just man. He was noted in all parts of the dominion for his fair judgment in all cases. In the city where this good king lived and had his home, dwelt two poor men. Both were very good, did the very best they could every day, and each had an old mother to support.

One day one of the men started to a village high up in the mountains carrying a jar of oil, selling it as he went. Walking along, he grew very tired and set his jar of oil on a rock by the roadside while he sat down to rest a while. As he sat there, his neighbor came down the mountain driving his donkey in front of him. There were two big loads of wood, stacked one on each side of the little donkey, which almost covered him. He didn't happen to see the jar, so came too near and knocked it off, breaking it, and spilling all the oil.

The man who owned the oil was very angry indeed, and the man who owned the donkey said it wasn't he who had done the damage, but the donkey. So they quarreled and quarreled and kept on quarreling. The man who owned the oil said he couldn't afford to lose it, as it was all he had in the world to sell for food for his mother and himself, and it couldn't have been his fault the jar was broken.

They both went to the king who questioned them very carefully about the matter and finally said he couldn't see that either one was to blame. They were both good men, took good care of their old mothers and were honest in all their dealings, and so far as he could see no one was at fault but the donkey and the rock, and he would judge them.

DONKEY AND THE ROCK

TIBET: Judges, both good and bad, appear in folk tales almost as often as brave heroes do. Here is a story about two odd defendants and a judgment that is both wise and tricky.

So the little donkey was led into prison with chains around his legs and his neck, while five of the king's men were sent out for the rock. The king ordered it wrapped with chains and tied outside the prison door to a post.

By this time the news of this strange case and the queer doings of the king had spread throughout the city. When the people heard their great king was having a trial about a donkey and a rock they thought he had surely gone mad. The next morning the king announced, by his runners through the city, that the case would be tried. The idea that a donkey and a rock could have a trial in court was more than the people could understand, but early next day everybody in the city was at the courtyard to see the result of the trial.

When the time arrived the judge came, took his seat, instructed the doorkeepers to shut and lock all the gates, thus locking in everybody, and then proceeded to pronounce his judgment on the case.

"As you very well know, there is no law by which a donkey and a rock can be judged. Why have you all come to see so absurd a thing? Now, because of your curiosity in the matter, every one of you shall pay a half-cent before he gets out."

The people, looking much ashamed, and glad to get out, handed over this bit of money and slipped through the gate. The cash taken in this way was given to the man who had lost his oil, so he was happy, the debt was paid, and the court closed.

THE WONDERFUL PEAR TREE

CHINA: Folk tales were being written down in China long before Europeans even knew how to write. This old story is still popular today.

ONE DAY a countryman came down the road to market wheeling a cart heaped with pears. He found a good corner where many people were passing by and began crying up his fruit. He soon had a large crowd gathered around his cart, for it was well known in the town that the countryman, although he asked a high price, always had particularly fine pears. But this cartful looked more luscious than ever before. They were golden with a tinge of red, they were full and firm. It could be seen at a glance that they were juicy and delicious—exactly at the peak of ripeness.

Several men in the crowd were beginning to examine their purses when a priest shuffled up to the cart. He was old, and so thin that his bones stuck out in knobs. His clothes hung on his gaunt body and his feet were bare. He carried a rice bowl and a pick tied to his bent back.

"Please, sir," said the priest, bowing humbly, "will you give me one of your beautiful pears?"

But the countryman had no thought of giving away goods he could exchange for money. He refused curtly and told the priest to move on.

The priest did not move. "You have hundreds of pears, good sir," he pleaded, "while I have nothing at all. Surely you would not miss one pear out of all you have?"

The countryman growled at the old man and called him a beggar and a thief. He swore and shook his fist in the priest's face. But the priest only drew back slightly and looked unhappy.

"It seems to me, sir," he said gently, "that your anger is too great for such a small request. How can I have offended you so much?"

195

At this, the countryman turned red with rage and, shouting, he started toward the priest threateningly. But one of the onlookers stepped between them and said, "Come, why don't you give him an overripe pear and make him happy? He's quite right. You would never miss it."

But the countryman stubbornly refused, and the crowd began to argue. The hubbub grew till the market constable hurried over to see what the trouble was. The mandarin would soon be carried by this place, and the constable wanted no disturbance in his presence. To keep the peace, he took a coin from his purse and bought a pear, which he handed to the priest.

The old man took the pear in both hands gratefully, made a low bow and turned to address the crowd. "As you all know," he said, "I gave up all I owned when I became a priest. I have no home, no family, no goods, no money. I must depend on the generosity of others even to eat. We who have given up everything find it hard to believe that others can be so selfish as to refuse food to the poor. We who live in poverty share what little we have. Now, I will show you. I have some exquisite pears of my own, and I will think it an honor if each of you will accept one from me."

"Why on earth, if you have pears of your own, didn't you eat yours instead of begging from others?" asked a man in the crowd.

"Ah, because I must grow mine first," said the priest.

With that, he held up his pear for all to see.

Then he bit into it with relish and did not stop eating until he had finished everything but one seed. Holding the seed carefully in one hand, he untied the pick from his back with the other and motioned the crowd to stand aside. With the pick he dug a deep hole in the ground. When he considered it deep enough, he carefully placed the seed in the bottom of it and covered it gently with earth.

"Now," he said, "I must have some hot water. Will someone be so kind as to fetch a kettle?"

One of the bystanders, chuckling, went to a shop and came back with a steaming kettle. The priest bowed, accepted the kettle, and, with great care, poured the water over the newly turned earth.

To everyone's astonishment, just as he poured the last drop, a tiny green sprout poked up out

of the ground. The people gasped and the countryman, who had been peering from the back of the crowd, elbowed his way to the front. The sprout grew taller as they watched. Presently, a leaf began to uncurl, then another, as the stalk rose higher and higher. Branches pushed out of the main stem and covered themselves with leaves. The tree reached over the heads of the crowd. They watched openmouthed as gradually buds appeared and the blossoms opened. The petals fell like snow on their upturned faces and tiny green pears grew in their stead. These swelled and yellowed and grew rosy. As they became heavier, the branches of the tree curved downward with their weight.

"Behold!" said the priest, beaming with pleasure. The crowd, startled out of its trance, realized that the pears were now fully ripe and so heavy with juice that the tips of the branches touched the ground.

A murmur of awe arose, but the priest took no notice. One by one, he picked the pears and, with a low bow, he handed one to each man. When the tree was bare of fruit, the old man looked around to make sure all the delighted onlookers had been served. Satisfied, he took up his pick and hacked at the base of the tree until it fell to the ground. He tied the pick to his back and, with a grunt, lifted the tree, leaves and all, to his shoulder. After a few steps down the road, he turned, bowed gravely, and disappeared around the corner.

The countryman now shook himself out of his daze and looked stupidly at the pear in his hand. Then suddenly he turned back toward his cart, pushed through the thinning crowd and stared unbelievingly. Every single pear was gone! And one handle of his cart was missing, too!

Now the countryman finally understood where the priest had got the pears he was so generous with. They had come from the countryman's cart! And now all that remained of the beautiful fruit was a few stems and cores lying on the ground at his feet and the single pear in his hand.

For a moment, he was too angry to move. Then he dashed his pear to the ground and went tearing furiously down the road after the priest. "Stop! Thief! Scoundrel!" he roared as he ran.

He rounded the corner and looked wildly to the right and left for the old man and the tree. The road was completely empty. There was no sign of any person at all! But out of the corner of his eye, the countryman saw a familiar object. Lying against the wall at the edge of the road was his missing cart handle, hacked off as with a pick. Then he knew without a doubt that the handle was the pear tree the priest had cut down.

Even from where he was, the countryman could hear the roars of laughter from the people in the market.

IN THE SHADE OF A DONKEY

CHINA: Many old Chinese fables teach lessons surprisingly like those an American parent might teach his children. By R. Pierce Beaver.

A MAN ONCE hired a donkey and went on a journey. The donkey boy went along to lead the beast and take care of it.

The day was very hot, and the travelers sought refuge from the sun in order to rest a while. They could find no tree nor building to give them shade, so at last the man and the donkey boy both crawled under the donkey's belly to shelter themselves from the hot sun. Since the donkey was not very large, there was not enough shade to cover two men. Both men wanted the shade and they quarreled violently.

The traveler declared, "I hired the donkey, and I have paid you money for the use of him. His shadow belongs to me now."

But the donkey boy protested, "I hired only my donkey to you. I certainly did not hire his shadow."

Neither man would give up his claim, and finally they came to blows. This frightened the donkey, and he ran away. The men ran after the beast, but could not catch him. They finally gave up the chase, hotter than ever.

The proverb says, "He who wrangles about nothing may lose something."

THE WOODCARVER AND THE PAINTER

MONGOLIA: Many Mongolians are Buddhists and believe that when a person dies, he is born again into a new life.

LONG AGES AGO in the kingdom of Kunsmon, there lived a Khan. He grew old and died, and his son became the Khan in his stead. In this same kingdom lived a painter whose name was Ananda, and a woodcarver whose name was Ananda also. These men seemed to be friends, but in their hearts each was jealous of the other.

One day the painter resolved to do away with the woodcarver and with crafty art he forged a letter in the name of the old Khan. Then he appeared before the new Khan and spoke thus, "Oh Khan, your father, born anew into the kingdom of the gods, called me to him and commanded me to deliver this letter unto you."

As he spoke, he handed the Khan a strip of writing on which were inscribed these words:

"To my son: When I last parted from you, I took flight from life on earth and was born into the kingdom of the gods. Here I live in plenty, having all that I desire. Only one thing is wanting. I am building a temple, and I can find not one man to adorn it who is as clever at his art as our woodcarver. Therefore, I charge you, my son, summon Ananda, the woodcarver, and send him up to me."

When the Khan had read the letter, the painter said, "Your father has told me how to send the woodcarver to the gods' kingdom."

The new Khan was filled with joy at knowing that his father had been born anew into the kingdom of the gods. He sent for the woodcarver and spoke thus to him. "My father, who

is new born into the gods' kingdom, is building a temple. But he cannot find a woodcarver as skilled as you. Now, he has written unto me to send you above to him at once." With these words, he gave the strip of writing into the woodcarver's hands.

When the woodcarver had read it, he said within himself, "This is indeed an unheard-of thing! Do I not smell some trick of Ananda the painter? I must find a way to protect myself against his mischief." Then, speaking aloud, he said, "Tell me, Oh Khan, how shall I, a poor woodcarver, attain the kingdom of the gods?"

"In this," said the Khan, "the painter shall instruct you."

He sent and fetched the painter into his presence while the woodcarver said within himself, "Have I not smelt you out, you crafty one?"

199

When the painter was commanded to tell the manner of the journey into the gods' kingdom, he answered thus, "When you have collected all your tools and materials, gather them at your feet and order a pile of beams of wood soaked in grain spirits to be heaped around you. Then summon the players of all the solemn-sounding instruments, and to the sound of the music kindle the pile. You will then rise to the gods' kingdom, borne on clouds of smoke as though on a swift charger."

The woodcarver dared not refuse the command of the Khan, but he asked for seven days in which to collect his tools and materials. He planned also to find out a means of revenge for the painter's trickery. Then he went home to tell his wife all that had befallen him.

His wife, without hesitating, proposed a plan by which he could save his life while seeming to obey the Khan's command. In a field a short distance from his house, she had him place a large flat stone. And under it, by night, she had him dig an underground passage to his house.

When the eighth day had arrived, all the people assembled around the pile of wood soaked in spirits in the woodcarver's field. The pile was the height of a man, well heaped up, and in the middle stood the woodcarver, calmly listening to the tones of the solemn-sounding instruments.

When the smoke began to rise thickly enough to hide him, the woodcarver pushed the stone aside with his feet and returned to his home by the underground passage. But the painter, never doubting that he had been consumed by the flames, rubbed his hands and pointed with joy and triumph to the curling smoke, crying out to the people, "Behold the spirit of our

brother rising on the obedient clouds as on a swift charger to the kingdom of the gods!"

And, believing his words, all the people cried, "Behold the spirit of the woodcarver rising to adorn the temple of the gods' kingdom!"

Now, for the space of a whole month, the woodcarver remained at home, letting himself be seen by no one save his wife. Every day he washed himself with milk and sat in the shade, out of the light of the sun. At the end of the month, his wife brought him a robe of white gauze with which he covered himself. Then he, too, forged a letter and took it to the Khan.

As soon as the Khan saw him, he cried out, "How have you returned from the gods' kingdom? And did you find my father well?"

Then the woodcarver handed him the letter he had prepared and the Khan caused it to be read aloud before the people of the court. These were the words on the strip of writing:

"To my son: Ananda the woodcarver has worked well on the part of the temple I assigned to him. I charge you to reward him richly for his labor. But now, to complete the temple, I am in need of a painter, to color the excellent sculpture the woodcarver has made. Send straightway for Ananda the painter, for there is none other like him, and let him come up to me in the same manner that you sent Ananda the woodcarver."

When the Khan heard the letter, he rejoiced and said, "These are truly the words of my father." And he loaded the woodcarver with rich rewards. Then he sent for the painter to come unto him.

The painter came with all haste. The letter was read to him and, when he heard it, he was seized with great fear and trembling. But when he saw Ananda the woodcarver standing before him, all white from the milk-washing and clad in the rich garment of gauze as if the light of the gods' kingdom still clung to him, the painter said within himself, "Surely the fire has not burned him, so neither shall it burn me. If I refuse to go, I will be put to death, while if I obey the command, I will receive rich rewards, even as the woodcarver has." So he consented to get his painter's materials ready in seven days and to rise to the gods' kingdom on the smoke of the burning beams.

When the seven days were past, the people assembled in the field of the painter. The Khan came in his robes of state surrounded by his officers and ministers of the kingdom. The pile of beams was again heaped up as high as a man and they were soaked in spirits. The painter was placed in the center of the pile and every solemn-sounding instrument rang out while the people set the pile on fire.

The painter strengthened himself against the pain with the thought that he would soon begin to rise on clouds of smoke. But when he found he did not rise, but began to sink to the ground, he shouted to the people to come and release him. But the clever plan he had formed to drown out the cries of the woodcarver was his undoing. No one could hear his voice above the resounding tones of the solemn-sounding instruments.

THE TONGUE-CUT SPARROW

JAPAN: As every American child knows the story of Little Red Riding Hood, so every Japanese child knows about the tongue-cut sparrow.

IT IS SAID that once upon a time a cross old woman laid some starch in a basin, intending to put it in the clothes she was washing. But before she was ready to use the starch, a sparrow, that her elderly neighbor kept as a pet, ate it up. Seeing this, the cross old woman seized the sparrow in her heavy hand.

"You hateful thing," she said, shaking the quivering bird, and she cut its tongue for punishment before letting it go.

When the owner of the sparrow heard that her pet's tongue had been cut for eating the starch, she was greatly grieved, for she had raised the tiny bird and nursed it in illness. She and her husband set out over mountains and plains to find where it had gone.

"Where does the tongue-cut sparrow stay?"

they called. "Where does the tongue-cut sparrow stay?"

At last they found its home. When the sparrow saw that its old master and mistress had come to see it, it rejoiced and brought them into the house and thanked them for their kindness now and in former days. It spread a table for them and loaded it with sake and fish until there was no more room, and made its wife and grandchildren all serve the table.

At last putting aside the dishes, it danced a jig called the sparrow's dance, and its wife and children and grandchildren danced, too. Thus, the old couple and the sparrows spent the day.

When it began to grow dark, and it was time for the man and wife to go home, the sparrow brought out two wicker baskets and said, "Here is a present for you. Will you take the heavy basket, or shall I give you the light one?"

The old people replied, "We are old, so give us the light basket. It will be easier for us to carry."

The sparrow then gave them the light basket and they returned with it to their house. "Let us open it and see what is in it," they said.

And when they opened it and looked inside, they found gold and silver and jewels and rolls of silk. They had never expected anything like this! The more they took out, the more they found inside. The supply was inexhaustible. So that house at once became rich and prosperous.

When the cross old woman who had cut the sparrow's tongue heard about their good fortune, she was filled with envy, and she went and asked her neighbor where the sparrow lived, and all about how to get there.

"I will go, too," she said, and at once set out on her search.

She finally reached the sparrow's home and the sparrow welcomed the cross old woman kindly, laid out fish and sake, and danced the sparrow's dance for her entertainment. As it came time to go, the sparrow once more brought out two wicker baskets and asked as before, "Will you take the heavy one, or shall I give you the light one?"

Thinking that the treasure would be great in proportion to the weight of the basket, the old woman replied, "Give me the heavy one."

So the sparrow gave it to her and helped her hoist it on to her back. The sparrows laughed as she struggled with the basket. It was as heavy as a stone and hard to carry, but at last she got home with it and, panting and hot, she put it down.

When she took off the lid and looked inside, a whole troop of frightful devils came seething out into her house and, without a sound, they tore the old woman to pieces.

THE BRIDEGROOM'S SHOPPING

KOREA: Far Eastern folklore is full of stories about mirrors, such as this one by Kim So-Un.

AWAY IN THE COUNTRY there once lived a long-established family of farmers. There was an only daughter in the family, who had just married. As is the custom in such cases, the bridegroom came to live with his in-laws.

A few days after the marriage it so happened that the bridegroom had to go to town on some business. As he prepared to leave, his bride asked him: "Will you please buy me a comb in town?"

"Why, of course," he answered, all eager to please his pretty bride.

However, his wife knew that her husband was a very forgetful man. Hadn't her in-laws told her so? As she was wondering how he could be made to remember, she chanced to look at the sky. There was a new moon, a thin crescent of pale light, shining softly in the sky. It was only three days old, and it looked just like the moon-shaped comb she wanted.

"There," she called to her husband, "look at the moon. Doesn't it look just like a comb? If you forget what you must buy, just remember to look into the sky. The moon will remind you that I want a comb. You will remember, won't you?"

This she repeated again and again, and after she was sure he would remember, she bade him farewell.

The bridegroom was soon in town. He was so taken up with his business that he completely forgot about his wife's comb. Several days later, his work finished, he packed his belongings and prepared to return home. As he looked around to see if he had forgotten anything, he happened to look out the window, and there he saw a big, round moon shining in the sky. Ten days had passed since he had left home. The moon was no longer a small sliver of light but a round, laughing globe of silver.

The moon suddenly reminded him of his wife's parting words. "Oh, I almost forgot," he told himself. "There was something like the moon I had to buy for my wife. Now, I wonder what it was?"

Try as he might, he could not remember. He knew that it had something to do with the moon —but what? His memory was a blank. "Was it something round like the moon?" he asked himself, "or was it something that shone like the moon?" But not for the life of him could he recall what it was.

"Well," he said at last, "I might as well go to a shop and ask for help."

So the young farmer entered a shop and said: "Good day, Mr. Shopkeeper. Please give me something that looks like the moon, something a woman uses."

The shopkeeper laughed at this strange request. Then looking around his shop his eyes lighted on a small round hand-mirror.

"Oh, I know," the shopkeeper said. "This must be what you want. Look, it's round and looks just like the full moon. You look into it and you can see yourself. A young bride would want it when she pretties herself. I am sure it could be nothing else."

Now, the bridegroom had never seen a mirror before, as they were very rare then. But he thought that surely his wife, the daughter of a rich old farming family, would know what it was. "Yes, this must be what my wife asked me to get," he answered, proud that he could thus get what his wife wanted.

Soon he was back home in the country again. As soon as he entered the house, his wife asked: "Did you remember to do my shopping for me?"

"Yes," he answered. "Here." And he handed her what he had bought.

The bride, expecting to receive a comb, wondered at the strange round object her husband handed her. She peered into the smooth glass. And what should she see there but the reflection of a young woman — and a very pretty young woman at that.

"What thing is this!" she cried. "I only asked for a comb, and here you bring home a pretty young woman." The wife turned angrily and ran to her mother.

"Mother, can you imagine anything so silly? I asked my husband to buy me a comb in town, and look what he brought home — a strange young woman!"

"Where? Where is she?" the mother asked, taking the mirror and peering into it.

Of course, the mother saw reflected only the face of a wrinkled old woman. "Why, my child," she said, "what are you talking about? This must be some old relative of ours."

"No, you are wrong. It's a young woman," the young wife cried.

"No, it's you who are wrong. Look, she's an old, wrinkled woman," the mother retorted.

Thus the two began quarreling.

Just then a small boy came into the room, eating a rice-cake. The boy picked up the mirror and peered into it. There he saw another boy eating a rice-cake. The boy thought the stranger had taken his.

"Give me back my rice-cake," he shouted, "It's mine!" He threw up his hand to strike the boy. The boy in the mirror also raised his arm. The frightened child began to cry loudly.

The room was filled with din, the two women arguing away at the top of their voices, and the boy crying his head off.

Just then the grandfather passed by and heard the commotion. Wondering what it was all about, he poked his head in the doorway. "What's going on here? What's the matter?" he asked. Then he caught sight of the boy looking at a round object and crying: "Give me back my rice-cake!" The grandfather flared with anger to think that someone or something should have taken rice-cakes from a small boy.

"Where, where?" he asked. "Show me the thief!" He grabbed the mirror and peered into it. There, staring at him, was a fierce-looking old man, anger written all over his face.

"Why, it's an old man. You ought to be ashamed at your age to jump out and interfere in a quarrel between boys." With these words

the grandfather rolled up his sleeves and was about to hit the old man in the mirror.

Suddenly the mirror slipped from his hand and fell to the floor with a loud crash. The grandfather, and the boy, and the two women, and the bridegroom all fell silent and stood staring, dumbly, at hundreds of pieces of broken glass beneath their feet.

Anthony D'Adamo

SALAM AND THE HORNET'S NEST

MALAYA: In Malaya, the small animal who regularly outwits powerful enemies is the delicate mouse-deer. His enemies are usually tigers or crocodiles. Rudyard Kipling based his *Just So Stories* on Malayan tales like this.

ONE FINE AFTERNOON the Mouse-Deer was stealing warily through the jungle, knowing full well that his most terrible enemy was not so very far behind him, when he suddenly heard a loud, continuous running sound, not unlike the noise of a giant, humming top, that seemed to come from some bushes near by. He crept up closer and saw it was a hornets' nest. So he picked up a fan-palm leaf, sat down on his haunches, looked fixedly at the nest before him, and began to fan it with the palm leaf until the fierce booming of the hornets gradually died down to a quieter note.

By and by, the Tiger tracked him to the spot, and pounced upon him quite unexpectedly out of the underbrush, snarling, "Now, you miserable little wisp of creation, you are caught at last, and I mean to devour you immediately."

But the Mouse-Deer only laughed and said, "You had better not try eating *me* just yet, Big Brother! For King Solomon has posted me here to keep watch over his Lullaby Gong, of which he is so fond that I am not allowed to leave this spot for even a minute."

"Where is this Lullaby Gong that you are commanded to guard, Friend Mouse-Deer?" asked the Tiger curiously. "I should like to try my hand at sounding it."

"Why there, in that bush, of course!" answered the Mouse-Deer. "Are you really so deaf as all that? Can't you hear how it murmurs, even when it is not being sounded? And when it is struck the note is wonderfully sweet! It has the irresistible, soft tones of the bamboo flute. If you were to beat it yourself I am sure its gentle, pure sound would continue to ring in your ears as it lulled you into a baby's sleep."

At hearing this, the Tiger's curiosity began, as usual, to get the better of him, and he said with a low growl, "May I beat the gong just once, my dear Friend Salam, just once before I have to eat you? I should so love to hear its tones."

"Touch it not, my dear Big Brother!" Salam answered. "Do you not dread the wrath of His Majesty, the Great King, who owns it?"

But the Tiger continued to plead, so Salam thought for a moment, and then said:

"No! I dare not give you leave to sound it. To do so would be as much as my little life is worth. However, if you will wait until I have asked his Majesty's permission, he might, perhaps, at my request, allow it. But you must promise not to touch it until you hear me call."

"I promise," said the Tiger eagerly. "Run quickly, and ask him for me, kind little Mouse-Deer."

The Mouse-Deer darted off and, as soon as he had reached a safe distance, about as far as a mouse-deer's shout could be heard, he stopped. After a few moments, he called out. "Yes, you may hit it, Brother. You may hit it hard just once. The great King grants you permission."

At this, the Tiger lifted up his heavy paw and, with one mighty blow, laid the nest in fragments.

He did not have to wait long for the music he desired. With a smothered roar like that of surf breaking on coral reefs, out swarmed the multitudinous black, hissing host of furious

insects. Each one was savagely bent on plunging his poisoned dart deep into the intruder's flesh.

"*Adohai, Adohai, Adohai!*" roared the Tiger. With his tough hide stabbed in a thousand places he fled like a lightning flash, and his howlings froze with terror the blood of all the jungle creatures for miles around.

Reaching the river at last, the Tiger stumbled blindly down the bank and plunged into the stream, his head still covered with a clinging,

up with mirth on a high bank above the stream.

"You have escaped me so far with your nasty tricks, my Friend," said the Tiger sulkily. "But make no mistake. The next time we meet, the very next time, down my throat you go—bones, hooves, and all, as sure as fate is fate."

The little Mouse-Deer, however, appeared not to hear the Tiger's threat. "So the gentle tones of King Solomon's gong did not make the great Tiger drowsy," he finally said when he

smothering cloud of stinging, frenzied, booming hornets. Presently, however, the swift current of the river washed the hornets down stream, and he lay in the water, hurting all over, trying to recover his breath.

Hearing peels of laughter nearby, the Tiger looked around and saw the Mouse-Deer doubled

could stop laughing. He shook himself, twitched his tail and trotted toward the jungle, calling back over his shoulder:

"Ah well, Old Hairy-face, don't be disappointed. Next time I'll try to think of a better game—a game that is more soothing for you to play."

208

THE FIRST NOSES

THE PHILIPPINES: Here is another creation myth—this one from Mindanao Island in the Philippines. It suggests that the gods could make some ridiculous mistakes. By Maria Leach.

IN THE BEGINNING there was Melu in the sky—a big white god with gold teeth. He was proud of his whiteness and kept rubbing his skin to keep it white.

The old dead skin that rubbed off he put in a heap; and when he had enough, he made the earth out of it. There was some left over, so he made two living creatures, just like himself, only smaller.

He finished one, all but the nose. Then he finished the other, all but the nose. While he was thinking about how to finish them, his stupid brother came along.

"Let me make the noses," he said. "You've had all the fun. Let me make the noses."

Melu didn't like it. He did not want to let this clumsy brother make the noses, but finally he consented. So the stupid brother made the noses, while Melu went off to do other things. But when he put the noses on the faces, he got them on upside down. Then he went away.

One day it began to rain in the new world, and it rained very hard. The two new people were very uncomfortable because the rain ran off their straight black hair right into their upside down noses.

All they could do was stand on their heads. So they stood on their heads under a big tree until the rain was over. They had to do this every time it rained.

One day when Melu noticed that there was a specially good rain falling on the earth, he thought he would look and see if the two people were thankful for it and enjoying it, as they should be.

So he looked—and there were the two little figures standing on their heads under a tree.

"What are you doing like this?" he demanded, and turned them right side up.

At once he saw that the rain was running down their hair into their noses. He could hardly keep from laughing at their ridiculous plight, but he set things right at once.

He took off the two upside down noses and fixed them right end up — the way noses are today.

THE PHANTOM BULLOCKY

AUSTRALIA: This story by Bill Wannan is a modern one, and is very much like our cowboy stories. Bullockies are oxen drivers, and the "cheers" used in driving the bullocks are words so strong that they are said to heat the air.

ONE TIME when I was the boss and needed a bullock-driver, a chap came to ask for the job. He was a bushman of the all-round type and talked as if he knew what he was about, so I said I'd give him a tryout.

"It's an eight-yoke team you'll have to handle," said I. "And I warn you, it has the wildest

cattle in Australia in it. See over there? Those are the graves of fourteen drivers killed at one time or another by this team."

He looked where I pointed, but the graves didn't seem to worry him. "I'll try 'em," he said.

I asked him if he knew bullock-driving language.

"You might say I do," he said. "Often, when I've been bogged down in the timber with a team, my conversation has set the stringybark trees on fire. Not the big ones, I admit, but the saplings."

"Well, I think you might suit," I said. "Suppose you give me an example of yourself starting a team."

"Where's the team?" he asked, looking over his shoulder.

"It's out now. But you take eight of those fence posts in the yard," I said. "Imagine that's your team, and get 'em going."

The eight fence posts were new timber, big posts. Each had four strands of galvanized wire run through, and at the end the wire was tied to a four foot thick stringybark tree.

"That'll do me," he said.

I handed him a whip. It was the same one the fourteen dead bullockies had used, one after another. The handle was six feet, the lash was eighteen feet of braided rawhide, and there was two feet of silk cracker at the tip. He bent the handle over his knee in two or three places, to test it for flaws. Then he ran the lash slowly through his hand as if feeling it for a loose strand.

Then he was ready to start the team. He walked along and tapped each post with the butt of the handle, as a hint to the bullocks to tighten the chains. Then he gave a mighty cheer and at the same time made a flourish with the whip that kept it cracking over and over. Presently, as he cheered and cracked the whip,

a little blue flame began to run along the top wire of the fence. He kept on cheering and urging the bullocks forward. I could feel the air getting hotter from where I was. The flame danced along the wire and the whip cracking sounded like the day of judgment.

Suddenly, he cheered like ten thousand, as if the outfit were really started and, to my amazement, the fourteen graves opened. Out of them jumped the fourteen killed bullockies, each carrying a whip. They walked right up to the new man who, seeing them, gave a louder cheer.

They surrounded him and yelled, "Hurrah for the King of the Bullockies!"

All together, the fifteen whips fell on the top wire of the fence and the flames ran up and down as if they were alive. Then—I couldn't believe my eyes—the posts began to walk forward, step by step, straining against the wires. Then the drivers gave a bigger cheer than ever, yelling louder and faster, and the posts strained against the wires until the four foot stringybark tree came out of the ground and fell in behind the team. The driver I was trying out cheered wildly and kept on going with the tree following behind him. The fourteen others gave him a last cheer as he disappeared around the hill.

Then they all rushed back to their graves.

Presently, I saw the driver coming back around the foot of the hill, driving the fence posts, and with the tree bringing up the rear.

He came up to me and brought the fence posts to a halt. "I think I could drive your team," he said.

"You can have the job," I said. "You're the best man with a fence I ever saw."

Then he laughed a great laugh and gave another wild cheer so strong that it lifted him up in the air. Last I saw of him he was rising straight up into the sky.

And he never came down again.

MA-UI AND THE LONG EEL

POLYNESIA: The God Ma-ui is said to have created the world in seven deeds. This story, by Padraic Colum, is about the sixth of these deeds.

HINA-OF-THE-FIRE lived in a cave that the waters of the river streamed over, a cave that always had a beautiful rainbow glimmering across it. While her sons were away no enemy could come to Hina in this cave, for the walls of it went up straight and smooth. And there at the opening of the cave she used to sit, beating out her tapa in the long days that came after Ma-ui had snared the Sun and had made him go more slowly across the heavens.

In the river below there was one who was an enemy to Hina. This was Kuna Loa, the Long Eel. Once Kuna Loa had seen Hina on the bank of the river, and he had wanted her to leave her cave and come to his abode. But Hina-of-the-Fire would not go near the Long Eel. Then he had gone to her, and he had lashed her with his tail, covering her with the slime of the river. She told about the insults he had given her, and Ma-ui drove the Long Eel up the river, where he took shelter in the deep pools. Ma-ui broke down the banks of the deep pools with thrusts of his spear, but Kuna Loa, the Long Eel, was still able to escape from him. Now Ma-ui had gone away, and his mother, Hina-of-the-Fire, kept within the cave, the smooth rock of which Kuna Loa could not climb.

The Long Eel came down the river. He saw Hina sitting in the mouth of the cave that had the rainbow glimmering across it, and he was filled with rage and a wish to destroy her. He took a great rock and he put it across the stream, filling it from bank to bank. Then he lashed about in the water in his delight at the thought of what was going to happen to Hina.

She heard a deeper sound in the water than she had ever heard before as she sat there. She looked down and she saw that the water was nearer to the mouth of the cave than she had even seen it before. Higher and higher it came. And then Hina heard the voice of Kuna Loa rejoicing at the destruction that was coming to her. He raised himself up in the water and cried out to her: "Now your mighty son cannot help you. I will drown you with the waters of the river before he comes back to you, Hina."

And Hina-of-the-Fire cried, "Alas, alas," as she watched the waters mount up and up, for she knew that Ma-ui and her other sons were far away, and that there was none to help her against Kuna Loa, the Long Eel. But, even as she lamented, something was happening to aid Hina. For Ma-ui had placed above her cave a cloud that served her—"Ao-opua," "The Warning Cloud." Over the cave it rose now, giving itself a strange shape: Ma-ui would see it and be sure to know by its sign that something dire was happening in his mother's cave.

He was then on the mountain Ha-le-a-ka-la, the House of the Sun. He saw the strangely shaped cloud hanging over her cave, and he knew that some danger threatened his mother, Hina-of-the-Fire. He dashed down the side of the mountain, bringing with him the magic ax that his grandmother had given him for his battle with the Sun. He sprang into his canoe. With two strokes of his paddle he crossed the channel and was at the mouth of the Wai-lu-ku River. The bed of the river was empty of water, and Ma-ui left his canoe on the stones and went up toward Hina's cave.

The water had mounted up and up and had

gone into the cave, and was spilling over Hina's tapa board. She was lamenting, and her heart was broken with the thought that neither Ma-ui nor his brothers would come until the river had drowned her in the cave.

Ma-ui was then coming up the bed of the river. He saw the great stone across the stream, and he heard Kuna Loa rejoicing over the destruction that was coming to Hina in her cave. With one stroke of his ax he broke the rock across. The water came through the break. He struck the rocks and smashed them. The river flowed down once more, and Hina was safe in her cave.

Kuna Loa heard the crash of the ax on the rock, and he knew that Ma-ui had come. He dashed up the stream to hide himself again in the deep pools. Ma-ui showed his mother that she was safe, and then he went following the Long Eel.

Kuna Loa had gone into a deep pool. Ma-ui flung burning stones into the water of that pool, making it boil up. Then Kuna Loa dashed into another pool. From pool to pool Ma-ui chased him, making the pools boil around him. (And there they boil to this day, although Kuna Loa is no longer there.) At last the Eel found a cave in the bottom of one of the pools, and he went and hid in it, and Ma-ui could not find him there, nor could the hot stones that Ma-ui threw into the water, making it boil, drive Kuna Loa out.

Hina thought she was safe from the Long Eel after that. She thought that his skin was so scalded by the boiling water that he had died in his cave. Down the river bank for water she would go, and sometimes she would stand on the bank all wreathed in flowers.

But one day, as she was standing on the bank of the river, Kuna Loa suddenly came up. Hina fled before him. The Eel was between her and her cave, and she could not get back to her shelter. She fled through the woods. And as she fled she shrieked out chants: her chants went through the woods, and across the sea; they came at last up the side of Ha-le-a-ka-la, where Ma-ui was.

There were many people in the places that Hina fled through, but they could do nothing to help her against the Long Eel. He came swiftly after her. The people in the villages that they went through stood and watched the woman and the Eel that pursued her.

Where would she go now? The Long Eel was close behind her. Then Hina saw a breadfruit tree with great branches, and she climbed into it. Kuna Loa wound himself around the tree and came after her. But the branch that Hina was in was lifted up and up by the tree, and the Long Eel could not come to her.

And then Ma-ui came. He had dashed down the side of the mountain and had crossed the channel with two strokes of his paddles and had hurried along the track made by the Long Eel. Now he saw his mother in the branch that kept mounting up, and he saw Kuna Loa winding himself up after her. Ma-ui went into the tree. He struck the Eel a terrible blow and brought him to the ground. Then he sprang down and cut his head off. With other blows of his ax he cut the Eel all to pieces. He flung the head and the tail of Kuna Loa into the sea. The head turned into fish of many kinds, and the tail became the large conger eel of the sea. Other parts of the body turned into sea monsters of different kinds. And the blood of Kuna Loa, as it fell into the fresh water, became the common eels. The fresh and the salt water eels came into the world this way, and Ma-ui, by killing the Long Eel, wrought the sixth of his great deeds.

BRANCHES OF THE HAND

MADAGASCAR: Its first settlers came from Malaya, and its stories are like those told in the Pacific Islands. This one is by James Sibree.

IN THE BEGINNING, when men were still new on earth, the fingers and thumb of a person's hand worked and thought as one, and they were called "branches of the hand."

But then one day, the branches of the hand started having independent thoughts. The little finger was the first to speak.

"I am so hungry!" it said.

"Well, if you're hungry," said the finger next to it unpleasantly, "don't just sit there and whine about it. Go and steal some food."

The finger next to that one chimed in, "Steal plenty while you're at it. I want some, too."

But the forefinger, the pointer, was shocked. "What do you two mean telling the little one to steal? You should be ashamed!" And the fingers began to argue hotly, pushing and bumping each other in their anger.

Finally the thumb spoke up. "You all make me sick with your arguing and shoving," it said disgustedly. "I want nothing more to do with the lot of you! I'm going to get away from your silly wrangling." And with that, the thumb moved away from the other branches of the hand.

To this day, the fingers have never patched up their quarrel, and they remain separate, with the thumb opposing them all. And in Madagascar, while the thumb, the pointer and the little finger are respected and have separate names, the two middle fingers have been punished for their bad advice. They have never been given names of their own, and they have no work that they can perform skilfully by themselves.

214

THE

A FARMER was coming home from his rice fields one evening. His mind wandered gently over thoughts of eating, sleeping, and playing his flute. As he walked along the trail he came to a pile of rocks. Protruding through a crack he saw a tail switching back and forth. It was a tiger's tail. It was very large.

The farmer was overcome with panic. He thought of running to the village. But then he realized the tiger was waiting for him to appear around the turn of the trail. So he dropped his sickle and seized the tiger's tail.

There was a struggle. The tiger tried to free himself. He pulled. The farmer pulled. They tugged back and forth. The tiger snarled and clawed. The farmer gasped and perspired, but he clung frantically to the tail.

While the desperate struggle was going on a monk came walking along the trail.

TIGER'S TAIL

INDONESIA: Like people everywhere else in the world, the Indonesians sometimes make fun of their holy men. This story is about a most untimely conversion. From *Kantchil's Lime Pit* by Harold Courlander.

"Oh, Allah has sent you!" the farmer cried. "Take my sickle from the ground and kill this fierce tiger while I hold him!"

The holy man looked at him calmly and said:

"Ah, I cannot. It is against my principles to kill."

"How can you say such a thing!" the farmer said. "If I let go this tail, which sooner or later I must do, the angry animal will turn on me and kill me!"

"I am sorry, brother," the monk said. "But my religion won't permit me to kill any living creature."

"How can you argue this way?" the farmer cried. "If you don't help me you will be the cause of my death. Isn't the life of a man worth as much as the life of a tiger?"

The monk listened thoughtfully and said calmly:

"All around us the things of the jungle kill each other, and for these things I am not responsible. I cannot take a life, it is written so."

The farmer felt his strength leaving him. The tiger's tail was slipping from his tired hands. At last he said:

"Oh, my holy, kind-hearted friend, if it is so written, it is so written! Do me then one favor. Hold this tiger's tail so that I may kill him!"

The monk looked into the sky and thought.

"Very well, there is nothing written that says I may not hold a tiger's tail."

So he came forward and took hold of the tail.

"Do you have it?" the farmer asked.

"Yes, I have it," the monk replied.

"Do you have it firmly?"

"Yes, I have it firmly."

The farmer released his hold. He wiped the sweat from his face with his head cloth. He picked up his sickle from the ground where he had dropped it. He straightened his clothes and brushed the dust from his hands. Then he started toward the village.

The tiger renewed the tug of war with great energy. The monk clung frantically to the tail. They pulled back and forth desperately.

"Kill him, kill him quickly!" the monk shouted.

The farmer continued toward the village.

"Where are you going? I can't hold on much longer!" the monk cried in alarm. "Kill him with your sickle!"

The farmer turned around placidly. His face was very peaceful.

"Oh, holy and venerable man," he said. "It was good to listen to your sacred words and to hear what is written. I have been moved by your feeling for living things. You have converted me. I now believe as you do. And as it is written, I may not kill any living creature. If you hold on with patience, other men who do not have such high ideals as we do may soon come this way and destroy the tiger for you."

And the farmer bowed and continued his way to the village.

GUNO'S HUNGER

INDONESIA: This story is from *Kantchil's Lime Pit* by Harold Courlander.

GUNO, the "helpful one," went one day from his village to Macassar to sell some knives he had made. He knew he wouldn't be home again before night, so he asked his wife for six rice cakes to feed him during the day. He walked briskly toward the city, but before the sun had risen high in the sky he was already hungry.

Guno sat in the shade of a large tree and looked at his rice cakes. He knew it was too early to eat, and that he must save his food for later in the day. But he was hungry, and he argued with himself. Finally he took one cake and ate it. But he was still hungry.

"Well, I will take one more and save four for the evening," he said to himself.

He took one more. But he was still hungry. So he ate the third.

Then he stopped arguing with himself, and he ate the fourth rice cake. Then the fifth.

There was only one left. Guno looked at it longingly, for he was still hungry. At last he said:

"Ah, let the evening take care of itself!"

And he put the last cake in his mouth and ate it. When he had eaten it he discovered that he was no longer hungry. His stomach was completely satisfied.

He looked into his empty basket and said:

"Oh, how foolish I was! Now there is nothing more to eat. It was the *sixth* rice cake that stopped my hunger. If I had only eaten the sixth one first, then my selfish stomach would have stopped its complaints immediately, and I would have had five rice cakes left for the evening."

216

DANNY KAYE'S
AROUND THE WORLD
STORY BOOK